THE Dark Fire

 **Also by Christine Silk**

Chase the Sun: Nine Short Stories of Passion, Betrayal, and Revenge

Creating a Private Foundation: The Essential Guide for Donors and Their Advisers
(with R.D. Silk, J.W. Lintott, and A.R. Stephens)

THE Dark Fire

A Novel

by

Christine Silk

CHARTWELL
PRESS

Chartwell Press, Reston, Virginia

For information about this title, written permissions, or to order other books and/or electronic media, contact the publisher:

Chartwell Press, LLC
12030 Sunrise Valley Drive, Suite 450
Reston, VA 20191
ChartwellPress.com
publisher@ChartwellPress.com

Printed in the United States of America
5 6 7 8 9 10 1 2 3 4

Cover illustration by Fez Silk
Cover and interior design by Rhion Magee

Publisher's Cataloging-in-Publication Data
provided by Five Rainbows Cataloging Services

Names: Silk, Christine, author.
Title: The dark fire / Christine Silk.
Description: Reston, VA : Chartwell Press, 2024. | Includes bibliographical references.
Identifiers: ISBN 978-0-9963498-2-6 (paperback) | ISBN 978-0-9963498-3-3 (hardcover)
Subjects: LCSH: Dracula, Count (Fictitious character)--Fiction. | Golem--Fiction. | Churchill, Winston, 1874-1965--Fiction. | Nineteen hundreds (Decade)--Fiction. | Historical fiction. | Paranormal fiction. | BISAC: FICTION / Gothic. | FICTION / Occult & Supernatural | FICTION / Historical / 20th Century / General | GSAFD: Gothic fiction. | Historical fiction. | Occult fiction.
Classification: LCC PS3619.I45 D37 2024 (print) | LCC PS3619.I45 (ebook) | DDC 813/.6--dc23.

Ebook ISBN: 978-0-9963498-4-0

To my traveling companions in Schooling for Life in 2014 and 2015.

Our adventures together helped to create this story.

Even the darkness is not dark to You,

and the night is as light as the day;

Darkness and light are one.

You created my mind;

You fashioned me in my mother's womb.

I will give thanks to You,

For I am awesomely and wonderfully made.

Wondrous are Your works,

and my soul knows it well.

My essence was not hidden from You

when I was made in secret,

I was knit together in the depths of the earth;

Your eyes saw my unformed limbs [גולמ];

and on Your book they were all written;

in due time they were formed, to the very last one of them.

–PSALM 139:12-16

This novel is my take on the golem legend, interwoven with elements of Bram Stoker's *Dracula*.

The golem legend is relatively new in the vast, millennia-old literature of the Jewish people. (It is not related to J.R.R. Tolkien's gollum.) The golem was a man-like creature shaped out of mud. He functioned as a bodyguard to protect the Jews of Prague from an onslaught of antisemitism and blood libel in the 16th century. According to Michael Weingrad, golems are "Judaically marginal" because, until the twentieth century, almost no Jewish writers have paid attention to them. Yet they have a hold on the modern imagination and have attracted many contemporary creators (both Jewish and non-Jewish), including: novelists, screenwriters, comic-book authors, and video-game designers. Weingrad argues that this is because "the golem is today the archetypal point of connection between Judaism and popular culture itself." Yes, he is right, but there is something more. The golem is a man-made creature who is fashioned from mud, not from electronic components. This fact alone brings us modern computer-users back to the chthonic roots of creation itself; however, it is a creation that is in the service of God, and made possible by Him.

The only golem novel I have read to date is Gershon Winkler's *The Golem of Prague*. I have read no other golem stories because I didn't want to overwhelm my own vision with cross-currents from the imaginations of other writers. Winkler's account was enough for me to take the concept and run with it, adding my own spin to the golem character as he might exist in Edwardian England.

Regarding the *Dracula* legend, most readers will already be familiar with it. Since its publication in 1897, Stoker's gentleman vampire has been the subject of countless derivative works, including novels, movies, comic strips, and stage plays. The vampire legend itself is old and can be found in many folklore traditions, especially those of Eastern Europe and Greece (See Dundes in the bibliography for more information).

Given the vast amount of commentary on vampires in literature, I don't have much to add, except to say that my own theory as to why vampires remain popular is that they are a metaphor for perhaps the darkest aspect of human nature: the desire to coerce, control, and forcibly convert others, which is a hallmark of tyrants everywhere. In the classic vampire legends, the conversion of an ordinary human into a vampire would start with a vampire bite. The bitten victim would then herself become a vampire. But I see the vampire metaphor as more psychological, with the "bite" being sophisticated techniques of persuasion and coercion. Right now, it is fashionable to talk of transgenerational trauma (that is, adaptive but harmful ways of behaving or thinking that are transmitted from one generation to the next). The abused child who becomes an abusive adult is but one example of vampirism. There is also geo-political vampirism in which less powerful actors are forced, by various means, to do the bidding of powerful oligarchs, and eventually become cooperative agents themselves (Stockholm Syndrome is a variation of this, in my view). There is ideological vampirism, in which vulnerable populations (especially the young and innocent) are conditioned to accept ideas and actions that are contrary to their self-interest, and they are persuaded to do the bidding of the head vampire(s), whomever that might be. In *The Dark Fire*, the main antagonist uses persuasion techniques that perpetuate psychological vampirism. This includes isolating the victim from her friends and family, and convincing her that utopia is just around the corner if she'll do what he wants her to do.

I noted above that *The Dark Fire* is historical fiction. These days, it is fashionable to take liberties with historical facts—and indeed, to completely re-write history itself without, at that point, calling the work of fiction "alternative history." Modern authors do this, I believe, as a means to advance the ideology that underlies their story, without making it obvious that that is what they are doing. So now, in contemporary literature, we have a situation in which history gets massively re-written in the service of a story's polemics, but the history is still accepted as accurate. The characters behave as if they are 21st-century activist-missionaries who have been sent back in time to enlighten the benighted rubes. This makes the reader (who already buys into the underlying ideology) feel vindicated, which is a nice feeling to have, but which extracts a heavy price on the quality of fiction and historiography that is currently on the market.

Don't get me wrong, every story has an underlying ideology. Or, to put it another way every story has philosophical premises on which it is based. Every fiction writer makes decisions about which historical facts to include or exclude. But not every novel aims to convert the audience to its ideology. Some of us writers just want to tell a good tale, and let readers draw their own conclusions. I have made an effort to remain true to the historicity and ethos of Edwardian England. I present men and women as conventional individuals (with normal-for-that-era attitudes about biological sex, class, and hierarchy). For some modern readers, this is going to be grating, if not offensive. So consider this a trigger warning. My novel is not a modern morality play set in 1908. It is a gothic-historical novel that attempts to remain true to the era in which it is set, with characters who (I hope) are believable for that time and place, and who are not anachronistic transplants (as so many contemporary fictional characters are). I could have written the story to genuflect to The Current Thing, but this would've gone against my vision for this particular story, and against my philosophy of how fiction is supposed to work.

Because this novel is composed of mostly British characters, I have retained the British spelling of certain words, and the British construction of certain phrases. I have also tried to capture patterns of speech and grammar of that time and place. I hope my British readers will forgive me if there have been lapses into American idioms. There is a glossary at the back to save the reader from having to look up unfamiliar words. There is also a bibliography for those who want to delve more deeply into some of the research that went into the construction of this story.

ᴀCKNOWLEDGMENTS

I am grateful to the following people for their insights and support: The Balogh & Clair families, especially to Mona for our long conversations about many of the themes in this novel. Kim Ziel for her enthusiastic support. Stephen Marmer for his insights into religion and psychology. Dennis Prager, Joseph & Dvorah Telushkin for their insights on Judaism and spirituality. The Torah Minyan, including Gilla Nissan, Susan Estrin, Miry Rabinovich, Orrie Frochtzwajg, Claudia & Shlomo Bobrow, Sarah Olsen, and Ron Gertz.

I am grateful to the Schooling for Life families who shared in the adventures in England and Israel when I was gathering material for this novel, including the following families: Allen, Balogh, Dunbar, Henderson, Malina, Rekedal, Silk, Stone-Rundblad, Stupin, and Uchida. Special thanks to Jessica Paliotto & family, and to Aryeh Leifert.

Heartfelt gratitude to the excellent scholars who answered my questions about various subjects that appear in this novel: Patrick Allitt, Michael Drout, Anton Howes, and Timothy Shutt.

I appreciate the knowledge so generously shared by: Mendel Adelman, Phil & Michelle Baron, Mendel & Sarah Cunin, Moshe Cunin, Robert Elias, Michael & Jill Gotlieb, Lee Ari & Rachel Greenberg, Dov & Rachel Greenberg, Michael Greenwood, Dennis Gura, Martin Heale, Levi & Chana Sputz, and Candace Smith.

These are yet more people who were willing to give advice and support when I needed it: Abigail Baisley, Andrew Cohen, the Elias family, Robert & Annette Florczak, Joseph & Dianne Iskovic, Shaili Jain, May Liang, Dolores Murphy, Kelly Murphy & Mark Graham, Joe Murphy & family, the OC and NL Silk families, and Naomi Silk. Special mention of Christine Jacobson (z"l), my parents-in-law Lawrence and Ellen Silk (z"l), and my father Joseph Murphy (z"l), all of whom would've been happy to see this novel published.

Kay ben-Avraham is one of the best editors I have worked with, and I appreciate her incisive comments. Thanks to her, this story is much better. Rhion Magee is the skilled graphic designer who made this book look as good as it does. The cover art is by the very talented Fez Silk, who captured the mood of the story.

Finally, love and gratitude to my husband and children. Without you all, I would not be the writer I am today. I am blessed.

It goes without saying that I alone am responsible for the contents of this novel (including all errors). My acknowledgements in no way imply that others agree with my approach or handling of the subject matter.

Christine Silk
September 2024

וְכָל מַעֲשֶׂיךָ יִהְיוּ לְשֵׁם שָׁמָיִם

And all your deeds be for the sake of Heaven.

–PIRKEI AVOT 2:12

CHAPTER ONE

Jonathan Drake glanced at his gold pocket watch. Nineteen minutes past four, time to go home. He gathered his things, put on his frock coat and top hat, and strode out of his office, down the corridor, to the front door. His clerk was nowhere to be seen. No matter. He'd see Mr. Dale tomorrow morning. Jonathan stood at the wrought-iron umbrella stand that stood next to the front door, and was careful to take the one that belonged to him—a Smythe & Fenwick with an ivory handle that his wife had given him for Christmas.

Jonathan felt a jostle as a man pushed past him without a word.

"Good afternoon, Mr. Miller," Jonathan said in a tone meant to reprove the man for his rudeness.

Miller stopped. He was shorter than Jonathan, and he looked up from under a hat brim that was too wide to be fashionable. A loose button dangled from his black overcoat. "Good afternoon, Mr. Drake."

"In a hurry, are you?"

"Not anymore," Miller said. "I've got nothing but time now. I expect I'll be given formal notice within days if not hours."

Jonathan was surprised that anyone at the firm would be stupid enough to do that. Miller might be a foreign Jew, but his work was impeccable. To let him go would be lunacy.

"But why?" Jonathan asked.

"Because I told Mr. Stoker I won't go to Klausenberg. The buyer of the Belgravia house lives there, and the papers must be signed before he can settle in London." Miller still had an eastern-European accent.

Jonathan stared at him. "Why the devil won't you go? Surely a cosmopolitan chap like you enjoys travel."

"I do not enjoy travelling to places where life is cheap, where people like me are killed for sport."

"But I thought your family were from there."

"That is how I know what I'm talking about." Miller's eyes narrowed. "Mr. Stoker will request that you go in my place. I'd refuse, if I were you."

Jonathan sneered. "Well, I'm not Jewish so I don't need to worry."

Miller said quietly: "Are you certain?"

Jonathan was stunned by the man's impertinence, and wondered whether Miller was referring to the need to worry, or about the question of Jewish heritage. There was no way this man could know such details—Jonathan had always been careful to never disclose more about his background than was necessary.

Jonathan drew the gold watch from his pocket and showed it to Miller. "This belonged to my paternal grandfather, Sir William Cecil Drake, a knighted admiral in Her Majesty's navy. It was given to him by the Duke of Marlborough. We English rule the world. Why should I fear some bounder in a backwater fiefdom?"

Miller's face was grim. "Because blood runs just as red, no matter who wields the blade."

This comment caught Jonathan off-guard. He retorted: "They wouldn't dare harm a subject of His Majesty."

Miller shrugged, clearly not convinced by Jonathan's reasoning. Then he asked: "Have you seen the Belgravia house?"

"The one to be finalized? No, I've not seen it."

"Evil place. Best to stay away." Miller turned abruptly and went outside, into the rainy London afternoon.

The interaction left Jonathan uneasy. For a man of his intelligence, Miller was a peculiar outsider who didn't understand native Englishmen.

Jonathan heard footsteps, and turned to see his clerk, Mr. Dale, standing nearby.

"Mr. Drake, sir, Mr. Stoker will see you now."

"But there was no meeting scheduled for this hour," Jonathan said.

Mr. Dale looked around to be sure no-one was listening, and took a step closer. He whispered: "It's on account of Mr. Miller, sir. He was to go to eastern Europe, but then he told Mr. Stoker he could not do that. He was threatened that he'd lose his job, but he doesn't seem to care."

Jonathan pretended he knew nothing. "Did Mr. Miller give a reason?"

"Something about a dangerous assignment, which is bollocks, given that it's just a real estate transaction. Miller's family are from that region, you know. He speaks the language." Mr. Dale shook his head. "If you ask me, sir, I believe Mr. Miller thinks he's too good for this assignment. No self-respecting Englishman would turn away from his duties. He changed his name to Miller, you know. It had been something unpronounceable. A lot of them foreign Jews do that when they come here, to blend-in like."

Jonathan didn't want to waste time gossiping with his clerk. He said: "Thank you, Mr. Dale."

"Anytime, sir. Anytime."

Jonathan paused to put on his gloves, and walked down the corridor to Mr. Stoker's office, with his overcoat and hat on, carrying his umbrella like a proper gentleman. It would be good for Mr. Stoker to see that he was unnecessarily detaining his solicitor at a time of the day when Jonathan should have already left. The meeting didn't take long. Stoker gave Jonathan an address. He was to see the agent of the estate straight away. Jonathan wasn't happy about the delay in returning home, but he was eager to distinguish himself from Miller. An Englishman's duty was to be carried out diligently, and with no complaint.

Jonathan left the building, and opened his umbrella against the rain. Whenever horses and carriages passed by, he was careful to dodge the splash of muddy water. Still, his shoes would need cleaning later, his wool suit would need a good brushing. His man McWilliams would take care of it.

After a ten-minute walk, Jonathan found the street and the building. The door was unlocked. In the vestibule, Jonathan closed his dripping umbrella and deposited it into an umbrella stand just inside the door. He placed his hat on the hat rack. He proceeded down the black-and-white tiled corridor.

At the end of the corridor an oak door opened, and a thin, balding man in wire spectacles and a chequered wool suit stood there. He gave a slight bow. Jonathan returned it.

The man said: "Welcome. I heard you clopping around. Terrible echo in this place. Been meaning to have a runner installed. I'm Triple-C, by the way. That's Charles Clayton Cowles, Agent of the Estate. And you are?"

"Jonathan Drake, solicitor. From Gershon, Stoker, and King. I'm here about the Belgravia house." He gave the man his card.

"Ah, yes. Come in, come in, Mr. Drake. Please take a seat."

Jonathan took a chair near Cowles's desk and looked around the office. There were scores of enormous leather-bound ledgers in book cases, brass hooks on the walls that held keys to various properties, and a fire burning low in the hearth. A window revealed the rainy gloom of the early-May afternoon. The lamps had been lit, throwing off a dull glow.

Cowles studied Jonathan's card. "So you're the Honourable Jonathan Drake, Esquire. Any relation to the judge named Drake?"

"He's my father."

"A fair-minded man when it comes to property disputes." Cowles plucked a smouldering cigarette from the ashtray and took a drag. "His ruling on the Ennismore estate was spot-on, no matter what the papers said. Anyway, your assignment is not a difficult one, as you'll see. You've travelled the continent before?"

Jonathan nodded.

"Do you speak any languages?"

"German, a little French. I studied Greek and Latin in school—"

"What school was that?" Cowles interrupted.

"Eaton."

"I'm a Harrovian myself. Now, our client is a German-speaker, although you know how it is with these continental aristocrats. They're all polyglots." Cowles lowered his voice to a confidential tone. "This is a crucial transaction. I've had a devil of a time with this particular property. Buyers always back out, even though it's one of the best addresses in London."

"Why do buyers back out?" Jonathan asked. He recalled the fact that Miller had called it an evil place.

4

"That is the question." Cowles fished a sheet from the stack on his desk and handed it to Jonathan. It was a pen-and-ink drawing of a mansion.

"The house is Greek Revival," Cowles explained. "It's right at the crossroads of Belgrave Place and Eaton Place."

Jonathan realised it was walking distance from his own house in Knightsbridge.

Cowles continued. "It blends with the other houses on that street because of the exterior finish. But it is a monstrosity when you actually take the time to look at the details." Cowles used his silver letter opener as a pointer. "The pediment over the front door is out of proportion. And the columns are more Egyptian in design than they are Greek Revival. Travesty."

"That would've escaped my notice."

"It escapes most people's notice. The fenestration is also wrong."

"Fenestration?"

"Windows, windows," Cowles said impatiently. "See how the windows are pointed arches at the top? They're Early English lancet windows, not at all in keeping with the Greek nature of the house. And there aren't enough of them."

"Maybe the window tax was a factor," Jonathan suggested.

Cowles shook his head. "The window tax was rescinded in 1851. This house was built in 1866. You'd think the architect would have taken that into account. Or maybe the owner was the architect. It happens, you know. Some nouveau riche merchant goes on the Grand Tour, sees some ruins and a few cathedrals, and comes back to London. He then draws up some horrible plans, all the while deluding himself that his self-designed, mishmash of a house is a wonderful tribute to his new-found architectural sensitivity—when in fact it only exposes his utter lack of taste." He moved his pointer along the balustrade at the roof line. "Here you would normally have pediment statues. Instead, there are gargoyles—gargoyles!—on a Greek Revival mansion." He moved the pointer to the front door. "The entablature over the doorway is a design of wings and snakes—clearly a copy of the entablature of the Temple of Isis. The owner couldn't make up his mind whether he was in Greece or Egypt. Or Medieval Europe."

Cowles paused, took another drag on his cigarette, and grinned.

5

"Now that I've got that out of my system, I'm ready to tell you about the owners."

Jonathan stifled a yawn. "Yes, go on."

"The original owner was a boring industrialist who made his fortune in the manufacture of mattresses. His son inherited the place, died there, and it got passed on to the son's wife. She lives in New York, but that hasn't stopped her from pestering me about selling it." He tapped a pile of unopened letters. "All from her. She writes the same thing every time— as if I don't want the thing sold and out of my hair." He paused. "We now have a buyer who is serious. I can't overstate the importance—to my own sanity at the very least." He chuckled, then added delicately: "Of course, your compensation will reflect your central role, as I am sure was mentioned already."

Jonathan ignored the allusion to money, discussions of which were beneath a man of his station. He said: "Why don't you tell me more about the buyer."

Cowles riffled among the papers. "I can't quite remember his full name. One of those German aristocratic concoctions. Ah. Here it is." He pointed it out on a letter.

Jonathan read the name aloud: "Baron Zoltan Vladimir Georg Tovis von Klausenberg."

The baronial seal at the bottom of the letter depicted a square-headed eagle clutching a curved sword. On closer inspection, Jonathan saw that the eagle was a fantastical creature, a hybrid of an eagle and a dragon. The date of the letter was 13 March 1908. Six weeks ago.

Cowles continued. "He lives in the Carpathian Mountains, not far from the city of Klausenberg, hence, the baron's surname. The city of Klausenberg also goes by the name Cluj and Kolozsvár." Cowles smiled apologetically. "You see how dreadful my accent is."

Jonathan took notes on a small pad that he had retrieved from his pocket. "So, I'll be meeting the baron in the city of Klausenberg?"

Cowles shook his head. "No, no. You will go to his estate. He will arrange a carriage once you are in the vicinity. It's a fascinating part of the globe, part of the Austro-Hungarian empire, an explosive cauldron of nationalities and ethnicities." He counted on his fingers. "Our client, the baron, is a full-blooded aristocrat, from what I can tell. His estate has been in his family for centuries." Cowles paused. "Now. We don't know whether our baron considers himself a Saxon or a Szekler or both, so tread carefully. Those distinctions are important."

"I'm afraid I've forgotten the distinction," Jonathan said in a dismissive tone.

Cowles lit another cigarette. "Saxons are the descendants of the German Goths who settled in the region. Szeklers are the Hungarian-speaking descendants of the Huns who settled there in the fifth century. Of course, he could also have a lineage that goes back to the Vikings, which would mean the berserker fury runs in his veins. Watch out for his temper, then!" Cowles chuckled.

Jonathan ignored the attempt at humour and asked: "Did the baron say what brings him to London?"

Cowles shrugged. "Any man of good breeding would want to live in London. Fortunately, our good baron is not one of those wretched Jews from Russia. And, he's not another Jewish millionaire from South Africa. Those Jews are buying up all our best properties, you know." He riffled a stack of papers on the corner of his desk. "All these have been sold to rich Jews." Cowles pointed to the drawing of the mansion. "You need to make yourself familiar with that house, Mr. Drake. Shall we go see it now?"

"Is that necessary?" Jonathan was eager to go home.

"Our good baron may have questions, and you'll need to answer them." Cowles took a key from a key rack on the wall. "I always keep an extra set of keys to every property, even after it has sold. A lord, whose name you would have seen in the papers, would get drunk, forget his keys, and harass me at an ungodly hour to come unlock his door for him. Of course, I did charge for my time, so it was remunerative. I sound like an American, don't I?"

Cowles donned a bowler hat and an overcoat. As the two men left the building and walked the wet streets to their destination, Cowles chatted amiably about architecture, pointing out features on the buildings they passed. Fifteen minutes later, they were standing outside the house, at the intersection of Eaton Place and Belgrave Place. In this part of the city, the streets were wide, but there was nobody about. An eerie greenish-yellow light emanated from the rainclouds and bounced off the immense white houses that lined the streets.

Cowles gestured to the house in front of them. "Do you see what I mean? It is a badly-executed mausoleum."

"I suppose you have a point," Jonathan said politely, not seeing how the house differed significantly from its neighbours.

The two men made their way through the front door into the foyer. Cowles left the door open in order to bring in fresh air and light from outside. An ornate marble staircase curved upward, curling around an immense pillar that funnelled up to the ceiling.

"This should do," Jonathan said, turning back toward the front door.

"But Mr. Drake, you need to actually *familiarize yourself*. And besides, another deluge has begun." Cowles gestured to the hard rain falling outside.

Jonathan resigned himself to the fact that Cowles was going to show him around the dark, musty house. Cowles was in high spirits, pointing out everything that was wrong with the place. His anticipation of finally closing the transaction was palpable, despite all the flaws—or perhaps with a perverse pleasure that it was *because* of all the flaws.

For Jonathan, the architectural details that annoyed Cowles didn't matter. But he hated the place even so. The gloom would not be dispelled, despite the fact that the cloudburst had now passed, and a late-afternoon sun was casting slender rays through the narrow, west-facing windows.

"Of course," Cowles said, "all the faults I've pointed out are simply my sensitivities to such things. And I've indulged myself by sharing them with you. No need to upset the client with my opinions when you see him. Remind him of the excellent taste everyone will say he has when they see this house. The location alone is worth the price."

He took Jonathan's arm and guided him to a back staircase. They made their way downstairs to the kitchen and servants' quarters.

Cowles pointed to a servant's entrance. "That door leads to the alley where the mews are located. In fact, there is an underground passageway between the larder and the mews. Comings-and-goings can be totally hidden. Be sure to mention that when you see him. Would you like to see it for yourself?"

"No."

Cowles sensed Jonathan's annoyance. "Let me trouble you for five minutes more and show you the pièce de résistance of the house, the one that has caused all previous buyers to back out. Forewarned is forearmed, as they say." He chuckled.

Cowles walked on, then stopped at a small door that was painted a muddy green to blend in with the wall. He grabbed a dirty oil lamp from a nearby table and lit it. He opened the small door.

"There is no rail, so step carefully," Cowles said over his shoulder, making his way down a stone spiral staircase.

Jonathan followed. He tried not to breathe through his nose. The cold air smelled faintly of decay, of an earthy, musty stillness that made Jonathan nauseated. At the bottom of the stairs, Cowles turned sharply to the left and led Jonathan to a door behind the staircase. It had been painted to look like the surrounding stone walls.

"Not a very good tromp l'oeil," Cowles observed. "But good enough because nobody would think to look for a hidden door here, now, would they?" He held his lamp high, and above the door, on the stone lintel, the word SERAIL was inscribed.

Cowles laughed. "Obviously they thought it didn't matter if they advertised what the room was *for*."

"I don't follow," Jonathan said.

"Seraglio," Cowles explained. "The private apartments of a sultan's harem. Mozart's *Abduction from the Seraglio*, remember that opera?"

"Of course."

Cowles threw open the door and stepped into the room. It was sumptuous—or it had been at one time. The lamplight bounced off the gilded ceiling. Around the perimeter of the room were low couches in red-and-black satin. The cushions had been chewed apart by rats, but in the lamplight, Jonathan could see that they had been of costly workmanship, with elaborate embroidery. In the middle of the room was a gilt brazier, low to the ground, with ball-and-claw feet. Persian carpets, now dusty, covered the floor. On the walls were alternating panels of watered silk. Moroccan sconces of coloured glass hung from brass chains. There were no windows.

Cowles said: "It was a fabulous room when it was newly appointed, even though that brazier is gimcrack."

"What do you mean, gimcrack?"

"A bad imitation. But it is alluring. No Turkish brazier would have ball-and-claw feet. Those feet are what you find on every sideboard in every low-class inn across England."

"What do you suppose this room was actually for?" Jonathan asked.

Cowles shot him a sly glance. "Come, come. Can't you guess?"

Jonathan said peevishly: "I'm not here to play guessing games."

"Well, the previous owner obviously had certain … appetites. One could keep at least three or four ladies in this room, and the servants—not to mention the wife—would be none the wiser."

Jonathan asked: "Would he keep them here permanently?"

"Probably not." Cowles paused, then added: "It may also have been a holding room for those waiting to proceed to what we're about to see next."

They walked down a short corridor that opened into a very large, stone-floored room. The air was fetid. A stone brazier stood in the middle of the room, with a hook and chain suspended over it. Next to the brazier was a tall rod of rusted iron, with a platform for the feet, and manacles for the hands. In a corner, there was an iron cage with a lock.

Suddenly, a terrifying picture popped into Jonathan's mind of people suffering here, in this room, while others looked on, amused.

"All that's lacking is a skeleton," Cowles joked.

"What the devil is this place?" Jonathan demanded. Fear had made his tone harsh and judgmental.

"I suppose one could call it a dungeon."

"Why on earth would anyone want to have a dungeon? Did the previous owner have medieval delusions about locking up his debtors?"

Cowles smiled, and his nicotine-stained teeth were dingy in the lamplight. "Oh, he was a pasha all right, and I don't think his proclivities had to do with punishing debtors. It's not hard to imagine that he was well acquainted with . . . certain practices. There were other artifacts we found here. Photographs and drawings, for example, that could lead to imprisonment by a puritanical magistrate. We found an outré merchant who bought the lot of it. They were the kind of things—"

"That's enough," Jonathan interrupted. "I really don't want to hear any more." He started toward the steps. "This place is evil. I'm leaving."

He realised he'd used the same adjective Miller had used: Evil.

Cowles stepped in front of Jonathan. "Better that I should lead the way. I have the lamp."

Jonathan kept so close to Cowles that he could smell tobacco smoke and camphor on the man's suit. Jonathan looked back to be sure nothing followed him up from the fetid darkness.

Out on the street, Jonathan tried to shake off the atmosphere of the house. He was glad he would never have to set foot in it again.

Cowles said: "I do find it interesting that people are typically offended by the dungeon, but not by the architectural monstrosities of the house itself."

"The dungeon is the worst feature," Jonathan retorted.

"But it is not pretending to be other than what it is," Cowles observed. "Its form follows its function. It is the only truly honest room in the house, unlike what's above ground."

"If buyers are so offended by that room, why in the world didn't you completely empty it of everything it contains so that it's not so sinister?" Jonathan demanded.

"Oh, but I was going to do exactly that right before our baron came along. Now it is a moot point."

"What do you mean, a moot point? Does the baron know about the dungeon and what it contains?"

"Oh, yes, he does indeed," Cowles said. "That's the curious thing. I wrote to him in great detail. I am bound to disclose everything, you know. I have my reputation to think of. I said I would oversee the removal of the remaining artifacts that our outré merchant had no interest in buying—the manacles, the cage, et cetera. But the good baron wrote back and told me to leave the dungeon as is."

"That's curious. Did he give a reason?"

"He said a man's castle wouldn't be a home without it." Cowles chuckled. "Our baron has quite a sense of humour, hasn't he, Mr. Drake?"

CHAPTER TWO

When Jonathan turned onto his street, the gloom he'd felt in Belgravia lifted. The Queen Anne style houses surrounding Cadogan Square were elegant, with their red brick exteriors and white trim. In the middle of the square was the communal garden. Young grass shoots created a fresh green haze across the landscape. Working men gathered their tools, and would be back tomorrow to continue painting the black rail fence that encircled the garden. Jonathan was gratified by the orderliness of it all.

His own house was a fine example of a traditional Victorian home, suitable to a man of his station. The marble stairs leading to the front door were regularly scrubbed by one of his servants—they gleamed white despite the black London soot that dusted less well-maintained properties. Jonathan unlocked his front door, and stepped into the vestibule, wiping his feet on the doormat. He placed his wet umbrella in the iron umbrella stand, his hat on the hat rack.

Beyond the vestibule was the entrance hall. The black-and-white tiled floor held a circular Axminster carpet that was decorated with a burgundy-and-gold medallion. Against a wall, a Regency demi-lune table held the mail and the newspaper. Jonathan glanced through the envelopes, and shuffled through the calling cards that had been left on the silver salver. There had been the usual visitors, including women who were friends with his wife, and two of his associates from his private club in Pall Mall.

Above the table was a gilded rococo looking-glass. He studied his reflection. In his well-cut coat, starched shirt and silk tie, he looked like the respectable London solicitor he was. He traced the outline of his nose, wondering whether Miller had thought him "of the chosen people" because of it. But that was impossible. Jonathan had inherited his father's aristocratic features. As for his thick, almost-black hair, well that wasn't so unusual. And Jonathan kept it trimmed as any man should. The only drawback to Jonathan's dapper appearance so late in the day was the dark shadow of stubble on his chin and cheeks, which he now rubbed in annoyance. His beard grew quickly and heavily, and he didn't like going more than twelve hours without shaving.

He went upstairs to his dressing room. His valet, McWilliams, had laid out new trousers, a smoking jacket, and house slippers, and was waiting to shave him. Jonathan told McWilliams of his upcoming journey, and gave him instructions for packing the portmanteau and the Gladstone bag.

After he was shaved and had changed, Jonathan made his way to the back parlour on the ground floor. His wife Anne was sitting by the hearth, on a brown velvet fireside chair, engrossed in her needlework. Jonathan was struck by her sensible prettiness. She was not the sort of stunning, sought-after beauty as Jonathan's mother had been at Anne's age. Jonathan knew from observing his mother's complicated life through the years that such great beauty had its burdens, and he was relieved that Anne would not be so burdened. He took a moment to appreciate how her hair was pinned up, and how her mauve dress showed off her trim figure. He knew he was a fortunate man.

He stood near her chair. She raised her face, smiling. He leaned over and kissed her.

"I worried that you'd been caught in the deluge," she said.

"I managed to avoid it," he replied. "But I am absolutely famished."

Anne set aside her needlework, and glanced at the clock. "I'll ring for it. You know how punctual our cook is."

They seated themselves at the dining table nearby. It was a heavy, solid piece of furniture with carved claw-and-ball feet that had cost more than he had wanted to pay, but Anne had convinced him that it was a good investment. Jonathan now wondered whether Cowles would consider it "gimcrack." He was immediately annoyed with himself for wondering that. This morning, the notion would not have crossed his mind, and he reminded himself to not care what some opinionated chatterbox like Cowles thought about his furnishings, or anyone else's.

The walls were covered with dark green wallpaper that bloomed with large butterscotch-and-teal flowers. Burgundy velvet drapes were festooned over a brass rod. Against the wall was a Welsh dresser, displaying a collection of fine English china in floral patterns. The ceiling was papered in Anaglypta, embossed with scrolls and acanthus leaves.

Anne would've preferred that they take their meals in the formal dining room, but Jonathan loved this room, so it had become a custom for them to take all their meals there when the two of them were not entertaining guests. Jonathan had mentioned on more than one occasion that he'd always hated dining in the cold, formal dining room of his parents' house. He'd been determined that, when he had his own house, he'd take all his meals in a cosy room warmed by a merry hearth.

"This lamb is excellent," Jonathan remarked halfway through the meal. "You're hardly eating. Is there something wrong?"

Anne sighed. "Our cook is talented, but she is asking for an increase in wages. She is also demanding a live-in scullery maid."

"I thought we had one."

"Yes, we had one. But she was not live-in, and she went back to Wales. Cook says she will not tolerate any entertaining until we've got a scullery maid, plus additional help when the guests number more than six. Our staffing problems are reflecting badly on us, Jonathan. We cannot have guests until this is all straightened out, otherwise cook will quit on the spot. I hired a new maid, by the way. Her name is Daisy. She did my hair. Do you like it?"

"Your hair is lovely. I noticed it first thing. Listen, my dear, I trust whatever decision you think is the right one." Jonathan was exhausted listening to her. He didn't like talking about household matters—it was not his domain. His mother never troubled his father about staffing issues, and he wished Anne would follow suit. Perhaps he'd ask his mother to gently advise her on this.

To avoid discussing this weary topic further, Jonathan said: "By the way, this afternoon I was at a house—a mansion, really—in Belgravia. It was big, but not nearly as nice as our house. You couldn't pay me to live there. It was the kind of place that would require far too many servants."

Her face perked up with interest. "Do tell."

"It's been up for sale for years now, and they finally found a buyer."

"Let me guess," she said. "Some Scotsman got it at a cut-rate price."

"Not quite, my dear. The buyer is an aristocrat who lives in Eastern

Europe. Somewhere near the city of Klausenberg. I'm starting off tomorrow, as a matter of fact."

Her face fell. "Tomorrow? When will you return home?"

"As soon as I can. I plan to get the papers signed, and then turn around for London post-haste. The baron has paid a rather large retainer for an actual solicitor to travel to him so that he may sign the papers before he actually sets foot here. Mr. Miller was supposed to go, but I am going in his place. It should be quite the adventure."

"I see." She paused. "Jonathan," she began.

"Yes, my dear?"

"Nothing, except that we've received two invitations. One from the Martins, one from the Wingates. What shall I tell them?"

"Tell them I'll be out of town."

"You'll be away for my birthday."

He said: "My darling, we'll celebrate in style when I'm back. I promise. We'll dine at the Savoy. No expense spared. And we'll go to a musical comedy. I know you love them. And we'll travel to Paris for new hats and gowns."

"That sounds wonderful," she murmured.

After they had finished eating, they made their way across the room to their chairs in front of the hearth. Jonathan built up the fire, then settled into the cushions of his chair and smoked a cigarette. He listened to the rain falling against the window pane.

"Tell me more about what that Belgravia house was like," Anne said.

"It was a monstrosity. Dreary. Hardly any windows. And there was even a dungeon."

"A dungeon? Whatever for?"

"The man who built it had wanted a dungeon for some reason." He would not burden his wife's delicate sensibilities with the information Cowles had revealed.

Anne asked: "What do you suppose the buyer looks like? Is he young?"

Jonathan shrugged. "Oh, he's probably haughty. Like Tsar Nicholas."

Anne laughed. "I hope he doesn't have the tsar's ridiculous beard." Her face changed to sadness. "I won't know what to do with myself when you're gone."

Jonathan reached over and took her hand. "Darling, it won't be long. The time will fly. I promise. You can ride with my sister around Hyde Park."

16

"I'm a dreadful rider, and the horses know it. Your sister only tolerates me because her other friends are not always available."

"Nonsense. She adores you, as do Mother and Father."

"I'm not a native Londoner. That gets in the way."

"Let them turn you into one." An idea occurred to Jonathan. "Do you want to go to Bristol to visit your mother?"

"I'd rather not. Besides, our house here needs tending."

"Mrs. Taylor can tend the house, along with McWilliams. You can take Daisy with you."

"You're not taking McWilliams?"

Jonathan shrugged. "Why should I? I won't be away that long. I'm not one of those men who needs his valet every second of the day." He watched the flames dance in the hearth. "Think of how amusing it'll be when I'm back home, recounting my adventures in this very chair. And you, in a brand-new dress at the height of Paris fashion, amused at my tales."

At seven o'clock the next morning, Jonathan stood in front of his bookshelf. He was freshly shaven and dressed in his best grey-wool travelling suit, his best overcoat, a grey top hat, and kid-leather gloves. He patted the waistcoat pocket where his grandfather's gold watch was safely tucked. He was trying to decide which books he should take with him. He found a primer on Eastern European languages. A good choice—he could pick up a bit of the local language in whatever country he happened to be travelling through.

A Book of Psalms caught his eye. It was on a high shelf and hadn't been opened in decades. He took it down and read the Hebrew title: *Tehillim*. He opened the cover and read his maternal grandfather's sprawled handwriting on the flyleaf: Simeon Manfred Rosen, Wein, 1836. This was the psalter that had belonged to his mother's father, back when he had still lived in Vienna.

He hadn't thought about Grandfather Manfred in ages. His memories of the old man were vague. Manfred had made a small fortune in business—but Jonathan could not recall what the business had been. When Jonathan was a boy, Manfred had lived in London, in a small but tidy flat not far from Hyde Park. Manfred would often visit his daughter Hannah, Jonathan's mother, during the day when Jonathan's father was putting in long hours in court or in the House of Lords. Jonathan remembered liking his grandfather very much, for he was kind and always brought sweets. Grandfather Manfred would converse with Jonathan in both Yiddish and German, and he taught him to read Hebrew. Jonathan remembered the old man telling the young boy that he had an aptitude for learning, and that he should study German and Hebrew when he was at school—advice that Jonathan later followed. Jonathan's mother listened to their conversations with silent benevolence, neither encouraging nor discouraging Manfred's efforts to teach Jonathan. The lessons had been cut short by Manfred's death when Jonathan was eleven years old. Jonathan always knew, without being told, that his grandfather's peculiar Jewish ways were not to be discussed. His mother clearly loved her father very much, but there was a rift between them because of her decision to marry an Englishman from a titled lineage, and leave her own Jewish heritage behind.

Looking back, Jonathan realised that Manfred never treated Edward and Hannah with the same deference that others showed toward them. Manfred and Edward were perfectly cordial to each other, and Manfred clearly adored his daughter Hannah. But the intricacies of the British peerage and social system was of no concern to Manfred. That marked the Viennese Jew as an irredeemable outsider—a position he seemed to find perfectly satisfactory.

Jonathan paged through the book, looking at the psalms in Hebrew with their German and English translations. He remembered the day he had received that book. It was the 30th of December 1891, the day of his thirteenth birthday.

His father had been sitting in his favourite chair, reading a newspaper. His mother had come into the room, her magnificent auburn hair pinned up in an elaborate coiffure.

"Jonathan," she said, "I'd like a word with you."

Jonathan's younger brother and sister stopped playing with their new toys, and watched silently to see whether their brother was in trouble.

Jonathan followed his mother to another room, out of earshot of the rest of the family. She gave Jonathan a small, paper-wrapped package tied with a ribbon.

"When your grandfather was on his deathbed, he insisted that I give you this book on your thirteenth birthday."

"Why did he wait until I'm thirteen, Mother?" Jonathan asked.

"Because he hoped you would have returned to his faith, and would consider yourself bar mitzvah by now."

"What is that?" Jonathan asked.

"A son of the commandment. It marks the time in a Jewish boy's life when he is no longer a boy, but is now fully responsible for his moral choices."

"But I'm not Jewish," Jonathan observed.

His mother's face was inscrutable. "Take good care of the book," was all she said. Then she left the room, her taffeta skirt whispering softly as she moved. He carried the book to the library and placed it on the shelf with other books he owned.

When Jonathan returned to the game with his siblings, his younger brother Michael whispered: "Have you gotten in trouble?"

Jonathan shook his head no and whispered back: "Mum forgot to give me a book—a boring old book for my birthday," he said. He knew that it was not to be discussed.

He'd never forgotten that episode. His English identity remained singular and untouched by his grandfather's lessons. He had been a student in one of the best public schools in London, a baritone in the boys' choir, the grandson of Sir William Cecil Drake of Her Majesty's Royal Navy, son of the Right Honourable Lord Edward James Drake, the Lord of Appeal-in-Ordinary. The Drake family lineage could be traced back to Sir Francis Drake.

His mother's past had been buried and forgotten. It was understood that her upbringing was never to be mentioned, that as far as everyone was concerned, Lady Drake was pure English and always had been. Occasionally she even set foot in church, although Jonathan was an adult before he noticed that she never actually said the prayers or sang the hymns.

He shook himself out of his memory, closed the Book of Psalms, and added it to the others he planned to take with him. He suddenly remembered his conversation with Miller, and he wondered again whether the clever Jew could sense Jonathan's background. Nonsense. Jonathan had never mentioned any of it to anyone.

He returned to the present, descended the stairs of his house, and took notice of the spotless burgundy carpet runner under his feet. The oak rails of the staircase were polished to a high sheen by the housekeeping staff. His luggage was ready at the front door, including his Gladstone bag. He opened it and slipped his books inside. Then he turned his attention to the portmanteau, and checked that it was properly locked. Like his Gladstone bag, it was crafted of French leather, custom-made by Vuitton of Paris. It had been his parents' wedding gift to him.

Baron von Klausenberg would know from the expensive luggage alone that Jonathan was no ordinary solicitor, but was in fact someone of breeding. Jonathan looked forward to meeting the baron, perhaps even striking up a friendship with him. He thought ahead to social events they'd attend together, once the baron was settled in London. They'd both travel in smart circles, and Jonathan would always be distinguished by his role in helping the baron become a resident of London. Foreign royalty from the Continent were a far preferable addition to London social circles than were the South African merchant-class immigrants that Cowles had mentioned.

At breakfast, Anne said: "You cried out in your sleep last night."

"Did I?"

He had forgotten about the nightmare until now. There had been two shadowy figures, a mysterious man and woman, trying to drag him into the same dungeon that he'd visited yesterday with Cowles. Recalling the dream made his stomach sink. He pushed it out of his mind.

At the front door, he held his wife tightly.

"I really don't want you to go," Anne said.

He inhaled the lavender scent of her hair. "My darling, I'll miss you every moment I'm away. But I'll be home before you know it. Then, we can sit in our chairs, near the hearth, and I'll amuse you with stories of my adventures."

"Ask Stoker to send someone else," she implored.

It wasn't like her to ask him to shirk from his duties. Her panic disturbed him. He had a sudden premonition to do as she asked: Cancel the trip and stay home. But he reminded himself of his obligations, of his reputation. He would not back out. He wasn't a shirker like Miller. Not at all like Miller.

CHAPTER THREE

The train ride across Europe gave Jonathan time to read. He brushed up on his German, and taught himself a bit of some of the other languages of the region, including Roumanian. Sometimes he tried to converse with fellow passengers who spoke those languages. He studied his grandfather's psalter, and spent considerable time looking out the window.

When the train pulled into the station at Klausenberg, Jonathan was gratified to see that the station building had good architectural details— the sort of sensible red-brick building that one would find in London. Granted, Klausenberg wasn't London, but it was a perfectly acceptable city. He was certain Cowles would approve.

The ride from the train station to the small hotel didn't take long. The porter took his luggage straight to his room. The hotel itself was clean and respectable. Jonathan decided to take a walk, see a little bit of Klausenberg so that he could converse intelligently with the baron when he met him tomorrow.

He left his room, and as he walked down the corridor, he noticed the figure of a man in the doorway of a darkened room. The man was facing away from Jonathan, and there was a choking sound. Jonathan put his hand on the shoulder of the man and said: "I say, are you alright?"

The man turned abruptly, and released the hold that he had on the neck of a young woman whom he had pressed against the wall just inside the doorway. The man was a rough-looking type, with eyes that were flat and remorseless.

"What the devil are you doing, you swine?" Jonathan demanded.

The man pushed past Jonathan and fled down the corridor. The woman rubbed her neck and took deep breaths. She was young, and her upper teeth formed a serious over-bite. She was dressed in a maid's uniform, and she wore a white bonnet on her head.

"Are you alright? Shall we find a doctor?" Jonathan asked in English. He asked again in German.

"Thank you, no," she said in Roumanian, shaking her head. She gestured to a cart of cleaning supplies that was in the room, making it clear that she needed to carry on with her duties. Jonathan again implored her to seek help in his primitive Roumanian, but she remained adamant that she had to continue with her work.

Jonathan went downstairs. He debated whether he should tell anyone about what he'd just witnessed. Perhaps it was better to stay out of it. After all, Jonathan did not know the details, and he didn't know the custom of how such matters were handled in this country. Besides, the maid seemed able enough to report it herself if she were so inclined. Jonathan tried to put it out of his thoughts. He went to the front desk to find out where the shopping district was located. He wanted to buy a gift for Anne.

The hotel desk clerk was a fastidious-looking young man with close-cropped blond hair. He gave the impression of an efficient staff sergeant.

Jonathan started off in halting Roumanian, asking where he should go to find a souvenir for his wife. The young man quickly interrupted in good English.

"Yes, you will want a walk before supper, most Englishmen do," he said to Jonathan. "Herr Siegfried, at your service, Herr Drake." He clicked his heels smartly and gave a small bow. "And, I must inform you, your carriage to Baron von Klausenberg's estate will be here at seven in the morning, sharp."

Jonathan was impressed with the young man's efficiency, and he told him so. Then he asked: "Do you know the baron? What is he like? Which properties here in town belong to him?" The success of the journey depended on good information about his client.

The young man's blue eyes glittered. "Oh, he does not actually own property here in Klausenberg, although the most notable citizens of Klausenberg know that their . . . how do you say it, that their *fealty* . . . is to the Baron von Klausenberg. They *voluntarily* pay him tribute."

"It is curious that he owns no property here, and yet his surname is von Klausenberg. Surely he must have a parcel of land or house here in town."

Siegfried shrugged. "It is the way of things."

Jonathan was disconcerted. Just how rich a nobleman was this baron? Perhaps he'd been forced to sell. Even in the United Kingdom, that sort of unfortunate decision had been made even by peers whose holdings had been in the family for centuries.

Siegfried continued: "Our beloved baron is a most interesting man. Most interesting. Do not believe the evil rumours you hear about him. The Baron von Klausenberg will one day be a great leader throughout Europe."

"I hope not *too* great a leader," Jonathan quipped. "We have quite enough of those as it is."

The young man's face grew deadly serious. "There will come a time when all the nations bow to men such as the baron. Take care to stay on his good side, and all will be well with you."

Jonathan was unruffled. All these provincial types were under the delusion that theirs was the most important region. "Well, thank you for the advice, Herr Siegfried."

As he headed for the front door, Jonathan passed a young parlour maid in a black dress and starched white apron, a white bonnet pinned to her black hair. She was dusting a side-table. She raised her face and met his glance. She was the young woman whom Jonathan had saved from the clutches of the rough man upstairs.

Jonathan smiled at her, and then proceeded to the front door. He walked down the street, and took note of his surroundings so that he could recount the details to his wife when he was back home. It was a perfectly nice city, not nearly as sophisticated and grand as London, but then again, no city could compare to London. He spent the better part of an hour strolling the area near his hotel, and during that time he bought a silver brooch and a pair of gloves for his wife. As he was about to cross the street to the hotel's front door, a pale young woman in a black overcoat touched his arm and motioned for him to follow her. It was the maid from the hotel. Jonathan followed her, his curiosity piqued.

He stayed several paces behind. She glanced back at him every so often. After another intersection, she turned down a narrow alley between two stone buildings. The young woman stopped at a heavy wooden side door, and knocked. The door opened. The young woman motioned for Jonathan to follow her inside.

Jonathan stepped over the threshold, into a large vestibule with stone walls and a stone floor. The door closed behind him. The place smelled of carbolic soap. A char-woman, who looked to be in her late fifties, held a mop. A white kerchief was tied around her head like a turban. She wore a clean apron over a brown dress. The two women exchanged information in low voices, in Roumanian. As they talked, and as Jonathan's eyes adjusted to the dim interior, he realised he was in a synagogue.

The young maid turned to Jonathan and said in broken German: "To the baron's castle, do not go."

Jonathan held up his hand and replied in German: "I do not know who you are. Why did you bring me here?"

The char-woman spoke in a mixture of German and Yiddish. "I am named Ruth. My friend here is Sofia. She says you stopped the man who was attacking her. He is a tradesman who seeks to harm Sofia because she has refused his advances in the past. He is married, which shows you what a low character he is."

Sofia said something more, and Ruth translated. "Sofia very much appreciates the fact that you helped her. Now she wants to help you. She says you should not go to the baron's. It is dangerous."

"But I have a business obligation," Jonathan explained. "And besides, Herr Siegfried says that the baron enjoys great fealty from among citizens here in Klausenberg."

"Only out of fear do people give him fealty," Ruth said in a contemptuous whisper. "He is a tyrant."

"And yet he owns no property here in this city," Jonathan said. "So how can he have any real influence?"

"He does not need to own property. His hold over the citizens is exercised by other means."

"What other means?"

Ruth shook her head to indicate that she would not answer that question. Instead, she replied: "Sofia is right. You should not go."

"I appreciate your concern. But I will go, and then I will return home as soon as all the documents are signed." He turned to leave.

Ruth said: "Wait. Then let us give you something that will protect you." She reached into the pocket of her apron and pulled out a tarnished silver tube about four inches long. At first, Jonathan thought it was a cigarette lighter. She pressed it into Jonathan's hand and said: "This is a mezuzah."

"The thing that goes on a doorjamb?" he asked. He suddenly remembered the one that Grandfather Manfred had had on his front doorjamb. It had been made of blue glass with a gold-leaf design.

Ruth nodded. "The sacred parchment is inside. Place it on your doorpost and no demons will enter."

"I don't believe in demons. And I don't believe in magic talismans, either."

"You should," Ruth said.

Jonathan examined it. The silver face was inscribed with a Star of David and the Hebrew letter shin. The back was flat and hollow, and a rolled-up parchment, written in Hebrew, was nestled inside. He handed it back to her and said: "I really cannot accept this."

"You must take it," Ruth insisted.

The young maid said something in Roumanian, and the older woman translated: "Sofia asks your forgiveness. She thought you were a Jew. That is why she brought you here."

Jonathan's eyes narrowed at the young woman. "What made you think I was a Jew?" he asked her.

The young woman's face turned pale, and she talked quickly. Jonathan could tell she was apologizing for her mistake.

Jonathan held up his hand. "I forgive you. No need to apologize."

Ruth said: "Sofia has the extra sense. She is not always right. But her soul is good. That is why we are friends. Even though she is Christian, and I am Jewish, we are on the same side. We fight the evil ones."

Sofia reached into the high neckline of her black dress, drew out a wooden crucifix on a jute string, removed it from her neck, and held it out to Jonathan.

"This would be comical if it weren't so absurd," he muttered to himself in English. Then he switched to German. "Thank you for your concern, ladies, but I do not need any of these … amulets."

Sofia talked vehemently in Roumanian, gesturing at Jonathan and then at the cross. Her eyes were full of worry. Ruth held up a hand, and Sofia stopped talking.

"What's got her so agitated?" Jonathan asked.

"Sofia fears for your safety. She overheard Siegfried and his assistant clerk laughing about your journey tomorrow, and taking bets on how long you'll be there. She says Siegfried is a wicked man. Please be careful. And do not say anything to anyone of our conversation. If they discover that Sofia had tried to help you, she will be punished severely. The baron's cruel hand reaches far and wide."

"You have my word," Jonathan said. He was suddenly touched by the concern that these two women had shown toward a stranger. He felt he owed them something to make up for his annoyance at Sofia, so he added: "I am not a Jew, but my mother had been born a Jew."

Sofia understood enough of what Jonathan had said to start talking again. Ruth interrupted her, and said something in Roumanian to calm her down. Ruth turned to Jonathan. "I told Sofia that you know to guard your tongue, so she need not worry. Do not tell the Baron anything of your background, especially about your mother. Do not let him know you speak German. Lock your chamber door at all times—especially when you sleep. Trust no-one. The rumours are true. Children have disappeared. Those who cross the baron have been killed. May the Lord bless you and keep you, Herr Englishman."

Jonathan slipped the crucifix and the mezuzah into his pocket. As he opened the door and stepped out, he noticed a brass mezuzah affixed to the doorjamb. On impulse, he reached up and touched it, then continued on his way toward the main thoroughfare.

The next morning, the carriage that would take Jonathan to the baron's estate arrived at the hotel promptly at seven, drawn by two stocky, strong horses with tassels of red wool plaited into their tails and manes. Herr Siegfried supervised the transfer of the luggage into the carriage. He barked orders to a muscular coachman with a large moustache who looked to be in his twenties. The coachman was dressed in white wool trousers, a white tunic with flowing sleeves, and a knee-length sheepskin vest. On his head was a tall fur cap. Another coachman was dressed in similar clothing. He was old enough to be a grandfather, and had a full, grey beard. He sat in the coachman's seat holding the reins. Once the young coachman was finished loading Jonathan's bags, he seated himself next to the old man and took the reins. Jonathan settled himself into the passenger seat, then leaned out the window to ask Herr Siegfried a question.

"Why do the horses have red tassels?"

"For the evil eye," Siegfried answered. "The country folk are superstitious. You'll see their amulets of garlic, and pouches of salt—and of course, the crucifixes. It's all so quaint! Do not listen to their prattle about demons and night spirits. They'll tell you their horses can sense them. It is all nonsense, the foolish talk of the ignorant. Safe travels, Herr Drake. You'll soon learn how remarkable our baron truly is. London will be much enhanced to have him there."

On the front steps of the hotel, beyond where Herr Siegfried stood, Sofia was sweeping. She paused her work, looked at Jonathan, and made a sign of the cross in the air with her right hand. She resumed sweeping before Herr Siegfried could turn around and catch her in the act.

When Jonathan's carriage was well out of the city, the scenery became more beautiful. Thick forests covered the land. Patches of snow gleamed not just on the mountain summits, but also on the north edges of lower-lying valleys. The paved roads became dirt roads on which geese waddled and chickens scratched. Sheep and cows grazed in the fields. The tallest buildings in the countryside were the churches, made of wood, with oak-shingled spires that were not even as tall as Jonathan's house. Houses and barns were strikingly rustic, with rough-hewn walls and grass roofs. The peasants had dignified features, and they wore clothing that was similar to that of the two men who drove the carriage in which Jonathan was seated.

At every crossroad, there was at least one crucifix (and often a group of them) fashioned of wood or iron that were about as tall as a man. Some had bulbs of garlic hanging from them, or smaller crucifixes fashioned of twigs or straw that dangled on twine.

Jonathan soon wearied of the sightseeing, and the carriage jostled too much for him to read. Eventually, he fell into a deep, dreamless slumber.

He awoke to the carriage shaking violently. He looked out the window. The sky was dark with storm clouds. They were on a steep incline, and there was no road. Stones bounced and tumbled down the mountainside as the beasts struggled uphill, trying to find their footing. The young coachman had his hands full with the reigns, and the old man whipped them and cursed, urging them to go faster.

Jonathan hated to see the horses mis-treated like that. If their load were lightened, the horses would have an easier time. He leaned out the window and shouted up at the coachmen.

"I will walk," he said in Roumanian.

The younger coachman swore, and the old one continued to crack the whip.

Jonathan held the door ajar, ready to spring out if the carriage began to slip out of control. His knuckles were white, and he sweated in fear. They were already at a treacherous height. If the horses stumbled, the whole carriage would tumble downhill.

They finally arrived at a level, grassy meadow that still had patches of snow. The rain had started, and was turning bare patches of ground to mud. The horses were able to find secure footing again. Instead of letting them rest, the old man whipped them harder, spurring them on. The animals were sweating and foaming at the mouth, their eyes frantic with exhaustion and panic from their dangerous journey uphill.

"The horses want rest," Jonathan said to the coachmen. "The horses want water."

The younger coachman turned around long enough to give him a contemptuous look and mutter an insult. Then he pointed and said something to the older one, and the two men laughed. Jonathan was certain they were laughing at him.

But he was wrong. The men were laughing at an overturned wagon. A peasant was beating his horse with a stick. The animal was on its side, tangled in his harness and reins, and could not stand. The animal whinnied as the peasant beat it, but it could not get on its feet.

Jonathan was infuriated. What was wrong with these peasants? Did they not know how to treat their animals? He leaped out of the carriage and made his way over to the peasant. Jonathan grabbed the stick out of the man's hand and threw it to the side. He noticed that the peasant did not have a right hand.

The younger coachman from Jonathan's carriage gave the reins to the old man, leaped down from his seat, and strode over to Jonathan, clenching his fists and yelling.

Jonathan stood his ground. He said in broken Roumanian: "I help him, you help him."

The coachman stared at him insolently, and made no move. The rain fell in a steady downpour.

A sudden fury seized Jonathan. He said in English: "Who do you think you are to ignore my orders, you bloody scoundrel? You savages abuse your horses, and I won't stand for it!"

The coachman made an obscene gesture of dismissal.

Jonathan punched the man in the nose. The man punched back and bruised Jonathan's cheekbone under his eye, drawing blood. Jonathan's top hat had been knocked off his head and was now lying in the mud. The old man on the carriage shouted, and the younger man retreated, the blood from his nose running onto his white tunic. Jonathan was surprised by the young man's sudden surrender, and at his own fury.

"Help now," Jonathan ordered. He removed his gloves and put them in his pocket.

The coachman grudgingly lent a hand, glaring at Jonathan. The three men freed the horse and got it to stand. Then they turned the peasant's wagon upright.

When the horse was re-harnessed and the wagon ready to go, the peasant grinned and thanked Jonathan and the coachman. Some teeth were missing, and his right eye socket was thick with scar tissue.

The younger coachman swore at the peasant, and then, in a spiteful, bitter tone, he told the peasant something that Jonathan could not understand except for the mention of the baron's name.

The peasant shrank back. His scarred eyelid twitched. With his remaining hand, he rubbed the stump where his other hand had been. Then he scampered onto his wagon and drove off, glancing back in fear.

Jonathan picked up his grey top hat, which was wet and muddy, and got back into the carriage. His cheekbone where the coachman had punched him was throbbing, and when he touched it, there was blood on his fingers. He drew out of his Gladstone bag a clean handkerchief and his small looking-glass, and tried to clean himself up. His suit was wet and muddied, and he hoped that the baron's valet was as talented at cleaning textiles as Jonathan's valet was. He slipped the looking-glass and kerchief into his pocket.

They travelled for another two hours. The carriage turned down a lane that led to a cobblestoned courtyard, and then came to a stop in front of a building. The rain had cleared, and a moonless night was fast approaching. The only light came from a single lamp next to a massive front door. Jonathan wondered why the baron's servants had not lit more lamps to herald his arrival. Surely a servant would appear with a lantern at any second, and summon a porter to carry the luggage.

The horses whinnied and stomped their hooves, straining against the reins. Their ears were flattened back. The old man held the reigns tightly while the younger coachman threw Jonathan's portmanteau onto the cobblestones. He muttered the words "vampir, satana, monstru."

Jonathan yelled at him. "Don't throw that luggage, you fool! It costs more than your yearly income."

But the young coachman ignored him, took the reins from the old man, and cracked the whip. The horses bolted into the night, leaving Jonathan behind.

The portmanteau had burst open, and the contents spilled out onto the cobblestones. Among the items were the crucifix and the mezuzah that the two maids had given to him. He had purposely left them behind in his room in Klausenberg, but now here they were. How did they end up in his portmanteau? It took Jonathan just a few seconds to realise that Sofia had probably slipped into his room when he had been at breakfast that morning, before his luggage had been taken to the carriage. No wonder her face had been serene when she made the sign of the cross as he was waiting to depart.

Jonathan put the mezuzah and crucifix into his jacket pocket. He stuffed his personal items back into the portmanteau and fastened the latches. He made his way to the front door. His luggage remained on the courtyard cobblestones. The porter would carry it in. There was no danger of rain. The sky had cleared and there were stars in the black sky.

He tried the door knocker and waited. The massive door was made of wood with heavy iron brackets and hinges, and it was carved with strange symbols. The black iron knocker was a fantastical eagle-dragon with a square head, looking to the left. Its talons gripped a sword. It was the same insignia Jonathan had seen on the letters from the baron, and on the jacket of Herr Siegfried at the hotel. Jonathan ran his finger along the curved blade of the sword. To his surprise, it was sharp and it cut his finger. The symbols on the door included a sun with rays that looked like lightning bolts, and the letter X with bent ends.

He put his finger in his mouth, and lifted the door knocker with his other hand to let it fall on the massive door. He waited a few seconds, and put on his gloves. Then knocked again.

The door opened to reveal a short, stocky man with a lantern. His thin hair was uncombed, and his beard was scraggly and untrimmed. His black eyebrows met on the bridge of his nose, forming one heavy line across his brow. He grinned like a country simpleton, but his dark eyes betrayed a calculating hostility that made Jonathan wary.

"I am Iosip," the man said in heavily accented English. "You are Mr. Miller?"

Jonathan didn't want to be out in the menacing dark a moment longer, so he stepped over the threshold, past the servant, without waiting for a formal invitation to enter. He had expected a grand entry hall, but it was an unremarkable rotunda of rough-hewn stone, probably from the Medieval period.

Jonathan presented his card, removed his hat, and held it out to the servant.

Iosip took the card but not the hat. Then he began laughing, and pointed out into the courtyard. "Your bags will stay there?"

"You may bring them to my room."

"We have no porter," Iosip said with a smug grin.

"Then *you* can carry them," Jonathan said, irritated at the man's impudence. "You *are* a servant, aren't you?"

"I do not carry bags."

Any servant who behaved this way in London would have been dismissed on the spot. Jonathan was about to upbraid the man, but he realised it was futile. He put his hat back on his head, and retrieved the luggage himself. Back inside the doorway, he dropped the bags.

Iosip stood at the threshold with the lantern, peering intently into the darkness outside. Then he turned and grinned at Jonathan. Jonathan knew he himself looked dishevelled from having been soaked and muddied in the rain. But that should not matter to a servant who knew his place.

"Do not go out at night," Iosip warned.

"Are there wolves?"

"Not wolves. Dogs." He held his lantern high and whistled out into the night. A few moments later, a large pack of German shepherds came running. Iosip gave another command, and the dogs stopped, waiting obediently on the courtyard cobblestones at the foot of the stairs. Their red eyes reflected the light from the lantern.

Jonathan was behind Iosip, peering out at the dogs in amazement and fear.

"They attack at my command," Iosip said. He whistled again for the dogs to disperse, stepped back inside, shut the door, and turned to his guest. "Come, I take you to the baron."

Jonathan was shaken by the strange display of the dogs' obedience. He needed time to freshen up before his meeting with the baron. "Please take me to my quarters first." He rubbed his chin, feeling the stubble that was already there. A shave would be nice, too.

"No. The baron will see you immediately. You are already late."

Jonathan debated whether he should carry his own luggage. It wouldn't do to meet the baron in the role of a common porter, but perhaps the baron would notice the laxity of his servants and upbraid them. Jonathan grabbed his luggage and followed Iosip down a dark hallway. The bare walls were smudged with soot. Jonathan was surprised that there were no paintings, no tapestries, not even hunting trophies. Had the baron already sent his things to London? Before the deal was finalized? Well, that meant he'd sign the papers immediately, and Jonathan would be on his way home tomorrow.

Iosip paused at a set of double doors. He opened one of the doors and motioned for Jonathan to enter. Jonathan knew this would be where he'd meet the baron. He was annoyed that he was being made to look like a commoner—a dishevelled, muddy one at that. So he dropped his luggage just outside the door, and entered the room. There was a blazing fire in the hearth, and a dining table set for one. A silver nine-branched candelabrum on the table burned brightly. Nobody else was in the room.

Jonathan took the opportunity to retrieve the mirror from his pocket. If he couldn't change his wet and muddy clothes, he could at least make sure his face was clean. He checked to be sure there were no mud splatters and no blood. The bruise where he'd been punched was swollen and discoloured, but it wasn't bleeding.

From another doorway next to the hearth, a tall figure entered the room, silhouetted against the blazing fire. "I am Baron von Klausenberg," the man said in a resonant, commanding voice. The baron's English was precise, but strangely accented.

Jonathan was at first embarrassed to be caught primping himself in such a dishevelled state. He quickly bowed to this aristocrat. When he straightened up, his embarrassment gave way to shock.

The baron's appearance was extraordinary. His long hair and white beard looked as if a barber's shears had not touched them in years. He wore a dingy yellow tunic over his torso, unfastened to the breastbone, revealing a pale chest covered with white hair. Over the tunic was a knee-length black robe, loosely fastened and elaborately embroidered with dragon-like creatures that clutched curved swords and globes in their talons. The baron's thin legs were emphasized by black stockings and red slippers that came to a point. He wore a strange scent.

The baron stood akimbo, and said: "Mr. Miller. Welcome."

He pointed at the looking-glass that Jonathan was still holding, and held out his hand to examine it. Jonathan noticed that his nails were long, polished, and filed to points—they were odd, but they were also the most fastidious aspect of his appearance.

"May I see that?" the baron demanded.

Jonathan gave the small looking-glass to him. The baron flung it into the blazing fireplace. He smiled at the surprised expression on Jonathan's face.

"We do not allow such objects of vanity here, Mr. Miller."

"I am not Mr. Miller. I am Jonathan Drake."

"I was not informed of this," the baron said with cold annoyance.

"I gave my calling card to Iosip."

"Your office ought to have notified me before you arrived."

"There was no time. Miller was … indisposed."

Jonathan held out another calling card in his gloved hand. The baron plucked it from his fingers.

The baron called out: "Iosip! Bring those bags up to his room. Our guest is not Mr. Miller, it is—" The baron read the card. "The Hon. Jonathan Drake, Esq." He did not pronounce the abbreviations as a full word.

Jonathan heard Iosip's footsteps approaching, and then receding.

Jonathan turned to the baron and said: "Your Lordship ought to be aware that Iosip made me carry the bags this far. The coachmen threw my luggage on the ground. It's unacceptable."

The baron said nothing. His eyes were cold and focused. Jonathan noticed that one eye was glacier blue, the other amber-brown.

Finally, the baron said: "I've had dinner prepared for you, Mr. Drake. Forgive me if I do not partake, but I have already eaten."

Jonathan was incredulous. "Your Lordship has just ignored what I said."

"Not at all, Mr. Drake. You are exhausted from a trying journey. Please sit down and refresh yourself."

Jonathan sat at the dining table, and helped himself to the covered dishes. He put two sausages on his plate, some fried potatoes, boiled beets, and sauerkraut. The baron sat at the head of the table, and offered bread from a silver bread basket. He poured wine from a crystal decanter into Jonathan's plain pewter goblet. He himself sipped from an enormous silver goblet that was elaborately engraved with strange symbols.

Jonathan cut a slice of sausage, and tasted it. He wanted to spit it back out, but that would be rude. So he forced himself to chew and swallow it.

The baron watched him intently. "What do you think?"

"I ... I've never tasted anything like it," Jonathan said. The truth was, he found it revolting.

"And you never will, outside of Iosip's fleischzimmer," the baron said. "Ah, forgive my use of German. In English, I believe you would call it a 'sausage room.'"

Jonathan would have translated it as "meat room," but he didn't reveal his knowledge of German. Instead, he asked: "Does your lordship fancy his culinary creations?"

The baron chuckled. "I myself don't eat flesh."

"What kind of animal is this particular sausage made from?" Jonathan asked. He wanted to know what to avoid should it appear on the menu at breakfast.

The baron waited a moment before answering. "A small creature that inhabits this area." He smiled. His teeth appeared square and grey in the firelight—like gravestones, Jonathan thought. The image made him shiver, and he told himself that the stress of travel was making his imagination run wild.

The baron clapped his hands together. "Now. Let us talk about punctuality."

"I beg your pardon?"

"You arrived later than expected."

"That is true," Jonathan said. "My apologies, Baron von Klausenberg. You see, I ordered the coachmen to stop so that I could help a man—"

The baron held up his hands. "In your country, that may be acceptable. But here, it is not acceptable. You are under my employ, so you should have had more consideration for my time."

"I take full responsibility for being late," Jonathan said, his tone hardening. "And I ask your lordship to not hold the coachmen responsible for my actions. They were following my orders. And rightly so."

"Their orders come from me, not you. When they obey you, that means they are disobeying me."

Jonathan was caught off-balance. "But you and I are both men of rank."

"Wrong, Mr. Drake. I am a baron. You are not."

Jonathan retorted: "In our country, foreign titles don't necessarily correspond to English titles. You will perhaps be called 'baron' as a courtesy once you get to London, but that does not signify that your rank is equivalent to that of an English baron. Furthermore, your lordship cannot possibly know that my paternal grandfather was Sir William Cecil Drake. He was an admiral in Her Majesty's Royal Navy, and he was knighted by Her Majesty Queen Victoria." Jonathan drew out his pocket watch. "This was a gift to him by the Duke of Marlborough. My father is the Right Honourable Lord Edward Drake, Lord of Appeal-in-Ordinary. His rank is equivalent to that of a baron. Our family's lineage goes back to Sir Francis Drake."

"And your point is what, exactly?" the baron asked blandly.

Astonished at the baron's reaction, Jonathan took a moment to put the gold watch back in his pocket, and formulate a retort. Then he said: "My original point is that servants ought to listen to whichever of their betters is present at the time the orders are given."

The baron scoffed. "You believe yourself to be of a similar rank to me. Well, in this country, we are not so taken with all these details as you English are. Keep that in mind, or there will be consequences." He paused, and then reached out to touch the wound on Jonathan's cheekbone with one of his long fingernails. Jonathan drew back, shocked at the man's audacity.

"How did you injure yourself?" the baron asked.

"The coachman and I fought. I ordered him to help me upright the peasant's cart—"

"My coachman ought to have killed you for your impudence," the baron said.

"A servant would never dare assault one of his betters. That would be outrageous."

"Outrageous?" the baron echoed with contempt. "Those are my rules. You'll notice there is no crime among my people."

"That is not true. Your people are superstitious. And they abuse horses."

The baron chuckled derisively. "The sooner those infernal beasts are replaced by motorcars, the better."

"Nobody has the right to abuse horses, or any other animal," Jonathan countered. He hadn't meant to get into an argument with the baron, but he was allowing himself to get carried away. The man was maddening. And perhaps mad.

The baron changed the subject. "You English think you are so superior because you care for the welfare of horses. And yet, your cities are filled with the poor and destitute. Here, we have no class of desperately poor as you have in London. We have no classes at all."

Jonathan gestured at the room. "So your lordship is that saying all of your subjects live in estates such as yours? I saw none on my way here from Klausenberg."

The baron chuckled. "What I mean is, everybody under my rule is equal. There is no merchant class to exploit the poor. Of course, the ruler himself must be above the common man, otherwise, how can he be effective?"

"So then your lordship believes in autocracy," Jonathan observed.

The baron said: "What I believe is irrelevant. The question is: What do the masses believe? If they believe in democracy, communism, socialism, republicanism, capitalism—then give them their beliefs. If they believe in aristocracy, monarchy, theocracy, oligarchy—then give them their beliefs. The content of their beliefs does not matter. What matters is how a ruler harnesses them to do the work that must be done. A shrewd leader tells the masses he agrees with them, that he shares their beliefs, that he is on their side. He tells them that he is their superior or their equal—or even their inferior—depending on what the masses want him to be. Then he leads them on the path that he chooses, all the while convincing them that they themselves are choosing their own perfect destiny. The masses believe themselves free, yet all the while their necks are in the yoke and the ruler holds the reigns."

"But that is deception."

The baron smiled. "Deception is a necessary tool for wielding the sword of power, Mr. Drake. And the sword of power is essential for ushering in a better world." He took a drink from his goblet and said, "But let us talk of something more congenial. Tell me about yourself."

Jonathan was put off by the man's unwarranted arrogance and outlandish political views. He said in a perfunctory tone: "There isn't much to tell. I live in London with my wife, and I am employed at a firm called Gershon, Stoker, and King. I have already told you of my family."

"And how long have you been married?"

Jonathan explained that they'd been married only since September, and they had no children.

The baron said: "One day I should like to marry and have children. Naturally, the woman I choose will be worthy of what I can bestow upon her, which is considerable since I am the only one of my bloodline who yet survives."

Jonathan wondered what sort of a woman would take him as a husband. Jonathan thought: *This man won't survive in London, except as a reclusive outcast. Well, that is his problem, not mine.* Jonathan reminded himself that he was here to get the transaction completed, and then his job was finished.

The baron stared at the flickering candles. "So, this Gershon, in your law firm. Tell me about him."

Jonathan was puzzled by the baron's interest in a dead law partner, but he answered as best he could. "Eli Gershon passed away in 1900, before I joined. I only know him from the portrait that hangs in the waiting room. He was a smart fellow, and those who knew him tell me he was kind and generous."

"He was a Jew, correct? You can tell by looking," the baron said. "The semitic profile is distinctive. It is all very scientific, and I have studied it in detail—" He interrupted himself and smiled. "But I am afraid I am boring you with details."

Jonathan wondered if his mother's heritage showed in his own features. He also thought of the charwoman's warning not to disclose his mother's background.

Jonathan chuckled to lighten the mood, and asked: "Why does any of it matter?"

The baron's eyes narrowed, and his smug expression vanished into a scowl. "You are not familiar with the epic struggle we face, are you?" the baron said. "It is the struggle between the forces of progress and stagnation, between forward movement and regression. And sometimes, the way forward is to go back to the old ways, to the ways before the interlopers came. I and my progeny are poised to change all that."

"You told me you have no children."

"Not yet. But I will."

From somewhere down one of the dark passageways, a clock struck the hour. The baron rose, and Jonathan followed his lead.

"It is time to bid you goodnight, Mr. Drake."

"I have the papers for you to sign here," Jonathan said, taking them out of his pocket. He was eager to get the transaction done and be on his way back home as soon as possible.

"Not now. Tomorrow."

"Would you like to hear about your new house? I have seen it—"

"If you'll excuse me, I have things I must attend to. Do not rush, Mr. Drake. Iosip will show you to your room. When you are ready to summon him, the bell pull is right there." The baron pointed to a tattered strip of needlework. "My estate is at your disposal. I have instructed Iosip to keep the dogs confined during the day, so you may take walks. You British do love your walks, I know. But at night, it would be wise to stay inside. The dogs roam free then. The library is extensive. I'm sure you will find it engrossing."

"Regrettably, I will not be staying long enough to enjoy all that you have offered," Jonathan said.

"Goodnight, Mr. Drake."

In his room, Jonathan felt exhausted, but could not sleep. He wished he had some brandy, and he thought about finding Iosip to ask for some, but everything was deathly quiet, except for the hooting of an owl outside and the occasional bark of one of Iosip's dogs. He surrendered to his insomnia, lit the candle, sat at the worn desk, and started to write a letter to Anne. He found that he was not in the mood to go into detail. Describing his current surroundings just made him miss his home even more. He dashed off a few lines, telling her that he was all right but exhausted. He'd write more later.

The room felt cold and forlorn, and the candle could not chase away the deep shadows that seemed to close in on him. It was a circular room, so he guessed he was in a turret. On the walls, large areas of stone were exposed where the plaster had fallen away. The furniture was sparse and not in good condition. A small casement window looked out into a pitch-black night. Jonathan opened the window and leaned out with the candle. It was impossible to see much of anything, but he did notice the glowing eyes of about a dozen animals at the base of the turret two storeys below—Iosip's infernal dogs, no doubt, keeping watch.

Jonathan shivered and withdrew, closing the window and making sure that the sash lock was fastened. Then he went to the door and wedged the desk chair under the door handle. He chastised himself for his late-night precautions, undoubtedly due to an over-active imagination that finds itself in a strange place, fuelled by exhaustion.

Jonathan changed into his night clothes, and hung his damp and muddy travelling suit on the only hanger he found in an otherwise empty armoire. He took the psalter out of his jacket pocket, and read it while in bed, with the candle nearby.

He dozed off at some point. He dreamed he was running in the dark, pursued by dogs. He woke up several times, impatient for the dawn to come. At one point, he re-lit the candle next to his bed to check his watch. He managed to fall asleep just as a grey dawn was showing through the casement window.

When he awoke and looked at his watch, it was almost half-past noon. In daylight, he was able to see the view from his window. He was definitely at the top of a turret, at the end of what appeared to be the eastern wing of the castle. If he leaned out of the window and craned his neck to the left, he could see the courtyard where he had arrived last night. Looking to the right, he saw nothing but thick green forest. Directly below his window was a sheer drop into a deep ravine, the bottom of which was concealed by a heavy canopy of trees.

He wanted something to eat. He moved the chair that he had wedged under the door handle and opened the door. A tray had been left there. He carried it into his room. Remembering last night's dinner, he would not touch the meat. Instead, he ate the bread and cheese, and drank the cold tea. He decided to take a walk and see when the baron was available to sign the papers. As soon as that was completed, Jonathan would make arrangements to return home.

The corridors were empty. No servants were about. In the daylight, Jonathan saw that the walls were painted a hideous olive-green. Some of the walls held an occasional dusty animal head or tattered pelt. Nails with bits of fur still clinging showed that other hunting trophies had once been mounted there. The dirty wall sconces looked as if they hadn't been used in ages. The whole place reeked of neglect. It would take a huge packet of money just to bring it up to acceptable standards—more money, perhaps, than the baron had. No wonder he wanted to move to more respectable quarters. Whatever architectural faults the baron's London house might have—and Jonathan didn't know enough to share Cowles's opinions—it was a vast improvement over this place.

Jonathan found the library. There were old volumes in various languages, but nothing that captured his interest.

Jonathan went outside, into the bright sunlight. Wandering around, he got a better feel for the estate.

The entire property sat on a mountaintop plateau, and could only be approached from a single road on the north side of the mountain. It was a sensible location for a noble family that had to defend their estate from civil unrest and foreign invaders. That would explain why the baron's family had been able to live there for centuries.

The place was not really a castle, though, it was a large, rambling country estate that had been added to, haphazardly, throughout the ages. Parts of it looked like the remnants of a medieval keep. Some parts were a Bavarian country house, still others were Gothic, with small spires and pointed-arch entryways. It was a jumble of conflicting styles, illogical outcroppings, half-finished additions that seemed to go nowhere. Jonathan was no expert on architecture, but he could see that the form did not follow the function. What was this place trying to be? There was a dishonesty about it, as if the empty corridors concealed their true nature. He wondered what Cowles would say if he were here. It would be scathing, that much Jonathan knew.

It suddenly occurred to Jonathan that the rambling, haphazard nature of the estate was similar to the baron's incoherent political philosophy: Harmony did not signify, history and tradition were of no consequence, nor were aesthetics and good taste. The only thing that mattered was expediency, the rapid put-up of another wing, the hasty addition of another a room, to serve an immediate purpose and further an immediate aim. Perhaps the baron's new mansion in Belgravia—with all of the faults Cowles had noted—would in fact suit him well. The Belgravia mansion was, after all, far more unified than this place, even if it bore the mark of the vulgar taste of the mattress-manufacturer who had originally built it.

To the east there had once been gardens. The broken outlines of

41

the planter beds were still visible. The adjacent stables were empty and dilapidated. Jonathan felt lonely and disoriented as he looked around the abandoned stalls, wondering why the baron didn't keep at least a few horses of his own. There was no livestock, not even chickens.

Jonathan found Iosip just inside the doorway of what used to be a gardening shed, not far from the wing where Jonathan's room was located. Iosip was sitting on a low bench, stropping a knife blade with a piece of leather. In front of him on the ground, knives, cleavers, scythes and axes were meticulously laid out. He held the blade very close to his eyes, and felt the edge with his thumb. Jonathan realised he had poor eyesight.

"When will the Baron be available?" Jonathan asked.

Iosip squinted at the sky. "Soon." Then he looked down at the knife in his hand.

From his breast pocket, Jonathan drew out a letter to Anne. "Please be sure to post this letter to my wife. And inform me the moment the baron is available."

"Yes, Herr Drake." Iosip took the letter, and dropped it on the ground next to where he sat.

"I need a looking-glass for my room. I cannot shave properly without it."

"We have none."

"Why the devil not?"

"The baron does not like them. He says people need not see what they've become."

"I can understand why *he* might not want to see his own reflection …" Jonathan stopped before he insulted his host further. "You seem to be the only one about. Do you cook my food?"

"No, my sister does. Her name is Mora."

"Please tell Mora to do a better job with housekeeping in my quarters. She is not carrying out her duties like she should. I need fresh linens and fresh water in the wash stand. And the chamber pot needs attention"

Iosip grinned, and his eyes held the same clever malice Jonathan had seen the night before. "The name Mora is Slavic for night demon. Do not let her into your room. She knows how to make the light go out of people's eyes."

"What the devil does that mean?"

"If you choose not to understand, I choose not to explain it," Iosip snapped.

Jonathan asked: "Have you no other servants who can do the work?"

Iosip gestured to the dilapidated gardens beyond the shed doorway. "You see how it is here. Only my sister and me."

"You have no livestock. How do you have enough meat for curing?"

"We hunt it."

Jonathan wondered how Iosip could hunt with weak eyesight. Maybe he paid some of the locals to shoot game.

"Why do you have no horses here?"

Iosip held up another blade to inspect it, and to feel it with his thumb. The sun glinted off the shiny metal. "The baron does not like horses. And they do not like him."

"Is that why he permits the peasants to abuse them?"

Iosip was silent. Then he said: "Many people here—including the coachman of your carriage—believe horses can sense things that we humans cannot. When supernatural beings are nearby, the horses become unruly. They flatten their ears and snort. They try to run."

"The horses did that last night in the courtyard. Is that why the coachman was muttering about monsters and vampires? Is that why he threw my luggage on the ground and hurried away?"

Iosip sneered. "You ask foolish questions, Englishman. The answer is plain, but you choose not to see it. The carriage coachman loves his horses. He drove them hard because he fears the baron. We make sacrifices when the baron asks us to, even if it means sacrificing that which we love."

For a moment, Iosip's lip trembled, and he looked as if he would cry. Jonathan realised that Iosip was admitting that he himself had been forced to make sacrifices of something—or someone—that he had loved. Fear overtook Jonathan, and his tongue was sharp when he was afraid.

"I really do not understand why you, or anyone else here, puts up with such tyranny," Jonathan rebuked him. "We English overthrow our tyrants. Why, we even beheaded our king, Charles the First, back in 1649. And the baron is hardly a king."

Iosip's face settled into its customary hostility. He retorted: "You do not fear the baron, but in time, you will."

Chapter Four

Jonathan spent the remainder of the daylight hours in the baron's library, perusing old volumes to pass the time. He went back to his room at sunset, and found that a tray of food had been left on his bed. That meant one of the servants—Mora, perhaps?—had been there.

His humble supper was interrupted by a knock at his door. It was Iosip, telling him that the baron had returned and wanted to sign the papers immediately. Jonathan hastily wiped his mouth, straightened his collar, and put on his suit jacket, making sure that the papers were in order. As he followed Iosip to meet the baron, he realised he had neglected to put the psalter in his jacket pocket. It must still be on the bedside table where he'd left it that morning. No matter, he thought, as he approached the room where the baron awaited him. His personal belongings would be safe until he returned. He looked forward to leaving for home tomorrow.

The baron was seated at the table, sipping a glass of red wine. His appearance was outlandish. He wore an old military uniform that looked Prussian. His hair was tucked under a seventeenth-century English cavalier hat. The black leather hat had an enormously wide brim, decorated with an ostrich plume. The effect was jarring: The hat did not match the military uniform; they were not even from the same country nor the same century.

The baron gestured for Jonathan to sit. He poured a glass of wine for Jonathan from a decanter.

"Now, my dear Mr. Drake, it has been quite an exhilarating day, but exhausting. So, let us sign those papers. I wish to leave for London tomorrow."

"As do I." Jonathan took the papers out of his pocket and laid them flat on the table, smoothing out the creases. The baron grabbed a pen and ink from the side board. With a flourish, the baron signed every required page. Jonathan handed the baron his copies. Then he slipped the remaining pages into his breast pocket.

Jonathan was relieved and happy. He could go home. He said: "The house you have just purchased is a spectacular piece of property, one of the most desirable locations in London. I can tell you about some of its history—"

"Yes, yes, I will see it all soon enough," the baron said, waving his hands dismissively. "How can I secure an introduction to Mr. Crowley? Can you write a letter of introduction?"

"Aleister Crowley? But, but I don't know him," Jonathan stuttered in surprise. "He's disreputable. Rumours of cannibalism and the like. Of course, it could all be nothing more than malicious tittle-tattle."

"Exactly the man I wish to meet. No matter. I'll find him. And Oliver Haddo, too." The baron took a small volume from his pocket. "I believe this is yours," he said.

It was the psalter.

"How did you get this?" Jonathan demanded.

"Why, you must've dropped it while you were exploring my estate today. Or you left it in my library. Something like that."

Jonathan racked his memory. Had he been carrying it around today? Or had he left it on the bedside table? It's possible that someone had nicked it from his room. He slipped it into his jacket pocket.

"Who is Simeon Manfred Rosen of Vienna?" the baron asked.

"My maternal grandfather."

"Ah. So you are a Jew."

"No, I'm not."

"Your grandfather was a Jew. Your mother is a Jew. That makes you a Jew." The baron's smile was cold. "And yet you deceived me about your true heritage."

"Not at all. I was raised in the Church of England."

46

"That does not erase your Jewish blood."

"Whatever blood is in my veins is unimportant," Jonathan said, taking a sip of wine. Why did the baron insist on pressing this point? It was uncivilized.

"Ah, now that is where you are wrong," the baron said. "Blood is everything. Everything. Our struggle cannot be won until we embrace the power of blood. Even the Jews know this. It is why their deity forbids them to consume blood. Their deity knows it contains the true power. That is what the serpent was referring to in the Garden of Eden. The forbidden fruit is blood. To consume the blood is to be like unto the gods."

Jonathan was suddenly disturbed that this eccentric man would be living in his home city. He asked: "Why does your lordship insist on coming to London? Why not go to Vienna or Berlin? Or Paris?"

The baron chuckled and lit a cigarette. "Oh, believe me, I did not want to go to London, Mr. Drake. You English disgust me, to be perfectly frank. But it became clear to me that London is where I must go. You see, the Austro-Hungarian Empire will soon be a mere footnote in history. It will flicker out soon, like a candle in an open window."

Jonathan wondered how the baron could be so daft, and believe such absurdities.

"I see from your face that you do not believe me," the baron observed. "Aristocratic rulers are doomed. The aristocracy will die. Titled men like me are outdated. The future lies with common men, men with a furnace in their belly. They'll burn down the world, reduce it all to ashes. But from the ashes will come a spark, and from that spark there will rage a fire that history has never seen. That fire will be a dark fire. It will cleanse Europe and the whole globe. My mission is to facilitate the coming of the dark fire."

"So, are we talking about socialism?" Jonathan asked. He really didn't know what socialism was, except that it was bad. But he was in a better mood now, and it wouldn't hurt to let this madman prattle on for a little while. He took another sip of wine.

The baron laughed. "Oh, the term 'socialism' is not large enough to describe what I mean. It is so much more than that. But if we need to use that term to herd the masses in our direction, then by all means, let us call it socialism. Or Marxism. Or Jacobinism. Or any other term that accomplishes my objective. It really does not matter."

The baron stood and paced the room. His gestures were animated.

"The important direction is this. We must destroy the old rules. We must free ourselves from the prison of our conscience. We must weed out the weak, the unnecessary. We must create a new order. These are the goals of enlightened progress." He paused. "Now, about mankind's enemies. We agree on who that is, do we not Mr. Drake?"

Jonathan suppressed a yawn, and resisted the urge to look at his pocket watch. "And who would that be?" he asked in an indifferent, patronizing tone.

"Why, the Hebrews. The western world has been tainted by them. We must return to the times before the vengeful deity of the Old Testament imprisoned us all with endless laws and prohibitions. The only hope is to return to the ancient faith of our northern forebears, to the old gods. This is why I must meet Mr. Crowley. He is a true visionary, and a fine poet, I might add."

Jonathan wanted to avoid this discussion—it was too dangerous. To change the subject, he asked: "I still do not understand. You mentioned the death of the aristocracy. Why go to London, then? We're rather fond of our aristocrats and we'll defend them to the death."

The baron sat down and lit another cigarette. "I want to ensure that the progress of the world is not hindered by your country's intransigence. It is war, Mr. Drake."

Jonathan was confused. "Are you saying that the Austro-Hungarian monarchy will try to take over British territories? Do they plan to start a war with us?" His mind was racing ahead, mentally assembling a list of those whom he'd need to contact in His Majesty's government.

The baron shook his head. "You misunderstand me. The war is hidden. The Habsburg monarchy is on its last legs. Your beloved Britain will outlast it, but barely. The true problem is, Britain will hinder a new world order."

"How?"

The baron gazed at Jonathan intently. "There are individuals in London who would try to stop our progress."

"Such as?"

"Churchill. And others."

48

"You mean Lord Randolph Churchill? He's been dead for a decade."

"No, not him. The son of the American whore."

Jonathan laughed. "Lady Churchill's son Winston? He's a shameless self-promoter. Nobody takes him all that seriously, except perhaps whoever is publishing his latest scribblings."

An amused smile played across the baron's lips. "You don't understand these things, Mr. Drake."

"Maybe not," Jonathan conceded. "But since nobody in London would have a clue as to what you are talking about, how can anybody there possibly be an obstacle?" Jonathan was thoroughly vexed at the baron's delusions. The man was now wasting time, ranting about some ridiculous scheme that was nothing more than a deluded fantasy.

"You are right, Mr. Drake," the baron said. "This is why I must go to London now and prepare the way for the future. I will have a free hand—for a short while." The baron launched into a monologue about politics and religion.

Jonathan suppressed a yawn and took another sip of wine.

After several minutes, the baron concluded: "Take note. The collective will of the masses is a living entity. The masses respond less to science and knowledge than they do to fanaticism, hysteria, and yes, even hatred."

Jonathan said: "That is uncivilized, and not at all true of my countrymen."

The baron shook his head in pity. "You British are naive. Hatred is useful. The mightiest upheavals on this earth come from the will of the masses, driven by their hatred of their enemies, and most of all, their fear. Of course, a good leader tells them what they should fear." The baron rose abruptly. "And now, my dear Mr. Drake, I'm afraid I've kept you up too late."

"What time do we leave tomorrow?" Jonathan asked. He was not looking forward to sharing a carriage ride with the baron, but once at the train station, he'd be able to avoid him.

"In the morning, after breakfast," the baron said. "You'll hear the carriage in the courtyard."

The next morning, Jonathan was dressed before sunrise. He finished packing, and made sure that his grandfather's pocket watch was in the suit he was wearing, along with the psalter and the signed papers. He slipped the mezuzah and crucifix into a jacket pocket. When he opened the door of his room, he found a tray of food. He put down his luggage and picked up the tray. A note was there:

My Dear Mr. Drake,

It'll be a long carriage ride to the train station, as you know. I asked Mora to provide your breakfast at your chamber so that you are fortified for the journey. She makes an excellent potato soup.

B v K

Jonathan heard the carriage in the courtyard. He quickly drank the bowl of soup, not bothering with the spoon. The flavour was strange and bitter, but he ate it anyway because he did not know how long before he'd get another meal. He put the bread rolls into his pocket.

He grabbed his bags and headed outside to the courtyard. His bags seemed impossibly heavy, and he dragged them toward the carriage. With each step, his strength decreased. By the time he neared the carriage, he was sweating profusely. He stumbled and fell. Iosip was by his side, and helped Jonathan to stand.

The early morning light was painfully bright. Jonathan shaded his eyes with his hands.

The baron was already seated in the carriage, and he grinned at Jonathan from the window, wearing the same cavalier hat he'd worn last night.

"How good of you to see me off," the baron said.

Jonathan turned to the coachmen. "Load my bags," he commanded, pointing to his portmanteau.

They ignored him. Their attention was on the horses, who were snorting and stomping, their ears flattened back. Jonathan recognised the one coachman as the old man who'd been in the coachman's seat when Jonathan had first arrived. Jonathan did not recognise the other coachman, a man who was middle-aged with a bald head and muscular arms. The old coachman turned in Jonathan's direction and spat at him.

The baron laughed. "He's angry at you, Jonathan, because you made his son stop to help that peasant whose cart had overturned. That was disobedience to me. The son was whipped yesterday, by my own hand. He'll eventually recover his strength enough to walk, but it'll be miraculous if he recovers enough of his eyesight to work again. Have I ever told you that I have pinpoint accuracy with a whip? It takes skill to strike the eye without striking any other part of the face."

Jonathan noticed that the baron was calling him by his first name.

Jonathan's tongue felt like cotton, and it was an effort to speak. "Let me in."

The baron said: "The carriage is quite cramped already. There is hardly room for me. I have so many trunks to transport."

"I don't care if I have to sit on top," Jonathan said.

"My dear Jonathan, you don't look well. You're pale, you need rest. Do you remember that I gave you back your Hebrew psalter last night? Why, I had no idea you were so *cosmopolitan*, Jonathan. You play the charade of the perfect English gentleman so well. And yet you lied to me about being a Jew. This was *after* you had ordered my servants to go against my wishes, and after you had kept me waiting. I do not take kindly to your disrespect and disobedience. I've killed my subjects for lesser transgressions. You have declared yourself to be my enemy. You will be treated accordingly."

Iosip yanked the gold pocket-watch out of Jonathan's waistcoat, and handed it to the baron, who now dangled it out of the carriage window.

"I'll be sure to give this to your wife. Goodbye. I leave you now to Mora's tender mercies."

Jonathan tried to grab for the watch. He lost his balance and fell onto the flagstones. The carriage moved forward. Jonathan wanted to run after them, but he could hardly move. He rolled onto his side and vomited. He was vaguely aware that his grandfather's psalter was still in the breast pocket of his coat.

Iosip stood over him, and kicked him with the tip of his dirty boot. "My sister is waiting for you."

51

CHAPTER FIVE

Anne re-read Jonathan's letter. He hadn't said much, just that he was at the baron's estate, that he was exhausted but doing well. And then, after that, no more letters, no clue as to where he was.

Anne did not begin to panic for a few more weeks after that. The postal service on the continent could be unreliable. Her in-laws assured her that if they'd heard anything, they'd tell her. After no more letters arrived, Jonathan's father had put out word among his contacts at home and in Europe to alert him should anyone have information about his son. Jonathan's mother Hannah, and his sister Sarah, did the same. They made it a point to write to Jonathan's brother Michael, in Berlin, and urge him to be on the alert for any information. Fortunately, the Drake family were not plagued with publicity or speculation. Edward's secretaries and clerks were able to deflect any unwanted attention—especially from the press. Friends of the Drake family were exquisitely well-manned, not asking impolite questions, nor offering unsolicited advice.

On Trinity Sunday in June, at around tea-time, the doorbell rang at Anne's house. Her maid, Daisy, answered the door.

Anne was resting in her bedroom. Daisy woke her. "Forgive me for disturbing you, m'lady, but it's your in-laws here to see you. They're in the front parlour. Shall I make up a tray o'tea?" Daisy asked.

"Yes, but help me get dressed first."

Anne got to her feet heavily, and glanced at her pregnant profile in the full-length mirror. Daisy helped her to change out of her muslin house dress into a loose-fitting day-gown of fine linen in cerulean blue. Over that, Anne donned a lace shawl with long fringes that covered her pregnant figure. Daisy arranged Anne's hair, and the two women descended the stairs to the front parlour. Anne could hear her parents-in-law, Hannah and Edward, talking in hushed tones. She also heard her sister-in-law Sarah's voice. As soon as Daisy opened the door to the front parlour, the conversation stopped.

Hannah immediately rose from where she sat, as did Sarah. Both women were at Anne's side, guiding her to the dark-blue jacquard sofa.

Jonathan's father, Edward, took Anne's hands in his. His thin face was grave.

"I trust you are feeling well, my dear," he said in a hollow voice. "At least the weather is sunny and warm…"

"We are sorry to have dropped by without warning," Sarah began.

Anne had no patience for the small talk. "This must be about Jonathan," she said.

Edward said: "I won't delay the news. Jonathan is dead. I'm sorry to have to be the one to tell you." His voice broke on the last words, and he exerted great self-control to keep his emotions in check. He let go of her hands, and paced the room. He normally held himself upright, but the tragic news made his shoulders slump forward.

"How do you know he's actually dead?" Anne asked. She was too numb to cry. Her own lack of emotion frightened her.

"The Baron von Klausenberg called on us this morning," Edward recounted. "Jonathan had been ill at the time of the baron's departure in May, which is why he could not take Jonathan with him. His servants had been trying to nurse Jonathan back to health, but to no avail. In the end, Jonathan succumbed to something called 'mountain fever,' which the baron says is common in that part of the world. The baron had gotten a letter at his Belgravia house here in London revealing the news, but he's only just come to town, and he came to call on us as soon as he read the letter."

Anne covered her face with her hands. No tears came. Hannah and Sarah sat next to her, lost in their own grief. Sarah wept quietly. Hannah twisted a linen handkerchief in her hands, murmuring words of comfort in an unsteady voice. Anne thought it odd that she herself could not cry.

It underscored the difference between her and her in-laws. They were in the full throes of their loss, but for Anne, grief sat outside, like an indifferent cat that had no interest in coming any closer.

Edward broke the silence. "I am furious that Jonathan cannot be buried in the Drake family mausoleum. The baron said he had been buried in the baron's private cemetery, but everything about this is all wrong. Our son needs to be here, back in England."

"We can see about re-interring him at a later date," Hannah said wearily. "Right now, we have to just get through the next few weeks."

"But we have to make arrangements," Edward insisted. "The longer we delay, the less likely that we'll succeed."

"I am not disagreeing with the need to make arrangements, Edward," Hannah snapped. "It's just that we have more pressing obligations."

"Maman is right," Sarah offered. She called her parents Maman and Papa, a habit since her days of studying French.

"I think you should stay out of this, Sarah," Edward said.

Anne found this bickering unbearable. "There is no point in arguing about any of this. It will not bring him back. Sarah, can you please ring for some tea. I'm very hungry."

Sarah went to the bell-pull. Anne noticed how youthful and energetic she looked, and yet she had a new maturity and gravitas that Anne had never detected before. It only added to her beauty, Anne thought. Anne put her hand on her abdomen where she felt the baby kicking, and she was seized by the sudden anxiety that her own youth was being eclipsed by motherhood, and now by the shadow of widowhood. It was all going to be so much more difficult. She was beginning to feel grief—but only for her own losses. She observed her own self-centredness with a detached curiosity, and found a certain strength and comfort in it.

When the tray arrived, Hannah asked if she could pour the tea. Anne nodded her permission. Anne could see how the loss of her son had visibly aged Hannah in just a few hours, although she was still beautiful in her middle age. It suddenly occurred to Anne that childbirth did not spell the end of her own attractiveness, nor her youth. She was only twenty-three. Plenty of women kept their looks well into their thirties, and comely young widows, like herself, had no shortage of re-marriage prospects. But all that was for the future. Right now, she had to get through the rest of her pregnancy and hope that her standard of living would not drop off so precipitously that she'd be left destitute.

"I have no idea what kinds of financial arrangements Jonathan had in place," Anne said. "I realise this may not be the time to mention it. But it has been weighing on me and I've had many sleepless nights. It has not been easy, to say the least, and it will only get worse once I am a mother."

Hannah said: "But of course we'll help you."

"Yes, that's right," Sarah chimed in. "You need not worry, Anne. I can be here every day to help once the baby is born, even though you'll want a nanny."

Anne was touched by Sarah's enthusiasm. "I appreciate that. I do not know whether I can actually afford a nanny."

Hannah ventured: "We can talk about how much to settle on you each month—"

Edward interrupted her. "Let's not get too far ahead of ourselves Hannah." He paced the room, and ran his hand over his carefully combed hair, which was showing a lot of grey. He tugged at his collar, as if it were too tight.

"What do you mean, Edward?" Hannah cried. "Anne is our family. We must do everything to help her."

"And we shall!" Edward gestured impatiently with his hands. "It's just that there is a slight wrinkle, that's all."

"What is the wrinkle, Papa?" Sarah asked.

"Your brother Michael—you know, the long-lost Drake who now lives in Berlin and has aspirations to be a great concert pianist," Edward added bitterly, "has amassed quite a pile of gambling debts. And the debtors are coming after us."

"Do they have legal standing?" Hannah asked.

"Does it matter?" Edward snapped. "All they need do is go to the papers with the story of Michael's debts, anecdotes about his little escapades, and our family name is ruined. I've already been visited by two creditors this week who have threatened exactly that if we don't settle his debts." He sighed in despair, and muttered: "It is as if I've lost two sons."

Hannah said: "So the choice is having our family name ruined, or having our bank accounts ruined?"

"That's the choice," Edward said bitterly.

"Oh, Papa!" Sarah was at her father's side. She took his arm and leaned against him.

"So are you saying I'm now on my own?" Anne asked.

"Of course not!" Edward said defensively. "It's just that I cannot even begin to talk about monthly allowances until I've had my advisors study our situation." He lit a cigarette, and his hands trembled. "We will do what we can to help, once I can see exactly what choices I have."

Hannah turned to her daughter-in-law and said in a low voice. "In the meanwhile, why don't you move in with us. Close up this house and save a packet on household expenses."

Sarah's face was cautiously optimistic. "Yes! That's brilliant, Maman. We could help each other through this time of mourning. And I could be with the baby all the time."

"I need to think about it," Anne said with uncertainty.

"Of course you do," Hannah said gently. "This is a shock for us all. No rush, my dear. We need to get through each day, one day at a time." She hesitated. "You are the widow, Anne. You have a say. Speaking for myself, I do not want a funeral. Just a small, private memorial service."

Edward nodded. "Yes, we need to keep this matter private. Even more vultures will swoop in once they find out about our loss. They'll attack us in our moments of weakness."

Anne was again struck by her own lack of strong emotions. "It makes no difference to me. I don't want to make any public appearances. I don't want anyone calling on me in my condition."

"That is sensible," Hannah agreed. "A quiet memorial service will spare you all that unwanted attention." Her eyes got a far-away look, and her face was creased with grief.

As they were leaving, Anne asked Sarah: "Did you see the baron when he called on your parents? What is he like?"

Sarah blurted: "He is odious!"

Before she could say more, her father interrupted. "You may not like him, Sarah, but he has proven to be a gentleman, and I have a feeling he is going to be a great good friend to our family—especially during these difficult times."

Hannah's eyes narrowed. "We'll see exactly what he turns out to be."

"Whatever do you mean, my dear?" Edward demanded.

"I don't completely trust him, that's all." Hannah turned to Anne. "I will invite you to a dinner party and you can meet him then. After your confinement, of course."

Edward had already stepped out the front door and was at his carriage, out of earshot. Anne said to her mother-in-law in a confidential tone: "Thank you. I am not quite like these modern women who are out and about until the moment of delivery." She ran her hands over her round, pregnant abdomen. "All I want to do is sleep and eat. I have little energy for anything else."

"Yes, I can't blame you," Hannah said. "I preferred to keep to myself for the entire time. It was a necessary respite. And I ate like a cart-horse, too! Mince pies were my preference. I could eat an entire one in a day. I didn't even bother to cut the pie into slices. I ate it straight from the pie dish."

"Maman, that must've been quite the sight—eating a mince pie right from the pie dish, like a commoner! Papa would've been horrified!" Sarah exclaimed.

"That is one reason I stayed in solitude," Hannah said.

All three women laughed. Hannah embraced Anne, and kissed her hair. "Eat and sleep, my dear. The baby will be here before you know it, and you can re-join society then. I will call again tomorrow. Think about coming to live with us."

"Yes, please think about it," Sarah implored her. "Goodbye, dear sister! See you tomorrow." She embraced Anne, then bounded down the stairs to the carriage where her father waited.

Anne locked the front door. Then she returned to the front parlour, and sat down at the oak writing desk to write a letter to her mother, Mrs. Prudence Hastings. As Anne wrote, she realised that the news of her husband's death had not been a complete shock. He had been missing for weeks, and what else was one to conclude? Her one regret was not having told him before he had departed that he was going to be a father. The grief that had remained outside now came inside. She suddenly broke down and sobbed, ruining the paper on which she'd been writing. After she had regained her composure, she threw out the tear-stained paper and started again. It wasn't a long letter—just enough to tell her mother the bad news and to assure her that she was managing as well as she could.

Anne addressed the envelope to the very house in which she had been born. It was one of the nicest houses in Bristol, and the Hastings family had become one of the most prominent. Anne's father had been a physician and a good manager of the family finances. He died when Anne was sixteen, leaving both Mrs. Hastings and Anne a decent provision.

Mrs. Hastings had always made it clear that Anne had been cut out for a better class of people than those who resided in Bristol. For centuries, Bristol had been an important port and a city of trade and industry, but it never had the kind of smart social sets one could find so easily in London. Doctor Hastings's patients had been mostly sailors, stevedores, factory workers, and their families.

Mrs. Hastings had been careful to give Anne, their only child, a proper upbringing. She never let Anne do menial work—that was the role of servants. She never let Anne mingle with those she considered "not quite." It was a phrase that never needed elaboration, because Anne knew that "quite" could be followed by any number of adjectives, such as "not quite wealthy enough" or "educated" or "up to snuff."

The "not quites" included the children of almost all of her father's patients, plus other prominent Bristol families who did not meet the high standards of Mrs. Hastings—which meant anyone from the merchant classes or lower, regardless of how much profit they earned in a year. Even before Anne was old enough to think about marriage, Mrs. Hastings didn't have to explain, it was understood that the common labour class and the merchant class were not the classes from which Anne should ever dream of finding a husband. No, Anne was made for much better opportunities. Perhaps a titled husband was asking too much, although by the estimation of Mrs. Hastings, nothing was impossible given Anne's pretty face, and the fact that she was one of the best singers in the church choir.

Besides singing, Anne had an interest in embroidery. Mrs. Hastings went to great lengths to be sure Anne was familiar with the classic designs of the nobility so that her work would never be confused with some ordinary woman's foray into the needle arts. Mrs. Hastings reminded her daughter that such notables as Jane Austen and Mary Queen of Scots had been accomplished needle-workers.

When Anne had met Jonathan and he had started to court her, Mrs. Hastings was behind-the-scenes, every step of the way, to guide Anne as quickly as possible to the ultimate goal: marriage. When that day came, nobody in that London church was prouder than Mrs. Hastings.

Anne had worried from the beginning that she could not live up to the high standards of Jonathan's titled family. Jonathan had spent many hours soothing her anxieties and reassuring her that her Bristol background made no difference to him or to his family. He loved her, and that was enough. He often told her that she wasn't like the boring hothouse flowers of his parents' social set, and that this fact pleased him to no end.

Such assurances could not entirely ease Anne's fears. Every time she spent an hour with Jonathan's sister, she was reminded that she lacked the native-born London sophistication that came so naturally to Sarah. Anne's Bristol upbringing, no matter how refined, could not compete. That was one reason she found visits with his family so trying. Sarah made every effort to put Anne at her ease and make her feel as if they were great friends, sisters even. Anne appreciated Sarah's efforts, but the whole thing felt forced.

Anne came back to the present moment, looked around the room, and put her hand to her pregnant belly. She realised that she did not want to follow Hannah's suggestion and give up her house here at Cadogan Square. This was her home. Anne was a proper lady, and she wanted to be the mistress of her own property, with her own staff, surrounded by her own furniture. She did not want to be the ward of her in-laws. She resented Edward for opposing Hannah's offer of a monthly allowance. It was the least they could do for her and for their own grandchild. Even if she could not depend on them, she could depend on herself, and this gave her some comfort.

As the summer days wore on, Anne found it increasingly difficult to sleep for more than a few hours at a time. Often, fear of her uncertain future would overwhelm her in the darkest hours of the night, and she would wake up, seized with anxiety. She would weep, alone in the big house, and cradle her swollen belly, vowing to never allow herself or her offspring to fall into poverty or indignity.

Anne had made the difficult decision to let go of all servants, including Daisy and McWilliams. Within a few weeks, Anne realised she needed a cook. She herself had never learned to cook, and her appetite was now finicky and voracious, so she hired Mrs. Rafferty, a kindly, middle-aged Irishwoman. She came to Anne's house four days a week (that was all Anne could afford). Twice a week, Hannah would send a housemaid from her own staff to help: a 15-year-old from the East End who was just starting out in service. Anne would assist the girl with the laundry—it took the labour of two people—and if there was time, the housemaid would scrub the pots and pans in the scullery. Anne found the physical labour exhausting. As the pregnancy wore on, she was able to do less and less. The house was falling into a state of neglect.

Anne had little desire or energy to deal with visitors. She had given Mrs. Rafferty and the housemaid strict orders to never open the door for callers. Not that she knew many people in London—she'd only lived there since she and Jonathan had been married, and any callers were invariably his friends and acquaintances, not hers. Still, in the wake of Jonathan's death, some had wanted to offer condolences in person, and Anne had avoided every one of them. She would open the condolence letters that came through the post. After she read them, she'd save them in a wicker box in her bedroom.

Gershon, Stoker, and King had given her a widow's allowance, which was a correct gesture, but not enough. Hannah would occasionally mention in a letter that she was eager for a monthly allowance to be settled on Anne, but progress was slow and, reading between the lines, Anne knew it was causing a great deal of tension between Hannah and Edward. In the meanwhile, Hannah would continue to send a spare servant over to Anne's house whenever possible. Anne would carefully fold the letter, put it back in the envelope, and place it in the wicker box. She appreciated her mother-in-law's constant concern, but resentment had hardened her heart. She was a widow, entirely alone. But she was also a survivor, and she would find a way to succeed on her own terms.

There came a September afternoon when everything changed. The day was hot and still. Anne reposed in the sitting room that adjoined her bedroom on the second floor. To distract her mind from her heavy discomfort, she concentrated on sewing a delicate piece of lace onto a blanket as part of the layette. She wore a simple muslin dress. But in the heat, she was wet with perspiration under her arms and down her back. Even though the windows were open, the air was oppressive, and the lace curtains did not stir.

The doctor had informed Anne that she was going to have twins. Anne had suspected this but had told no-one. She was due any day. She pushed on the tender spot on the right side of her ribcage where one of the babies continually kicked her.

Mrs. Rafferty, the cook, came into Anne's bedroom, too out of breath to speak, and shoved the silver salver at her. A calling card was on it.

"He's in the front entrance hall, waitin', m'lady," Mrs. Rafferty said breathlessly.

"Who?"

"An aristocrat, m'lady, with one of those foreign names that me Irish tongue cannot pronounce."

"I've told you to never allow callers in," Anne admonished her. "I don't want to see anyone."

"M'lady, it happened while the boy from Turner's was delivering a leg o'mutton at the service entrance at the kitchen. He appeared right there—a nobleman at the servants' entrance! Imagine! Me and the boy, we just about fainted on the spot. I tried to dissuade him, m'lady, but he insisted. So I bade him wait in your husband's library while I came to fetch you."

Anne read the calling card. Baron Zoltan Georg Tovis von Klausenberg. The address under the name was a prestigious one in Belgravia. The insignia was a strange-looking eagle clutching a sword.

Anne's heart stopped, and she grew pale. "How am I to receive him? Look at me. I'm in no condition for this."

"Let's get you arranged on the sofa in the front parlour," Mrs. Rafferty said. "Then we'll put that brocade coverlet on you, and it will hide everythin'. Tell him you're a little under the weather, and you can't stir from your spot. Even if he suspects otherwise, he is a nobleman, and he won't press the issue. I'll be within earshot. Ring the bell on the side table, and I'll bring refreshments."

She was obviously a cook and not a maid, but she would have to do. There was no other staff in the house.

When Anne was reclined on the sofa, with the brocade coverlet arranged to hide her swollen body, she waited anxiously for the mysterious guest to arrive. Brilliant sunlight streamed in from the large bay window that overlooked Cadogan Square. Anne noted with dismay how the rays illuminated the dust motes that floated through the air. She hoped the baron would not notice. There was no breeze from the open window. The air was hot and still.

Mrs. Rafferty was at the doorway of the drawing room. "Mr. Baron Closs-berg," Mrs. Rafferty announced, mis-pronouncing his name.

The baron strode in. Anne's first impression was that he was tall and regal. His white hair, just above shoulder-length, was pomaded back from a distinguished, clean-shaven face. He fixed his gaze on Anne as he strode across the room. He took Anne's hand in his gloved hand before she had a chance to offer it, and he held it too long. Did the man not understand the manners of the English? Anne was startled to see that one of his eyes was blue, the other light brown. He wore an exotic cologne that Anne found overpowering. She put a linen kerchief to her nose.

"My dear Madam Drake," he said in a resonant voice with a strange accent, "I am distraught over the news of your dear husband Jonathan."

Anne was flustered by his lack of manners, and by his overpowering scent. "Is it customary for your lordship to always reach, uninvited, for the hands of women you've not met before?"

The baron chuckled, and removed his gloves, revealing his unconventional long nails, lacquered an ox-blood red. "I have not yet mastered the manners of English society," he confessed. "My speech betrays that I am not an Englishman. Forgive my audacity. I feel as if I already know you so well, because of all Jonathan had told me." The baron reached into his pocket, and dangled Jonathan's gold pocket watch in front of her. "He asked me to give this to you."

Anne was shocked to see her husband's prized possession. It jolted her unexpectedly, and brought back memories of him, and she had to force herself to stay composed.

"I thank your lordship," Anne said in an unsteady voice, taking the heavy watch in her hand.

"He had wanted me to give this to you when it became clear that he would need to delay his journey. He had expected to make a full recovery, and I was devastated when I got the news. My devastation pales in comparison to yours, naturally."

Anne remained silent.

He went on: "I had the obligation to deliver his pocket watch myself. It is too valuable to leave in the hands of a servant. So, I have kept it safe all these months. When I saw your in-laws in June, to deliver the most tragic news about your husband, I had been told you were not receiving visitors. I have respected your solitude, otherwise I would have called sooner."

"Yes, of course," Anne replied. "So why has your lordship decided to visit now?"

"I simply could not delay. The pocket watch belongs to you, Mrs. Drake. For me to have kept it an hour more would've constituted theft." He paused. "And, I simply had to meet you in person."

"I see." To cover for her reclining posture and bad manners, she said: "One must forgive my indisposition. I have … not been well. I beg your lordship to have a seat. I can have Mrs. Rafferty bring refreshments." Anne reached for the small bell on the mahogany table nearby.

The baron took it out of her reach. "No need to ring. I am more interested in talking to you than in taking refreshments."

He looked around the room, and saw the chair that he wanted at the far corner: a straight-backed, Regency mahogany with Egyptian motifs and no cushions. It was an antique from Jonathan's parents. The baron strode over to it, seized it with one hand and placed it near the sofa where Anne reclined. She wondered why the baron hadn't chosen the much more comfortable cushioned chair nearby.

The baron skilfully turned the conversation into a light-hearted interview of her, asking her about her interests, her hobbies, her dreams.

She answered warily at first, but as the minutes wore on, Anne found herself relaxing and actually enjoying the conversation. He made her feel as if she were the most fascinating woman he had met in London. Anne heard the clock strike the quarter-hour, and she was amazed that the conversation with a total stranger was so natural, and so entertaining. Well, perhaps he wasn't a total stranger. He had, after all, known her husband, and he had told her how Jonathan had spoken so lovingly of her.

At one point, he asked: "What, my dear Madam Drake, is your deepest desire, the thing that if you had to do it all over again, you would have focused more of your energies on?"

Anne hesitated. Nobody had ever asked her that question, especially not on the first meeting. And truth be told, she'd never thought about it in those terms. But it seemed a natural question.

The baron saw her hesitation. "In my case," the baron continued, putting her at ease, "I would have dedicated more time to music. I'm a baritone, you know, and I'm quite good at piano. As it is, I surround myself with talented people, and feed vicariously off of them." He leaned closer, and said in a confidential tone: "I have salons at my house once, sometimes twice a week. The talent that gathers at my place—artists, musicians, actors, actresses, poets, along with ambassadors and royalty—would make the king green with envy." He paused and leaned back in his chair. "Ah, but I'm prattling on and on. Perhaps the arts are not your métier. Perhaps you are a genius at cultivating roses, or applying watercolour paints to paper—all worthy accomplishments, I assure you. One thing I do know, madam, is that you have hidden talents. A woman of your intelligence does not confine herself to merely attending to her beauty, essential as that is."

Anne felt she could trust him. "As a matter of fact, I like to sing."

The baron clapped his hands with delight. "I knew you had a musical side! I could sense it. Then you would fit right in to my salon gatherings. Please, madam, please be my guest. I know you would be an enchantment." The baron then proceeded to skilfully drop the names of some of the most prominent people in London—names that Anne had seen in the newspapers. She was impressed.

"Of course, these eminent personages do not come to every salon gathering," the baron explained. "The regulars who do come may not have famous names, but they are just as talented." And the baron began to describe two or three of those talents.

It all sounded so fascinating. His descriptions made her feel as if she were missing out on the smartest gatherings in London. She badly wanted to go, to see it for herself. As soon as her babies were born, she would go.

Before he readied himself to leave, the baron mentioned one more thing. "Mrs. Rafferty looks as if she's been a faithful part of your household for a long time."

"She has," Anne agreed, not wanting to explain the truth.

The baron wrote down an address on the back of one of his calling cards. "Here is the name of one of the most diligent young women in London. Her name is Minerva. As you can imagine, it is not exactly easy to find a position in London right now. If you know of anyone who can use her excellent services, please be sure to mention her."

Anne took the card. "Thank you. She expects standard wages, I assume."

"Right now, just room and board. She is an artist, and is accustomed to living in poverty. Having regular meals and an actual house to stay at—even if she took a shabby garret room—would be a luxury for her."

"Her name is unusual," Anne observed.

"Yes. An ancient name, far more noble than the commonplace names you give your servants here." The baron seemed to hesitate. "Madam, I feel an obligation. Your husband had been an exceptional man. You are no less exceptional. Please do not hesitate to come to me for help, should you ever need it. I have a special place in my heart for those who have been widowed, as my own mother had been."

"I thank your lordship, but I do have in-laws who are more than capable of helping me. In fact, they have offered to take me into their household at Hyde Park." Anne realised that she had admitted to more than she had intended, but she felt she could fully trust the baron.

"And have you accepted this offer?" He sounded troubled.

Anne was confused by the disapproval she heard in his question. "Not yet. I am considering it." It was true. As the birth of her children drew nearer, she realised she did not want to be alone in a big house at night—

not until she got used to taking care of the babies. Having her in-laws and servants under the same roof would be an immense relief.

The baron said: "Notice that I give help without … attaching ropes. I think that is the expression in English."

"Attaching strings," Anne corrected him.

"Yes, strings." He went on. "A woman like you deserves to be in her own household, not under the care of her in-laws. You are not subservient to them. You are independent. You should act as such."

Anne realised that he had voiced her own thoughts and feelings, and she was relieved that he could capture her inmost thoughts so accurately. He showed her that she was not mad for wanting her own independence.

"It would only be … it wouldn't be forever," Anne said, catching herself from mentioning her upcoming delivery date.

"No? The sticky webs of in-laws have ways of entangling vivacious young women such as yourself."

"What do you mean?"

He leaned close, and the smell of his cologne enveloped her. "May I be frank? I am the only one who has the insight and courage to tell you this because I am not from here."

"Of course," Anne said. This whole conversation was extraordinary, but she was too enchanted to cut it short.

He hesitated, and then sat back in his chair. "Perhaps I should not. I do not wish to offend you."

"I beg your lordship to continue."

"Then I will be frank. You are young and beautiful. If you are living with your in-laws as a widow, how easy will it be for you to find another husband? Do you think they would let any other man court you? Do you think you would have the freedom to go out dining at the Ritz, or would they be too afraid of scandal?"

Anne knew the answer, but she was silent.

The baron continued. "They would use their money to control you, if they have not done so already. Do not let them clip your wings, madam. You deserve to fly as high as you can go. Unlike other women I have met here, you have some undefinable quality that they do not have. I cannot explain more than that, but in time I shall, as I get to know you more."

He swiped his finger along the side table, and glanced at the dust he'd picked up on his glove.

Anne was mortified, but her embarrassment receded when he said: "Another thing I admire about you is your refusal to be a slave to your housecleaning, as so many London women are. Dust is natural. Filth is natural. Chaos is natural. We must embrace it all." The baron stood, then took Anne's hand and kissed it. "Goodbye, Madam Drake. Do not trouble Mrs. Rafferty. I can find my way out."

But Mrs. Rafferty was already outside the doorway, waiting for him. He murmured a polite farewell to the old woman and left the house.

"He seems to be an important man," Mrs. Rafferty later said to Anne. "But I'd be careful about him, m'lady. He seems to want something."

Anne was too distracted to hear Mrs. Rafferty's warning. She meditated on what the baron had told her. He was the only person she'd ever met who saw her for what she was, and—more important—for the woman she wanted to be.

CHAPTER SIX

Jonathan did not know whether it was day or night because there were no windows. The room was cold and smelled of rats. His arms were numb from the manacles on his wrists. Thirst and hunger were a constant distraction, but they were forgotten when Mora was there. He could hear himself screaming, but he didn't recognise his own voice. The pain was a force bigger than himself, engulfing him until he thought he would die. Sometimes he saw Iosip lurking in the doorway. But it was Mora he most feared—the silent Mora at whose hands his dark world became a universe of agony.

His brain was continually foggy, and he was aware that it had something to do with whatever she put in his food. He wanted to stop eating what she gave him so that he could regain his senses. But hunger drove him to eat whatever there was, and to suffer the consequences. The hour came when Jonathan found his senses to be clearer than usual—perhaps she had forgotten to drug his food?—and he overheard Iosip and Mora whispering in the doorway, just beyond a circle of candlelight. They were speaking German. Jonathan pretended to be unconscious, his head dropped forward onto his chest.

"He's been here for months," Iosip said. "How much longer will you let him live?"

"Until he bores me," she said.

"He grows thinner and uglier by the day," Iosip observed.

"He is handsomer than you. And the others. But when he no longer amuses me, I will feed him to your beastly dogs."

"Last time you disposed of a prisoner, you made a mess, and I had to finish it. Am I going to have to clean up again this time?"

Mora said contemptuously: "I had been too exhausted then, too distracted. I'll have better concentration this time. I won't need your help."

"Tell me when you are ready. I want to watch."

"Soon," Mora said.

They left him alone in the dark cellar. Jonathan could hear rats scratching somewhere in the corner. A plan began to take shape in his mind. He tried to think through all the possibilities of escape.

He realised he had fallen asleep when he was awakened by cold steel on his neck. Jonathan could not yet tell what was in store for him, but now he had a strategy, and his head was clearer.

"Mora," he whispered in English. "I want to know more about you."

"I don't understand," she said in German. She began humming some strange melody.

Switching to German, he said: "Mora, I want to talk to you. I want to see your face. That's all."

She stopped humming. He could hear her rummaging around in the dark. She struck a candle and held it up, so close to his face that he was afraid he would be burned. The light made his eyes water with pain. Jonathan watched her through half-closed eyes. She was thin and lanky, and she wore a black dress. Her skin was bone-white, and her heavy brow line made her small eyes appear as empty sockets in the candlelight. Her unkempt blond hair was the colour of tallow.

"Tell me again," she commanded. Jonathan could not tell whether she was surprised that he was speaking German to her.

"I just want to talk to you," he repeated.

She laughed. "This is nothing new. I decide about the talking."

"That is why I want to ask you a favour. Something only you can do."

She tilted her head to one side. "What is that?"

"Free my hands."

She laughed and snuffed the candle out on his chest. He cried out from the sudden pain.

Then Jonathan felt one of her long white nails pressing on his eye, harder and harder. He turned his head away and fought to keep panic down. She had the mentality of a twisted child. What would a child-like mentality bargain for? What might appeal to her?

Secrets. Maybe she would want to know secrets.

"Mora," he said. "I know things. From far-away places. Magical things that can give you incredible power. You could be more powerful than Iosip. And the baron. They wouldn't be able to order you around anymore."

"My brother says you are a Jew. Is it so?" she demanded. "They found a Jew talisman and a crucifix in the pocket of your coat. And Iosip says you are a Jew here." She brushed her hand across the crotch of his filthy trousers. He reflexively crossed his legs and twisted away from her, straining at the manacles that held his arms.

"How can I be a Jew if I have a crucifix?" he said. "Crucifixes are Christian."

"It is forbidden to have those things," she said. "The baron has told us that only if we go back to the old ways can we find progress."

"How can I know the old ways unless somebody teaches me?"

"The same way they taught me," Mora said.

"Who did?"

"Iosip. And the baron. And others you don't know. They all taught me how to master the purifying pain. And how to take the light out of someone's eyes. I am very good at that." She paused. "The darkness becomes your friend. Even you are not so afraid of it anymore. We are all equal here in the dark."

"Mora, listen. I can be more interesting if you just free my arms. Iosip doesn't know what magic I can do, but I'll show you. It'll be our secret. You'll know something he doesn't. You'll have real power."

The seconds passed in silence. Then he heard her strike a match to light the candle again. She unlocked the manacles, her breath sour and hot on his face.

He shook his arms and rubbed them. When the numbness subsided, pain shot through his nerves. He slid down the wall until he was sitting on the cold flagstone floor. He forced himself to breathe through the pain, but his breath came in ragged gasps.

Mora held the candle high and looked down upon him with curiosity.

"You're thin, but still nice. Iosip tells me appearances should never matter Still, I prefer a nice-looking man to an ugly one like him."

"How old are you?" Jonathan asked. He guessed she was in her late twenties.

Mora shrugged. "I don't know. Iosip was born first. And we had another child, but the light got taken out of his eyes, and we buried him in the garden."

"Do you plan to take the light out of my eyes?"

"Of course."

"But why?"

"Because it is necessary. It is the way of things. But first, I want to know the secrets that you promised to tell."

Jonathan needed time to gather his strength. He began talking of far-away places, of magic spells and witches from the fairy tales of his childhood.

He saw the glimmer of a blade that she was trying to hide behind the folds of her skirt. He suddenly kicked at her ankles. She fell to the ground with a cry, and the knife clattered out of her hand. He pounced, and his hands were around her neck. She scratched his arms and chest, drawing blood. He rapped her head against the stone floor until she lay motionless, her blood pooling where he knelt. His breath came in dry heaves, and he tried to get to his feet, but he realised he had no strength to stand, so he rolled onto his side and concentrated on gathering his strength. After some minutes, he grabbed the guttering candle from the floor, set it upright, and proceeded to search her pockets. He found the key ring she always carried. He forced himself to stand and walk, closing the door behind him as he left. He fumbled with the keys until he found the one that would lock her in.

Stumbling ahead, he came to a stone staircase, climbed to the next level, and made his way to the kitchen. He didn't care that he was naked from the waist up, he needed to find something to eat. In the pantry, he found cheese, stale bread, and a jug of cider. He ate them all greedily until his stomach hurt. Cider had spilled down his chin, and he wiped his face with his hand. It was then realised then that he'd grown a full beard from the months in captivity.

He ransacked the pantry and larder for more food. He found an empty basket, and used it to hold apples, and lumps of sugar in a paper bag. He found stale biscuits and dried plums, and a knife.

His skin was caked with dirt and filth. His trousers were squalid, tattered rags. He made his way to the scullery, where cooking and cleaning utensils were strewn about. The place had a depressing air of neglect and chaos. He found a rag, and he washed himself at the sink.

He carried the basket up to the room in the turret where he'd stayed when he'd first arrived. Being back in that room gave him an eerie sense of déjà-vu. His bags were there, as if the months of horror had never happened. He needed to get dressed and leave as soon as possible. His plan was to walk back to Klausenberg and get a train back to London from there. Maybe he'd even happen upon someone on the road who could give him a ride.

He searched his portmanteau. The muddied travelling-suit was there, the one he'd been wearing when he'd helped to upright the peasant's cart that had overturned. He currently wore the trousers of the suit he'd been wearing the day of the baron's departure, but he had no idea where the rest of the ensemble was. There was one ensemble in his portmanteau that was clean: full-evening dress consisting of a tail coat, trousers with a galon down the side seams, patent-leather court shoes, black silk socks, a white starched-shirt and tie, a white waistcoat, and a black top hat. He got dressed, ruefully remembering that he had expected to wear that ensemble to one of the baron's evening events, as if the baron were a normal, respectable aristocrat who actually hosted such events, instead of a reclusive eccentric in a dilapidated estate with sadistic servants.

The trousers were too loose—he'd obviously lost weight—but the trouser braces would keep them in place. He didn't feel fully dressed without the collar and tie, so he put them on, which he knew was ridiculous. He put the white gloves into a coat pocket, and straightened the pocket square. The extra accessories gave him a sense of completeness, like a knight donning armour down to the last detail. His wedding band was missing from his finger (he was convinced that Iosip or Mora were guilty of that theft). His nails were long and dirty.

He slid the knife into an inside pocket of the waistcoat. He searched his luggage again. Any currency he'd had was gone—undoubtedly stolen by Iosip or Mora. His grandfather's psalter was nowhere to be seen. He searched his luggage for it. It had been in the coat pocket of the suit he'd been wearing before he'd been thrown into the dungeon. If he could find that coat, perhaps he'd find the psalter. He knew it was a foolish risk to hunt it down, but he could not leave that book behind—it would be as if he were leaving a piece of himself and his history in this infernal place.

There was no point in going back into the dungeon where he'd been a prisoner. He knew his clothing was not there. He made his way to the servants' quarters near the kitchen, unlocking doors as needed with the keys he'd taken from Mora. Room after room yielded nothing—there were hardly any furnishings in most of the rooms he searched, even though Jonathan could see that the place had the capacity to house ample household staff, and must've been quite impressive in its heyday.

Near the kitchen, Jonathan found a room with a wooden table that held equipment, including knives and hatchets laid out in a row, a meat grinder with a crank handle, salt, pepper, and spices. Hooks were suspended from the ceiling. The table, floor and walls were mottled with dried blood stains. This was obviously the room—the fleischzimmer, the baron had called it—in which Iosip made the revolting sausage that Jonathan had tasted the first night he had arrived.

In the corner, Jonathan noticed a pile of rags. On closer inspection, he realised that the rags were actually clothing. It was filthy clothing that stank and probably had lice, but he rummaged through the pile anyway. He noticed that most of the clothing was child-sized, made of the kind of rough cloth that peasants would wear. He found his coat. It was dirty and blood-stained. He turned the coat upside down, and shook it. The psalter fell out, along with the crucifix and the mezuzah. He put these three items into the pocket of the tail coat he was wearing.

His search was interrupted by the sound of dogs barking in the distance. He hurried back to his room to retrieve his Gladstone bag. The portmanteau would have to stay behind—it was too unwieldy.

Jonathan went to the casement window of his room, opened the sash, and leaned out to scan the area and see what his best route of escape was going to be. Overhead, the sky was dark with rainclouds, and in the western sky, the sun glowed red from a break in the clouds. A movement caught his attention below. Iosip appeared from nowhere, a pack of dogs surrounding him. He raised his shotgun, fired a round, and hit the window, causing glass to shatter across the bedroom floor.

Jonathan went to the door, ready to escape that way. From the other side, he heard dogs scratching at the door and whining. His escape route was cut off. He jammed the chair under the door handle. Some minutes later, the knob of his bedroom door turned.

"Jonathan," Iosip called. "I know you are there. We will have a meal together, just the two of us, so that we can discuss your departure."

Jonathan refused to answer. Iosip pounded on the door, and the dogs barked and scratched the door. Iosip threatened him, commanding him to open the door so that they could negotiate, or else there would be consequences. Jonathan went back to the window and cautiously peered out. Eight dogs waited at the base of the wall. Two of them looked up, and their eyes seemed to glow from the fiery red of the setting sun.

A cloudburst released a torrent of rain, causing the dogs at the base of the tower to scatter. The dogs at the bedroom door remained. Jonathan could hear them scratching and whining.

His best escape route was now to scale the tower wall so long as the rain continued. He removed the linens off the bed and tore them into strips. He plaited the fabric strips until he held the coiled rag-rope in his hand. He had to be ready at a moment's notice, and he double checked to be sure he had whatever he could carry in his pockets, including the psalter—and the knife.

A break in the rain came. Now was his chance. Jonathan made sure his hat was secure on his head. He tied the end of the rope to an iron sash lock, then threw the rope out the window, and climbed onto the sill, holding the rope tightly. The outside wall was slick from the rain, but the stones were rough-hewn enough that he could find some purchase, despite the fact that his shoes were not designed for such activity. Slowly, he made his way down, one step at a time. He fought the panic of descending a high wall in the rain, and he tried not to think about what waited for him in the shadows below. He concentrated on finding secure footing and keeping his balance. He could feel how weak he was, and he hoped his strength would not give out before he reached the bottom.

As his feet touched the wet grass, he made a dash for the edge of the ravine. In a moment, he felt dog's teeth on his arm, biting through the fabric. Jonathan panicked and rolled over the edge of the ravine. As he fell, the dog let go, and Jonathan flailed. He grabbed foliage and vines, and managed to break his fall. He was now cradled in the branches of a small tree, and he held on to the wet branches.

Against the grey twilight sky, Jonathan could see Iosip's silhouette, shotgun in hand. The pack of dogs had gathered around Iosip, and were barking wildly. With his poor eyesight, and fading daylight, Iosip's aim would be bad. Iosip tried to quiet his dogs so he could use sound to locate Jonathan, but Jonathan didn't move. Iosip shot the second shell anyway, and it was so wide of the mark it was almost comical.

As Iosip paused to reload, Jonathan started to descend into the ravine, keeping a tight grip on tree branches.

Suddenly, Jonathan heard a yelp and felt something heavy crashing through the foliage nearby. Iosip had pushed one of the dogs over the side in hopes of dislodging Jonathan. Iosip stood still and listened, and Jonathan didn't move. Then Iosip picked up another dog and threw it over the side. This time, the dog managed to scratch Jonathan's arm on the way down, twisting and yelping as it fell.

Jonathan maneuvered himself as close to the slope of the ravine as possible. Another dog plunged past him, then another. Then there was silence. Jonathan could hear the remaining dogs above panting and pacing, occasionally whining with frustration. He could not tell where Iosip was. He also could not hear whether the dogs below were still alive.

He waited for what seemed like hours, straddling a small tree trunk. It was now dark. He heard Iosip call the dogs away from the ravine.

Was Iosip trying to lure Jonathan out of the ravine by pretending to leave? Or was Iosip himself going to go down into the ravine from another route to hunt for Jonathan at the bottom?

One thing Jonathan knew for sure was that Iosip would not be able to capture him in the darkness with his poor eyesight, even if his dogs were with him. There were too many roots and rocks that could injure Iosip if he tripped on them.

Jonathan descended slowly, feeling his way along. His wet clothing often caught on branches, and he pulled it free, sometimes tearing the fabric. His hat was gone. The air was cold, and he began to shiver. Occasionally, he paused to listen for the dogs, but there was no sound of them.

When he reached the bottom, he gingerly felt with his feet among the rocks and boulders. He ran into something furry. It was one of the dogs, and it was dead.

Jonathan could hear the stream gurgling nearby. He also heard a cry. It was eerie and not-quite-human. Something was crawling toward him.

In the dim twilight, Jonathan could see it was a young dog, about half the size of the typical canine of Iosip's pack. It clawed its way forward on its belly. Jonathan realised the dog was too badly injured to attack. Jonathan was moved to pity for the animal's suffering. He got his knife ready, and crept closer, thinking about how to kill it quickly and put it out of its misery. The dog wagged its tail weakly, and whined in submission. It wanted to live.

Jonathan put the knife away, and gathered the dog in his arms, taking care not to aggravate its injuries. It whimpered and yelped, but also seemed to sense that Jonathan meant to help. Jonathan carefully settled the animal onto his shoulders, and began walking downstream. Some of Jonathan's strength had returned, but he found himself getting exhausted as he carried the dog. His shoes were filled with water and mud, and his feet were numb from cold.

The dog suddenly stiffened and growled. Jonathan heard a rustle, and something leaped at him, knocking him off his feet. The injured dog fell off his shoulders, letting out a cry of agony as it hit the ground. The attacking creature was now on top of the lame dog. At first Jonathan thought it was a wolf, but then he realised it was one of the German shepherds Iosip had thrown off the cliff. It was twice the size as the lame dog he'd been carrying.

Jonathan rushed forward, knife in hand. He stabbed the big dog behind the shoulder blades. The dog turned on Jonathan and clamped down on his shoulder with its jaws. Then it let go of Jonathan's shoulder and went for his neck, breaking the skin.

The lame dog dragged itself forward and bit down on the big dog's hind leg. As the big dog swung its head to see what was attacking from behind, Jonathan stabbed it in the neck, hitting the artery. The beast collapsed to the ground in a pool of blood.

The lame dog whimpered. Jonathan was trembling. He put the knife back in his pocket, and wiped his hands on his trousers.

In an unsteady voice, he said to the lame dog: "Don't worry, I'll take you with me. You saved my life."

He hoisted it onto his shoulders again, grimacing from his own pain. He continued downstream, trying to remember whether Iosip had thrown three or four or five dogs off the cliff. He thought it was four, but he could not remember. Sorting this out became an obsession because if he didn't get the number right, there might be more lurking in the darkness, waiting to attack. He worried he'd drive himself mad trying to recollect. Finally, he talked out loud to distract himself.

"Well, we sure showed that other dog what we were made of, didn't we? Was he your friend? I hope not. You two were in the pack earlier today and got along fine. Then down here, you two were fighting like mortal enemies. Maybe we've both been in hell. I know I have. And all the rules have changed. Did you see the way the other dog's eyes glowed red? Your eyes don't look that way. Why not? Maybe it's because you're a good dog, and he was a demon. I'm talking rubbish, I know."

The dog didn't stir. For a moment, Jonathan was afraid it had died, and he stopped, listening to be sure that the dog was still breathing. It was, but it was breathing in small gasps.

"Listen, dog, you and I must find some help. You need to stay alive until someone can patch us up. My shoulder is chewed to bits. I can feel the blood running. But I'm not going to die. Neither are you. They want us to die, but they won't have that satisfaction, will they? No, they won't."

The rainclouds had cleared, and an almost-full moon lit the way. Jonathan kept talking in order to maintain some sort of composure against the terror he felt and the darkness that closed in around them.

"Now that we're traveling companions, I need to give you a name. I once had a spaniel named Sasha, and a dachshund named Hesby. They were spoiled lap dogs. You're a fighter. The way you gripped his leg, you were like a terrier chomping a rat." Jonathan paused. "Maybe that's the name for you. Chompsworth. Chompsie for short. It's a proper British name. If we call you Sir Chompsworth, you'll be able to mingle with the best of them. Anne will be so happy to meet you. And you'll adore her."

At the thought of his wife, Jonathan began to weep as he trudged onward.

"Foolish and sentimental," he said, not bothering to wipe the tears from his cheeks. "I want my old life back."

The dawn was beginning to light the sky, and Jonathan noticed an old wooden bridge ahead, spanning the stream.

At the bridge, he scrambled up the embankment. He lost his footing in the mud and slid backward. He tried again, and when he reached the top, he stood on the bridge looking upstream. He thought he heard the barking of dogs, but Chompsworth was heavily draped on his shoulders, not stirring, so he must have imagined it. Jonathan gazed downstream, seeing nothing but water, trees, and rocks. His shoes were wet and heavy with mud. He trudged along the road, and found himself at a crossroads. Typical for the region, it was marked with several iron and wood crucifixes festooned with garlic and red threads.

There was a ringing in his ears. He was too exhausted to go on, and he sank to the ground, letting the dog gently roll off his shoulders. He laid his head on the dirt road and was grateful for the crucifixes that stood guard over him, like sentinels. He silently asked them to keep evil away so that he could have just a few minutes of rest.

CHAPTER SEVEN

Anne's children were born just hours after the baron had called at her house that day in September. There had hardly been any labour pains. Looking back, Anne wondered whether there had been something about the baron's very presence and his interest in Anne that had hastened the arrival of her children. Her own superstition scared her. She was a woman of great common sense, and she chided herself for imagining things that weren't real.

The baron sent a note of congratulations. After that, he sent regular letters, enquiring after her health and keeping alive the invitation to the salon gatherings—when she was feeling up to it, of course. Anne was too exhausted to reply. After some weeks had passed, and she was stronger, she wrote back, thanking him for his concern and filling him in on small details, such as the fact that she had hired Minerva as a nanny after Anne's mother had gone back home to Bristol. Of course, Sarah had been true to her word, and was at Anne's house whenever possible to help look after the babies. Hannah often visited, too, and Anne was grateful for her mother-in-law's help, but also jealously protective of her own independence.

Exactly seven weeks after Jack and Lily were born, Anne attended her first salon gathering. She squeezed herself into her corset, with Minerva's help. She was able to barely fit into one of her best dresses, a gown of silk taffeta the colour of claret.

Anne remembered how, before he left for his journey, Jonathan had described the baron's house in Belgravia. But nothing prepared her for actually walking through the front door, as a guest. Yes, it had the sort of things one would expect of an aristocrat: walls in rich shades of red and gold, oriental carpets, upholstered furniture with carved mahogany legs of birds' talons, tasselled velvet drapes in sumptuous colours.

What she did not expect was his taste in artifacts. Anne's in-laws, by comparison, had a collection of oil paintings and Chinese porcelain. The baron's tastes were far more unconventional. He had a fancy for gargoyles and primitive tribal masks, swords and other tools of war, and these artifacts decorated the rooms, along with collections of oil paintings, ostrich plumes in vases, leopard and zebra skins, stuffed heads of ilex and bear, and shadow boxes of curiosities such as animal bones and teeth. Anne even caught sight of a human skeleton.

It took a while for Anne to realise that the unconventional-looking guests (some dressed in outrageous outfits) were in fact more distinguished than she could have dreamed. They were far more interesting than the boring, stuffy guests who attended the dinners hosted by her in-laws. There were actors and actresses whose names Anne had seen regularly in the papers, along with viscounts, dames, and baronets. There were bishops, ambassadors, heads-of-state, and other foreign dignitaries. Musicians, painters, sculptors, writers, political agitators, and financiers were amply counted among the guests. There were certain rich, idle nobles who had no permanent home or country, but who considered the world their playground and whose vocation in life was to never let the ordinary overtake them. So they made it their mission to find the most brilliant parties across Europe, and they found themselves at the baron's gatherings. Even the notorious Mr. Crowley made an appearance in a flamboyant outfit with his latest mistress on his arm.

There was Ursula, an American actress whom Anne had never seen in the newspapers, but who was well-known among the more sophisticated set. She performed an exotic dance with veils. Anne stood off to the side, amazed. She had never seen a woman's body painted with henna designs. Anne would not have described Ursula as beautiful, but rather as striking and hypnotic. Her body was thin and sinewy, and she had a hardness and sophistication that Anne both feared and admired.

The artist who had painted the henna designs on Ursula's body was named Lucien. He sat with his sketch pad, laughing and drinking. Lucien wore a powdered wig, breeches, a tobacco-coloured velvet jacket, and a lace-trimmed shirt. He looked like a nobleman from the eighteenth century. After the veil dance, Anne watched the two of them disappear together to another part of the house. There were whispers about a "serail room"—whatever that was.

Anne chatted with other guests, entranced by the fact that everyone she met was unlike anyone she had ever met before. For a half-hour, she was monopolized by a brooding man with a Russian accent who called himself a revolutionary communard, whatever that was. Anne could not follow most of what he said. When he suddenly lost interest, he turned away and strode to an adjoining room without saying another word. The rooms were heavy with the smoke from water pipes. Absinthe dripped over sugar cubes; goblets were filled with wines from around the world.

Anne's attention was caught by a display case. It contained small, shrunken heads mounted on wooden stakes. They looked like grimacing, macabre dolls' heads fashioned of scraps of leather and bits of fur. The eyes were hollow.

"They are real human heads," an American-accented voice said at Anne's elbow.

Anne turned. It was Ursula, dressed in a flamboyant purple-and-scarlet robe, trimmed in ermine. She looked theatrical, as if she had chosen her clothing from the wardrobe closet of the Old Vic. Nearby, within earshot, Anne noticed that Lucien was sitting on an elaborately carved chair, with a sketch-pad and pencil, completely absorbed in his work.

Ursula continued. "The baron acquired these from actual head hunters in New Guinea."

"Did he?" Anne said. She still did not believe they were genuine.

A wall hanging caught her eye. It was a circular piece of black wood with mysterious carvings, and thirteen rays shaped like elongated lightning bolts surrounded the circle. Compared to the shrunken heads, it didn't look ugly or macabre, just unusual.

Ursula followed Anne's gaze.

"Do you like it?" Ursula asked.

"Yes," Anne said hesitantly. "I don't know why, but it seems ... compelling."

"It is the Black Sun."

Anne had never heard of that. She nodded to hide her ignorance.

As if reading her mind, Ursula said: "The Black Sun symbolizes creative destruction, and creative re-birth. It is the vanguard of the new world order, against which all others will be powerless." She traced her finger along one of the lightning-bolt rays. "It is said," Ursula went on, "that when this particular sun wheel is given as a gift, the recipient is forever in the thrall of the giver."

"How did the baron acquire it, then?"

Ursula smiled. "It was given to him. Naturally."

"Who gave it to him?"

Ursula shrugged. "You'll have to ask him."

The baron was whispering something to Lucien, who smiled and looked over at Ursula and Anne. The baron straightened, and approached the two women. "I see that you are showing her my collection, Ursula."

"It's all so very interesting," Anne said.

The baron took down a sword from a wall. It had a curved blade that gleamed in the lamplight.

"This is a scimitar," he explained, "given to me by an Ottoman sultan who claims it has killed exactly six thousand, six hundred, and sixty-five enemies. I think it is hungry for one more life, to make an even four sixes in a row." He chuckled at his macabre joke. "It is my favourite object in my entire collection. It's why it is part of my heraldic insignia."

"Lucien wants to re-design your insignia, bring it up-to-date," Ursula remarked.

"He likes change for the sake of change," the baron countered. "He may think my insignia is old-fashioned, but it carries the weight of a distinguished history. There will come a day when it will be new again."

"Speaking of new," Ursula said, "I need to refresh my wine glass. Excuse me." She glided away, and Anne followed her with her eyes until the baron spoke again.

"Pay attention to me, Mrs. Drake, my time is more valuable than hers," the baron said playfully. He put the scimitar back and took down another sword. "This one is a real sacrificial sword, from Bengal. It's called a ramdao. This blade is also thirsty for human blood."

"How very macabre!" Anne cried.

The baron asked: "Do you know the goddess Chhinnamasta?"

Anne shook her head.

The baron grabbed a small framed picture from a nearby table and showed it to Anne. It depicted a decapitated woman standing up, holding her own head in one hand and a ramdao in her other hand. She wore a necklace of skulls and a lotus-flower-shaped skirt embroidered with gold. From her open neck, fountains of blood spurted into the open mouths of her handmaids. She stood upon a couple lying on the ground in an embrace.

The baron said: "The goddess Chhinnamasta is the headless one. She is the duality of the feminine, the Great Mother—the one who creates, but also the one who destroys. She is but one of a multitude. History is replete with such goddesses: Athena, Diana, Artemis, Isis, Cybele, Aphrodite. They all create life, and they take it away. That is the true essence of femininity."

Anne was puzzled. "How so?"

The sacrificial sword glinted in the baron's hands. "You Englishwomen have been told that you are soft, gentle creatures of home and hearth. But that is only half of it. You have within you another power, a power equal to that of men who engage in wars. You have your own terrible aspect that can destroy. The question is, have you the strength to take away the life you've given?"

Anne laughed. "Really! What an absurd question! Why would any woman want to do that?"

"For the sake of something higher," the baron explained, replacing the sword on the wall. "True creativity and true progress cannot exist without the ability to destroy, especially the ability to destroy that which you love."

He plucked a flat, square stone off a display shelf and handed it to Anne. It was obviously very old. It was the figure of a woman, seated on a chair (or maybe it was a throne— Anne could not tell), and she held a staff in one hand and what looked like a long axe in the other hand, raised over her head.

"Egyptian?" Anne enquired.

"It is Canaanite," the baron corrected her. "It is a stone relief of the virgin goddess Anat. Do not let the epithet 'virgin Anat' fool you. Virgin goddesses were 'virgins' only insofar as they refused to dedicate themselves to a single lover or husband. Anat was worshipped in the land of Canaan thousands of years ago, long before the infernal Hebrews invaded and settled there. Anat was both a fertility goddess and a fearsome warrior, a great slayer of men, and the consort of both her father and her brother. Have you heard of Anat's brother Ba'al, the god of the storm and vegetation? Great fiery furnaces were erected in the honour of Ba'al, and children were sacrificed to him, while the beating of drums drowned out their cries."

Anne shivered. "How horrible!"

The baron continued, and his voice was mesmerizing: "Anat went on a rampage when her brother Ba'al died. One can imagine it was more than just a sister in mourning, since they were lovers. She slaughtered multitudes of men, and she enjoyed every minute of it. She frolicked in the blood that came up to her knees, in the gore that came up to her neck. They say human heads were under her feet. In the sky above her were human hands like locusts. She plucked the severed hands from the sky and bundled them like a bouquet of flowers. And all the while she laughed. Her heart was full of exultation." He paused, and brought his hands together as if in prayer. "That, my dear Mrs. Drake, is victory. That is strength."

"It sounds so cruel," Anne murmured.

"Have I not told you that cruelty is simply another word for strength?"

"I've not heard that," Anne replied. "It is all rather ... contrary."

He chuckled and replaced the stone back on the display shelf. "Ah, you modern Englishwomen think that you are so revolutionary because you demand to vote. Now, I agree that you *should* be allowed to vote. But can you imagine what this country—no, what this *world* would be if more of you smart Englishwomen took on the more fearsome aspects of Anat or even Cybele?"

Before Anne could respond, Ursula returned, and held out a drink for Anne.

"Absinthe," Ursula explained. "It is simply marvellous. Although it is an acquired taste."

Anne took a sip of the green liquid, and found the flavour far too strong, but she hid her distaste. She immediately felt a warm glow as the absinthe began to flow in her system.

"The hookah is also marvellous," Ursula suggested.

The baron exclaimed: "Anne's voice is too lovely to pollute with that filthy smoke, my dear Ursula. Leave the hookah to others who have nothing to lose. Let us ask our darling Mrs. Drake to sing for us."

Anne began to protest. "But I haven't prepared anything—"

"Nonsense," the baron said, taking her hand. "Karol is a world-class pianist and he'll accompany you."

The baron led her across the room to the piano. He clapped his hands to silence the room. "Our darling nightingale, Anne Drake, will sing for us."

Karol, a thin-haired man with a sad face and delicate hands, seated himself at the piano.

"I don't know what to sing …" Anne told him.

"One of Schubert's lieder?" Karol suggested. "'Gretchen am Spinnrade' would be a good choice."

"Oh, I'm afraid I don't know that one," she said. "How about 'Three Little Maids from School.' It's from The Mikado. My mother used to sing it to me."

Karol played the opening notes. Anne closed her eyes, and sang, concentrating on the words.

Three little maids from school are we
Pert as a school-girl well can be
Filled to the brim with girlish glee
Three little maids from school!
Everything is a source of fun
Nobody's safe, for we care for none!
Life is a joke that's just begun!

She finished singing, and opened her eyes when she heard the applause.

The baron cried: "Brava, my dear Mrs. Drake! Brava! How many singers would've insisted on an aria from Verdi or Mozart, but our nightingale has the confidence to sing a Gilbert and Sullivan ditty!"

Anne took another sip from her glass of absinthe, and felt the glow of accomplishment. The glow stayed with her until long after she returned home—a home without a husband, but with her two babies who were being cared for by the nanny.

Two days later, a wooden crate was delivered to Anne's house, along with a smaller box. Anne opened the smaller box and found, in a silver frame, a curious pencil-and-charcoal sketch of a woman surrounded by birds and rocks. Inside the box, there was also an exquisite perfume bottle of amber-coloured glass. The note from the baron read:

Dearest Mrs. Drake,

In the wooden crate is the sun-wheel. Put it in the place of that ugly looking-glass in your foyer. While you're at it, banish every looking-glass from your house. They are tools of shallow vanity. The small bottle contains perfume that is called ambergris, what the Arabs call anbar. It is one of the costliest perfumes in the world. Do you recognise the sketch of the woman in the silver frame? It is the goddess Anat, your patron-saint-goddess. (Am I a heretic for saying this?) If Anat had a perfume, ambergris would be it. It smells of decay and seduction, both death and life in a single embrace. She was the Virgin Goddess, and yet also the warrior goddess. Wear the ambergris and think of me.

Yours, Zoltan B v K

Anne noticed the way he'd signed his name. Anne looked at the sketch again. The goddess's face was Anne's own face. In the lower left corner was Lucien's signature. Anne flipped the frame over, and read the inscription on the back:

Anat gives battle
Powerfully she cuts into pieces the sons of the two cities.

She strikes the people of the seashore,
She destroys the men of the sunrise.
Beneath her are heads like rocks,
In the air over her are hands like birds,
like grasshoppers without number are the hands of the quick ones.
She hangs severed heads on her back,
She fastens severed hands on her girdle.
She plunges her knees in the blood of swift ones,
Her thighs in the gore of fast ones.

Anne examined the sketch again. The goddess was standing, not on rocks, but on severed heads, and three were hung around her neck. In the sky above her, and on the girdle around her waist, those were not birds, they were severed hands. It was a ghastly drawing, and yet Anne found it compelling and strangely flattering.

She opened the perfume bottle and dabbed a tiny amount on her wrist. She could not make up her mind as to whether she liked it. It was so different from the rose and lavender perfumes she had on her dressing table.

Anne summoned a tradesman to the house that day. After the black-sun-wheel was in place (and the old looking-glass removed from the house—it really was ugly and old-fashioned, Anne told herself), Mrs. Rafferty gave the new sun-wheel a suspicious look and said nothing. Minerva complimented Madam on her excellent taste. The framed sketch of the goddess was placed below the sun wheel.

Anne wrote a thank-you note. The baron's reply was prompt.

It was an inspired sketch from Lucien, who had been eavesdropping on us. Had you noticed he was nearby, sketching furiously, when I was showing off to you my sword collection and my other objets d'art? You had been wearing a wine-red dress that evening. Did you know that the land of Canaan got its name from the red-purple dye for which they were famous, probably the colour of your dress? It is so fitting that you had been wearing that colour, as if the comparisons between Anne and Anat could not be clearer. Even your names are similar!

As Anne tended to her babies on that bleak November day (Minerva was out), she wondered when she could attend another salon gathering. It had been glorious to sing for such a distinguished gathering! It had been an island of happiness in a sea of loneliness. Visits to her in-laws' house in Hyde Park were a crashing bore in comparison. What would they all think if they knew about the bohemian company she'd been keeping? About the absinthe and water pipes? About swords that had cut off actual human heads, and the shrunken heads themselves? About the sketch of her as a warrior-goddess? They'd be scandalized. And Anne was certain that they'd withdraw their offer to financially support her and the children. No matter. She was too young and too ambitious to spend the rest of her life as a lonely widow. She had a bright future ahead. She was sure of it.

CHAPTER EIGHT

On the day that his children were born, Jonathan was lying on a dirt crossroads somewhere not far from the baron's estate. He opened his eyes to a man's face hovering over his, backlit by a bright sky.

The man was a peasant, speaking Roumanian, and insisting that he would help Jonathan. The peasant tugged Jonathan's injured arm. The pain made Jonathan scream and sit up. Morning light glinted off the wood and iron crosses that surrounded them.

When the pain subsided, Jonathan looked around and cried in English: "Where is my dog?"

The peasant pointed to his horse-drawn wagon nearby. Jonathan stood and tried to climb into the wagon. The man wrapped his arms around Jonathan's filthy trousers and heaved him up and over the rough-hewn side board. Chompsworth was already there, lying on a dirty goatskin. Jonathan lay down next to the dog. The peasant covered Jonathan with an old wool blanket to conceal him. The man was nearly toothless and had scar tissue covering his right eye. Where had Jonathan seen him before?

Jonathan fell asleep in the wagon, and then awoke from the clatter of hoofs and wheels on cobblestones. He sat up in a panic, ignoring the pain that shot through his body. He feared they were back at the baron's estate. But this place was different. The stone walls were old, but not decayed. The architecture harmonized; it was not a confusing jumble of additions. Jonathan noticed that one of the buildings had stained-glass windows.

Nuns in black surrounded the cart. Jonathan remained sitting in the wagon, next to the dog. He scratched his head. His hair was matted. He looked down at his clothes, a custom-made evening suit from one of the best tailors in Savile Row, now filthy and torn, and splattered with blood, not much better than the rags of a beggar. His expensive shoes were ruined.

Two nuns closed and locked the heavy iron gates of the entryway from which the cart had just come. The peasant was talking rapidly with a nun who stood at the front of the group. She was quite plump, and wore the largest, most ornate crucifix of all the nuns. Jonathan guessed that she was the abbess.

As the peasant talked, he gestured with his arms. Jonathan noticed that he was missing a hand. The abbess listened without interrupting, occasionally glancing at Jonathan. Her eyes were inscrutable. Jonathan wished he could understand what the man was saying, but he could only decipher occasional words.

The other nuns who stood nearby included both old and young faces, all surrounded by black fabric. They kept their eyes fixed on the peasant, occasionally glancing at Jonathan with a mixture of revulsion and pity.

Jonathan looked down and noticed that the dog was perfectly still. He cried: "The dog is dying! Please help him!" Three nuns moved closer. The peasant leaped up next to Jonathan and slid his arms under the animal. He lifted the dog down to one of the nuns, whose upraised hands were ready to receive the animal.

The abbess said in German: "Sister Athanasia, please find Sister Ruperta and tell her to tend to this animal right away. Sister Rosa, please go with her."

Two nuns scurried away, one carrying the dog. Jonathan slid down off the wagon, stumbling as his feet touched the ground. He started after the nuns, but the peasant blocked him with his arm and said something he didn't understand.

The abbess said in English: "Do not worry, we will help the dog. I am the Reverend Mother Margarete, the abbess of this convent."

Before Jonathan could reply, the peasant began talking again. The abbess listened, occasionally asking a question. Then she gave orders in German to other nuns. Some were to prepare sleeping quarters for Jonathan, others to find clean clothes, and others to prepare a meal.

She turned to Jonathan and said in English: "Our Lord Jesus Christ would never forsake a man in need, so we will not forsake you. Sister Bernardine and Sister Francesca will show you to the balneum—the bathhouse. We will give you something clean to wear, something to eat, and a place to sleep."

"What about the dog?" Jonathan said.

"Sister Ruperta will heal the dog. She can talk to animals, you know, just as Saint Francis of Assisi could." The abbess smiled, as if she were making a joke, but Jonathan could tell that she actually believed what she was saying.

The two nuns who accompanied Jonathan to the balneum led him through a passageway that eventually ended at an arcade surrounding a cloister. They crossed the grassy cloister garth, and went through another passageway that must have been near the kitchen, because he could smell food. His overwhelming desire was to find the food and gorge himself until his stomach could hold no more But he forced himself to follow the nuns past the barns and stables and a vegetable garden, through a vineyard that had dark clusters of grapes under yellow-and-green leaves. He grabbed handfuls of grapes and ate them furtively, ashamed at his lack of self-control, but tantalized by the sweet juiciness of the fruit.

The nuns unlocked the double doors of the small stone building and threw them wide open. Then they handed Jonathan an oil lamp and a small block of soap, gesturing for him to go inside. There was a coarse linen towel hanging on a wooden peg, and a dark-brown garment on the peg next to it.

In the middle of the stone building was a sunken pool. The pool was lined with blocks of grey stone that were streaked rust-red and sulphur-yellow from the minerals in the water.

The nuns waited outside, sitting on a bench to the side of the door, overlooking the vineyard. They talked in quiet voices, and faced outward the whole time as Jonathan disrobed and lowered himself into the bath.

The water stank of sulphur and iron. As he washed away the dirt and blood of his ordeal, wounds and bruises became visible all over his body, some of them inflamed. The dog bites on his neck and shoulder bled as he washed them out. His hands were scratched, his rib bones protruded, and his legs were pitifully thin.

The garment they had given him was a brown friar's robe. He slipped it over his head and tied the rope girdle around his waist. He transferred items from the pockets of his old garments to the new robe. The crucifix that Sofia had given him went around his neck. He put the mezuzah into the pocket of the robe, along with his grandfather's psalter. He no longer wanted his old garments, as expensive as they were. They were ruined beyond repair, soaked with blood and dirt, and they had too many bad memories clinging to them. He rolled the old garments into a bundle, and made a mental note to bury them at the first chance he got.

He grabbed the oil lamp and went outside to where the nuns sat. They stood up. The one nun looked down at the ground, but the other one glanced at Jonathan's face and then at the crucifix around his neck. She took the oil lamp from him and started walking in the darkness toward the convent with the other nun. Jonathan followed at a respectful distance behind them both, grabbing and eating more grapes as they passed through the vineyard once again.

They reached the Norman arcade surrounding the cloister and went through a doorway, to the refectory. It was a large room with vaulted ceilings where meals were taken, furnished with simple wooden tables and benches.

Jonathan sat down at a table with three place settings. The abbess appeared. Her black robes flowed around her ample figure as she walked. She wore a white wimple that completely concealed her hair.

She took a seat at the table across from him. "Forgive me that I didn't ask your name before. The wagon driver had a lot to say."

He deliberated on whether he should give his full title and that of his father. He decided against it. "I am Jonathan Drake. And I do speak German, by the way."

The abbess smiled. Jonathan immediately took a liking to her. Her round face glowed with kindness and strength. He estimated her age to be early-forties, but she had the vitality of a woman in her twenties.

She said: "Let us keep this in English. The walls have ears."

Jonathan eyed the bread basket. The abbess noticed this. She hastily recited a blessing, then clapped her hands and called out in German: "Bring out the food, please."

Bowls of hot soup were set in front of them, along with goat-cheese, yogurt, and hard-boiled eggs. She chatted amiably the whole time, explaining the history of the convent and her own upbringing in Bavaria.

When Jonathan had eaten his fill, he gestured to the extra setting and asked: "Is a guest missing?"

"He'll be here soon. He's an old friend of mine. Father Milosz."

"If he doesn't get here soon, he may find I've eaten everything. Rather like the locusts in Egypt." Jonathan took the last piece of bread.

"Please eat as much as you like, Mr. Drake. Father Milosz has the appetite of a bird. I believe he sustains himself on nothing more than prayer and wine, and the holy eucharist."

"What is the name of this place?" Jonathan asked. He didn't realise she had told him all that while he'd been eating. He had been too focused on the food.

She said patiently: "We are the Abbey of Saint Hildegard. We are an old German order, dating from the middle of the thirteenth century. Have you heard of Saint Hildegard von Bingen?"

Jonathan shook his head.

"Saint Hildegard was a mystic who received visions directly from God. I will tell you about her another time." The abbess poured wine into clay goblets. "I think you'll like this. One of our better vintages."

Jonathan took a sip from the heavy goblet. The warmth of the wine, along with a full stomach, gave him a feeling of well-being that he hadn't felt in a long time. Just a short time earlier he had been running for his life. And before that, he had almost lost his life at Mora's hands in a dungeon. He was grateful to be alive.

The abbess gestured at the doorway. "Ah, here is Father Milosz. Good evening, Father. We didn't wait, but you are certainly welcome to a meal now."

The emaciated priest, dressed in black, looked older than he was. He held up a thin hand. "I have already had my meal for today, Reverend Mother. But I will take some of that that excellent wine." He spoke English with a heavy Slavic accent.

Father Milosz remained cordial when the abbess introduced Jonathan, but Jonathan could see wariness in the man's watery eyes.

She re-filled Jonathan's goblet. "Please tell us about your adventures. We're all so curious about you."

Jonathan looked from the abbess, who waited expectantly for his answer, to the priest, who fingered the cuff of his sleeve nervously while eyeing Jonathan's crucifix. Father Milosz's shoulders slumped forward, as if he were accustomed to defeat. He had a timidity about him that contrasted strongly with the Reverend Mother's strength.

Jonathan said: "I left the baron's estate, I think it was yesterday. Somehow I ended up here."

The abbess said: "The wagon driver who brought you here said he found you lying on the road with the dog. He said you were too weak to even lift yourself into his wagon."

"That is true," Jonathan said. "I had not eaten for some time."

She raised her eyebrows. "That surprises me. The baron certainly has enough money to afford food to feed his guests. His wealth is legendary."

"The baron is no longer at his estate," Jonathan said. At this news, both of his companions exchanged a surprise glance.

"Where is he?" the priest asked.

"In London. He bought property there. I came here to finalize the deal."

"When did he leave for London?" Father Milosz asked.

Jonathan tried to think. When was that day, the day he tried to run after the baron's carriage, but collapsed on the cobblestones? And then there were those countless hours of horror, at Mora's cruel hands. He tried to count backward, but it was all a blur.

"Some months ago," Jonathan said. "Early May."

"It is now September," the priest remarked.

"Never mind," the abbess said. "The man who brought you here said you had helped him right his wagon. That had been in the spring, he said."

Now Jonathan remembered where he had seen that toothless peasant with the scarred eye and missing hand. Jonathan told his companions of the baron's anger at the fact that he had helped the peasant, and that the younger coachman had been whipped for it.

Father Milosz's face grew even more pale. The abbess flushed with anger.

"Yes," she said acidly, "the baron is known for his lavish punishments that he likes to administer himself. But the peasant rescued you precisely because of your kindness all those months ago."

The priest clutched his wine goblet, a look of worry on his pinched face. "Rescued you? From what?"

Jonathan was silent a moment. Then he answered. "The baron's servants imprisoned me. I barely escaped."

The priest said: "I have heard …" He let the sentence trail off.

"What have you heard?" the abbess asked sharply.

"That a dangerous man is on the run. They say he is English and a Jew," Father Milosz shot a glance at Jonathan. "They say he murdered a female servant."

"That is a lie!" Jonathan snapped. He immediately regretted his outburst.

The abbess asked calmly: "What else do they say, Father?"

"That anyone harbouring him will be punished." The priest rubbed his mouth, then took another drink of his wine.

"Yes, yes," she said impatiently. "The peasant told me all about this rumour. That is why he brought Mr. Drake here. He knows Mr. Drake is suspected by some to be that man. But in talking to Mr. Drake, I know he is not that man."

Jonathan was caught off guard at how quickly malicious lies about him had spread. That meant Iosip was worried that Jonathan was still alive.

The abbess folded her plump hands on the table. "We all know the baron's evil nature. Why should we believe what he says? Both truth and lies are equally useful tools that he'll deploy to get what he wants."

The priest held up his thin hand, a finger upraised in triumph. "Ah, yes, that's it, Sister. The baron uses both lies and truth. If he told only lies, then we'd know what not to believe. But he does tell the truth, and we ignore that at our peril. Do you remember, just a few years after the Roumanian war of independence, when a fearsome band of Turks threatened our region? The baron had warned us all. Those of us who believed the baron were not taken by surprise. Those who dismissed his warning … well, remember what happened to them."

The abbess had no answer. Jonathan was suddenly frightened that the priest's favourable views of the baron would lead to Jonathan's discovery. He came up with a retort.

"I hardly look like a Jew," Jonathan remarked dryly, fingering the crucifix around his neck. "I am a solicitor, from London, from a respectable family." He didn't feel the need to go into detail about his family's pedigree. That history belonged to the man he used to be, and it would be a waste of time to detail his lineage to a nun and a priest in this remote location. Right now, more basic instincts such as food and shelter, and finding his way back to London, were foremost in his mind.

"Maybe they think that little slander will inspire a quicker capture," the abbess observed.

"Will it?" Jonathan asked.

"Among some of the ignorant, perhaps."

Father Milosz fixed his gaze on the table. "Again, we don't know what the truth is," he reminded her.

"Don't we?" she retorted. "At this abbey, we welcome all those in need, no matter their faith. I would even welcome a Jew. After all, our Saviour was a Jew."

"Yes, everyone knows that this abbey does not turn away Jews," Father Milosz said, "even when a pogrom flares up." The priest took a deep breath. "I don't mean to sound indelicate, Reverend Mother, but do you think it is safe for Mr. Drake to stay here? Now that they are looking for him, perhaps he needs to move on, so that you and the others are not at risk."

She replied: "This abbey is a fortress, Father. It has been here since the thirteenth century. It has survived wars and marauders, the Turks and Martin Luther. It can certainly withstand a rumour."

"How did the convent manage to survive all that?" Jonathan asked, eager to turn the conversation in another direction.

The abbess smiled with pride. "This place is difficult to find. There is only one road leading here, and unless you know what to look for, it is not an easy road to follow."

"What if they cut off your food supply?"

"We are self-sufficient. We have food stores. We have our own spring, as you know from the balneum. Most important, God blesses us and protects us."

Father Milosz said: "If the local magistrates decide to put pressure on you, Reverend Mother ..." He didn't finish the thought.

"Nobody tells me how to run my convent," she snapped.

"But the baron is influential—"

"The baron has no jurisdiction over us here."

The priest clapped his hands over his ears. "Ssh! Do not say that so loudly!"

The abbess's cheeks were red. In German, she said: "It's my convent, and I will say what I damn well please!"

Jonathan was surprised to hear a nun use profanity.

The priest trembled. "He is lord of us all."

"Baron von Klausenberg is not my lord. God the Father is my Lord," she repeated, first in German, and again in English, in a voice loud enough to be heard by anyone listening in the shadows.

"That's easy for you to say," Father Milosz whispered nervously. "You sit up here, secluded from the world. I'm down in the village, with people who will be harmed if the baron gets wind of any disobedience. In fact, there have already been even more reports of children disappearing." His hand shook as he raised the cup of wine to his lips.

"I've heard those rumours, too," she said. "But when I ask for names and witnesses, nobody ever comes forward."

"They are afraid," the priest murmured. "And besides, the rumour is that the Jews are behind it. A gypsy woman and her son went missing in the late spring. In retribution, a Jew and his family were burned to death, in their house, by a mob in Klausenberg." The priest added: "Then there are accounts that have been circulating for years that the baron himself has ordered the hunting of children."

"Which only proves that it is the baron, and not the Jews, who are behind it," she said, visibly shaken at this news. After a few moments, she added: "Tell the people that the baron is gone to England. That should calm their fears." She turned to Jonathan. "You must be tired, Mr. Drake. Let me have one of the sisters show you to your room. May God grant you a restful sleep."

The priest added with nervous relief: "Be well, my son, and God speed to you."

A nun waited in the shadows to lead him. She held an oil lamp and walked three paces ahead. They passed the chapel, and arrived at a small stone building next to the gateway. The nun opened an ancient wooden door, and stood aside for him to enter. It was a dark room, sparsely furnished with only a bed. Stone walls, no window. It reminded him too much of the dungeon where Mora had imprisoned him.

He turned to the nun, and said in English: "I cannot stay here." She did not understand. He repeated it in German.

"Where do you want to sleep?" she asked sharply.

"Not here."

She turned and walked briskly back toward where they had come from. Jonathan followed.

Outside of the refectory door, where Jonathan had dined with the Reverend Mother and Father Milosz, the nun stopped.

"Wait here," she said.

A few minutes later, the abbess appeared from the shadows of the arcade, accompanied by a sizeable group of curious nuns.

The abbess gestured to the nun who had escorted Jonathan to his quarters. "Sister Francesca tells me you do not like your accommodations," she said in German. Clearly, she wanted this conversation to be understood by the other nuns.

"Forgive me, but I cannot sleep in that room," Jonathan replied, also in German.

"May I ask what is wrong with it?"

Jonathan waited a moment, unsure of how to answer. Finally, he said: "It reminds me of the place I was forced to stay when I was at the—"

The abbess interrupted him. "I understand. Where do you prefer to stay?"

"I can sleep in the barn. I saw one on the way to the balneum," Jonathan said.

Sister Francesca spoke up. "It is unseemly for a gentleman to sleep in a barn with animals."

The abbess turned to her. "Our Lord and Saviour was born in just such a place."

"But no visitor has ever been allowed to stay there," she retorted. "It is dangerously close to our dormitories. We do not know this man or where he comes from."

An ancient nun with a wrinkled face limped forward. "I will stay in the barn with him. I am far too old to attract scandal. Sister Athanasia, bring the man's dog to us there, please."

"Thank you, Sister Ruperta," the abbess said to the old nun. "Goodnight, my holy sisters. Goodnight, Mr. Drake."

In the barn, Jonathan saw a mule with a bandaged ear in one stall and a cow in another. In a third stall, there was a lamb with a blood-stained fleece. Sister Ruperta pointed to the lamb and the mule, and said, "Wolf attack." She pointed to the cow and said, "Foot rot, but she'll be healed soon."

Jonathan spread a blanket on top of some straw. As he settled onto the blanket, Sister Ruperta was speaking to a nun who had appeared in the doorway.

"Sister Athanasia, put the dog here," Sister Ruperta said, pointing to a spot next to Jonathan. The dog's leg was bandaged, and the creature looked weak and exhausted. Jonathan scratched the dog's ears and chest.

"Hello, Chompsie old friend," Jonathan said. "You're looking a lot better, old boy."

"She is female," Sister Ruperta corrected him.

"Ah, so she is," Jonathan said.

The nun pointed to the wounds on Jonathan's hands and forearms, and to the one on his neck. "You must let me attend those."

"Tomorrow. I want to sleep now."

"Infections get worse quickly if nothing is done." Sister Ruperta turned to Sister Athanasia and instructed her to fetch medical supplies.

When the younger nun returned, Sister Ruperta bade her a goodnight and dismissed her. Then the old nun kneeled on the straw next to Jonathan, organised her supplies, and started to clean his wounds. As Sister Ruperta pushed the sleeve of his robe toward his shoulder, she frowned. A rivulet of blood had trickled down from his shoulder to his elbow.

"I must repair the bleeding," she said. "But I cannot do that through the robe."

He got to his feet wearily and took off his robe. Sister Ruperta had meanwhile turned her back and riffled through her medicine chest while he arranged the robe around his waist so that his lower half was covered. Then he lay down again on the straw.

Sister Ruperta gasped when she saw the wounds on his shoulders and back. She ordered him to turn so she could see his torso.

"Gott im Himmel," she muttered. "My son, who did this to you?"

He covered his eyes with his hand. "Sister Ruperta, does it matter? The lamb in the stall there was torn up by a wolf."

"Wolves don't know any better. Your disfiguring was done by the hand of man. Those are symbols carved into your flesh."

"Actually, it was the hand of a woman. Or perhaps she was a witch. Or a she-devil. I don't know what's real anymore."

"Where did this happen?"

"In Baron von Klausenberg's dungeon."

At the mention of the name, the old nun closed her eyes for a moment and her lips moved in prayer. Then she opened them and resumed inspecting his wounds

"I have never seen this kind of skin carving before. Not even on victims of war."

"At least everything is healed now," he said, trying to reassure himself.

"No, everything is not healed. You have infections in some of the wounds still." She touched the wounds on his shoulder and neck. "What animal did this to you? A wolf?"

"A dog. From the baron's estate. It had red eyes. But that must have been a trick of the light."

"No, my son, that was not a trick of the light. The beast was a demon, sent to destroy you."

"Sent to destroy me, that's true," Jonathan agreed, "but as for the demon part, well, that's hard to accept." He patted the dog lying next to him. "She helped me to kill it."

"Demons are real. You and your dog fought and won. You have skill in battling the forces of darkness. God is with you."

Jonathan was once again struck with what a superstitious lot these Easterners were. As Sister Ruperta tended to his wounds, he found his eyes getting heavy. At one point, through half-closed eyelids, he thought he saw a halo of light above her, but he convinced himself it was an optical illusion of the lamplight.

Jonathan slept through the night and awoke late in the morning.

Sister Ruperta was not there, and neither was Chompsworth. Only the injured lamb was there, placidly chewing grass. Sunlight streamed in from the open doors.

He went outside and made his way to the refectory. Two nuns were sweeping the floor. They seated him at the wooden table, and brought food. While he was eating, the abbess came to talk with him.

"Sister Ruperta said you were calling out in your sleep during the night," she said.

"I don't remember any of that, but I believe her."

"Perhaps some work will help you get your bearings. The remaining grapes need to be harvested. Some fences need to be mended, and wood needs to be cut and stacked. Are you strong enough?"

"Yes," Jonathan said.

CHAPTER NINE

The abbey gave Jonathan a sense of peace he had not felt in a long time. He worked alone, repairing whatever needed repairing, milking the cows and goats, harvesting grapes and squashes. He split firewood, and drove posts into the ground. Chompsworth followed him everywhere he went, limping along with her bandaged leg. He kept to his solitude and spoke to nobody, except to the abbess and to Sister Ruperta.

The trees were in their full blazing glory of red and gold. On sunny days, when he worked in the fields, he stripped down to the waist, giving his wounds a chance to air out. Sister Ruperta kept an eye on every scab, which were now much fewer in number, thanks to her healing skills. His body—which had been painfully thin and weak at the hands of Mora—slowly became healthier. He was no longer a filthy, starving prisoner. He looked like an itinerant labourer, lean and wiry and bearded. His hair was now shoulder-length. He tied it back with a leather lace.

Once or twice when he was in the field, he thought he saw a nun watching him from a grove of trees. He pretended not to see her, and continued with his work.

As for his previous life as a solicitor in a prestigious London law firm, that was someone else. He could not recall the fine antiques in the reception room of Gershon, Stoker and King, nor the china and linens of the home where he used to live. Anne belonged to another man—a man he used to be. That other man was well-fed, with a clean-shaven face and smooth skin on his torso, unblemished by hideous carvings.

He didn't know how long he'd stay at the Abbey of Saint Hildegard. All he knew was that time had stopped. He could rest, gather his wits, drown the nightmares in hard work. He asked for nothing more than something to eat, a safe place to sleep with his dog at his side. The misty dawn, the frost on the leaves, the sunsets that turned the mountaintops a blazing gold, all that was an unexpected gift. He strived for nothing more than an honest day's work.

At night, Jonathan was alone in the barn with his dog, except for whatever sick animals were recuperating there. Exhausted from the day's labours, he would lie down on the straw, with Chompsworth curled up nearby. He would read his grandfather's Book of Psalms. The words gave him comfort, and seemed to speak directly to him.

Psalm 22:16: "For dogs surround me, a pack of evil-doers encloses me." He remembered how Iosip's dogs had attacked him at the edge of the ravine.

Psalm 107:10 "Those who sat in darkness, and the shadow of death shackled in affliction and iron…" He remembered how he'd been imprisoned in the dungeon.

Psalm 107:14 "He brought them out of darkness, and the shadow of death, and broke open their shackles …" He remembered how he'd found the strength to escape the dungeon. Whether it was due to God, or to sheer luck or both, he could not be sure. Reading the psalms and meditating on them gave him the serenity he needed to fall into a dreamless sleep.

One early morning in December, when Jonathan was outside stacking firewood against a wall next to the kitchen, Chompsworth pricked up her ears and wagged her tail. The abbess approached them. She was wrapped in a heavy black woollen overcoat.

She held up an envelope. "Father Milosz sent a letter. He said that the authorities will be here soon to make the arrest of the Jew."

Jonathan took the envelope and read the letter, and handed it back to her. "Who betrayed us?"

"We have only speculations," the abbess admitted. "There had been a novitiate here. She left last week without a word. We think she was the one who may have spoken to the authorities."

"Why would she do that?"

The abbess shrugged. "The baron inspires a lot of fear, but he also rewards those who are loyal to him. Perhaps she was hoping to win his favour for herself or a loved-one, or avoid his punishment."

Jonathan suddenly remembered an incident from last week. "Did this novitiate have large black eyes and olive skin?"

"Yes. Her name was Sister Francesca. She came from Marseille."

Jonathan had been washing his hands and his robe in a small room near the refectory, before his evening meal. The front of his robe was soiled from cleaning the stables, and he used a wet towel and water from the lavabo to clean the stains. He had removed the psalter and mezuzah from the pocket of his friar's robe, and had placed both items on a nearby stone shelf. Sister Francesca had come in unexpectedly, and had seen the mezuzah sitting on top of the psalter. She had immediately left the room without saying a word.

Jonathan removed those items from his pocket now, and showed them to the abbess while he recounted that incident. He also told her how he'd acquired the mezuzah from the cleaning woman at the synagogue in Klausenberg. He concluded: "It's been more than three months since I escaped the baron's estate. Why should they care at this point?"

The abbess's face darkened. "The baron's thirst for revenge never stops." She paused. "I'll tell you a story. There is a tiny village near the baron's estate. That village was founded in the fourteenth century. About a hundred years later, when the baron's family conquered the region and turned it into their fiefdom, they set up a golden chalice in the town square. The chalice is of real gold, and it is not fastened to the pedestal atop which it rests. It has never been stolen. Why not? Because whoever merely touches it will have his hand cut off. Whoever tries to steal it will pay with his life. And the baron's ancestors—and eventually, the baron himself—personally administered the punishment. Some years ago, a visitor touched it. Word got to the baron. The villagers would not disclose who had done it. So the baron decided that he'd begin chopping off hands until the culprit was found. He started with the children. It didn't take long before the villagers were forced to give up the transgressor."

"Is that why the peasant who brought me here was missing a hand?"

The abbess nodded. "He was one of the unfortunate children. Later, when that same peasant was a teenager, the baron punished him for lending a few coins to one of the baron's debtors, which is why his one eye socket is thick with scar tissue. The baron prides himself on accuracy with the whip. The peasant told me all this when he brought you here."

Jonathan looked up at the December sky, which was grey and bleak. A few flakes of snow drifted down to the ground.

"How much time do you think I have?"

"You need to leave today," the abbess advised him. "The day after tomorrow is Christmas. That will spur their determination to find you."

Jonathan looked around at the fallow fields dusted with snow, the barn, the stone buildings where the nuns dwelled, and the looming church with its ancient stone and stained-glass windows. "I like it here and I don't want to leave."

"I do not want to see you go. You do the work of three of us. And," she added with a smile, "I've enjoyed our conversations. But the choice is no longer in our hands. There is a mule waiting for you, with a saddle bag of provisions."

"I'll have no money to reimburse you until I'm back in London."

"We don't expect payment. You've earned it by working."

She handed him a slip of paper. "Memorize this name and address, then destroy the paper. He is a Jewish merchant in Budapest. His name is Yitzhak Loew." To an English speaker, she pronounced the surname as somewhere between the words "love" and "lev."

"Why are you sending me to a Jew? I'm not a Jew," Jonathan protested.

"The rumours are strong. The ignorant ones, those whose ears have been poisoned, may betray you if you remain among Christians. Loew is a good man. He will not turn you away. Tell him all that has happened. He will help you."

Jonathan looked down at his dog. "It looks as if we're going to travel, Chompsie old girl."

The dog wagged her tail in reply.

When Jonathan appeared at the entry gate of the abbey, in the same courtyard he'd arrived with the one-handed peasant, he saw the mule standing there, twitching its ears, burdened with saddlebags. Every nun in the convent had gathered to bid Jonathan farewell. Some blessed him by making the sign of the cross over his head. Their breath was visible in the frosty air.

Sister Ruperta cradled Chompsworth's face in her wrinkled hands, and murmured a farewell. She ran her hand along the neck of the mule, then turned to Jonathan.

"The mule is named Cinnamon. Be patient with her. Never beat her, and she'll do what you want."

"I don't beat animals."

The nun replied: "I know it, and the animals know it. You are good to them. May God bless you and protect you on your journey, my son."

"Thank you, Sister Ruperta, for healing my dog, and for healing me, too."

The old nun smiled, and a tear ran down her wrinkled face.

Jonathan turned to the abbess. She gave him a sealed envelope. "It is a letter from me." She held out a square filet of lace. Jonathan took it.

"Herr Loew will recognise this lace. Tell him you have seen it, that I showed it to you and told you the history behind it." She pointed to the figures depicted there. "That is Balaam and his donkey. Herr Loew gave it to me as a gift because I helped him and his family some years ago. He told me that I had been one of the few who had blessed them rather than curse them at a time when the curses were causing blood to run in the streets."

Jonathan returned the filet of lace to her. "You've been a true friend, Reverend Mother. I'll never forget you or my time here."

She bit her lip, and her eyes were moist. "Take care," she said. "God be with you and protect you, Jonathan Drake."

Jonathan put the envelope into the deep pocket of his robe. He placed the dog on the mule's back.

Sister Elisabetta and Sister Bernardina walked ahead of him and the mule, picking their way down the treacherous mountain path. It was an impossible path to find if one did not already know where it was. At the bottom of the mountain, the two nuns pointed out the road he must take, and bade him farewell. They turned to head back up to the abbey.

He recalled the Reverend Mother's words about God protecting him, and hoped she was right. If it had been his choice, he would not have left the abbey—not so soon, anyway. It had become his sanctuary, a place of healing where the only things that mattered was the hard labour, humble food, and the dreamless sleep in the barn with his dog nearby. The smell of the barn animals and their soft noises in the darkness were a comfort, for they reminded him where he was, that all was well.

He wore the brown friar's robe because he had no other clothing. He had buried the clothing he'd been wearing when he arrived at the abbey because it had been ruined beyond repair. His current ascetic-Christian appearance would deflect suspicion. A heavy wool cloak was draped around his shoulders, a hood covered his head, and the crucifix that Sofia had given him dangled from his neck. The winter boots on his feet were common to the region. They consisted of roughly sewn hides padded with wads of wool and secured with leather laces. His full beard and uncut hair gave him additional insulation against the cold. In the solitary hours of travel along the road, he told Chompsie and Cinnamon stories from his younger days. Those stories helped him to remember that he was connected to a past, and that maybe he could return to a semblance of his old life.

But could he truly return to his old life? He didn't know whether that was possible—not as the man he used to be, anyway. Right now, he couldn't afford to think about the exact details of how he was going to re-build a life in London. There were too many things that demanded his attention, such as staying warm and fed while he made his way to Budapest.

Each day he set out on his travels just as the dawn broke, even if it were snowing. He endured occasional snow storms. By sunset, he would settle in for the night. He always offered to pay for his lodging with the few coins that the Reverend Mother had given him. But innkeepers and farmers did not charge him. They treated him with deference, believing him to be a man of God. It was a different kind of deference than the sort he'd been accustomed to as the son of a lord and lady, and he appreciated it. They gave him food, fed and watered his animals. Often, they would ask for a blessing, and Jonathan obliged. It was the least he could do to repay their kindness. Before going to sleep each night, he would read from his grandfather's psalter.

On the day he arrived in Budapest, it was near sunset. He asked directions to Dohány Street. Those he asked looked at him quizzically, pointed in the general direction, and watched him as he set off with his animals. As Jonathan neared the address he sought, he realised he was in the Jewish quarter—hardly the place for a friar. Jewish men with beards, dressed in black suits and black hats, stopped to watch the friar travel down the street with his mule and dog. Jonathan ignored their stares. He was tired, hungry, and eager to make contact with the man who would help him get back to London.

Yitzhak Loew's door was hidden in a stone alcove off the main street. Jonathan knocked and waited, holding the rope that was tied to the mule. Chompsworth sat upon the mule's back, alert and curious.

The door creaked open. There on the threshold stood an old man with small round glasses, rounded shoulders, and a long grey beard. A black silk cap topped his bald head.

"Good day," Jonathan said in German. "You are Yitzhak Loew?"

The old man nodded. His eyes went to the crucifix around Jonathan's neck.

"My name is Jonathan Drake. The Reverend Mother Margarete of the Abbey of Saint Hildegard von Bingen sends her regards." He held out the letter from the Reverend Mother, and said: "She showed me the lace that depicts Balaam and his donkey."

Yitzhak read the letter. He looked at Jonathan, his eyes went to the crucifix around Jonathan's neck, and then at the mule at the end of the rope. "So, you are here to bless us, not to curse us?" he asked. Before Jonathan could answer, he said: "I will not turn away one of Sister Margarete's friends. Come in."

Jonathan gestured at his mule and dog. "Where shall I leave them?"

Yitzhak leaned inside the doorway and yelled in Yiddish: "Rivkeh! Shmuli! Please come here!"

Moments later, youngsters came running out. The boy was about

111

thirteen years old, and wore a black kippah. The girl was about eleven. Her hair was tied back in a dark blue kerchief, and she wore a long, blue skirt.

Yitzhak instructed the children to take the animals to the stable, and feed and water them.

"You must be careful with the dog," Jonathan said in German. "Her leg has been badly broken and is still healing."

"I will take care of her," the girl Rivkeh replied. "I love animals, and I know just what to do." She paused a moment, then asked: "Are you poor? Your clothing is so dirty. And why do you speak German with such an accent?"

"Rivkeh, those are not nice questions," Yitzhak reprimanded her. "You must apologize."

"I'm sorry," Rivkeh said to Jonathan.

Jonathan said: "You are correct, I speak with an accent. I look poor because I have been on a very long and difficult journey. At the moment, I have only a few coins because the rest of my money was stolen by some bad people."

"We can give you money from the tzedakah box," Rivkeh offered.

"But not on Shabbos," Shmuli observed.

Yitzhak said: "That is why you both must tend to the animals right away. Shabbos is almost here, and your chores must be finished by then."

They led the animals away. Jonathan watched them go. Yitzhak noticed the sad, anxious expression on Jonathan's face.

"Do not worry about the animals," Yitzhak said. "They will be cared for. Rivkeh will cry when you must leave and take them away from her."

They climbed one flight of stairs, to a door that opened into a parlour.

Books lined the walls. A large bird cage with twittering canaries occupied a corner of the room, near the lace-curtained window. In the adjoining dining room, a large table was set with a lace table cloth and white china. On the back of every chair was a lace antimacassar. These were not wealthy people, but they were not poor, either.

The place smelled of baked bread, cake, boiled vegetables and roasted meat and potatoes. Jonathan's stomach rumbled with hunger.

"Dinah!" Yitzhak called out in Yiddish. "We have another guest for dinner."

From out of the kitchen came a sturdy woman wearing an apron. A lace kerchief covered her hair.

She stopped, her mouth agape, when she saw Jonathan. He knew he looked totally out of place, with his dirty friar's robe and crucifix.

She recovered her composure and said: "Welcome. Guests are coming soon. You can wash downstairs. My husband can give you fresh clothing."

"I would greatly appreciate that," Jonathan said.

Yitzhak led Jonathan to a bathroom on the ground floor. There was an iron tub there, with a tap, and some bath towels draped over a towel rack. Yitzhak left a stack of neatly-folded clothing on a wooden table. Then he left Jonathan alone. The room was cold and the water was barely lukewarm, but after spending his days travelling in the winter air, it wasn't hard to endure. Jonathan washed quickly, soaping his hair and beard, and scrubbing his body. The symbols carved there were now red scars, still visible in contrast to his pale skin. There were no more infections, no scabs, no bleeding. He again felt gratitude toward Sister Ruperta for healing him.

Jonathan got dressed. The clothing Yitzhak had given him consisted of a starched shirt that had yellowed with age, and an outdated black wool suit. The pants were too loose at the waist, but he cinched them with the worn belt. The shoes were old and needed a polish, but they fit well enough. There was a black hat that needed a brushing.

On the wash stand, was a comb and a looking-glass. Jonathan gazed into the looking-glass and barely recognised his own reflection. He was a bearded itinerant with long hair. His cheekbones were hollow, and his eyes gazed back with a dark intensity that he had never seen in himself before. He was nothing like the well-dressed, well-fed, clean-shaven solicitor who had left London in the spring of 1908. He combed back his hair and tucked it up under the hat. Fully dressed, he looked like the other men of that neighbourhood.

Outside the door, Yitzhak said: "Herr Drake, may I come in?"

"Yes, yes of course," Jonathan said.

When Yitzhak saw him, he said: "You could go out on the street now and nobody would look twice at you. So different from an hour ago. So, tell me about yourself," Yitzhak said delicately. "How did you learn German so well?"

"Some people in my family spoke it."

"The abbess wrote that you're from London."

"Did she? I have no idea what was in the letter she had me deliver to you, only that she requested that you help me."

"Tell me about your family."

Jonathan hesitated. What had been important, in terms of his family pedigree, seemed no longer important when one had survived torture and starvation.

Jonathan finally answered: "The less that is said about me, the better."

Yitzhak faced Jonathan squarely. "I am helping you because the Abbess Margarete is my friend, and I trust her. She saved my life. But I want to know: Is another pogrom on the horizon? Are my people in danger here? This is why I am asking all these questions."

Jonathan could not blame the man. He answered honestly. "I do not know. The Baron von Klausenberg has gone to London."

Yitzhak's eyes narrowed. "And how do you know this? Are you a friend of the baron?"

Jonathan heard the fear and suspicion in Yitzhak's voice. He replied: "I am a solicitor from London. I had been sent to the Baron von Klausenberg's estate to finalize a real-estate transaction. I had never even heard of him before then. I expected that, after we had signed the papers, I would be free to go home. But the baron's servants had other plans for me. They imprisoned me for several months. I managed to escape and find refuge at the abbey. I had to leave there when the abbess got word that the authorities were going to come to the abbey to arrest me."

"For what would they arrest you?"

"They said an English Jew was on the run, guilty of murdering one of the baron's servants."

"So you are this Jew they are pursuing?"

"I am not a Jew."

Yitzhak gestured to the wash-stand. "And yet you have a mezuzah, and a book of Tehillim that is both in German and in Hebrew. On the other hand, you ride on a donkey, dressed as a friar. It is all very confusing. This is why I need to talk to you."

Jonathan took a deep breath. Full honesty, however unpleasant, would be most expedient. "My mother had been born Jewish. Her father had been a rabbi. He is the one who taught me."

Jonathan picked up the psalter and showed Yitzhak the inscription that his grandfather had written, and explained how his mother had given it to him on his thirteenth birthday.

Yitzhak asked: "So you told the baron of your mother's background?"

Jonathan shook his head. "No. I had been warned not to say anything. But the baron's servants went through my things and stole what they wanted, including my wedding ring."

"I see," Yitzhak murmured. He pointed to the psalter. "Have you a favourite?"

It was an odd question, but Jonathan realised that Yitzhak was trying to further gauge Jonathan's identity and honesty.

"When I was at the abbey, every night before I went to sleep, I'd read the Psalms. They comforted me," Jonathan answered. "I like number ninety-four. 'My God is my sheltering rock. He will make their evil recoil upon them, annihilate them through their own wickedness.'"

Yitzhak said: "Have you ever heard of Rabbi Naftali Berlin, the Netziv of Volozhin?"

Another test question. Jonathan answered honestly. "No, I have not heard of him."

"He believed that King David composed those Psalms, with divine inspiration, of course, so that each man would find in them a parallel to his own circumstances." Yitzhak changed the subject. "I have asked you endless questions, and yet I've told you nothing about how the Abbess Margarete saved my life."

"I would be grateful if you could relate that story to me," Jonathan replied.

Yitzhak took a deep breath. "It was 1905. I'm a lace merchant, you see, and I had business near Klausenberg. My wife was travelling with me. A pogrom started like that—" he snapped his fingers. "Margarete was a nun at the abbey, but she was not yet the abbess. There is a very small village down the mountain from the abbey. She happened to be there that day, and saw me and my wife, we had become surrounded by an angry mob. Margarete got them to release us. Then she persuaded the abbess to hide us until the danger was past—at a great risk to everyone's safety at the abbey—and then she helped us get back here to Budapest. This is why trust her, and also why I am worried about your being here, you see. You may be a sign of bad times coming, God forbid."

Jonathan retorted: "I am a man who is just trying to survive and get back home. There is no larger significance than that. You have just as much hatred for the baron as I have. That makes us allies, even if I am not a Jew."

"We are not the only two who hate the baron," Yitzhak said in a whisper. "The hatred goes back generations. They say that the baron's father was descended from Vlad Tepes—Vlad the Impaler, a fifteenth-century Wallachian prince who was renowned for his cruelty. They say the baron's mother had been descended from Countess Elizabeth Báthory of Hungary. In the sixteenth century, the countess and her servants were accused of torturing and murdering hundreds of girls. It is not an auspicious ancestry."

Jonathan recalled the pile of children's clothing he'd found in the fleischzimmer when he'd been searching for his travelling suit. He pushed that horrifying recollection out of his mind.

Yitzhak changed the subject. "And your wife, have you told her you are now here?"

"Not yet."

Yitzhak said: "There is no time to write and post a letter before Shabbos begins. We can write to her once Shabbos has finished. Let us go upstairs. My wife will not be happy if we are late."

CHAPTER TEN

Yitzhak's flat was crowded with guests for Shabbat dinner. Two of Yitzhak's married daughters were there with their husbands, along with their children, ranging in age from infants to teenagers. Another woman named Berthe, a plump seamstress and a friend of the family, helped Dinah with last-minute preparations. Berthe's daughter, a plain young woman named Lotte, tagged along and did what her mother ordered. Rivkeh and Shmuli, the two youngsters who had tended to Jonathan's animals, played with their siblings and cousins.

Rivkeh broke away from the group to talk to Jonathan. "You smell better now. And you don't look poor anymore."

Jonathan smiled at the girl's earnest expression. "I am happy that the bath had its intended effect. How is my dog doing? And the mule?"

"They are both happy. The mule is in the stable and I gave her lots of food and water. Your dog is here. I put her in a room off the kitchen." She pointed in the direction of the kitchen. "I gave her water and food, too. I taught her how to sit and give me her paw."

In a gentle tone, Jonathan said: "Is the dog even allowed inside? I don't want to take advantage of your grandmother's hospitality."

Rivkeh laughed. "Oh no, Grandmother won't mind, so long as the dog doesn't harass the canaries. She doesn't want to eat birds, does she?"

"Well, I honestly don't know," Jonathan admitted.

"How can you not know? She's your dog."

"Yes, but I haven't had her very long."

"What is her name?"

"Chompsworth."

To the girl's ears, the English name sounded strange. She laughed.

"What does it mean?" she asked.

"It means she is good at chewing on her enemies. She is a good defender."

"But she is so sweet. That is why I think Zusa is a better name for her. 'Zusa' means sweet like honey."

"You can call her Zusa, then."

"I will."

Rivkeh's mother called her to come sit in her chair. Rivkeh took her place at the table, among her siblings and cousins.

Jonathan looked around the room. At least he was not conspicuous. All the men in the room had full beards. All wore black suits.

The room was noisy, crowded, and hot. Dinah Loew opened the window just an inch. An unusually warm breeze blew in, stirring the curtains.

She glanced at the empty chair next to Jonathan, and then at her husband. She asked: "Does anyone know when Dovid will be here?" She pronounced the name "David" the Yiddish way.

"Don't wait, Mamma," one of the married daughters said. "It is time to light the candles. And the children are hungry." As if on cue, the small child in her arms started crying.

Dinah struck the match, lit the candles, and covered her eyes while singing the Shabbos blessing in Hebrew. The other women also covered their eyes until the prayer was finished.

The women took their hands away from their eyes. Just then, a strong gust blew in from the window and snuffed out the candles. Dinah looked at her husband with a worried expression. Murmurs went around the table. One of the husbands got up from the table and shut the window.

Yitzhak remained calm. "Light them again, please, Dinah."

Dinah lit the candles again, and recited the prayer for a second time.

Sensing the unease in the room, Yitzhak said: "Nothing can extinguish the light of Shabbos. Hashem's light glows in each one of us, in our love for each other and our love for Hashem and His Torah."

Prayers and blessings were recited: the blessings for the children, the blessing over the wine, the prayer and the washing of the hands, and the blessing over the two loaves of challah.

Jonathan was moved by the celebration. He took a piece of the challah and ate it. He vividly remembered his grandfather's table. He had not gone often to his grandfather's on Friday nights—only when his father was traveling or otherwise occupied and his mother would take the children to visit their grandfather. During those times, Jonathan caught a glimpse of the devoted Jewish daughter that his mother had been, before she had married Lord Edward Drake.

Bowls of soup were set in front of each diner. Around the table, everyone was talking and laughing. The conversation stopped abruptly when a knock was heard at the door.

"He is here, finally," one of the husbands said.

Lotte, the plain young woman in the yellow kerchief, blushed as her mother nudged her to sit up straight.

Shmuli sprang to his feet. "I'll answer the door," he cried.

"I want to open the door for him!" Rivkeh dashed ahead of her brother.

Within seconds, all the children who were old enough rushed down the stairs to the front door.

Shouts and squeals of laughter floated upstairs to those waiting at the table.

"He takes the time to speak with each child," Yitzhak explained. "It may be a while before he actually appears at the table."

"That means he would be a very good father," Berta said significantly. She nudged her daughter again, and the blushing Lotte once again remembered to sit up straight.

Finally, after several minutes, the gaggle of children came back with their trophy: Uncle David, who was carrying a four-year-old, while a seven-year-old was riding on his back. The rest of the children crowded around him, tugging on his coat and talking all at once in excited tones.

David swept his hat off in a dramatic gesture, and said to the room: "A good Shabbos everyone!" His voice was a rich baritone. He was a tall man, with a good profile and a wide smile that revealed perfectly white, straight teeth. His hair and beard were a deep auburn. He wore a grey pinstripe suit that Jonathan thought was remarkably elegant and au courant, especially for this part of Europe.

David lowered the child in his arms, and the one on his back hopped off. He made a dramatic bow to all assembled there, and then reminded one of the girls to give Dinah the huge bouquet of flowers she was holding.

"Thank you, Dovid," Dinah said. "You are always so thoughtful." She turned to the young woman. "Lotte, will you please put these flowers in the green vase in the kitchen?"

Lotte rose from her chair, blushing a deep red, and carried the flowers to the kitchen. Her mother Berthe watched her go, and then gave David a significant look. David was not looking at either Berthe or Lotte. He was making his way around the table, greeting his cousins and their spouses.

David took his seat next to Jonathan. Unlike the other men at the table (including Jonathan) who had bushy, untrimmed beards, David's beard was closely trimmed and shaped along his jawline. He looked smart and aristocratic.

He finally arrived at the empty place next to Jonathan, and said in German: "I don't believe we've met. I'm Uncle Yitzhak's nephew, David Lowe." He pronounced his last name as "low," not "lev" as Yitzhak's was pronounced.

"Pleased to meet you, Mr. Lowe," Jonathan replied.

Yitzhak interrupted in Yiddish. "Dovid, our guest is an Englishman, newly arrived from . . . Klausenberg."

"Klausenberg?" David said. "Why, if he's an Englishman, I thought perhaps he'd come from England." David said to Jonathan in perfect English: "I'm so glad you're here. Now you and I can have a good chat."

David had a slight accent, almost undetectable, in his otherwise flawless diction.

"Where did you learn to speak English so well?" Jonathan asked.

"Why, at Oxford, of course," David said. "That's why I changed my surname to L-o-w-e. It's so much more congenial among Anglos. Oh, and please drop the 'mister' bit, if you don't mind. We're actually old chums who have yet to get acquainted. You see, I dreamed about you recently. It was really a vision. We're friends, like David and Jonathan from the Book of Samuel."

Jonathan was shocked by such an outlandish statement. Was the man mad, or was he just being flamboyant on purpose? It occurred to Jonathan that he could not dismiss David's statements out of hand—not after the ordeals he'd been put through. And that realization was more frightening than the statements themselves.

As if reading his mind, David said: "Don't be frightened—I don't think our lives are in danger. At least not yet."

"When will I know for sure?" Jonathan asked.

David laughed. "Oh, you'll know. We both will."

Jonathan wanted to change the subject. This was all too strange, and he didn't want to spend the evening discussing danger and death. So he asked David: "How did you get to Oxford?"

David sighed. "You can't imagine how hard I pressed my parents to consent to that little adventure. And then when I changed the spelling and pronunciation of my last name ... well, let's just say they were so angry, they almost sat shiva. But the problem was, you see, that Loew sounded too ... foreign. And I had to fit in, didn't I? I might as well tell you right now, Drake, that I'm an incurable anglophile, and somewhat of a snob, which will become increasingly obvious the more you get to know me. And, I'm a wine merchant by trade, which brings me into contact with all sorts of interesting people. But I am rich, so there's that."

Jonathan laughed at David's candour. Such statements would never be uttered in the Drake family dining room, no matter how truthful. It would have been regarded as bad taste. But coming from David, it was oddly charming.

Dinah interrupted their conversation. She was speaking Yiddish.

"Dovid, I'm talking to you. Dovid. Listen. I want to introduce you to my good friend Berthe Schwartz and her daughter Lotte. Berthe's father-in-law was the great scholar Moshe Wisse of Würzburg. Lotte herself is a talented seamstress. She takes after her mother."

David smiled amicably. "Nice to meet you both, and good Shabbos."

Lotte was staring down at her plate, red and petrified, while her mother Berthe smiled and nodded, trying to compensate for her daughter's awkwardness. Berthe launched into a monologue about how pleased and grateful she was to finally meet Herr Lowe after all she had heard about him from her dear friend Dinah. Her monologue was interrupted when one of the children accidentally tipped a water glass and got another child wet. The two children started quarrelling, and the parents stepped in to calm the situation.

David whispered to Jonathan in English. "Ah. Just as I suspected. There is a conspiracy here to make a match. Unless you're the target." He glanced at Jonathan's hands. "I suppose you're not married."

"I am married. My wedding band was stolen."

"You're lucky you're not in their sights, then. Things get tedious when family members debate precisely when an itinerant like me should settle down with a wife and have children. There is a new prospect every time I come for a visit. And regular letters urging me to court this woman or that woman. This has been going on since I was twenty. I'm now twenty-nine—just to save you the guesswork." David stood abruptly, brandishing a bottle, and announced: "I have a fine Tokaj here, if anyone is interested. You need not wait for dessert to enjoy it."

David walked around the table to fill wine glasses. When he resumed his seat, he whispered to Jonathan: "I have another bottle here you should try." He opened a second bottle and filled Jonathan's glass, then his own.

David raised his and said to Jonathan in English: "Let's drink to England, shall we?"

"Cheers," Jonathan said.

David asked: "During your recent travels, did you find yourself pining for merry old London?"

"In ways you can't imagine."

One of the men at the table said: "Dovid, tell us where you've been."

David said: "Two nights ago, I was in Szeged. Before that, Timisoara. In November, Constantinople and Ankara. In October, Helsinki, Saint Petersburg, and Kiev." He added, in a self-deprecating tone: "I'm a wanderer, a vagabond. I am not the kind of man to settle down in one place. That's how I've lived my adult life, at any rate."

Bertha and Dinah overheard this comment, and frowned at him as they placed on the table hot platters of food. David took no notice of their reactions.

Jonathan avoided the meat. Dinah saw this and remarked: "Mr. Drake, why won't you try the beef at least? I buy it at the best kosher butcher in the city. I make the best beef sauce in Budapest. And you are our guest of honour, so you get extra."

"I thought I was your guest of honour, Auntie," David said.

"Oh, Dovid," she said in an exasperated tone, "you are sometimes so silly."

She placed a slice of meat on Jonathan's plate. "Enjoy!" she said, beaming a proud smile.

"Thank you," Jonathan said.

David whispered in English: "Vegetarian, are you?"

"One could say that."

In a deft move, David speared the meat on Jonathan's plate and moved it to his own, glancing to be sure Dinah hadn't noticed.

"Whatever I don't finish can go to your dog," David said quietly.

"How do you know about Chompsie?"

"Rivkeh was telling me all about her when she answered the door. She's totally in love with her, you know." David paused. "What made you decide to be a vegetarian?"

Jonathan was silent. Then he finally said: "Travelling. Sometimes I develop an aversion for one reason or another."

"Same thing has happened to me, many times," David remarked. "I was a vegetarian for a full year after visiting China. The food there could be sublime or revolting, depending."

Rivkeh was at David's side, tugging at his sleeve. "Excuse me, but have you got sweets for us? You always bring them."

Her brother Shmuli overheard everything and said: "Rivkeh! You're not supposed to ask for gifts. It's rude."

David tapped his knife on his wine glass to get everyone's attention. "Now, children, I have Turkish delight to give to each of you. But first, you must answer questions. Whoever gets the right answer gets a sweet."

Rivkeh spoke up. "Shoshi is only three. How can she answer questions? Then she won't get any candy, and she'll cry when she sees us eating it."

"You, my darling, will earn candy for her," David said. "In fact, each of you older children will first earn candy for the younger ones, and then for yourselves."

"Why do we have to answer questions?" Shmuli grumbled.

"Because your parents and grandparents don't like it when I hand out candy for nothing. They want you all to earn it, and learn some Torah in the process. Both of which are noble goals, by the way. Now, first question: Who was Menashe's brother?"

Shmuli rolled his eyes. "That's so easy. Ephraim."

"How do you know?"

"Because we hear the blessing every week that asks God to make us boys fine and strong like Ephraim and Menashe."

123

"Good!" David said, giving the boy a candy. "Now, here is the next question. Who are the matriarchs in the blessing for the girls, and what did Rashi have to say about them?"

"I'll answer that!" Rivkeh exclaimed.

Yitzhak leaned over to Jonathan, and said: "My nephew has an incredible mind. He could have been a great scholar. But he instead chooses his life of wine and travel."

David continued with the questions, and told jokes. The children laughed, and were delighted with the candy they had earned. The women cleared the plates and dishes. Dinah brought out a sponge cake and a large bowl of tinned fruit.

After dessert, the mothers with young children gathered their belongings. Yitzhak began singing the after-dinner blessing, the birkat hamazon, and other voices joined in.

Once the singing was finished, Rivkeh came up to Jonathan.

"Your dog wants a walk," she said "I can take her outside."

"Why don't we all go for a walk," David suggested. "You can still hold the dog's lead, Rivkeh."

David and Jonathan accompanied the guests as they walked back to their respective homes. The children took turns riding on David's back as they made their way through the moonlit streets. Some of the children took turns riding on Jonathan's back, but only because they couldn't secure a spot with David, their clear favourite. Jonathan found that he enjoyed being with the children, and he suddenly wished for a family of his own. Rivkeh was engrossed in caring for the dog. She talked non-stop to Zusa (as she called the dog) explaining what street they were on and which people she knew on that street. Jonathan was touched by her compassion for the dog.

Suddenly, in the midst of the merriment, Jonathan had the feeling that he was being watched. He glanced around, and tried to peer into the shadows, but he saw nothing out of the ordinary. He securely held the child (Rivkeh's younger sister Leah) who was riding on his back.

They turned down a side street. At door to her house, Rivkeh reluctantly gave the lead to Jonathan, and asked if she could see Zusa tomorrow. She hugged the dog, and then went into the house with her family. Jonathan and David were now the only two people on the street.

Chompsworth stood between them. Jonathan insisted that he and David wait a few minutes to be sure everyone got upstairs safely. When lights on the upper floor were lit, Jonathan said: "All is well. We can go now."

David said: "You are vigilant. Are you always like this?"

"Just a feeling, that's all."

As they walked, Jonathan glanced around constantly, trying to dispel the feeling that he was being followed. The dog was too distracted by the new smells to alert on Jonathan's anxiety.

"You're scanning the landscape like a fugitive," David said.

"That's because I am one," Jonathan admitted. "There's a rumour in around Klausenberg that an Englishman who is also a Jew is on the run with a dog. I had been a prisoner there not too long ago. I managed to escape."

Jonathan waited for David's reaction, and all the questions he thought would follow. David finally said: "Klausenberg. Interesting. An aristocrat in that vicinity had started a pogrom against the Jews there. Uncle Yitzhak and Aunt Dinah were there when it erupted. They found refuge in a convent—Hildegard, I think it was called. When the worst was over, they came back to Budapest."

Jonathan looked at him sharply. "I fled to that very convent. The abbess advised me to find Yitzhak. That is why I am here." Jonathan paused. "I hesitate to ask, but what happened to the rest of the family in Klausenberg?"

"Some were murdered. A branch went to England and changed their name to Miller."

Jonathan knew, without asking, that that was the same family to which his colleague Mr. Miller belonged. No wonder that man hadn't wanted to come back to this part of the world.

David said: "What about your wife? Does she know where you are?"

"Not since I left the convent."

David took Jonathan by the arm and walked faster. "Good God, man, we've got to get word to your wife that you're all right."

Jonathan protested. "But your Uncle Yitzhak says it's Shabbos, no writing on Shabbos, not even letters to one's wife."

"Dear old pious Uncle Yitzhak," David said. "We're talking about your wife. She must be in agonies not hearing from you. To hell with a letter. We're sending a telegram, right now."

"But they're expensive—"

"I'm paying."

"I thought you weren't supposed to spend money on Shabbos."

"God will forgive me. Just don't tell Uncle Yitzhak."

They arrived at a darkened building in another part of town, about ten minutes away. David pounded on the door. No answer. He pounded again. A window opened over the door, and a man leaned out, swearing in Hungarian.

David looked up at him and addressed him in a charming tone. The man shut the window, and Jonathan could hear him stomping down the stairs.

"I'll handle this," David whispered.

"Good, because I don't speak the language," Jonathan replied.

The door was flung open. A fat, bald man with angry eyes stood on the threshold.

David smiled, reached into his pocket and brought out a coin purse. As he counted out the coins, chattering the whole time, the man's eyes got bigger and less angry. Finally, the man grudgingly let them inside the storefront. The man's keys jangled as he opened the door. He refused to let the dog inside, so Jonathan tied the lead to the door handle.

It was a post office and general-goods store. The bald man went to the telegraph machine. David wrote a brief sentence in English and handed it to the man. The man read it, and rattled the paper in David's face, spewing a torrent of angry words. David calmly explained the situation, gesturing to Jonathan.

The man calmed down and began to send the message via telegraph. David leaned over him, making sure he got it right. When the process was over, David thanked him and gave him a few more coins. The man grudgingly pocketed them, muttering something that made David laugh.

A few minutes later, when they had travelled down the street, Jonathan asked: "What did he say that made you laugh?"

"He called me a crazy, demanding Jew, who should be home with his family on a Friday night instead of harassing gentiles like him." David paused. "Funny how he got all upset because the message was in English. You'd think he'd be accustomed to that sort of thing, given his line of work. But then again, the people here can be so narrow-minded. It's why

I could never settle in one place."

"Have you got any brothers or sisters?" Jonathan asked.

"My sister lives in Jerusalem with her husband and five children. She and her husband are so pious they make Uncle Yitzhak look like a pagan."

"And your parents?"

"Venice."

"Why aren't you married?"

David's voice was wistful. "There was someone, a long time ago. I was young then."

"And there have been no opportunities since?"

"Opportunities, yes. Plenty of those. The right one, no."

"If you wait too long, you'll miss your chance."

David gave Jonathan a sidelong glance. "But there can be no chance if the right woman is nowhere to be seen. If I met her, and frittered away her love by not marrying her, that would be missing my chance."

Jonathan sighed. "I suppose. But sometimes you marry the one who is good enough."

"Is that what you did?"

"No. Anne is more than good enough. I really do love her, you know." *I just hope she still loves me*, he thought. *I'm no longer the man she knew.*

David said: "I'm not questioning your love for her. I'm just curious."

"I could have kept looking, ticking off items on a list. But she had eighty, no, ninety percent of what I was looking for. I was struck by her beauty and refinement."

"Is she your bashert? The one you were destined for?" David asked.

"Yes." Jonathan had never thought about it that way before. "Anne and I are well matched. It was logical to marry her."

"I'm not logical when it comes to falling in love," David declared. "I've been in love many times, and it was never logical."

"How do you know it wasn't logical?"

"Because none of the women had a hundred percent of what I was looking for. When I meet my bashert, she'll have the hundred percent."

"And what will that hundred percent comprise?" Jonathan asked, curious.

"I won't know until I meet her."

"Good luck finding her," Jonathan said. "Whoever she is."

When Jonathan and David returned to Yitzhak's flat, there was a crowd of people on the pavement out front.

Near the entryway, a hussar in uniform held the bridles of three hussar's horses. He yelled at the crowd to keep their distance. David pushed through the crowd and went up the stairs. Jonathan followed, keeping the dog on a short lead.

As the two men entered the parlour, two uniformed hussars pushed past them, their faces scowling. They muttered to each other in Hungarian, and made their way down the stairs, their riding boots clopping on the stairs as they descended.

Dinah sat at the table where dinner had been served. Her face was streaked with tears. Yitzhak sat next to her. A few neighbours stood nearby.

"What happened?" David demanded.

"Two men were here. Strangers. They wanted to know where he was." She pointed at Jonathan.

"Do you mean the hussars who just left?"

Dinah shook her head. "No. Not the hussars. Two men who wore black masks. The fancy kind your parents gave me, that only cover your eyes and nose and you wear to a party."

"You mean, the kind of mask you find in Venice," David clarified.

"Yes," Dinah said. "But theirs had strange red designs."

David signalled to the neighbours to give them privacy. The neighbours left the apartment, shutting the door behind them.

"Can you draw the design for me?" David asked Dinah.

"It is Shabbos," Yitzhak reminded him. "She should not write or draw."

"Uncle, I know. But lives may be a stake."

David gave her a piece of paper and a pen. She drew some figures and handed it to her nephew. One figure was an X with bent arms. Another was a crescent and a circle.

Just then there was pounding on the door. Yitzhak got to his feet to answer it, but David moved swiftly and flung the door open. There, on the threshold was a thin man dressed in black, with a wide-brimmed hat and a black beard.

David said in Yiddish: "Ah, Feuer, I'm not surprised to see you. Where there is smoke, there is Feuer."

The man came into the room, and Chompsworth started barking furiously. Jonathan quieted her and kept her at his side.

Feuer sneered. "What is all the commotion?"

"That's what I want to find out," David said. "You seem to have your nose in business that's not yours. As usual."

Feuer folded his arms across his chest. "I heard there was some kind of trouble here, and I am the one who informed the authorities. Surely you see the wisdom of my actions."

"Wisdom?" David repeated with contempt. "All I see is a trouble-maker."

"Who is the man with the dog?" Feuer asked, nodding in Jonathan's direction. "And what has he to do with all this?"

David's eyes narrowed. "He is my friend, and he has nothing to do with any of this."

Feuer rubbed his hands. "So many remarkable things today. First reports of a strange man in a friar's robe, with a mule and a dog, looking for Yitzhak Loew's residence. Then, intruders wearing masks. None of this is normal. If your friend is the problem, then you need to turn him out. Immediately."

David said: "Don't tell me what to do, you kochleffel."

Feuer ignored the insult, and continued calmly, "If a stranger comes into our part of town, and he brings trouble, he must be removed, otherwise the trouble falls on all our heads."

"If anyone brought trouble, it was you by calling the authorities," Dinah cried.

Feuer raised his chin defiantly. "And what would you have me do? Risk the chance that they'll investigate us tomorrow while we're all at schul, when the rumours build up that there is someone suspicious among the Jews? Then the officials would think we were hiding something, and they'd send in the hussars anyway, and there'd be the cracking of whips across the backs of our people. It would be the start of another pogrom." He crossed his arms in a self-satisfied manner. "As it is, I saved all of us from unnecessary trouble. The hussars were here, now they're gone. You ought to thank me."

David said sharply: "So, who are the people who saw the masked intruders walking on the street?"

Feuer sneered again. "Nobody saw them, as a matter of fact. It's easy enough to sneak around after dark, dressed in black, and put on a mask once you've entered the building."

Jonathan was staring at Feuer, and strange visions flashed through his mind. He began speaking in German, and his voice had a strange cast to it: "Pinchas Feuer, you need to let your daughter marry the man she loves, and stop spreading lies about him. Apologize and tell the truth. He is a pious man. He did not eat unkosher food."

The blood drained from Feuer's face. He turned to David. "What lies are you spreading about me? What have you told him about my family?"

"I've told him nothing," David said calmly. "In fact, I'd forgotten you exist until you showed up here."

"How did you get your information?" Feuer demanded of Jonathan. "Who told you these things about me?"

"Nobody told me," Jonathan said. "I just know it. Don't ask me how. It all suddenly came into my head." Jonathan was badly frightened by what he'd just said. He didn't know where the words had come from, but he'd seen the vision in his head, and he knew it was real. He sat down in a nearby chair to keep himself from trembling.

"I guess he can't be the dreaded stranger everyone is looking for," David observed. "Else, how could he know your business, Feuer?"

"The man is insane!" Feuer yelled. "He's a liar and a charlatan. I'm going to tell Rabbi Gerde about him—"

Yitzhak interrupted him. "Now it is time for you to go, Feuer. Good Shabbos."

Casting a hostile glance at David, Feuer stomped out, slamming the doors behind him. There was silence until they were all sure Feuer was gone.

Jonathan said: "That man was right. I might put you all in danger."

Yitzhak said wearily: "The danger is past."

"I have a strong feeling it's not," Jonathan said. He looked at Yitzhak. Another vision came into his head, and the words were out of his mouth before he could stop himself. "The man you signed a contract with last week is going to accuse you of cheating. Review your account books, and find the error."

Yitzhak's mouth was agape, and the blood drained from his face.

Dinah looked at her husband in shock, and then at Jonathan. Jonathan was too frightened to notice their reactions. He began shaking. Chompsworth sensed his distress, and put her paw on his knee, whining.

"Now this is getting even more interesting," David said.

Yitzhak said to Jonathan: "You need to see my brother. He lives in Prague."

"I'm not going to Prague, I'm going home," Jonathan said. "I've spent far too much time in this part of the world."

David said to Jonathan: "Rather than argue about your next destination, let's get some sleep, Drake. I have a suite of rooms at the Hotel Nemzeti. You can stay there, as my guest."

Jonathan was wrapped in a blanket, lying on a comfortable sofa. It was an elegant sitting room, located on the top floor of the Hotel Nemzeti. Chompsworth was curled up on a Persian rug next to him. A soft light came from the bedroom beyond the doorway, where David sat reading and smoking.

Jonathan fell asleep. Sometime later, he suddenly woke up. The room was dark, and so was the bedroom beyond the doorway where David slept. A pale beam of moonlight came in through a chink in the drapes. Jonathan felt a wave of panic coming over him, and he sat upright, in a cold sweat.

He tried to focus his eyes. He saw an enormous spider's web just beyond reach. A black mass sat at the centre of the web, but it was not a spider. Jonathan swatted at it, hoping that the movement would dispel the illusion. Then he withdrew his hand, sensing the presence of something. It wasn't a presence, exactly, but an absence—an absence of light and life, a black hole of nothingness at the centre of the web. It moved closer and Jonathan recoiled, but he could not take his eyes off it.

Pictures moved in the web, a succession of images whose meanings Jonathan could not understand.

There were wounded men in war trenches, women and children immolated in enormous ovens, crowds waving red-white-and-black flags, train tracks leading to a central stone tower flanked by two rectangular buildings, a slave master in a loincloth beating a slave and then himself being killed by another man, a cathedral on a grassy slope that was catching fire, gaunt men who looked like walking skeletons smoking cigarettes, an Egyptian Sphynx, a man with black hair wildly gesticulating, farmers tilling land in the desert, a man striking a rock which then spouted water, a man with a big moustache brandishing a gun, a star of David, a hammer and a sickle, an explosion, a smiling image of the baron squeezing a dove to a bloody pulp, a vision of himself in a top hat and morning coat running from a burning building, an image of Anne holding two babies with a look of terror on her face—

"No! I don't want to see anymore! Go away!" Jonathan screamed.

Chompsworth barked, then jumped up and put her paws on Jonathan and licked his face. He felt David's hand on his shoulder, shaking him.

"Drake! Are you alright?"

Jonathan stared wildly at the spot where the spider's web had been, and pointed to the empty space. "The visions were all there. I saw it all." He grabbed the sleeve of David's robe. "You've got to help me. I don't know what to do."

"Calm yourself. Tell me what you saw."

Jonathan squeezed his eyes shut, and recounted the images out loud.

"The worst was seeing my wife holding two babies. She was terrified," Jonathan said.

David scribbled rapid notes as Jonathan talked. He looked up and said: "You didn't tell me you had children."

"I don't!"

David finished making notes, then sat in silence, thinking. After a while, he said: "Do you think you were seeing the future?"

"The distinction between past, present, and future doesn't exist," Jonathan intoned. The voice didn't feel like his own.

Fear flashed across David's face. "What is your name?" he demanded.

"Jonathan Charles Edwin Drake."

"Whom do you serve?"

"I serve His Majesty King Edward the Seventh," Jonathan said in an imperious tone. He added peevishly: "What in bloody hell do you expect me to answer? I'm an Englishman, so of course I serve my king."

132

David looked relieved. "That is a good answer, my friend. My esteemed uncle Yehuda Loew would no doubt say it means you're probably not possessed by a demon, which is a good thing, in case you were wondering. Now then, let's figure out what happened. When did the dog wake up? Was it when you first saw the spider's web?"

"No. I felt the dog licking my face right before you shook me."

"So the dog didn't perceive anything," David observed. "She didn't bark or whine. She reacted to you only, not to anything else in the room."

"That's right. I was the only one who saw the web and the images. That proves it was all a delusion."

"I wouldn't say that," David answered thoughtfully. "Let's get some sleep now, and examine everything in the cold light of day."

"How can I sleep after something like that?" Jonathan snapped. He covered his face with his hands. "Bloody hell, I'm going insane."

"Listen, old chum. I've got a bottle of cherry brandy. You and I are going to have a drink and a smoke, and I'll sit with you until you're ready for sleep."

True to his word, David sat with Jonathan. The cherry brandy loosened Jonathan's tongue, and he recounted his time at the baron's. He felt as if he were rambling, but David listened with full attention, and never glanced at his watch or even let a yawn escape, despite the lateness of the hour.

"I'm realizing now the connection between the pile of children's clothing I found in the fleischzimmer, and the revolting sausages I'd been served the night before," Jonathan said despairingly. "It's too much. The darkness at the centre of the web is going to swallow me whole. All those months at the hands of Mora and Iosip ..." His voice trailed off.

David's face was resolute, but kind. "You must make yourself steadfast, Drake. You are not the first to encounter great evil, and you won't be the last. All your experiences—especially the worst ones—are a crucible for you to become an even stronger man, so that you can rise to the challenges that you'll face in the future."

"I don't want any more challenges," Jonathan said. "I just want to go home." He suddenly felt exhausted. "Now I want to sleep."

"Goodnight, my friend," David said.

The sun was shining brightly the next day when there was a knock on the door. The knock awakened Jonathan. David, fully dressed, opened the door to a messenger, who handed him an envelope. David gave the young man a tip, then closed the door and opened the envelope. David's face was a mixture of surprise and amusement.

Jonathan raised himself to his elbows. "What is it?"

"Uncle Yitzhak says he got a telegram from my Uncle Yehuda. On Shabbat, which means it is very serious. Poor old Uncle Yitzhak almost had a heart attack when the messenger delivered it, and I don't blame him."

Jonathan said: "I'm just remembering. I dreamed of an old man sitting in an enormous purple chair."

"I dreamed of him, too," David said "He is my Uncle Yehuda who lives in Prague. He told Uncle Yitzhak to urge me to come to Prague with my friend, if I am still able."

CHAPTER ELEVEN

Anne helped Minerva to put the babies in their cribs for their afternoon nap. Then Anne went downstairs, and tried to concentrate on her needlework, but it was no use. She put the needlework aside, and sat in her chair, waiting. Her mother-in-law would be here any minute.

Anne went to the front parlour, and stood at the window that overlooked Cadogan square. A few flakes of snow drifted down from a grey sky. She realised that her husband's birthday, the thirtieth of December, had come and gone without much agony on her part. She believed she had finally accepted the fact that he was dead and gone, and that she needed to pick up the pieces of her life and come up with a plan so that she and her children would be cared for. She was determined that nothing would stand in the way of a brilliant future for each of them—including a brilliant future for herself.

A motorcar parked in front of Anne's house, and the liveried driver opened the door for Hannah Drake. Anne was surprised that her in-laws now had a motorcar, what with the financial difficulties that her father-in-law had mentioned last time they had discussed money. Surely a motorcar was an extravagance that they could do without. But maybe it was necessary to keep up appearances. Her mother-in-law was elegantly dressed in a grey cashmere overcoat with a silver-fox-fur collar. She looked every inch the smart wife of a judge, with her auburn hair pinned up in the latest style, a fashionable hat from the best milliner in London.

Anne opened the front door, and stood aside to let her in. Hannah removed her hat and gloves, and chatted about the increased traffic on the London streets, and her sympathy for those horses who had not yet gotten used to the motorcars. The two women made their way to the front parlour.

Anne said: "May I offer refreshments?" Anne would have to fetch them herself from downstairs because the cook had the day off.

Hannah said kindly: "I appreciate your hospitality, my dear, but no thank you."

Hannah had settled herself into a nearby chair. Anne sat on the sofa— the very sofa that she had been reclining on when the baron had called on her all those months ago just hours before the twins had been born. How much lighter and more attractive Anne felt now that she was no longer pregnant, and was able to perch at the edge of the seat with perfectly straight posture, without a heavy pregnant belly resting on her legs.

Hannah took a deep breath. "You know that I've wanted to help in whatever way I can. I hope that the assistance I've been able to send your way, along with boxes from the grocer and butcher, have helped."

"They have," Anne admitted. "I very much appreciate what you've done." She didn't add that life was still difficult, and that she needed absolute certainty that she and her children would not eventually fall into poverty.

Hannah acknowledged Anne's gratitude with a slight incline of her head. Then she continued. "There is no delicate way for me to do this, my dear, so let me just plod through, however clumsy I may be." She withdrew an envelope from her purse, and placed it on the nearby tea-table. "I promised we would support you. This amount should keep you in comfort for the next two years."

Anne thought it excessively delicate that she'd put the envelope on the table instead of handing it over directly. It was exactly the sort of gesture from Hannah that Anne admired, and yet found infuriating, because it smacked of a patronizing attitude toward Anne and her situation. Anne realised this was not fair. After all, her mother-in-law was trying to help and stay true to her promises. Anne felt guilty for her secret fury, and also touched by her mother-in-law's kindness. But this latter emotion was tempered by remembering the baron's warning: "Your in-laws attach too many strings. Don't become ensnared. Stay free, my song bird."

Anne said: "I thought this would not be possible, owing to the other problems that have needed attention."

Hannah knew that Anne was referring to her son, Michael Drake, whose gambling debts were affecting the Drake family fortune.

Hannah took a deep breath. "I sold off some of my personal items— some jewellery and trinkets that I could part with. Edward has no idea, and I'd appreciate if it remained that way."

Anne had to give her credit for selling off her things. It was exactly the course of action she'd wondered whether the Drakes would take. Still, it had been over six months since they'd had the conversation about settling an allowance on Anne and the children. Anne's own mother, in the meanwhile, had sent money, and Gershon, Stoker and King had given her a small widow's compensation for Jonathan's death. But none of that had been enough to restore her to the standard of living she'd had when Jonathan was still alive.

As if reading her mind, Hannah explained: "It has taken me all these months to gather that much—" here she gestured toward the envelope on the table. "Edward has this preternatural sense when something is missing, except when it came to Michael's ability to get his hands on our bank accounts. Edward has always had a soft spot for Michael—" Her voice, tinged with rebuke, trailed off and she got a faraway look in her eyes. After a moment, she pulled herself back into the present. "I had to be extremely careful in what I sold so that Edward wouldn't notice. And it took time to find a broker who could keep a confidence. I regret that it took this long, but now it is done, and you need not worry."

"Thank you," Anne said.

Hannah sighed. "This whole affair with Michael is taking a terrible toll. We've been on tenterhooks, all of us, wondering if it's going to blow up." She added: "I do worry for Sarah's prospects."

"Sarah will be fine," Anne said. "She is beautiful and she has her pick of suitors."

Hannah sighed. "The problem is, she won't decide on one. She keeps telling me that the right one has not come along. Sarah has always had a poetic side to her, and I'm afraid she's caught up in one of her romantic daydreams. But she's not getting any younger. Perhaps you could have a word with her when the two of you are next together. You are so much more mature than she is when it comes to marriage and children. Your advice carries weight."

Anne nodded. "Of course."

Hannah looked lost in thought. "One more thing, my dear. There has been talk of you being seen at salon gatherings, at the baron's house. Do you think it proper for a woman of your standing to be at such events? I'm told they can be quite … unconventional. Of course, I put no stock in any of those rumours. I realise that my personal opinion carries little weight, in the scheme of things. But there is the opinion of others, in society, whose opinion does count—that is, if you want certain doors opened. After all, you are beautiful and still young, and quite capable of a brilliant marriage once the year of mourning has passed."

Anne raised her chin. "Are you telling me not to go?"

"I suppose I am," Hannah said gently. "I don't expect you to wear black all the time, but showing up at outré parties in gaily-coloured dresses … well, it seems a bit beyond the pale during a time of mourning, even for our modern times, don't you think?"

Anne took a deep breath to steady herself before answering. "Those gatherings have been the only bright spot in an otherwise dull and sad existence."

"But my dear Anne, if it is smart company you crave, why have you not accepted any invitations from us? We entertain regularly."

Because your guests are far too conventional, and your parties are a crashing bore, Anne thought. Instead, she said: "But those are your friends. And while I appreciate being included, I want to cultivate my own set of friends. After all, I've not had the advantage of being in London as long as you have."

"What you say is reasonable," Hannah conceded. "But there are rumours that the baron … that he …"

"That he what?"

"That he is not all he appears. Oh yes, he is handsome and urbane and all that, but I've heard rumours that there is a darker aspect. Word reached me—rumours from eastern Europe—that the locals live in fear of his cruelty—" Hannah stopped short, unwilling to go on.

"If you truly believe those lies, why has he been a guest at your table?" Anne countered.

Hannah smiled ruefully. "If I had to choose my guests according to whom I actually liked, my parties would consist of the same dozen people, over and over. It is for political reasons that my guest lists are composed the way they are. The baron is too well-connected for us to snub him." Hannah paused, then added: "Why don't you come to one of our dinner parties? I've told you before that the invitation is always open. That way, you can interact with him there, and then there will be no fodder for rumours."

"I don't go to the baron's salon gatherings just to see the baron," Anne said. "I have befriended many of the regulars there, and I don't want to let go of those friendships."

"But there have been rumours of very unconventional activities …"

Anne snapped: "Stuff and nonsense. It is true that his guests are not conventional. But I have been treated with the utmost courtesy and honour."

Hannah countered: "You are a Drake. You have a family reputation to uphold. Where one is seen is just as important as who one is seen with, and at what venue. Surely you realise that, my dear Anne."

Anne's face was hard. "I don't give a row of pins for the opinions of people I've never met."

Hannah stood. "Very well, then. You've made yourself clear. May I see the babies while I'm here?"

"They're sleeping and they can't be disturbed," Anne said coldly.

Anne grabbed the envelope from the table and held it out to her mother-in-law. "Please take this back. I don't want to be beholden to the Drakes if it means I must give up my friends."

Hannah protested. "Oh, no. I'm not trying to exert that kind of control. Please keep it. I spoke frankly because I fear for my family's reputation. I'm already worried it's going to founder on the rocks of Michael's follies."

Anne would not be deterred. "Please take it. I will not accept this."

Hannah hesitated a moment, then took the envelope and stuffed it into her purse. "If you change your mind, just say the word."

"I won't," Anne said.

Hannah deliberated. "One more thing. I know you loved Jonathan. We both wish he were here with us now. You are young and beautiful and need not be resigned to widowhood. I can help you find a suitable husband, when you are ready for that. I have excellent connections."

"Thank you," Anne said stiffly.

She walked with her mother-in-law to the front door and watched as the driver helped the older woman into the motorcar. Anne suddenly had the strong intuition that she and Sarah were competitors for the affections of the baron. Perhaps that is why Hannah was warning Anne away from the baron's company and offering to help Anne find a different husband. Hannah wanted her own daughter to wed him, even though Sarah had deemed him "odious" back in June. A woman's heart could change, especially under the charm of a man like the Baron von Klausenberg.

Anne was left with a glow of self-satisfaction that she'd avoided what amounted to social blackmail from her in-laws. Yes, money was still going to be a problem, but the baron was a true friend on whom she could depend. He would help her if she just said the word—he had told her that more than once. She was certain that, when she recounted to him all that had just happened, he would praise Anne's strength in fighting for her independence. The only question was whether she should write everything in a letter and post it right away, or wait until the next salon gathering.

She was still debating this when Minerva appeared in the front parlour.

"M'lady, the babies are still sleeping. I had forgotten to give this to you when it arrived yesterday." She handed over an envelope. It was a telegram.

"Why hadn't you left it on the silver salver?"

"Oh, it seemed too important to leave about," Minerva said.

"If it's so important, why had you waited until today to give it to me?" Anne knew her peevishness largely stemmed from her annoyance with her in-laws. She would not normally be so annoyed with Minerva.

"M'lady, you know the babies have been fussy. We've both been very distracted taking care of them." Before Anne could reprove her further, Minerva tilted her head. "I hear one of them waking up." She rushed out of the room.

Anne opened the envelope and read:

SAFE IN BUDA PEST. WILL WRITE SOON. ALL MY LOVE.
JONATHAN.

She let the telegram drop to the floor.

140

CHAPTER TWELVE

Along the narrow, winding streets of Prague, Jonathan felt that he had gone back in time, to a medieval town where the inhabitants believed in the unseen, deferred to the mysterious, and took precautions to keep the dark forces at bay. Even though many of the building facades were cream or white, or painted pastel shades of yellow, green and blue, these cheerful colours were not enough to dispel the mystical atmosphere of Prague. David led him through twisted alleyways, beneath vaulted archways, past buildings whose Gothic towers soared into the sky like grim sentinels keeping watch over the old city. Elaborately-decorated Gothic doorways promised a portal to supernatural realms.

Jonathan was grateful that David had not mentioned the upsetting incidents he had experienced. David was the perfect travelling companion, striking the right balance between entertaining conversation and rejuvenating silence.

The two men had left their luggage at a small but elegant inn, and were now making their way through the Jewish Quarter. Chompsworth was distracted by the new smells and sounds. Jonathan kept her on a short lead. The two men stopped at the wrought-iron fence of a cemetery. Beyond, there were thousands of old headstones of varying shapes and sizes, tightly packed together and tilted at odd angles. They were worn and stained with lichen and moss. The skeletons of the bare trees were silhouetted against a darkening winter sky.

"By some counts there are a hundred thousand bodies buried there," David said. "Dozens beneath each headstone, in layers, like an archaeology site. The town would not let Jews bury their dead anywhere else, nor make the cemetery bigger." He paused. "I mentioned I'd once been madly in love with someone. I met her when I was nineteen, visiting here in the spring, for Passover. She was my age. I returned to Venice at the start of that summer. We wrote letters to each other every day. She died at the end of that year of tuberculosis. She never let on that she'd been ill. They weren't supposed to bury her here—the place has been closed to new burials for at least a century—but her parents had it done it secretly."

"Did you go to the funeral?"

"No. I didn't even find out about her death until after she was buried. My heart was shattered."

They made their way along another street called Maiselova.

David gestured to a large building with a Late-Baroque façade, topped with a Gothic-steeple. Directly below the bell tower was a clock with Roman numerals, and under it, a clock with Hebrew letters. Those clock hands moved anti-clockwise.

"That's the Jewish Town Hall," David said. "It was built in 1562, back when the Jewish community of Prague was self-governing." David pointed to a building adjacent to it, a medieval yellow-and-brown stone synagogue with red tiles on the roof and a steep, notched gable that followed the roof line. "That's the Altneushul, built in 1270."

"Does it always glow blue like that?" Jonathan asked.

"What do you mean?"

Jonathan pointed. "Do you not see that blue light coming off the tip of the gable there, at the very top? It's rather eerie. It flashes like a sapphire in sunlight."

David gazed at the spot Jonathan was pointing at. "No, I don't see it."

Jonathan closed his eyes and rubbed his temples. "Another hallucination. I'm truly going insane." Chompsworth sensed his distress, put her front paws on his leg, and whined for attention.

David put his hand on his friend's shoulder. "Steady there, Drake. You are not going insane. You're merely seeing things I cannot see."

"And that's not lunacy?" Jonathan snapped.

"Just because I cannot see it does not mean it's not there."

"I don't know how much longer I can take this," Jonathan said with despair.

"Be strong, man. Be strong."

"Why am I seeing this strange blue light?" Jonathan demanded angrily. "What is so special about that building?"

David said gently: "I don't know why you can see something that I cannot. I will tell you this. There is an old legend that there is a creature up there in the garret, sleeping. The creature is called a golem. It was created out of mud to protect the Jews of Prague from an evil priest. When the golem was no longer needed, it was interred in that garret. It sleeps there until it is needed again. Have you heard those stories?"

"Never. When did this happen?"

"In the year fifteen-eighty." There was a pause. Then David asked: "Do you still see the blue light?"

"Yes, it's still there."

"And yet, the sun has set and the full darkness of night is almost here," David observed sombrely. In a cheerful voice, he said: "Come, let us hurry to my uncle's house. He will be able to explain more."

"He'll explain while laughing into his sleeve at the lunatic standing before him," Jonathan said drily.

"Oh, you do not know Uncle Yehuda. What others call lunacy he takes seriously, for he sees into places that ordinary humans cannot."

David led them through narrow, twisting streets with alleyways dark in shadow. Jonathan found the medieval atmosphere of the town haunting and yet, oddly comforting, as if his visions and hallucinations would not be regarded as so uncommon here. They stopped in front of a polished wooden door with ten carved panels, each panel depicting one of the Ten Commandments. David reverently touched the wooden mezuzah that was affixed to the doorpost, and then tugged the bell-pull. A stern, middle-aged woman in a black dress opened the door.

David said in Yiddish: "It is so nice to see you, Mrs. Prijs. We are but two poor beggars wanting some supper."

Her face lit up when she realised it was David. She led the men up a flight of stairs, chatting with David the whole way.

"Your uncle is over-taxing himself, even now. Fortunately, he took my advice that he confine his receiving hours from ten in the morning until sunset. I had to insist, you know, for his own good. He's eighty-three, and if he doesn't start acting his age, who knows how long his strength will last. Did I tell you that my son Eliezer is now the rebbe's secretary? Maybe you can convince your uncle to cut back his visiting hours even further, and let some of the younger rabbis share the burden of counselling those who seek advice."

She brought them to the door of the rabbi's study. At that moment, the door opened, and two younger men in suits and expensive wool overcoats walked out, holding their hats in their hands. The rabbi was behind them, and he immediately recognised his nephew.

"Ah, Dovid," the rabbi said in German. "So nice that you're here. I'd like you to meet Mr. Hugo Bermann, and Mr. Franz Kafka. We were just discussing Zionism and the future of the Jewish people, a topic about which you could've offered valuable opinions."

David bowed to his uncle, and to the two men, and said: "I wish my uncle a good evening, and good evening to you two gentlemen."

Jonathan noticed that David addressed his uncle in the third person, as was the custom with addressing royalty.

"Allow me to introduce my friend Jonathan Drake, a solicitor from London," David said.

"Good evening," Jonathan said in German, and the men exchanged bows.

The one named Kafka was cool and detached. He looked into Jonathan's eyes with his intense grey eyes, and Jonathan found it disconcerting, as if the younger man could see things he could not possibly know.

Kafka said to Jonathan: "A man could hold himself back from the sufferings of the world. That is certainly his choice. But perhaps this holding back is one suffering that a man could avoid. To jump into the chasm with both feet, and dance with death itself—maybe that is another sort of courage that makes the other suffering worthwhile."

Jonathan was speechless.

Mr. Bermann said: "Forgive my friend for articulating such a blunt pronouncement. He has a morose temperament because he is a serious writer who sees tragedy everywhere."

"Perhaps he is not wrong," Jonathan remarked, recovering his composure and wishing he could talk more to these two men.

The rabbi said to his two departing guests: "Gentlemen, I look forward to our next conversation." He said to his housekeeper: "Mrs. Prijs, please see Mr. Bermann and Mr. Kafka downstairs to the door. And now, Dovid, and Mr. Drake, let us have a seat in the study."

The study was a cluttered, comfortable library with one large leaded-pane window that overlooked the street. Rabbi Yehuda Loew sat behind an enormous cherry-wood desk. He was a thin, wizened man with a white beard. He wore a yarmulke.

"So, Dovid," the rabbi said, "I am eager to talk to you and your friend. The dreams are not ordinary." He gestured to some nearby chairs. "Please sit, both of you."

The two men sat. Jonathan commanded the dog to sit at his feet. Jonathan kept the dog on a tight lead. He could tell she wanted to get closer to Rabbi Loew. She sniffed the air in the direction of the rabbi and wagged her tail.

The rabbi turned his gaze to Jonathan, and said in heavily accented English, "Welcome. I hope your journey was good."

Jonathan nodded. "I thank the rabbi for his good wishes."

"Now please tell what has happened that has caused me to have visions about you both, such that I had to send a telegram to my brother Yitzhak of Budapest on Shabbat," Rabbi Loew prompted.

The way the rabbi worded this made Jonathan feel tremendous relief that David had been right, that he was not about to be singled out as a madman suffering from delusions.

David said: "We both had a dream, and that is why we thought it best to come here." Then he recounted the events in Budapest.

While David talked, Jonathan studied the old rabbi's face to determine what was so unusual about him. Men in their eighties usually had large features and bushy eyebrows. But Yehuda Loew's face had small, regular features. His white hair was neatly combed around delicate ears, and his eyebrows were well-shaped. Nobody would have mistaken him for a young man; his skin was creased, his white beard came to a point well below his chin. The contrast between his delicate child-like features and his old-man traits was startling—and the contrast was accentuated by his slight build and the enormous, high-backed purple velvet chair in which he sat. Jonathan suddenly remembered that the purple chair had been a part of the dream he'd had in Budapest—and variations of that dream had been experienced by David and Rabbi Loew, which was why the three men were now meeting.

David concluded: "We are disturbed not just by the dreams that we've all had, but by the strange events that preceded the dreams."

Rabbi Loew turned to Jonathan. "Have you a wife, children?"

"I have wife, in London. No children. We sent a wire to my wife from Budapest to let her know I'm still alive."

The rabbi raised an eyebrow. "Still alive? Why would there be a doubt?"

Jonathan shifted in his chair. "Well, it had been a while since she'd heard from me. Several months, in fact."

"So, did you have no wish to communicate with her?"

There was an uncomfortable silence. Jonathan said in a quiet voice: "The baron's servants held me in a dungeon against my will. After I escaped, I had no will to write, not even to tell her I was alive. But David sent a telegram from Budapest, telling her I am alive."

Rabbi Loew was still. "Please explain what happened."

Jonathan recounted his ordeals at the baron's estate, and his time at the abbey.

Rabbi Loew pointed at Chompsworth. "This dog was kept by the baron?"

Jonathan put his hand on Chompsworth's head. "Yes. But this dog is gentle. She's not like the others, the evil dogs whose eyes glowed in the dark."

Jonathan described how he'd climbed down the tower and then down the ravine, and had found the dog. He then recounted how he had been rescued by the one-handed peasant and brought to the abbey. He explained how he had helped the peasant untangle his horse and turn his cart upright. Jonathan added: "The baron punished the coachman for helping, even though I had ordered him to help. It was an outrage."

The rabbi said with disgust: "What can you expect from a tyrant who will cut off the hand of anyone who touches the golden chalice in the town square?"

"You know about that?" Jonathan asked. He was so incredulous that he forgot to address him in the third person.

"Anybody who has spent time in that region knows about it," Rabbi Loew said quietly. "And they know of other horrors as well." He studied Jonathan. "Dovid says you revealed things about one of Yitzhak's neighbours, and about Yitzhak himself. How long have you had this ability?"

Jonathan said: "That was the first time. Later that night, I saw visions in the spider's web."

"Describe the visions," the rabbi said. "Every detail. Do not leave out a thing."

Jonathan recounted the succession of images he saw. The old man was still, listening closely but deeply alert. Jonathan had never met someone who could listen like that, fully attentive and fully focused on every word, every nuance, every gesture. Jonathan knew that the rabbi was gleaning information that even Jonathan himself was not aware of.

When Jonathan finished talking, the rabbi waited a full minute, lost in thought. Then he asked quietly: "Is that all you remember? Were there any other visions?"

Jonathan said: "That is all. The most terrifying one was of my wife holding two babies, screaming. I don't know why it affects me so. We don't even have children."

The rabbi closed his eyes and appeared to be meditating. The only sound in the room was the clock ticking.

After some time, Rabbi Loew said: "Some of these visions are images or stories found in the Torah. The slave master beating the slave and himself being killed by another man, the man striking the rock to get water— "

"That's Moses, of course," David said.

Rabbi Loew nodded.

"I don't understand why I would have a vision of Moses," Jonathan cut in.

Rabbi Loew shrugged. "Why you're having any of these visions is a mystery. Your ordeal has been extraordinary. But clearly, there is some message here, some sign. What that sign is, that is our task to discover." He paused. "Mr. Drake, tell me again about the vision of the burning building. You said you were running from it. Describe what you were wearing."

"I was wearing a suit, including my top hat. It was the same hat I had been wearing when I escaped from the baron's estate. It was lost when I descended into the ravine." Jonathan paused, remembering something more. "One of the visions was of a burning church on a grassy hill. But I'd forgotten that I'd had another vision. I was running from a burning building, wearing my top-hat and formal day dress, but it was nighttime. Somehow the two visions are connected. That second burning building may have been a church, or even a synagogue. It had a rosette window. The smoke was billowing. You know how it is with dreams. A thing can be two things at once, and it makes sense in the dream, but not in the real world."

Jonathan took out of his pocket the crucifix and the mezuzah, showed them to Rabbi Loew, and explained how he had acquired them.

The rabbi examined them, and handed them back. "The young woman named Sofia who thought you were a Jew, did she say why she thought that?"

Jonathan shook his head. "I asked her exactly that, but she refused to answer."

"Is there anything else I should know?" the rabbi asked.

"Not that I can recall."

David said: "Mr. Drake saw a blue light emanating from the roof of the Altneushul when we passed it on our way here."

The rabbi nodded. "That is interesting. Please describe that, Mr. Drake." After Jonathan gave his account, the rabbi asked: "Did you know about that synagogue before you came here?"

Jonathan replied: "Of course not. I've never been to Prague before. I'd never even heard of that synagogue before today."

"Had my nephew mentioned the golem?"

"Only after I saw the blue light."

"And? What do you think?"

"It all sounds like a fantastical legend that no rational man could possibly take seriously." He desperately wanted to believe this. He'd seen enough of the eerie and unexplained, and he found it all so confusing and frightening. He craved the order, stability, and predictability of the world he used to take for granted, before all these things had happened.

"Do you find it curious that some people do, in fact, believe that the golem is real?" the old rabbi asked gently.

Jonathan realised that the rabbi was confessing to that very belief.

"People are entitled to their opinions, however wrong-headed they may be," Jonathan said. "I personally don't believe a word of it. I saw a blue light because my eyes were playing tricks, and nothing more."

He was suddenly aware that he was in a trap. On the one hand, he wanted the rabbi to believe his accounts, and to tell him that he was not insane. On the other hand, he was not ready to take the leap into believing all that the rabbi believed in. The contradiction made him very tired. He wanted to have something to eat, and then go to sleep and not have to think about any of this.

As if reading his mind, the rabbi said: "Gentlemen, let us have supper and then continue this discussion tomorrow. It has been a long day."

Jonathan was still sleeping when David looked in on him the next morning. Chompsworth stayed next to Jonathan. She perked her ears up when David came into the room, and wagged her tail. She wouldn't leave Jonathan's bedside, except to go outside briefly to relieve herself. The day was unseasonably warm, and brilliantly sunny. David attempted to take her for a walk around the neighbourhood, but the dog would not stray far. As soon as she had relieved herself, she immediately returned to the inn to go back inside. She darted up the stairs to Jonathan's room, jumped onto the bed, and settled herself next to Jonathan.

David left the dog with his sleeping friend, and made sure that her water bowl was filled. He walked to his uncle's house.

"The dog senses something," Rabbi Loew said when David told him about the dog's behaviour. "She guards him. We must prepare ourselves for anything. Anything."

"I have my revolver ready," David said.

"Good. But physical defences may not be enough. We must prepare ourselves mentally and spiritually. I have been praying for guidance." The rabbi went to his bookshelf and pulled down some heavy tomes. "You and I must pray and study. And your friend Jonathan must do the same, once he is awake."

David moved the books to the dining room where he sat at the polished table, smoking and studying the books that the rabbi had taken down from his shelves. Mrs. Prijs silently dusted the room. Her housework was regularly interrupted by having to answer the door to visitors. Many were from the neighbourhood, some from far away, and they all came to seek the rabbi's advice or to study with him.

David walked back to the hotel and looked in on Jonathan at noon and again at three o'clock. Jonathan continued to sleep. The dog stayed at Jonathan's side, going out only once more to relieve herself. David fed the dog, and then returned to his uncle's house. The afternoon was late, and the sun was low in the sky. The two men davened minchah, the afternoon prayers, together. Each was so engrossed in prayer, they did not hear Mrs. Prijs respond to the door bell, nor did they notice that Jonathan had come into the room and had seated himself nearby, and was watching them. The dog was lying at his feet.

When the prayers were over, David exclaimed: "Hullo, Drake! How are you feeling?"

"I'm still exhausted," Jonathan said. His face was pale, and his eyes were rimmed with dark circles, despite the fact that he had slept all night and all day.

Rabbi Loew said: "Tell me, Mr. Drake, did you have any dreams?"

"Not that I remember. I feel as if I've been in a heavy, dreamless sleep for a week."

David observed: "You haven't eaten since yesterday. You must be hungry."

"A bit," Jonathan said.

"Let us dine at Gruenbaum's," David said. "I know the owner. I've sold rivers of wine to him over the years. He'll have a table for us."

Jonathan gestured to his dog. "I can't leave her alone."

"She can come along," David said.

It was a short walk from the rabbi's house to the restaurant. Jonathan saw a notice in the front window, alerting customers that it was a kosher restaurant. The restaurant's owner, a wiry man in a perfectly tailored suit, greeted the three of them warmly. He was hesitant to let the dog in the main dining room, but David persuaded him that she'd be no trouble at all. Soon Chompsworth was safely installed under the table, at Jonathan's feet, with her own bowl of chicken scraps and a gristle-covered beef bone that had come from the stockpot in the kitchen. She was happily preoccupied with this feast.

The three men ate heartily. Jonathan revived under the good food and gaiety. The three men traded stories and jokes. He could not remember the last time he had enjoyed himself that much. He suddenly realised that he loved these two men as if he'd known them for his entire life. They'd listened to his horrific ordeal, his strange delusions, and not only didn't deride him for it, they respected him and took him seriously.

Jonathan and David finished a bottle of wine. The rabbi had refused even a sip.

David noticed his uncle's uncharacteristic abstinence, and tried to mask his concern for his uncle's behaviour under a light-hearted comment: "I hope my good Uncle is not taking the vow of the nazarite."

Rabbi Loew chuckled. "No, my dear nephew, I still drink wine. It's just that tonight is not a night for wine."

"What is the vow of the nazarite?" Jonathan asked.

The rabbi explained: "It is a vow to dedicate oneself to God by abstaining from all things made from grapes."

"Why would one want to take that vow?"

"For some, it is a bargain," the rabbi said. "The nazir asks something of God, and makes the vow. When the vow is undertaken correctly, the nazir seeks the attainment of a more elevated, holy existence."

David added: "It is telling that the nazir must make a sin offering when the time period of his vow comes to an end. The nazir risks falling prey to the sort of self-important vanity one commonly finds among the sanctimonious. Maimonides—he was one our greatest Jewish sages—said that one ought to abstain only from those things the Torah specifies, and allow oneself all of the permitted pleasures. After all, the life of a Jew is hard enough." He turned to his uncle. "Well, since my dear uncle the rebbe is not a nazir, it would be most welcome to indulge in one of the greatest pleasures in Prague, namely, Mrs. Prijs's raisin cheesecake. Do you suppose I can persuade her to bake one tomorrow? Is there anything on this earth as delicious as her raisin cheesecake?"

"Not a thing," the rabbi agreed, "except, perhaps, oranges from Jaffa."

"I will be sure to buy some for you next time I am there," David promised. He quaffed the rest of the wine in his glass, and said: "This evening is too enjoyable to end early. Let us crown our outing with a visit to the old marionette theatre."

Rabbi Loew's face brightened. "The marionette theatre! How long since I have visited, I don't even know. The hot-air balloon is magnificent. It has always been my favourite."

David said: "My favourite is the Trojan horse marionette. It opens with an ingenious mechanism to reveal the soldiers inside. Truly a marvel." David turned to Jonathan. "It's a charming place. I think you'll find it worthwhile, Drake."

"Let's go, then." Jonathan was in high spirits from the food, wine, and good friends. He thought the world was perfect in that moment.

The three men walked to the marionette theatre. Chompsworth kept her nose to the ground, sniffing and alerting to every sound. Jonathan noticed that Rabbi Loew watched the dog closely, and kept an eye on what was happening around them.

A warm wind scattered dead leaves across the pavement. Spires of a gothic tower were silhouetted against the moon, which illuminated wisps of fast-moving clouds. The rabbi held on to his black hat. David held his uncle's arm, making sure the old man didn't lose his footing on the pavement.

The entrance to the theatre was on a side street, under a Baroque stone archway. The door was narrow and tall, carved with theatrical designs, such as musical instruments and circus animals. The brass knocker was cast in the figure of a court jester holding a heavy ring.

The narrow door opened into a large hallway, carpeted with an antique Persian runner. The place smelled of wood polish, dusty old silk, and candle wax.

An older man with an elaborately curled moustache and ebony walking stick appeared from one of the rooms. He introduced himself as the curator and offered to show them around.

The entrance to each room was framed in heavy velvet curtains drawn aside with tasselled tie-backs. From the high ceiling to the dark wainscot, the walls contained marionettes of every size, shape, and design from kings and queens, to chimney sweeps and washer women, from the fairest Northern European, to the darkest African, and others in full oriental splendour. Some marionettes were suspended from the ceiling. Many were animal figures: horses and unicorns, lions, giraffes, dogs, cats, and elephants. Others were of machines: steam engines, sailing ships, motor cars, chariots, bicycles, along with the Trojan horse that David had described, and the hot-air balloon of which the rabbi was so fond.

The curator recited the history of particular marionettes, recounting the performances in which they appeared, along with notable people who had been in attendance. David and the rabbi asked detailed questions, and the curator was delighted to have interested guests.

Jonathan was bored. The conversation was in Czech. David did his best to translate, but he was caught up in the conversation and forgot to translate most of it.

Jonathan needed to find the privy, and he asked directions.

"Of course," said the curator. He gave him a candle lantern and pointed down a dim corridor. In broken English, he gave directions. "Go down stairs. Then straight, then left and right. Picture of vater bucket on door is vater closet."

David held Chompsworth's lead while Jonathan excused himself.

Jonathan descended the wooden stairs, holding the lantern high. As he proceeded down the cellar corridor, he remembered how much he hated cellars, and he wished he had just gone out the front door and found a dark corner, as uncivilized as that was. Too late now—he was too uncomfortable to delay. He pushed away unpleasant thoughts, and found the door with the water bucket painted on it.

He locked the door. While he was in there, he thought he heard something out in the corridor. Laughter? Voices? He couldn't be sure. He finished, and cleaned his hands at the sink. Then he paused, one hand holding the lantern, the other resting on the door knob. He listened. Nothing. In some ways, the silence was more unnerving. He took a deep breath, and reminded himself that in about sixty seconds, he would be back upstairs with his dog and his friends.

Jonathan turned the knob, but it was stuck. He moved the lantern closer to the knob to see whether a latch had fallen into place. Then he felt around the knob plate. There was no lock. He turned it again, and this time, it gave way easily. He gripped the lantern tightly and stepped into the dark corridor, trying to remember if he needed to make a quick right and then left, or vice versa. He guessed at the direction, and found himself down a different corridor. Frantically, he turned back, but he could not find the way. He felt freezing air creep over him, as if someone had opened a door into the most frigid winter's night.

He walked quickly, and turned left this time. Certain that the staircase was just ahead, he quickened his pace.

But it turned out to be another room in the cellar, lined with hundreds of marionettes of all shapes and sizes, in various stages of assembly. It was obviously the workshop where the puppets were created and repaired.

Movement from the corner caught his eye. A marionette on a string had started to dance. Mesmerized, Jonathan was drawn to see what could possibly be causing the motion.

As he got closer, he realised that the marionette was a perfect likeness of the baron. The face, eyes, and body were an exact copy, even though the marionette was not even as tall as a man's leg. From the corner of the baron's smiling mouth, a faint trickle of red paint dribbled down. The jaws moved up and down. Jonathan reached out to touch the trickle of paint—he wanted to see if it was still wet—but the marionette's arm shot up and there was a flash of metal. Jonathan withdrew his hand quickly, realizing he'd been cut. The marionette was holding a scimitar. The small, curved blade was stained with Jonathan's blood.

On the floor, under the baron, were other marionettes. They were broken and heaped in a jumble, with red paint splashed all over them, as if they were bleeding. Jonathan found himself kneeling in front of it all, as if he were obeying a silent command.

The marionette spoke. "My symbol is a chimera of a dragon and an eagle. The dragon is the chaos that brings the fire. The eagle represents self-immolation by fire. We must die in order to live. There will be mass death and destruction across Europe. The corpses will pile up like those beneath me now, and they'll all be burned away. A phoenix will come up out of the ashes of that dark fire. I told you all this before, but you didn't pay attention. We are going to conquer your country."

"Who is we?" Jonathan could barely speak. He felt as if the marionette could actually read his thoughts.

The puppet said: "We are the masters of the dark fire."

"Who are you, exactly?"

"That will be revealed in time. We will conquer all of Europe and make a new world order."

"We will fight, damn you!" Jonathan snarled. "The British Empire is the most powerful force in the world. We'll fight and win!"

The marionette laughed, its jaw working up and down. "How do you think victory will appear? Your countrymen will fight at first, but then they will become tired and wracked with guilt. They'll sell their honour for peace. All over Europe, they'll torture themselves with the memories of their sins. They'll let the dark fires burn, hoping that the flames will expunge their guilt and soothe their conscience. Across Europe, they'll make concessions, give up their land, sacrifice their children. They'll congratulate themselves that they've purchased freedom. When, in fact, they've put their own wrists into the manacles of their imprisonment."

"You think no Englishman will fight? That is a lie!"

"There may be a few who will try, but these few won't prevail. We'll kill them first."

Jonathan gazed at the ugly, grinning marionette. "Who are the few who will try to fight you?"

"The worst is he who was born to the American whore at Blenheim."

Jonathan had to think for a moment about who that was. Then he remembered. Winston Churchill. An arrogant upstart. "Why him? He's nobody important."

The baron-puppet jiggled on its strings. "Oh, but he will be. He will be. But do not worry about world affairs, Jonathan. Worry about your precious family, about your precious Anne."

"No!" Jonathan screamed. He lunged for the marionette, and tried to twist off the grinning head. He got tangled in strings, and they encircled his throat, pulling tighter. Jonathan tried to work his fingers under the ligatures so he could breathe, but the strings were already cutting into the flesh of his neck, and blood made his fingers slip. The sound of the marionette's laughter echoed in his head as he lost consciousness.

CHAPTER THIRTEEN

Jonathan opened his eyes. He couldn't focus on David's face, but he could see the glow of his friend's auburn hair back-lit by the daylight coming in from the window.

"Had a good sleep?" David said. "Try to stop picking at the bandages around your throat. They're keeping your sutures from breaking."

"Sutures?" Jonathan repeated hoarsely.

"Yes, sutures. They're keeping your head on, like the Frankenstein monster."

Jonathan struggled to sit up. David helped him.

"Frankenstein monster?" Jonathan repeated. His head was cloudy, and his throat felt like he had swallowed sand. "I need some water."

A middle-aged woman poured water from a carafe into a glass and gave it to Jonathan.

"Do you remember Mrs. Prijs?" David asked. "She is my uncle's housekeeper, and she's been taking care of you. We're at Uncle Yehuda's house, in case you haven't noticed. And, of course, Dr. Berg has been here regularly."

Jonathan saw that a man in a black suit stood just behind David, to the right. He moved forward and said in an American accent: "How are you feeling?"

"Very thirsty." Jonathan drank the remainder of the water in his glass. It hurt to swallow. He touched the bandages again.

"You've got some lacerations there," Dr. Berg said. He was a balding man of medium height, with a neatly trimmed moustache and round, wire-framed glasses. His waistcoat was a little too tight on his podgy torso. He had a kind face, and his eyes conveyed both benevolence and intelligence.

Jonathan said: "You sound as if you're from the other side of the pond."

"I am. Philadelphia, as a matter of fact. But my home is now in London. I'm a surgeon at Saint George's. Ah, but I'm forgetting my manners." He held out his hand. "Dr. Samuel Berg at your service. Pleased to meet you."

The two men shook hands.

"Your home is in London but you're in Prague," Jonathan observed.

"I'm lecturing at Charles University for the next few months."

Jonathan suddenly remembered his dog. "Where is Chompsie? Is she safe?"

"Yes, yes," David assured him "Mrs. Prijs's son is taking her for a walk. But she's been by your side non-stop, except for short excursions outside. You've been saying some interesting things in your delirium. Do you remember any of it?"

"No. I don't remember a thing, except being in that museum and having to find the water closet."

Sam asked: "How are you feeling now that you've had some water?"

"I feel ghastly. I have a pounding headache."

"More liquids and some food should take care of that."

"I'll bring up a tray," Mrs. Prijs said.

Sam looked at his watch. "I have to leave for the university."

"I'll walk you to the door," David said.

When David returned to the room, Jonathan was sitting up in bed, eating soup and bread. Rabbi Loew sat in a chair nearby.

Jonathan said to David: "I was just telling your uncle that I'm beginning to remember more. I need to go back to London as soon as possible."

Rabbi Loew said: "Tell us again what you saw at the marionette museum."

"The baron was there, in the form of a marionette that moved on its own. You must have seen it when you found me."

"We did not notice it," David said, "but then again, we were rather distracted by your condition."

"The marionette had blood trickling out of the corner of his mouth.

He was holding a curved sword." Jonathan held up his hand. "That's where he cut me." With his other hand, Jonathan tapped his forehead to remember more details. "He said there was going to be a dark fire. Corpses would pile up. He said he would kill my wife. That's why I want to leave for London right away."

The rabbi tugged his beard. "About this dark fire, did he say anything else?"

"No. He just said 'we are the masters of the dark fire.'"

"Who is 'we'?"

"He wouldn't tell me. He said all that would be revealed in time."

"What else?" the rabbi prodded.

Jonathan was exasperated. "You mean, aside from the fact that the marionette looked like the baron, and was communicating with me, and said my wife is in danger, and cut my hand? That's not enough?"

"Everything that happened I need to know. From the beginning, please," Rabbi Loew said patiently.

Jonathan recounted the events as clearly as he could remember.

"The marionette said he was friends with her," Jonathan remembered. "He threatened to become her lover. It's all such a contradiction."

"Friends with your wife?" David asked.

"Yes. But I don't believe it. Anne would never permit a man like that through the front door. She'd see him for what he is."

The rabbi said: "Your visions are recurring. Twice is no coincidence. It is a message."

Jonathan was agitated, and forgot to address the rabbi properly. "Yes, you are right. So forgive me for making a hasty departure."

He swung his legs to the edge of the bed. But before he could stand, David put his hand on Jonathan's shoulder, and gently restrained him. "You're not well enough to travel, my friend."

Jonathan pushed his hand away. "If you'll excuse me, gentlemen, I've got to get to London."

"Drake, don't be a fool," David said. "You've got to recuperate first."

"Bloody hell I do. I need to protect my wife."

"You just said she'd never open the door for a man like the baron," David pointed out. "Besides, if your neck starts to bleed again, it will be bad for you."

Jonathan sank back onto the pillows. He noticed he was still in the clothing he'd worn the night before. He wanted a bath and fresh clothes.

The rabbi continued as if he were conducting a study session, reviewing the steps of a proof in a math problem. "There was freezing air in a cellar on a night in which the air outside was not freezing. That tells us we are dealing with the supernatural."

"The freezing air was just cellar air," Jonathan said. "Nothing unusual."

"Cellar air is never freezing," David observed, "no matter what the weather is outside. Cellar temperatures remain a fairly constant 55 degrees Fahrenheit, which is why they are preferred for storing wine."

The rabbi continued. "You were almost strangled to death. By the baron, you say, and yet there was no earthly soul down in that cellar with you."

"*Earthly* soul," David repeated.

Jonathan caught the wording, and he was again frightened by the strange events. He touched the bandages on his neck, and remembered the terror that had seized him in the cellar.

"You cannot face these phenomena alone," Rabbi Loew said quietly.

"I'll contact Scotland Yard when I get home," Jonathan promised.

"Not sufficient. You'll need a companion."

"I can travel with him," David volunteered.

Jonathan shook his head. "That is unnecessary, because I am perfectly capable of riding a train myself."

The rabbi tugged at his own beard, lost in thought. Then he said: "There is danger that you don't understand. You need a companion who understands that danger."

David was surprised. "Surely the rebbe my uncle isn't thinking of making that journey."

Rabbi Loew shook his head. "Oh, no. I'm too old. My work is here, in Prague. But I can prepare Mr. Drake for the battles he faces. The baron is a formidable adversary, and should not be underestimated."

Jonathan laughed bitterly. "This is all sheer nonsense. A wicked old aristocrat from some back-water fiefdom is no match for a Londoner, like myself, who is a crack shot. And I happen to come from a well-connected family, which I have not yet elaborated upon to either of you gentlemen. The fact is, the baron cannot defeat my father's power, nor our police force, our courts, nor the Royal Navy, nor the Crown—no matter what delusions he has."

Rabbi Loew said slowly: "Mr. Drake, you do realise these events are abnormal—no, the English word is … paranormal. So your father and your authorities will have no effect, no matter how powerful."

"We British are exceptional," Jonathan reminded him. "My family members are also exceptional."

The rabbi smiled as if he'd just won the debate. "You yourself do have special abilities, yes?"

Jonathan frowned, sensing a trap. "I was speaking of law and order."

The rabbi continued. "The rules of the game you are playing, none of this do you understand?"

Jonathan's temper flared. "I beg your pardon, but I understand very well, Rabbi Loew. I'm dealing with a bloody maniac who tried to kill me and is now making threats against my wife. He thinks he and his imaginary army can conquer my country. I'm going to finish him off once and for all."

"Who is this 'he' you mention?" the rabbi asked gently.

"You bloody well know who I'm talking about," Jonathan said, exasperated, and forgetting his manners. "We're talking about the Baron von Klausenberg."

David said: "Please don't excite yourself, Drake. And please remember whom you are addressing."

Jonathan exclaimed: "I won't stand by while a crazy old baron makes threats against my wife! He's already kept me from her all these months, the blackguard."

"Mr. Drake," Rabbi Loew said in a commanding voice, "you do not know what you are doing or with whom you are dealing. You are like a child tinkering with a furnace that's about to explode."

The force of the rabbi's statement stunned Jonathan. He retorted: "I respectfully differ. I do know what I am dealing with. I actually spent time with him."

Rabbi Loew's eyes were intense. "I'll prove it. Was the baron, the very same baron you met at his estate, actually with you in the cellar when you were strangled?"

Jonathan paused. "The marionette who looked like him was there."

"But was the marionette actually the baron? Are they one and the same?"

Jonathan turned the question over in his mind. Finally, he stammered: "I … I do not know."

"Was any human being in the cellar with you?" the rabbi asked.

"No … no, I don't think so."

"And you *saw* nobody?"

"Correct. I saw no ordinary humans in that cellar."

"Did you *sense* another presence?"

"Yes," Jonathan admitted reluctantly.

"So, do you agree that we're talking about the non-physical?"

"The wounds on my neck are quite physical," Jonathan said.

David interrupted. "Listen, old chum. What Uncle is getting at is this. Whatever attacked you in that cellar is not an ordinary being. The freezing wind came from … well, we don't know where it came from, exactly. A marionette, who just happened to look like the baron, was making threats. Marionette strings somehow got around your neck and nearly strangled you to death."

"You're saying I imagined it all?" Jonathan demanded.

"No," Rabbi Loew said. "To the contrary, it's all very real. But it is of *another realm*."

Jonathan suddenly looked deflated. He stared at nothing in particular. Chompsworth jumped up onto the bed and licked his ear. He gently elbowed her away.

David said: "Listen, Jonathan, do you remember at Uncle Yitzhak's house when I told you I'd had a dream about you?"

"Vaguely."

"Well, I hadn't remembered the details until just now. But I did dream about you. I dreamed I was fighting by your side, against some figure in black. It was terrifying, but exhilarating at the same time."

The rabbi added: "And, Mr. Drake, those things you said about the neighbour Feuer, and about my brother's account books, and the visions of things in the spider's web. All that signifies an ability to see things that ordinary people cannot see. So you are in an extraordinary situation, and that is why we need to take extraordinary measures."

Jonathan closed his eyes. "Why me? I didn't ask for any of this. I just want to go home."

There was silence for a few moments. Then the rabbi spoke. "You are part of a larger plan. Who knows what is in God's designs? You survived an ordeal. That is uncommon strength, tempered by suffering, like metal in a crucible. Now, your mission is before you. To fulfil it, that is what you must pray for."

A tear of frustration rolled down Jonathan's cheek, and he wiped it away in anger. "But don't you understand? I don't want any of this. I don't want to have a special vision, or a mission. I just want to go home to my wife. I want us to sit in front of the fire, and talk about the day's events. I want to stand at my window and smoke a pipe, and watch the fog swirl around the square where I live, and watch the seasons change. I want to leave the dirty business of war and politics to the professionals."

Rabbi Loew said: "The responsibility that has been placed on your shoulders, Mr. Drake, do you think anybody would choose it? When Moses was chosen by God to lead the people out of their bondage in Egypt, do you think Moses wanted to do it? He did not. He had a wife and children. He had a nice life in Midian. But God had other plans for him. Moses obeyed."

"I'm not Moses."

"But you are an instrument in a larger design. As Moses was. As we all are. And so you must accept it. Otherwise, the comfortable life you yearn for will vanish like a scrap of paper in a flame. The evil ones will win. They will destroy you and everything you love."

"I don't want to fight."

"You will have no peace, and no life, if you do not fight them."

Jonathan let his irritation show. "Please forgive my frankness, Rabbi Loew, but you get to sit in your big purple chair, in your comfortable library, and while away your hours in peace. I just want to do the same."

Instead of being angry, the rabbi said: "Don't you see that I also have a responsibility in all this? I have seen many strange things in my life. I have been in situations where I lost those I love. I almost lost my own life, more than once. I have had to counsel people out of doing evil. I have my own battles to fight, and I fight them. It is no accident that our paths have crossed. You're not the only one who carries the burden of a responsibility. And one of my responsibilities is to help you."

"What do you mean?"

"I have a responsibility to prepare you for the ordeal ahead." The rabbi closed his eyes for a moment, then opened them and continued: "We Jews know that in every generation, evil must be fought. We remind ourselves of this every year at Passover. And not just at Passover. At Purim, in the Scroll of Esther, we are reminded of the evil Haman who wanted to destroy us, but the good Queen Esther saved us. You see? We know that the tyrants never go away. They rise out of the ashes to destroy us in every generation. There have been pogroms everywhere through the centuries. The Bialystock pogrom of 1906. The Kiev pogrom of 1905. Kishinev 1903. Russia from 1881 to 1884. The Chmielnicki massacres of 1648. Andalusia in 1391. Those are the ones I can recount quickly. There have been others."

"Like the one your brother Yitzhak survived?"

Rabbi Loew nodded. "The baron's father had orchestrated it, and the baron himself was there to help."

"Then you understand my hatred of him," Jonathan said through clenched teeth.

"I do."

There was silence for a few moments. Then Jonathan said: "I found refuge at the abbey of Hildegard, same as your brother."

"Then you know that our allies come from unexpected places." The rabbi's bony hands were raised, as if trying to hold up a memory that was too heavy. He deliberated about saying more, and decided not to. He let his hands drop into his lap. "But the important point is this. It's not just Jews who are oppressed. The tyrants start with the Jews, but they never end with the Jews. They always move on to the next victims, and before you know it, everywhere there are victims, everything is chaos and destruction. Even now I hear rumours from Klausenberg—women and children who disappear, animals found dead and mutilated. The baron brags that there is no crime in his realm, but he deceives. He himself is the biggest criminal. And there are no Jews left there, so the victims are all gentiles. But they are not safe."

David lit a cigarette and blew out the smoke. "What the rebbe is saying, Drake, is that we Jews are the canary in the coal mine. Once we've been attacked, you can be sure that eventually, everyone else will be a target."

"Fair enough. But I don't have the strength to fight," Jonathan said, looking hollowly at the floor.

"I can help you find that strength," Rabbi Loew said.

"But time is of the essence, and Anne needs me right away—"

Rabbi Loew held up his hand. "If you do not first heal yourself, and allow me to help you regain your strength, there is a very good chance, God forbid, that those unseen forces that have already attacked you once will do so again. If that happens, the consequences may be far worse next time. You are here because my house offers better protection than any other place in the city."

"All this is too fantastical," Jonathan protested. "Your house is inviting, but I really don't see how it is better than the inn, and besides, we can alert the police—"

"Listen," David interrupted. "You're up against a formidable opponent, along with forces from another realm. If you don't prepare yourself, you'll be hurt. And then you won't be able to protect Anne at all."

Jonathan's face was grave, and he made an effort to get the words out. "If something happens to me, you must swear, as my friend, that you'll protect my wife."

David said: "You have my word. I will protect not just your wife, but your entire family, to the best of my ability."

Jonathan closed his eyes, exhausted. "That puts my mind at ease. Now I need to rest."

ᴄ Chapter Fourteen ᴄ

That evening, Jonathan was well enough to dine with Rabbi Loew, along with Sam Berg and David Lowe.

Rabbi Loew ate in haste. He kept glancing at the clock, and then out the window at the gathering twilight. The other three men talked about the price of real estate in European cities as compared to American cities.

The hour was getting late. Mrs. Prijs bade the four men farewell from the doorway of the dining room. The rabbi listened for the sound of the front door closing and being locked by her from the outside. He broke his silence. "Gentlemen," he said, "Please finish quickly. We must fast until night-time tomorrow."

David said in a half-joking tone: "But the rebbe surely knows that Yom Kippur has already passed, and the next fast day is some weeks away. My beloved uncle must not exert himself, especially now that winter is here."

"And fasting is bad for Mr. Drake, given his condition," Sam added. "It is not recommended for the rabbi, either. I do not need two patients convalescing in this household."

The rabbi said: "All this I know."

"Then I ask that Rabbi Loew follow my advice and not insist that anyone fast," Sam pressed.

Rabbi Loew held up his hands in surrender. "I will leave it up to each of you to decide whether to fast. I must tell you something." He turned to his nephew. "But first, please light a lamp, Dovid, and go around the house. Check that everything is secure, that a mezuzah is yet securely on each door post. All windows and doors locked. All curtains drawn.

Take the dog with you. Then we shall all gather in my study."

After David did as the rabbi requested, the four men gathered in the rabbi's study. Chompsworth usually sat at Jonathan's feet, but this time she went to the middle of the carpet, circled and then settled down, facing the doorway.

The rabbi noticed the dog's behaviour. He sat behind his desk, in his large purple-velvet chair.

"It feels immediately as it was before the pogroms that have happened during my lifetime." He rubbed his forehead.

"Surely my dear uncle exaggerates," David said with great concern. "Prague is safe. There are no pogroms here."

"But there is danger," the old rabbi said. "Can you not sense it? This is why I insisted that you and Jonathan stay here, in this house, and not at the inn. Evil forces gather, but this house offers protection."

Jonathan said: "I do feel safer in this house than I have felt anywhere else, except my own home."

Rabbi Loew was silent. After a few minutes, David broke the silence.

"Why did my uncle want me to check to be sure the house is secure? Surely Mrs. Prijs did all that before she left."

"One cannot be too cautious." Rabbi Loew held up an envelope. "Today I received a letter from my brother Yitzhak. He tells me that the Abbey of Saint Hildegard was attacked."

Jonathan's face was suddenly pale, and he felt sick. "Attacked? But why? Who did it?"

"That is not clear. Animals were slaughtered, and their blood was used to draw symbols on the altar in the chapel. The head of a lamb was impaled on a cross." The rabbi was silent a moment. Then he said in a quiet voice: "The rumours are that it is retribution for the fact that an English Jew took refuge there. They say he had been a guest at a particular nobleman's estate, and had killed one of the nobleman's servants, and then escaped to the abbey."

"That's outrageous," Sam said. He looked at Jonathan. "Why would they accuse you of such a monstrous crime? You're not even Jewish."

Jonathan's voice was hollow. "She was going to stab me. I stopped her."

"So you actually *did* murder her!" Sam exclaimed in a shocked tone.

"It's not murder if it's self-defence," David pointed out.

"But even so," Sam countered, "taking a life is a serious matter. A very serious matter."

"I had no choice," Jonathan said. "She was going to kill me. She had already … done unspeakable things. I could not take it any longer."

Sam folded his arms. "Really. That's an unbelievable accusation."

"I'm surprised you think so," Jonathan said acidly. "Didn't you see my scars when you bandaged my neck?"

"You have no injuries, other than the ligature wounds from the marionette strings," Sam insisted.

Jonathan stood and took off his jacket, his shirt and under shirt. He was now naked from the waist up. David stared at his friend's torso, his mouth agape. He covered his mouth with his hand.

The rabbi muttered something in Yiddish that Jonathan didn't catch. It was clear he was distressed.

Sam pointed at Jonathan, and said triumphantly: "See? He has no injuries other than what's under the bandages on his neck."

"You cannot see anything on his torso?" David asked incredulously.

"Of course not. There is nothing there to see," Sam insisted.

The rabbi said: "You may dress, Mr. Drake." When Jonathan had put his clothes back on, the rabbi said: "Tell us, Mr. Drake, who did all that to you?"

"Did what? There's nothing there!" Sam exclaimed. "It is wrong to feed into this man's delusions." He turned to David. "You didn't see anything, did you?"

"He's got strange symbols carved into his skin. They're ghastly."

Sam had a note of panic in his voice. "Why can I not see them? I'm a man of science. I can see physical reality. I've been *trained* to see it."

"There is a supernatural dimension at work here," the rabbi explained in a quiet voice. "That may be why you cannot see it, Dr. Berg. Even the injuries to his neck are no mere coincidence. The neck is significant—it connects the head to the heart, uniting our intellect and body, our higher Godly self to our lower animal self. The fact that the injury is to the neck means that the dark forces want to sever that connection, to neutralize Mr. Drake." The rabbi turned to Jonathan. "Tell us what happened to make those scars on your torso."

Jonathan took a deep breath. "The baron's servants did it. Iosip and

Mora. They imprisoned me. They … carved my skin. They said they'd kill me. I had to do something, so I—"

Sam interrupted. "This is all too much. Was there really no other way to avoid hurting a woman?"

"If there had been, don't you think I'd have done it?" Jonathan snapped. "Good God, man, I'm no scoundrel. I'm a gentleman from a distinguished family. My father is a law lord. My grandfather was—" he stopped himself. "It doesn't matter what my pedigree is. I was fighting for my life. Any man with an ounce of sense would've done the same. I didn't have the luxury to test other alternatives. But I got out of there alive, and that was my only aim."

The rabbi said: "You were right to defend yourself, Mr. Drake. It is not for us to second-guess." His delicate features took on a far-away, tragic expression, as if he were remembering something terrible from long ago. Then he looked at Sam. "Sometimes there is no choice, Dr. Berg."

Sam's face was a mixture of doubt and repulsion. "It's all so distasteful."

"Agreed," David said. "However, I would have done the same in that situation."

"Let's hope none of us has to put any of our resolutions to the test," Sam concluded.

In the silence that followed, the clock chimed the half hour. Rabbi Loew glanced at it. Then he tapped his fingers on his desk. "Now then. The day after tomorrow, Jonathan will be leaving for London, with Dovid."

"Leaving?" Jonathan repeated. "For London?" He rose from his chair. Chompsworth raised her head and pricked up her ears. "Let me start packing. And I want to send a wire to my wife."

The rabbi held up his hands and slowly lowered them. "Please sit. And listen carefully. There is so much to do. I have told Mrs. Prijs and her son to take a holiday until you have departed, Mr. Drake. I will not be allowing any visitors here until you are gone. Please do not contact your wife to let her know you're coming home."

"But she'll be shocked if I just show up."

"Announcing your plans will give your enemies forewarning. You are a target. That is why I am sending someone with you. A protector."

Sam spoke up. "If Rabbi Loew will forgive my objections, I can't just leave the university. I have an obligation until the end of March."

David corrected him. "He means me, Berg. I'm to be Drake's escort. Didn't you hear him say that?"

"There will be a protector in addition to you, Dovid," the rabbi said.

"See? We were both right," Sam interjected. "The university will not be pleased, but they can be persuaded."

The rabbi closed his eyes and smiled briefly to himself. "I have something else in mind." He opened his eyes. "We will pray and study. Tomorrow night, we will purify ourselves. If you do not want to do this, please leave now."

"Is that why my uncle the rebbe has suggested that we all fast?" David asked.

The rabbi nodded. "I know the doctor objects, so I leave that decision to each of you."

Jonathan interjected. "Why are we delaying? I want to get to London as soon as possible. We can leave tomorrow."

"Soon all will become clear," the rabbi said. "Since you are all agreeing to this, I will explain more. The mikveh in which we will purify ourselves will be the Vltava River."

"But it's winter," Sam said.

Rabbi Loew continued. "We must use the mayim chayim—the living waters—of the river, because it is on the banks of that very same river that the Maharal shaped the mud of the Vltava River into the semblance of a living being, just as God shaped Adam from the earth into a living man."

David's face was drained of all colour. "We're going to do *that?*" He obviously grasped the implications of what the rabbi was saying, but Jonathan and Sam did not.

Rabbi Loew continued. "We ourselves will follow in the Maharal's footsteps and touch that mud and the water there so that we are properly prepared for what we need to do afterward."

Sam said: "I realise I'm being a block-head, but I don't understand what we will be doing afterward."

The rabbi's voice was equally quiet. "After the mikveh, we will go up into the garret of Altneushul and wake up the golem. And the golem will then accompany Jonathan and Dovid to London."

"I thought that's what my dear uncle the rebbe had in mind," David said, rubbing his temple.

Jonathan stood. "What a waste of time. We all agree that every minute counts, and yet here we are, squandering precious hours on some old legend."

"I agree with Mr. Drake," Sam said. "This is crazy."

"I will pack my bags tonight and leave for London tomorrow," Jonathan announced. He turned to David. "There is no need to accompany me. I can make the journey myself, with my dog."

The rabbi said: "You are free to do as you like, Mr. Drake. My only request is that tonight you pray before going to sleep. Pray for guidance about what action Hashem desires that you take tomorrow."

Jonathan said: "That is a simple request. I will pray. But I will be on the train tomorrow, on my way home to see my wife."

"Then goodnight, Mr. Drake. I shall see you early tomorrow morning," the rabbi said affably.

Jonathan left the study, with Chompsworth trotting behind him.

The rabbi stood and said: "It is time for me to retire as well. I would ask that you two gentlemen also pray for guidance tonight."

"I will do as my uncle asks," David said.

"As will I," Sam added.

When the rabbi had left the room, and the door had been closed again, Sam Berg stood up. He was so agitated, he could barely contain himself. "Lowe, you and I need to have a word." He paced a few steps, then turned to David. "You can't trust Drake. He admitted that he is a murderer."

"To kill in self-defence is not murder," David said.

"How do you know it was self-defence? He could be lying. His delirium after the museum incident was alarming. He's been raving about things I've never heard anyone rave about. War, corpses, dark fires. I'd put him in an asylum, if I had that power." Sam was silent a moment. "Listen, you know I have nothing but respect for you and your uncle. Who is this man Drake, and what brings him here?"

"I brought him here, from Budapest." David recounted how he had met Jonathan. Then he concluded: "He had been a prisoner of Baron von Klausenberg, as he explained. Surely that counts for something."

"Klausenberg?" Sam repeated. "I'm an American. I can't keep up with all these European names."

David said: "The Baron von Klausenberg is from an old, aristocratic family whose estate is about a day's ride from the city that bears his name. That family ruled with an iron fist, and has a history of inciting the locals to carry out pogroms. These days, there are no Jews left in the area, but among the locals there is a lingering fear of the baron, especially as one gets closer to the baron's estate. From what Jonathan reported, and from what I've heard when I've travelled to that area, the fear is justified." He paused. "I brought Drake here so that Uncle could help him. Now, it is possible that I am wrong. Maybe you, as a man of science, can come up with a better plan."

Sam tugged at his moustache. "Lowe, you know I am not a religious man. I haven't been to synagogue since my wife died, and that was eleven years ago. But I must admit, there is something at work here that even I cannot explain."

David chuckled and took a cigarette out of a silver case. "Even the man of science detects the spiritual vibrations affecting us all."

"Yes, I do." Sam was defensive. "Your uncle says I have a spiritual sensitivity, if only I would develop it."

"Develop something which you don't believe in," David said in a gently mocking tone.

"I didn't say I was a total sceptic. But I don't have time for it anyway."

"Maybe that's why you cannot see Jonathan's scars," David observed.

Sam was offended. "You say that as if I want it that way. Don't you think I'd prefer to see them so I could help him heal?"

"Forgive me, Berg. It's just that Jonathan has been having quite a difficult time." David paused. "Listen, Berg, if he's not stable mentally or spiritually, then his physical state is somewhat irrelevant."

"Exactly," Sam said. "That's why I'm worried about you and your uncle. How can you be so sure he won't try to hurt you both?"

"Since I met him in Budapest, I've spent almost every waking hour with him. By now, I would've detected some idea that he's a threat. Besides, Uncle is very sensitive about these things, and he is not concerned. He even insisted that Drake stay here, under his roof."

"Then what are the spiritual vibrations you mentioned?" Sam pressed.

"He has supernatural abilities," David said. "When we were in Budapest, he was able to read things about people he could not possibly have known. This was followed by a vision he claimed he had, in which he saw many things, events of the future and the past. Uncle has been able to piece together only a fraction of what it means."

"And?"

"It sounds incredible, even to my ears."

"And you don't fear for his mental stability?"

"Uncle told me in private he thinks we are facing a manifestation of the dark side. In fact, he …" David stopped himself.

"He what?" Sam pressed.

David shook his head. "I've said enough already."

"In for a penny, in for a pound. You might as well let it all out."

David hesitated. Then he said: "Since Jonathan arrived here, Uncle has been praying for divine guidance. He said that on the night Jonathan was attacked, a messenger of Hashem had appeared and spoken directly to him, telling him that he must help Jonathan prepare for what awaits him in London. That is why Uncle was uncharacteristically reserved at dinner that night. He didn't even taste a sip of wine. Uncle has been inspecting each mezuzah around the house to be sure that each klaf—that is, each parchment scroll—is properly inscribed and in good condition, because if one of them is in any way defective, the dark forces will be able to enter more easily."

Sam folded his arms. "I thought we Jews weren't supposed to believe in all this superstitious nonsense."

David said good-naturedly: "Why don't you ask him about all that tomorrow? I'm sure he has an answer that will satisfy even your sceptical mind."

"You say that as if it's bad. Don't you think it's wise to always question?" Sam pressed.

"Of course. But I've noticed how many times I've been wrong, so I don't take my scepticism as an accurate description of the way things really are."

A soft knock sounded at the door of the study, and a moment later, Jonathan let himself in, the dog following behind. He was wearing an overcoat over his pyjamas. "Forgive me for interrupting, and for being dressed like this. I can't sleep, and I wanted to talk to you both."

He took a seat, and the dog sat at his feet. "I don't really understand why we need this, this … golem person to go to London with us," he said in an exasperated tone. "It's an unnecessary delay."

"It's a necessary delay," David corrected him. "And the golem is not a person."

"Then, what is it?" Jonathan asked.

"It is a being that the Maharal made from mud to protect the Jews of Prague from the forces of evil."

"What is a Maharal?" Jonathan asked.

"Maharal is the shorthand name for Rabbi Yehuda Loevy ben Bezalel, the Head Rabbi of Prague, in the sixteenth century. Uncle is a descendant, which makes me a descendant, too."

"Is the legend really true?" Sam asked.

David shrugged. "I suppose it depends on what you want to believe. The Maharal himself was certainly real."

Sam waved his hand dismissively. "Wouldn't it be a joke on us all if it turned out that the golem was probably some eccentric recluse, the synagogue's retired shammash, whom nobody ever saw, except those who brought him food."

Jonathan asked: "Have either of you seen this golem creature?"

David shook his head. "Nobody has been up there. It is off-limits. They say that in the eighteenth century, Rabbi Landau decided to defy the warning and go up there to verify it for himself. He fasted, and purified himself in a mikveh."

"Like we're going to do," Sam observed.

"Right." David continued. "He dressed himself in a tallit—a prayer shawl—and told ten of his pupils to recite psalms on his behalf. Then he ascended the stairs. When he came back down, he was white as a sheet and trembling with fright. He announced to those around him that the warning still stands, because the golem was indeed there."

There was silence. The wind had started to blow, and Chompsworth raised her head and listened for unusual sounds. A low growl came from her throat as she alerted toward the window.

David walked over to the window and drew the drapes aside. He looked down onto the street. Tree branches tossed in the wind, and intermittent flakes of snow fell from the sky. A solitary figure in black stood outside, near an illuminated window, across the street. David could not tell whether the figure was looking up at him. He closed the drapes and returned to his chair.

"What does this golem look like?" Jonathan asked.

Sam joked: "I would imagine muddy, since that is what it is made from."

"Uncle has told me the legends," David said. "The name 'golem' comes from a Hebrew word that means 'indeterminate matter,' 'imperfect substance' or 'unshaped form.' The word appears in Psalm 139, when the psalmist is talking about God: 'Your eyes saw my unshaped form.' Does this mean that the creature in the garret has an extraordinary appearance? I do not know, but we shall find out soon."

"Why, exactly, did the Maharal make a golem in the first place?" Jonathan asked.

"In the time of the Maharal, here in Prague," David explained, "there had been an evil priest named Thaddeus. He was always scheming to get the Jews expelled or executed. At first, Thaddeus tormented only the Jews. But eventually, even that was not enough for him. One day, he got the idea of killing a young gentile boy and blaming it on the Jews. He kidnapped the boy, murdered him, and put all the evidence—the body, the blood— here in the Jewish Quarter. Then he tried to blame the Jews for the evil he'd committed with his own hands. But with the help of the golem, the Maharal was able to foil this nefarious plot and expose the evil Thaddeus. Notice how wickedness progresses. Thaddeus started off by tormenting the Jews, but in the end, that was not sufficient. He also had to torment the Christians. Evil has an insatiable appetite, and it never confines itself to what it consumes first. It always wants more and more victims."

Sam said: "I still find it hard to believe there is some entity in the attic of the Altneushul who is supposed to help us."

"We'll find out tomorrow, won't we?"

"Yes, I'm certain we'll see that it's really nothing more than a fiction that survives only as dust and cobwebs," Sam declared confidently.

Jonathan said: "You gentlemen will have to have the next adventure without me, because I'll be on my way to London tomorrow. Please write and tell me what you find. I'll be reading your letter in my comfortable chair near the fireplace, with my wife next to me."

CHAPTER FIFTEEN

When the rabbi came into his study just before dawn the next morning, he found Jonathan asleep in a chair with books on his lap. Chompsworth was lying at his feet, and her tail thumped on the carpet when she saw Rabbi Loew.

David came into the room after the rabbi, and he gave his uncle a questioning look. The rabbi shrugged as if to say: "I have no idea why he is here."

David gently shook his friend. "Drake, if you want to catch that train back to London, you need to get dressed."

Jonathan sat up and rubbed his eyes. "I'm not leaving today. I've had terrible dreams all night. I came here, to this room, because I could not sleep. It was better to read here than to toss and turn in the bed. I hope Rabbi Loew will forgive me for perusing his library."

"There is nothing to forgive, Mr. Drake," the rabbi replied. "I should like you to describe the dreams."

"They were dreams about all the things we talked about last night: the golem, and the river, and the synagogue—all that. I don't remember the details."

"I had dreams as well," David confessed. "Dreams of waking the golem."

"As did I," Rabbi Loew said. "So, we will go to the river after sundown this evening. In the meanwhile, we shall spend the day in prayer and study." He turned to Jonathan. "You may get dressed, Mr. Drake. Then, we shall begin our day by davening shacharit."

David whispered to Jonathan: "He means we're going to say the morning prayer."

When Jonathan was dressed, he returned to the rabbi's study. Rabbi Loew helped Jonathan to put on tefillin: He showed Jonathan how to wrap the leather straps around his forearm and head, securing the small box that contained parchment scrolls with verses from the Torah inscribed on them.

As the three men were praying, Sam quietly slipped into the room and joined them. When the morning prayers were finished, David turned to Sam and said: "You're here early, Dr. Berg. We thought you'd be here closer to noon."

Sam had a sheepish grin. "The truth is, I was plagued by dreams, and I didn't sleep well at all."

Jonathan said: "You've come to the right place. We've all been plagued by dreams."

The four men spent the day in prayer and study. They each fasted, against Sam's wishes, but the doctor realised it was useless to argue.

Rabbi Loew had imparted to Jonathan insights about the nature of evil, supernatural creatures, and unseen forces. The rabbi had explained that there were schools of thought in Judaism that had developed a full arsenal for dealing with those phenomena. At the heart of it all, the rabbi stressed, was the indisputable fact that Hashem is the Ruler of All of Creation—including all of His creation that we humans cannot see. Any use of supernatural tools wielded by the righteous must be done in His service, according to His laws as He set forth in the Tanakh. The rabbi explained that the creation of the golem is done only through God's will, using the raw materials that God Himself had created. Humans were but subordinate partners in that creation.

Rabbi Loew did not have time to educate Jonathan in the intricacies of all he knew—that would take years. He urged Jonathan to pray every day at home, to wear tefillin during morning prayers, to recite specific psalms, along with passages from the Torah, and the prophets Isaiah and Ezekiel.

At sundown, the four men donned overcoats and hats, and left the house. Jonathan had wanted to bring Chompsworth, but the rabbi convinced him that she would be a distraction. Jonathan reluctantly left the dog behind. Jonathan's stomach was in knots, both because he was uneasy and because he was hungry.

They made their way in the frigid night air through the streets of Prague. The cadences of the prayers Jonathan had been reciting all day echoed through his head as they walked. The rabbi had warned each of them to keep a sharp eye out for anything unusual. "The forces of darkness are on the march, and we need to make sure we do not attract their notice unnecessarily," he had said.

The air was still. A few flakes of snow fell. Although the rabbi was old, he moved with a swift, wiry energy that had Jonathan breathing hard to keep up. The rabbi carried a rolled-up towel under his arm. Jonathan wondered where the old man had got his energy since they hadn't eaten in over twenty-four hours.

They continued at a brisk pace and didn't stop until they were well beyond the outskirts of town, on a road that paralleled the river. The rabbi suddenly veered off the road, into a thicket of trees that lined the bank of the river. They emerged into a small clearing, with the river flowing a few paces away.

Jonathan could barely see the outlines of the other men. The rabbi's voice was just loud enough to be heard above the moving water.

"I will go first," he said.

The other three turned their backs as the rabbi disrobed and plunged into the river. The darkness provided privacy.

Jonathan heard him murmuring a prayer in Hebrew. He paused the prayer each time he completely submersed himself in the water, for a total of three times. Then he emerged from the river, dried himself off with the towel, and got dressed.

David went into the river next, reciting the same prayer. He also fully submersed himself three times, and then returned to the riverbank to dry himself and get dressed. Sam did the same.

Jonathan's turn came. When his clothes were off, he shivered in the cold night air. He hesitated to let his feet touch the water, but he told himself that if an old man of eighty-three could go in without hesitation, so could he. As he plunged in, he had the revelation that the cold could not chill him so long as his mind was focused. It was as if a Higher Power had suddenly put a protective layer around him, so that the frigid water could not affect his earthly body. He submersed himself three times, and the rabbi helped him to recite the prayer. As he was emerging from the river to return to the bank to dry off and get dressed, he noticed that the symbols that had been carved into his torso seemed to glow faintly for a split second, and then diminish. He told himself that this was an optical illusion. But the truth was, he couldn't be sure it was just an illusion. Too many strange things had happened. And there was Rabbi Loew, a wise and learned scholar who not only took Jonathan's strange experiences seriously, but seemed to have additional insights and explanations for them. The rabbi could not be dismissed as a superstitious fool. He was, for Jonathan, an inspiring example of courage in the face of malevolence and uncertainty.

After Jonathan was dressed, the four men made their way back to the Jewish Quarter of Prague. The hour was late, the streets deserted. Jonathan felt strangely renewed, as if he'd never need to sleep or eat again.

The four men stopped at a side door of the Altneushul. Rabbi Loew unlocked it, then locked it again after everyone was safely inside. David lit a lamp.

The rabbi led the way up an old staircase. David held the lamp high to light the way, making sure to be ready in case the his uncle lost his footing. Sam followed close behind. Jonathan was last.

At the top of the stairs, the rabbi fumbled for the proper key to the door there. Outside, the wind could be heard beyond the stone walls of the synagogue.

David remarked: "The air was still when we walked to the Vltava, and now there is a storm coming in."

A cold wind suddenly blew along the stairwell.

Rabbi Loew asked: "The door downstairs is closed and locked, is it not?"

"Yes," Jonathan replied. "I checked twice to be sure it was locked."

"The unearthly forces follow us," the rabbi observed.

Jonathan shivered and anxiously looked back down at the shadows of the stairwell, half-expecting something to come up after them. He was reminded of the time that he and Mr. Cowles were at the house in Belgravia, climbing the stairs from the sinister cellar. Jonathan wished he were back at the rabbi's house, where it was safe.

Rabbi Loew found the correct key. The door was now unlocked, but the rabbi still could not open it. David had to put his shoulder to it and push with all his strength.

It creaked loudly as it swung open on its hinges. The four men made their way into the room.

A small circle of light was cast by the lamp that David held. The wooden beams of the roof were festooned with cobwebs. Most of the place was in deep shadow.

As Jonathan's eyes adjusted, he noticed that there was a pile of what looked like rubbish—old books and tattered cloth—not far from the window. The rabbi made his way to the pile, and motioned for the other three men to wait nearby.

"This is a genizah," David whispered, gesturing to the pile. "It's a depository for old holy books and manuscripts that are no longer in circulation."

Rabbi Loew took a book out of his pocket and began reading Genesis chapter 1, verse 1 in Hebrew. His voice was drowned out by thunder and by the sound of wind blowing across the roof. Lightening flashed outside, illuminating the room in ghostly shades of white. Rabbi Loew continued.

After some time, the rabbi stopped reading. He moved close to the other three men, and in hushed tones, instructed each of them in the proper recitation of the Divine formula in Hebrew. David went first, circling the genizah seven times clockwise, then seven times counter clockwise, reciting the formula as he paced. Sam was next, circling exactly seven times in each direction while reciting a slightly different formula.

When Sam was finished, it was Jonathan's turn. The rabbi helped him to recite the Hebrew words.

A strange sensation came over Jonathan. As he circled, he knew he was in a trance, but his mental and emotional state was unlike anything he had ever experienced before. He felt a profound sense of peace, as if all the trials and fears of the last several months were as insignificant as a speck of dust on the floor. That was the most amazing part—the absence of all fear, and the absence of all worries and anxieties about what had been and what was going to be. Time didn't exist. He could have been circling for a minute or for a year. He was simultaneously outside of his physical body while being one with everything around him, from the cobwebs strung across the rafters, to the knots in the floorboards, to the flame of the lamp that was now in the rabbi's wrinkled hands. There was no meaningful difference between him and everything around him. He was one with it all.

Rabbi Loew put his hand on Jonathan's arm and gently drew him away from the perimeter of the circle. Jonathan took his place next to David and Sam, not wanting to break the spell. The rabbi began to circle the pile of discarded books and documents—the genizah—while reciting another prayer.

A faint glow emanated from the pile of old books and manuscripts, as if lit from within.

By the time Rabbi Loew was finished circling, the glow had intensified, and the storm was at the height of its fury. A gust of wind shattered the windowpane and extinguished the lamp. David searched his pockets for a match to re-light it. He turned so that the lamp was protected from the gusts. As he touched the match to the wick, and the flame once again illuminated the room, the pile heaved. Books and manuscripts tumbled to the floor, their pages blowing about in the gusty wind. A figure sat upright. It was shrouded in a tallit—a prayer shawl with fringes—and its face was hidden by another tallit wrapped around its head and shoulders.

Jonathan trembled, unable to move. Rabbi Loew went over to the golem and spoke quietly to it. Thunder and wind made it impossible for the other men to hear what the rabbi was saying.

Rabbi Loew adjusted the tallit so that the creature's line of sight was unobstructed. Its head was still covered with the tallit, and its face was still in shadow. It stood. Jonathan estimated its height to be over six feet.

Rabbi Loew took its arm and helped it to stand. He led it to the staircase, and the two of them descended the stairs together. Compared to the slight build of Rabbi Loew, the golem looked massive.

Sam, David, and Jonathan followed. In the stairwell, the noise of the storm was not as intense, but the stairs themselves seemed even more narrow and treacherous on the way down. The rabbi waited at the bottom. The golem stood nearby, a solid figure hidden by the shadows, his head and shoulders still covered by the tallit. He stood as a servant would stand, obedient and deferential, waiting for orders.

Each of the men wanted to examine the creature more closely, but the rabbi said: "Let us hurry. We will be safer at my home."

They rushed along the few short blocks to the rabbi's house. Jonathan shivered as snow and freezing rain fell down upon them. The thunder and lightning seemed dangerously close overhead, and Jonathan would not have been surprised to see bolts of lightning strike at them between the buildings, like the fingers of a malicious giant trying to kill them.

David jogged ahead and unlocked the door to the rabbi's house. As soon as they were all safe inside, he locked it against the tempest outside.

$\curlywedge$ CHAPTER SIXTEEN $\curlywedge$

They all sat at the dining table in Rabbi Loew's house. Rabbi Loew took his place at the head of the table. The golem sat to his right, still wrapped in prayer shawls, its face obscured. Chompsworth went up to the golem for the second time, sniffed, and found nothing interesting or unusual. Then she returned to Jonathan's side, circled a few times, and lay down. From time to time, she raised her head, twitched her ears, and alerted to the sounds outside the window. The wind was still raging, and wet snow pelted the window panes.

Rabbi Loew removed the prayer shawls from the golem's head and shoulders. Jonathan hadn't had a good look at the creature up to this point—there hadn't been enough light in the dim synagogue and dark streets, and he'd been too distracted by the whole ordeal.

The golem looked like an adult man, but completely without hair. His skin had a faintly swarthy cast, like a miner who cannot clean off all the earth in which he continually toils. The golem's head was round and smooth, his face was hairless and unremarkable. Mud-brown eyes peered out from under a heavy brow. The golem had the physique of a stevedore: a muscular build, large square hands. But for the fact that he was taller than most men, he looked as undistinguished as any ordinary labourer. His demeanour was calm and watchful. His clothing was shabby and dusty.

At supper, the men ate silently, and each of them watching the golem The creature was able to use a fork like a common man. Nobody would mistake his table manners for those of an aristocrat. Among servants, he'd blend in nicely.

When they had finished eating, Sam addressed the golem: "I've noticed you're awfully quiet. You haven't even asked for second helpings of the bread, which is quite delicious." Sam offered the bread basket, and the golem took all slices at once in his large hand, dropped them onto his plate, and began eating again.

Rabbi Loew said: "Our friend cannot speak. But don't let that mislead you. He has a keen intelligence, and can comprehend everything."

"Whom does he serve, exactly?" Jonathan asked.

"He will take orders from any four of us because we all helped to awaken him. But—" Rabbi Loew raised his hand for emphasis "—he is not to be used as an ordinary servant. His task is to keep us all safe—well, you two, at any rate." The rabbi pointed at Jonathan and David.

"Let us hope he doesn't have any of the vices one finds in an ordinary servant," Jonathan said, remembering how his mother had to sometimes manage the embarrassing problems of her household staff.

Rabbi Loew shook his head. "He is not moved by primitive impulses. He needs food and water for physical sustenance. He needs to sleep. He isn't plagued by the flaws that we humans suffer: greed, gluttony, the desire for fame or wealth, compulsions with gambling or drinking. He has no libido, therefore, he is not a menace to women." The rabbi paused. "Our golem needs a name."

There was silence while the men pondered the answer. They looked at the creature. The golem's face was inscrutable, and his eyes rested on each man's face in turn.

Finally, Sam spoke up. "What was he called last time he was, er, summoned?"

"During the Maharal's time here in Prague? He was Yossi," the rabbi said.

"Well, that's it, then," David said. "Since we're going to London, let's simply call him Joe."

"That name works well enough," Jonathan said, recalling the ordinary names of the servants in his parents' household and in his own household.

"Does he have a moral sense?" Sam asked.

The rabbi nodded. "He can sense evil and resist it. If you were to order him to kill an innocent person, he would not do it. Even so, you are each accountable for the orders you give him insofar as those orders create foreseeable consequences."

"What would my uncle the rebbe say is his Achilles's heel?" David asked.

The rabbi was pensive. "He looks human, and yet he is not. Others will expect him to have the full range of human emotions and capacities. You may even come to expect it, forgetting that he is a facsimile of a human. The lack of a fully human soul may cause errors, even tragedy. Part of your responsibility is to be sure that this does not happen." He gestured at the golem. "Our friend here understands language, so guard your tongue. Do not abuse him. The way you treat him reflects on you for better or for worse."

Sam said: "I was once at the sickbed of a rich old widow. She complained about her maid—and the maid was right there, in the same room. The widow said: 'Helga is a good worker, like an ox. I just wish she weren't so much like an ox, stupid and clumsy.' The maid carried on as if nothing had been said. My heart broke for that poor girl."

Jonathan recollected that although his mother had been strict, she'd never been abusive toward her servants. Such abuse was common, and he'd overhear his parents' disapproving judgements upon their peers who thought nothing of doling out such abuse. He remembered that his mother would say out loud that to treat servants shabbily was the mark of bad character.

Rabbi Loew said: "Our Torah teaches us that such abusive words are forbidden to be spoken aloud in front of anyone, including a lowly servant, even if the servant is deaf. We are required to treat not only our servants, but also our animals with consideration. Even animals of limited capacity, such as chickens, are sentient enough that we must not cause them unnecessary pain."

David said: "The rabbi is referring to Deuteronomy chapter twenty-two, verse seven, in which one must shoo away the mother bird before you take her eggs so that she does not see them being taken."

"Just so," the rabbi said. "We can always count on Dovid for the exact citation." He turned to Jonathan. "This is how I knew you were a man of high character. You helped the peasant untangle his horse from the overturned cart. I know you will treat the golem well."

Sam interjected in an approving tone: "Good for you, Mr. Drake. I am one who loves horses. They are noble creatures."

The rabbi continued in a grave voice. "We must keep our eyes on what is happening. The unseen forces we used to awaken the golem are powerful. To use them unwisely, or without God's permission, only invites disaster. It is essential—essential—to be humble before God at every step of the way. This is why you must pray every day, three times a day. Put on your tefillin. Recite the Psalms."

Sam asked: "I would like to ask the rebbe why we have been dabbling in these occult arts. We Jews are told to have nothing to do with all that."

"A little late for that objection," Jonathan observed drily.

The rabbi said: "The doctor's question is a good one. Do you remember the story of Nadav and Abihu?"

"No," Jonathan said.

David spoke up. "In the book of Leviticus, chapter ten, there are two sons of Aaron. Aaron is the brother of Moses, and he is the high priest of the Israelites. The two sons, Nadav and Abihu, bring an alien fire into the sanctuary. This was a serious transgression, and it displeased God so greatly, that they were both struck dead on the spot because of it."

The rabbi said: "They used their power improperly. They violated God's instructions about how to wield the knowledge and the responsibility He gave to them. Another example. Deuteronomy, chapter eighteen, verses ten and eleven. There, we Jews are commanded to not use divinations or to converse with familiar spirits. Why? Is it because occult practices are just a bunch of silly superstitions?"

"That's what a lot of people believe," Sam agreed. "And given the marvellous advances in science, it is a valid claim."

The rabbi pointed a finger into the air. "If you read carefully, the Torah says time and time again that idols and pagan gods are worthless, detestable, and not real. There is only One Eternal Ruler, and that is the God of Abraham, Isaac and Jacob. But the Torah does not say that divination and augury and spirit-summoning are all nonsense. It just tells us that to traffic with it, this is something we Jews should not do. And so, this leads us to another point." He took a sip from his cup before continuing. "What if certain aspects of the occult arts are real? What if it is possible for us humans to get in touch with the unseen, to harness the forces of the beyond?"

Sam looked doubtful. "Just because it is possible—and I'm not convinced it is—does not mean we should do it."

The rabbi was pleased. "Exactly, Doctor Berg, exactly. God forbids us to use occult powers because He knows we humans have a high chance of abusing those powers, and we will forget to be in His service. And, besides, only a very few of us have even an inkling of what we're actually doing. There were Jewish scholars who knew magic. They knew they were ultimately relying upon God, not upon their own abilities. But even then, danger lurks. None of this is to be taken lightly. One must allow one's faith to shine forth."

"But I don't have faith," Jonathan said. "Not after everything I've been through."

"Nobody is asking for an emotion or a feeling," the rabbi said. "It is about your actions. You must act righteously, and do what God wants, in spite of your fear. That's a special kind of courage, a special kind of faith."

"I'm afraid I am not as courageous as I ought to be," Jonathan muttered, looking down.

"I beg to differ," David said. "You've been through hell, and you haven't gone to pieces."

"Or, perhaps I *have* gone to pieces and I just don't know it yet," Jonathan said with a bitter smile.

The rabbi shook his head. "The ordinary world regards extraordinary abilities and perceptions as a form of insanity. But the ordinary world is wrong. The extraordinary is the true warp-and-weft of the fabric of existence. Most people cannot, or will not perceive it that way." Then Rabbi Loew said: "You've been given a unique task, Jonathan Drake. Use your abilities to serve His ends. Pray, and He will give you strength to do what you must do."

CHAPTER SEVENTEEN

When the train arrived at Victoria Station, Jonathan was both relieved and filled with dread. The relief was that he was home, in the largest, richest, most productive city in the world. The dread, which sat like lead in his stomach, was the prospect of trying to pick up the pieces of his life and return to a normal existence with Anne. He was not the man who had said goodbye to her all those months ago. It was now January of a new year, 1909. The man who had departed London in the spring of 1908 was another man from a world that no longer existed.

David and Jonathan went their separate ways at the train station, and Joe went with David. They would all meet at Jonathan's house the next day. They had discussed this plan during the journey, agreeing that Jonathan needed to see his wife without the distraction of others being there.

Jonathan took a hansom cab to Cadogan Square, holding Chompsworth on his lap. The noise and bustle of London made his nerves jangle. He held Chompsworth tightly.

Although the air was cold, they both had their heads out the window, surveying the constant activity as the hansom made its way through the streets. For Jonathan, the sounds and smells were familiar, but they also shocked him with their intensity. For the dog, they were new and exciting. Her ears were constantly pricked up, alerting on every sound, her nose twitched constantly at the unfamiliar smells. On Chesham Place, Jonathan held her fast as she tensed to leap out of the window to chase a stray cat.

There was no snow on the ground, but the grey sky threatened freezing rain that could very well turn to snow once night fell. He was looking forward to a hot cup of tea in front of his blazing hearth, and a hot supper in the comfort of his own home.

The carriage pulled up to his front door. The coachman leaped down from his seat and chattered away in a cockney accent about how "noice it is to be 'ome at last to see one's lady and little 'uns." He offered to carry Jonathan's small bag to the door, or hold the dog's lead, but Jonathan tipped him and said he could manage by himself. The man doffed his cap with a "thank 'ee" and drove away.

Jonathan climbed the marble stairs to the front door. They had once been white, but now they were dingy and grey with soot. He wondered why the maid had not scrubbed them. He rang the bell.

Anne opened the door, and it took her a moment to recognise him. Jonathan dropped his bag and took her into his arms. She began sobbing. Chompsworth put her paws on Jonathan's leg.

Jonathan remained silent and simply held her. When her sobs had quieted, he said gently: "I was not able to send a cable to tell you I was on my way back home."

Anne's face was pressed against his chest. "Since June, we all thought you were dead. And then I got your telegram from Budapest, telling me you were alive and you'd write. I waited for your letter. Now here you are."

"I'm so sorry, Anne. I had my reasons."

She pulled away from him and looked at him with a bewildered expression on her face. "I didn't recognise you with the beard. And you've lost weight." She took a deep breath. "I have something important to show you."

Jonathan closed the door and locked it. He dropped the dog's lead. Chompsworth darted around, sniffing and exploring.

There was a strange black circle hanging on the wall, over the table in the entry way.

Jonathan pointed. "There used to be a looking-glass there," he said. "It was a wedding-present from the Wingates."

"Yes," Anne said, "I did some re-decorating."

He noticed a framed picture below, on the table next to the silver salver, drawn in bright colours. He didn't bother to examine it. He could see that Anne was nervous, yet she was also in high spirits.

"I need to show you something," Anne repeated.

Jonathan followed her to the back parlour. A cheerful fire blazed in the hearth. How many times had he dreamed of being in this room, sitting in his chair, next to Anne, telling her of his adventures? Except for a wooden bin between his armchair and Anne's, the room was exactly as he had left it. It was surreal. A small sound came from that direction.

"Meet the new family additions," Anne said, going over to that side of the room and lifting out an object wrapped in a blanket. "This is Jack." Anne pointed down. "Lily is sleeping, so we won't wake her. But Jack eats about every hour, and he's probably hungry again."

Anne had a baby bottle ready.

"Are you caring for somebody's children?" Jonathan asked, too dazed to understand what was happening.

Anne's face was grave. "Why, no, darling, they're our children. I was already some weeks along when you'd left, and I planned to tell you when you returned. I had sent a letter to you at the baron's estate, but I suppose you hadn't seen it."

"No, I had not," Jonathan murmured in a daze.

She continued. "At any rate, it doesn't matter now. They were born on the sixteenth of September. Early, but the doctor said that's normal with twins."

Jonathan was too shocked to answer. He sank down into his armchair and stared at his son in his wife's arms. The baby was gnawing on his fist, eyes closed. There was no doubt that Jack was his child. The chin, ears, and shape of the eyes were Jonathan's. He looked over at the sleeping girl baby. She had Anne's features.

Anne glanced at him anxiously, waiting for him to say something more, but he was too lost in his own memories. He thought back to the fact that September had been the month he'd arrived at the abbey. Anne could not have known to send a letter there. And anyway, why should she have written? She had thought he was dead. A shiver ran through him as he pushed away nightmare images of the horrors he'd endured.

Finally, he said: "These are beautiful children, Anne. We have been blessed."

A smile of relief spread over Anne's face. "Yes, they are beautiful," she agreed. "And so well-behaved. They are the most perfect children anyone could wish for." She went on to describe all the wonderful compliments that her mother and Jonathan's mother had said about the children. As she spoke, her mood lightened considerably. Everything was going to be alright. Her husband was home, and he loved his children.

Chompsworth trotted into the room, satisfied with her inspection of the house. She sniffed Jack, her tail wagging. Then she went over to Lily's cradle and sniffed the blankets.

"This is a sweet dog," Anne said, patting Chompsworth's head. "Where did you find it?"

"On the baron's estate," Jonathan said. "I named her Chompsworth."

"So the baron gave you the dog as a gift?" When Jonathan didn't answer, she said: "In June, he paid a visit to your parents to tell them you had died of mountain fever. And now here you are. How I've dreamed that this moment could happen. What on earth has happened to you, Jonathan? Why didn't you write me to tell me you were alive? Why did you wait until just a few weeks ago to send that telegram from Budapest?" The words rushed out in a torrent, and she held back tears.

Jonathan rubbed his face. "Good God, Anne. I have so much to tell you. It's all so complicated. Where should I begin? I can't talk about any of it now. I'd love a cup of tea."

"I'll ring for Mrs. Rafferty to bring some up before she leaves."

"Does she live here?" Jonathan asked.

"No. We can't afford *that* luxury. She comes in a few days each week."

As Anne fed the baby with the bottle, Jonathan sat in silence, watching his children, watching his wife care for them, and then gazing into the fire. He could only guess what Anne thought of him now. The man who had been her husband had left in the spring, and now a stranger had returned in the winter—a gaunt stranger with a bearded face and inscrutable eyes. There was a hardness about him, a turning-inward to his own thoughts and memories that hadn't been there before. He knew he was hardly making a proper fuss over his own children, or over Anne, for that matter. Well, the shock was very great, not just for her, but for him as well.

Jonathan's thoughts were not interrupted when old Mrs. Rafferty came shuffling into the room with the tray of tea. Jonathan didn't realise she was there, so he didn't notice her peering at him with a perplexed expression. She left without saying a word.

Anne poured the tea and gave her husband a cup just the way he liked it, with cream and just a touch of sugar. He sipped it absently, still staring into the fire.

"I'm glad you're home. So are Lily and Jack." She turned and fussed with the baby's blankets. She looked as if she'd start crying again. She steadied herself, and reached into the folds of her dress and took out his grandfather's old pocket watch.

"I'm so happy that I can now give this back to you," she said, handing to him.

Jonathan took it without a word, and slipped it into his own pocket. He didn't want to ask how, exactly, it had been returned to her, nor did he want to tell her about the day it had been taken from him. There'd be time for all that later. Anne was puzzled by his silence. She had expected him to be happy to be back home, and to have his pocket watch again.

Jonathan was not sure what to say next. He had never felt this uncomfortable with her before.

"Did you get along without me?" he asked in a hoarse voice. "It must have been very difficult."

"It *was* difficult. My mother came from Bristol to help. And Mrs. Rafferty was a pillar of strength. I also hired a nanny. You'll meet her soon enough."

"What about my parents? And my sister? Did they not offer to help?" He was bewildered and angry.

"Oh, yes, they offered to help," Anne said. "Your mother sent one or two of her servants here every week to help. Of course, this house requires more attention than that, but it was better than nothing. Then your mother got this idea that I should live with them. Even your sister Sarah joined her campaign, raising the issue every time she came here to visit, which got quite tedious. Your mother was prepared to give me the entire third floor, with my own staff, and have it redecorated any way I wanted." Anne laughed as if it were the most ridiculous proposition she'd ever heard.

Jonathan was astonished at her lack of common sense. "Why in the world didn't you take her up on it?"

"And let this place go to ruin?"

"This place would not have gone to ruin in just a few months. Closing it up would've saved a bundle."

Anne's eyes flashed with annoyance. "How could I have known it would be just a few months? I thought it would be permanent."

"And what would be wrong with that?"

"You would have me live at your mother's house like a charity case? Like a poor abandoned widow who has to live with her in-laws? What would people think?"

"I'd say that living at their Hyde Park address doesn't exactly signify common charity. Mayfair is hardly the part of London that is down-at-the-heels, you know."

Anne raised her chin. "My independence is worth something."

"I'm so sorry, Anne," Jonathan said quietly. "I wish I could have come home sooner."

"Why didn't you?"

"I … I was gravely ill." He adjusted his shirt collar to be sure the dressing on his neck was concealed. "I cannot explain it all now." He took a sip of tea. "Listen, I have a friend in town. His name is David Lowe. I'm eager for you to meet him. Perhaps he can come for tea tomorrow. And there's Joe. A servant."

"Yes, that would be wonderful," Anne said. "Minerva—that's the nanny—will be here later tomorrow. I gave her the day off until then."

That wasn't exactly true. Minerva had demanded the time away with no notice, and Anne did not dare insist otherwise. Anne knew it was a bad position to be in—at the mercy of one's own servant—but she had come to depend on Minerva so much that she didn't dare ruffle Minerva's feathers.

"The name Minerva is rather unusual," Jonathan observed. "We ought to re-name her with an ordinary Christian name while she is in our employ. And, as you know, it is an honorific to call nannies by their surname preceded by missus, as in Mrs. Smith."

Anne said: "It's rather unfair to re-name a girl just because we don't like her given name."

"People do it all the time," Jonathan pointed out. "In some houses, whoever is the footman is always called Roberts, or whatever. The house parlour-maid is always Rose. It doesn't matter what their given names are, their new names are what they're called."

"Well, that's all so old-fashioned," Anne said. "Let's be modern. Minerva can keep her own name. And she doesn't have to be Mrs. So-and-so. She's just plain Minerva."

Anne's heart was lighter than it had been in a while. Now that her husband was home, he'd return to work. She would be able to hire more servants and appoint her house in the style it deserved. She was ready to pick up where they'd left off, and begin life again as a proper lady with a proper household.

Anne stood up. "Let me have a word with Mrs. Rafferty before she goes home. Please mind the babies until I return."

Jonathan sat alone before the fire, staring at his children. He was still in shock that they even existed. Jack was fast asleep. Lily stirred and let out a small cry, then settled back to sleep. Jonathan put a hand on both of the children and was suddenly grateful that he was alive to see them.

CHAPTER EIGHTEEN

The next day, the doorbell rang at Jonathan's house in Cadogan Square. Jonathan opened the front door to find Sam and David standing there. Joe was behind both men, dressed in a suit that was appropriate for a servant not in livery.

"Berg, what the devil are you doing here?" Jonathan exclaimed.

"I couldn't remain in Prague any longer. After all that has happened, I had to be in the thick-of-it."

"Let's hope there is no thick-of-it," Jonathan said grimly.

Jonathan led the three guests to the front parlour. He announced: "Anne, I'd like to introduce my friends, Dr. Sam Berg and Mr. David Lowe."

Anne greeted her guests with poise, and bade them to take a seat. She was splendidly dressed in one her finest afternoon gowns of watered silk in a shade of blue that made her eyes look brilliant. Her hair was nicely arranged. Jonathan was proud of her. She was a fine woman.

Anne turned to Joe, who had taken a seat in the corner. "How do you do. I'm afraid I did not catch your name."

There was a moment of silence. Jonathan spoke up. "His name is Joe. He is a servant. He is a mute."

Anne smiled graciously. "Then he should feel free to make himself at home, downstairs in the servants' quarters."

"In due time, my dear. There are a few things that need explaining first."

Anne thought this highly irregular, but instead of arguing, she turned her attention to the silver tea service before her, one of her prized possessions.

Sam remarked: "That is a splendid tea service, Mrs. Drake. And it is polished to a perfect sheen."

Anne replied: "Thank you, Dr. Berg. It had once belonged to Princess Mary, Duchess of Gloucester. Jonathan's parents gave it to us on our wedding day. They have excellent taste, as you'll discover if you ever have the chance to see their house."

"You husband has spoken very highly of you, Mrs. Drake," David said, taking a cup of tea that she handed to him.

David's sensitive nose picked up on the fact that she wore ambergris perfume, and this fact surprised him. Usually, the preferred scent of Englishwomen was rose or lavender. He wondered whether Mrs. Drake was far more sophisticated than Jonathan had let on. In his experience, it was only worldly women with a strong artistic disposition who could wear such a scent successfully. It also happened that such women had access to great wealth, because ambergris was one of the costliest perfumes in the world.

Anne's eyes went to Joe, who was sitting quietly in a corner. Light glinted off his bald head. He looked like an ordinary labourer, with his common face and faintly muddy complexion.

Anne brought a cup of tea to Joe, but he refused it with a shake of his head.

"He only drinks water," Jonathan said. "I'll ask Mrs. Rafferty to bring some up. Ah, never mind. I'll fetch it myself. I forgot that she is not here today." He left the room, closing the door behind him.

Anne offered her guests sandwiches and scones.

"Oh, I can never refuse," Sam said, selecting from the plate she offered.

Anne offered the plate to David, but he politely declined. Anne decided he was not as amiable as Dr. Berg. David Lowe was a man every woman would notice. He knew it, and didn't care. She wondered whether David was some sort of an aristocrat. He certainly carried himself like one. Anne found that off-putting and worrisome, because she dreaded having David discover the extent of the come-down in her financial status since Jonathan had been away. She would have to manage this meeting carefully. Not even Jonathan knew the extent of it.

David said: "Mrs. Drake, I noticed the fascinating piece you have hanging over the table in the front entrance hall. Where did you get it?"

Anne froze for a moment. She was glad that Jonathan was out of the room.

"Well, it's from an auction," Anne lied nonchalantly.

"Has anyone explained the symbols on it?" David asked. "It's probably a type of far-east sun wheel. I believe it is called the black sun. What is the provenance of the piece?"

"I really don't know."

"And you have a small drawing on the table below it, in a tortoise-shell frame. It looks Middle-Eastern."

"Yes, I saw that," Sam said. "A woman revelling in the gore of her victims. Quite ghastly, but also beautifully rendered. She resembles you, you know, Mrs. Drake, which is quite a coincidence."

Anne's mind was racing for a way out of this dangerous conversation. "It is of some goddess, I don't recall her name. A London artist drew it, and a friend of mine gave it to me. He thought the resemblance was quite amusing." She smiled brightly. "Now, who needs more tea?"

Jonathan returned with a glass of water for Joe. Anne excused herself without giving a reason—it was time to look in on the babies, but she didn't say this.

After Anne left, David turned to Jonathan. "Did you tell your wife about Joe?"

"No. I really haven't had a chance," Jonathan said. "I keep thinking I'll wake up any moment and find myself back *there*."

"You won't," Sam said. "This is reality."

Jonathan looked at his friends. "I didn't get a chance to tell you two, but I'm the proud father of twins."

David sputtered on the tea he was sipping. Sam nearly dropped his sandwich.

"But that's marvellous news!" Sam exclaimed.

"Mazel tov, my friend," David added.

"They were born while I was . . . away. I didn't even know Anne was pregnant."

David said: "This calls for cigars. Have you got any?"

Jonathan went to a cabinet, and pulled out a humidor. The three men sat smoking in happy silence. Joe watched them calmly. Chompsworth pricked up her ears, growled, and both the dog and Joe alerted on the sound of the front door opening and closing. A moment later, Anne returned.

David explained. "We want to congratulate you and your husband on the new members of your family, Mrs. Drake. Dr. Berg and I had no idea until a moment ago, otherwise we would've offered our congratulations sooner."

"It really is wonderful news," Sam added. "Children are a blessing."

"Well, thank you both very much," Anne said. "I'm afraid it was a bigger shock to my husband than it was to me."

"Yes, that is true," Jonathan said, "but I am happier than you can imagine." He beamed at his wife. "Why don't you bring Lily and Jack in here so David and Sam can meet them."

"They're out at the moment. The nanny likes to take them for a walk at this hour."

"But the gas lamps are already lit," Sam said. "Isn't it too dark to be out?"

Anne said: "The fresh air will do them good, no matter the weather. Even rain doesn't deter Minerva from walking them twice a day. She is quite diligent about that. Of course, the pram is covered and the babies are bundled up nicely."

The men chatted about exercise regimens, and which ones were currently touted as being the most healthful. Some minutes later, Anne heard the front door opening and then closing. She said: "I think the nanny is back with Jack and Lily now. I'll bring them in."

Anne left the room. A moment later, Anne appeared, pushing the pram into the room.

"And here are our darlings," Anne announced proudly.

Sam said: "I would like to hold the babies, if that's okay with you, Mrs. Drake."

"Both at once?" Anne asked, surprised at his request.

"Why not?"

Sam settled himself at the corner of the sofa, and Anne nestled the babies in his arms. He happily gazed down into the faces of Lily and Jack.

"Do you have children, Dr. Berg?" Anne asked.

"Yes, I have a daughter. Her name is Deborah, and she is married to a printer. They live in Philadelphia with their three children. My granddaughter Rebecca is ten, my grandson Daniel is eight, and the baby, Eli, just turned two. I see them about every other year, and I miss them all terribly. But we write letters back and forth. My older grandchildren are excellent letter-writers."

"I knew from the moment you spoke you were American," Anne said. Her mood had improved now that her children were with her. She turned to David. "And what about you, Mr. Lowe? Do you have children?"

"No, unfortunately, I do not, Mrs. Drake. I'm not even married. And please don't tell me about your friend or cousin that I should meet. I've just been badgered by my dear old aunt to come back to Budapest to consider a seamstress they want to foist on me."

"Oh, you mean Lotte," Jonathan chuckled.

Anne turned to her husband in surprise. "You know her?"

"I met her at the same time I met Mr. Lowe. I'll tell you all about it later."

Anne again offered the platter of sandwiches and scones to David and Sam, but they both declined. She walked up to Joe and offered the platter. "Would you like something?"

Instead of selecting one or two items, Joe took the platter, placed it on his lap, and began eating straight from it, making sure to share with Chompsworth, who sat next to him, watching his every move.

Anne returned to her spot with a perplexed expression. Jonathan knew she was shocked by Joe's behaviour.

"Tell me about him," Anne prompted, referring to Joe.

"There isn't much to tell," Jonathan ventured. "He is from Prague . . ."

"But he understands English," Sam cut in.

"Very well, in fact," David added.

"And what is he, exactly?" Anne asked.

Each man waited for the other to explain. Anne tapped her fingers on the arm of the chair, waiting for an answer.

"What is he?" Jonathan repeated slowly. "What do you mean, my dear?"

"I don't understand why you're all being so thick," Anne said, looking from one man to the next. "Is he a coachman? A footman? A valet? Whose man is he? Or is he not a servant at all? He certainly doesn't have the manners of even the commonest footman."

"Oh, he's a servant all right," David said. "A very particular kind of servant, in fact. He is a guardian," David ventured, "or if you will, a type of security guard."

Anne said: "Our house, such as it is, cannot accommodate such arrangements." She made it sound as if they already had a full staff, and could take on no more domestic help. Jonathan knew this was far from the case, but it would have been unseemly to press the point in front of guests.

Anne drew herself up a little higher. "Forgive me for being so direct, Mr. Lowe, but here in London, servants don't have tea with those whom they serve. Nor do they take the whole platter and eat from it as if it is their own personal plate. He ought to have been downstairs from the start. This sort of mingling isn't done in our country, although it may be done in yours."

"He's my man, darling," Jonathan said gently. "We can make space for him. He doesn't have any worldly possessions."

"That's curious. Is he a religious ascetic?" Anne asked.

David answered. "That's an interesting question. In a sense, he is."

"What church will he want to go to on Sundays?"

"Church will not be one of his requirements."

"He's not Christian?"

"No."

"What is he, then?"

"I guess he's Jewish," David said. "As am I, and Dr. Berg. And Jonathan, for that matter."

Anne retorted: "Jonathan's *grandfather* was Jewish. *We* are Church of England. Did he not mention that to you?"

"Perhaps he did," David said amiably. "My error. Please forgive me."

Jack started to whimper and chew at his fist. Anne took him from Dr. Berg's arms, and placed him back in the pram.

"He is always ready to eat," Anne said. "In fact, I'm sure Lily also wants feeding." She placed Lily back in the pram. Then she rang for Minerva.

Minerva was at the door right away. She opened it without knocking or waiting for a summons. She was a striking woman in a black dress, with black hair and extremely pale skin. As soon as she stepped into the room, her eyes went to Joe and the dog. Joe stood, and held tight on Chompsworth's lead. The dog lunged and began barking wildly, straining at the lead. The babies started to cry. Minerva drew back her lips and hissed at Joe and the dog.

"Minerva!" Anne shouted over the racket. "Take these children to the nursery and feed them!"

Minerva's face transformed into that of a dutiful servant. She backed out of the room, wheeling the pram as she went, and never took her eyes off Joe or the dog. Anne followed her out, and shut the door. The dog immediately settled down. Joe remained standing, his eyes on the door, until Jonathan asked him to be seated.

"What the devil was that all about?" Jonathan demanded.

David went over to Joe.

"Do you like her?" he asked the golem quietly in Hebrew.

Joe shook his head no.

"Is she bad?"

The golem nodded yes.

David returned to his seat and told Jonathan what Joe had just answered.

Jonathan rolled his eyes. "This is absurd. How on earth can he tell in such a short time?"

David said: "Joe is a supernatural creature. He can sense these things. And the dog senses something, too."

"There is no doubt that they took an immediate dislike to each other," Sam observed. "Although don't you think it is an overstatement to believe that Joe's opinions about her character are accurate? After all, he has never seen her before."

"I'd wager that Joe is correct," David said firmly.

Jonathan rubbed his face. "This is going to be a brilliant situation to negotiate with my wife. Just brilliant."

CHAPTER NINETEEN

The next evening, Jonathan and Anne walked up the steps to the front door of his parents' house, which overlooked Hyde Park. Jonathan's hair and beard had been trimmed. He wore a top-hat and an evening overcoat. He was pleased to have access to his own clothes after having had "sartorial limitations" (as he wryly called it) during his time in Eastern Europe. He suddenly pined for the top hat that had dropped into the ravine when he was fleeing the baron's dogs. He made a mental note to buy another one exactly like it.

Anne looked lovely, but she hardly spoke to, much less glanced at, her husband. The tension between them was palpable. She was furious at Jonathan. They had not agreed on how to resolve the situation between Joe and Minerva. Anne had wanted to send Joe and the dog back with David and Sam. Jonathan had insisted that Joe be allowed to stay at their house. The compromise was to keep Joe and Minerva under the same roof, but as far apart as possible. Minerva was to stay upstairs in the nursery, and use the front door to go outside. Joe was to stay downstairs with the dog, in the scullery maid's bedroom off the kitchen, and use the door to the kitchen garden to go outside.

The scullery maid's bedroom had been dusty and full of cobwebs because there had been no live-in scullery maid since before Jonathan had left. Anne had reluctantly cleaned it and put fresh sheets on the old bed. The mattress could've used airing—in fact, it should have been replaced, it was so old and lumpy.

Anne had seen this as an opportunity to have her way, and went back upstairs to have a word with her husband. "The bed in the scullery maid's room will hardly be comfortable for a man of Joe's size. He won't want to sleep in it. And we won't be able to get a replacement for at least a few days. Perhaps he should find lodgings elsewhere."

"He's accustomed to far more primitive sleeping conditions," Jonathan had retorted drily, remembering how the golem had been interred for centuries in the dusty, cobwebbed garret of the Altneushul, amid a rubbish pile of manuscripts and tattered cloth. He hadn't mentioned any of this to his wife, though.

Jonathan still believed that Joe had mis-read Minerva. Even a golem could not possibly know someone's heart in such a short time. But Jonathan had to admit that there was something about Minerva he did not like. He couldn't put his finger on it. It wasn't that she was foreign (Jonathan never did ask where she came from). There was a little too much of the vulgar music hall about her. Her dress, although a respectable colour, had a theatrical flair about it that was not appropriate for a woman of her station. He couldn't quite identify what was too theatrical. The black-and-red beads sewn around the neckline? The strange bauble she wore around her neck? The too-short hemline, which actually wasn't improper? Maybe that was Joe's problem with her—the golem was reacting as a creature from a previous time and place would react to a modern woman in a modern city. But Rabbi Loew had said that the golem had no libido, so why should he react to a woman's dress any differently than a man's? Jonathan could find no good answer.

All this went through Jonathan's mind as they stood at the threshold of his parents' house. His thoughts were interrupted when the butler opened the door.

"Good evening, Peters," Jonathan said.

"Good evening, sir. Good evening, madam."

Jonathan asked: "Have my parents started serving cocktails yet?"

"Not yet, sir. His lordship has taken a telephone call, and I have not yet seen her ladyship."

"Where is my sister?"

"In the library, sir. Shall I announce?"

"No need. We'll find our way just fine."

The butler took their hats and coats. Then he retreated.

Anne said: "I'm sure you and Sarah can get along without me for a few minutes. I want to see your mother's orchids. I'll make my way to the greenhouse."

"Are you sure? You needn't absent yourself on my account," Jonathan said.

"I am sure. I'll join you both in a little while."

Anne was relieved to have some time to herself, away from the constant demands of being a mother with barely any staff to help her keep a house and children. She was also relieved to be away from her husband, who was now a stranger to her. Since he'd been home, he had refused to talk about what had happened to him. She consoled herself with the thought that it had only been less than forty-eight hours that he'd appeared on the doorstep, wearing strange clothing that looked out-of-date and a bit shabby. One could hardly expect a man as dignified as Jonathan to begin pouring out the whole account of his adventures in such a short time, even to his own wife. At this realization, her step was lighter, and she found herself in an optimistic mood.

As she made her way to the greenhouse, she noted the elegant Georgian décor of her in-laws' house. Each room was done up in a different colour, ranging from shades of pastel yellow, to light green, to powder blue. Oil paintings, watercolours, tapestries, and marble statuary adorned every wall and every niche. The elaborate mouldings around the doorways and wall panels, painted a glossy white, gave the house an airy, Neoclassical feel. Anne was determined, now that her husband was alive and back home, to have her own house as well-appointed as this one. She suddenly felt more certain than ever in the correctness of her decision to stay in her own home, despite the repeated invitations to have moved into this grand house when they thought Jonathan dead. More than ever, she wanted to be the mistress of her own house, not dependent on her in-laws. The fact that she had maintained her independence through the darkest days spoke well of her. She was proud of herself, and she let her thoughts wander to someone else who was also very proud of her.

As she seated herself on an elaborately-carved stone bench in the greenhouse, and ran her finger across the velvety petal of a white orchid, she began planning how she could dedicate the bay window of the front parlour in her own house to the hobby of raising orchids. She herself would choose the more exotic colours: magenta, purple, and yellow-maroon tiger-striped varieties. The thought raised her spirits, and kept her in a pleasant reverie.

Jonathan paused at the massive oak door of the library, and adjusted his collar to be sure it fully covered the bandages on his neck. He opened the door quietly. A fire was blazing, and his sister Sarah was standing in front of it, feeding sheets of paper into the crackling flames. The fire glinted off her rich red hair and her dark teal dress.

Jonathan said: "Hello, Chippers."

It was a nickname he had called her since she was a small girl. Her hair used to have the russet hue of chipmunk fur. But now her tresses had deepened to a fiery copper, and they cascaded down to her waist.

Sarah turned, and let go of the sheet of paper she was holding. It drifted to the floor. She ran to her brother, and put her arms around him.

"Ozzie! Oh, Ozzie!" She buried her face in his lapel. She had called him Ozzie since she was three. At the time, she thought Jonathan resembled their cat Ozymandias, because both the cat and the boy had black hair and hazel eyes. It was only natural, to her three-year old mind, that her brother should have the same name as the cat.

She took a step back and appraised her brother, hiding her surprise that he had grown a beard, and that he looked thin and gaunt.

Jonathan noted how she had changed, too. The last time he'd seen her, her cheeks had been as round and puffy as a chipmunk's, but now her face had thinned out and matured into an elegant profile. There was a track of a tear down her smooth cheek.

"Ah, you've been crying, my poor Chippers."

"Don't bother about me. Have you seen Maman yet?"

"No, I've just arrived. How is she?"

"Much better now that she knows you're home safe. Oh, Ozzie, I don't even have a birthday present for you. Or a Christmas present. We never expected—" She stopped herself.

Jonathan knew she was going to say "We never expected to see you again." Christmas and his birthday had passed, and he hadn't noticed. "Don't worry, Chippers. I don't need presents. Being home is enough. How is Michael, by the way?"

Michael was their older brother.

"He's on holiday in Lucerne right now, then he plans to go back to

Berlin." Her voice was flat.

"Is that good?"

She sighed. "Yes and no. Maman and Papa have managed to pay off many of his debts. There are some influential people who would make Michael's life difficult if he came back here to London. He burned some bridges. I'll tell you about it all later." She rung her hands. "Oh, Ozzie, we were all so worried. What happened to you? I know you were sick, but why did you stay away so long? Aren't you glad to be home now? Don't you think Jack and Lily are the most adorable little bunnies in the world? Is Anne ecstatic to see you? Tell me all about your trip, and don't leave out a thing."

"Let's not get into all that now, Chippers. I'm sure Mother and Father will be down any second."

"Oh, I hope not this second," Sarah said, picking up the paper she had dropped. She threw it into the fire.

Jonathan stood next to her and watched it curl into flames. "Poems or love letters?" he asked.

"Both," she said sadly. "His name was Roderick Hadley-Baldwin, son of the prominent historian. He thought that by penning some verse, he'd win me over. But the verse was dreadful—he'd never written poetry before—and worst of all, he was an arrogant boor, so naturally he thought he was the next Shelley. I've had to consign his letters to the flames."

"Is that why you were crying?" Jonathan asked softly.

"Yes," she said in a whisper. "I always cry. You know that."

"Why, Chippers?" Jonathan said in a quiet voice. "I've never understood why."

"I mourn the lost opportunity, the children we will never have together, the life that could have been. Every time I burn a love letter, I feel as if I eradicate a world of possibilities in the flames."

Jonathan studied his sister's tear-streaked face. "You know, Chippers, a lot of women would gloat over the stack of love letters they've collected and suitors they've rejected. They'd show them off to their friends as trophies. You destroy all evidence and then you never talk about them. That's good."

She gazed mournfully at the flames. "Well, I don't enjoy putting a needle through a man's heart, like a lepidopterist pinning up a live butterfly. It's too cruel."

"You're right. There's too much cruelty in this world already without making sport of some poor chap."

His sister heard the break in his voice, and looked at him with alarm.

Before she could ask about it, Jonathan began talking again. "Hasn't there been anyone who's been good enough, Chippers?"

She sighed. "There was one—a nephew of the Wingates, the only son of Viscount Hesilridge. He turned out to be a philanderer. Fortunately, I discovered that before he reached the proposal stage. But it was heart-breaking, even so."

Jonathan could tell she didn't want to talk about it. He pointed to the riding boots on Sarah's feet. "Does mother still chastise you for wearing those boots instead of 'proper slippers as befits a lady'?"

"Yes," Sarah laughed. "And I must remember to pin up my hair before the guests arrive. Maman constantly reminds me that wearing it loose is fine for a young girl, but now that I am a grown woman, I must wear it pinned up 'as befits a lady.'"

They both laughed at Sarah's impersonation of their mother uttering that phrase. The door opened, and Sarah and Jonathan turned to see their mother and father enter the room.

"My dear, sweet Jonathan," Hannah Drake said in a voice choked with tears. The green of her dress contrasted elegantly with her auburn hair, which was pinned up elaborately. She clasped her son, then released him, holding him at arm's length. Tears glistened in her eyes. She gazed at him as if she could not believe he was really standing before her.

Edward Drake shook his son's hand, and then clasped him in an awkward embrace. "Welcome home, my dear boy. We've missed you terribly. Just terribly." His father's voice broke on the last word.

"We hope your illness wasn't as bad as it sounded, although we were told you were in excellent hands," Hannah said, glancing at her husband.

"Yes, well," Edward said, recovering his composure, "Jonathan can catch us up on all that later. Right now, let's have a drink. Our guests will be arriving at seven-fifteen sharp, and we all want to be relaxed and in a festive mood by the time they get here."

Hannah mixed the gin pahits, Sarah helped her to distribute them. By this time, Anne had joined them. She sat quietly, listening to the conversation.

Jonathan sipped his drink slowly, while his father quaffed his way through two, talking about the latest political news and intrigues in Parliament. Jonathan could see that in the months he'd been gone, time had etched itself into his father's face with a vengeance. And his father had lost a great deal of weight. His impeccable evening jacket and trousers were too loose on him. Grief did that to a father.

As his father talked, a hazy vision crossed Jonathan's mind, but he couldn't bring it into focus. He found himself asking: "And Mr. Churchill. How is he doing?"

Hannah cut in. "Jenny's son Winston? Oh, he's just married Clementine Ogilvy Hozier, the daughter of Sir Henry Hozier. The wedding was this past September."

"He got quite the sartorial rebuke in the papers," Edward chuckled. "They said his morning coat made him look like a glorified coachman because it was too long and heavy to be a morning coat, but too short and skimpy as a frock. We'll see if he gets a better tailor."

"Do you think I could meet with him sometime?" Jonathan asked. "Could you arrange it, Father?"

Jonathan could not remember exactly why he wanted to meet with Churchill. Perhaps to tell him about the baron's rantings about a new world order? But then, why would Churchill care about any of that? The baron was another foreign eccentric, secluded in his Belgravia mansion, unknown to the people in this city who really mattered. Even so, Jonathan tried to remember what message he was supposed to convey. Perhaps when he saw Churchill it would jostle his memory.

"Meet with Churchill? Whatever for?" Edward knitted his brows, puzzled.

"I thought he might be interested in hearing about things in Eastern Europe. You know how he loves to keep abreast of developments abroad."

"Yes," Hannah chimed in, "and he loves to write such tales, too. His book, *African Journey*, was just published. I hear it's quite the thing to read now."

"He can certainly write," Sarah said. "I had read *Ian Hamilton's March*, and thought the prose quite good."

Anne said: "I had no idea you were fond of Churchill, Jonathan. I thought you considered him callow and self-promoting."

"I still do," Jonathan said. "But I'd like to talk with him even so."

"Mr. Churchill is a difficult man to see," Edward said. "Always on the go."

"Surely you can arrange it, Father."

"I'll see what I can do."

The butler opened the door and announced: "Lord and Lady Stanton Kirkbridge Trask."

"They're far too early, as usual," Sarah murmured.

"Stanley! Hilda!" Edward exclaimed when his guests walked through the door. "Welcome! Come share in our joy that our dear Jonathan is home."

"What a delightful surprise to see you, dear Jonathan," Hilda Trask said. She was an older woman with white hair and a magnificent sapphire necklace that glittered against her lace neckline.

Stanton Trask, a short, round man with hair the same shade of white as his wife's, shook Jonathan's hand. "A pleasure to see you again, Jonathan. We were so pleased to hear the good news of your safe return. Do tell us of your adventures."

"Let me recount it when we're all seated," Jonathan replied diplomatically.

"Yes, we do want all the guests to hear what he has to say," Anne added proudly, taking her husband's arm.

As the clock reached seven-fifteen, the butler announced three more couples: The Right Honourable Lord Advocate Nelson Borthwick and Lady Borthwick, the Right Reverend Bishop of Southwark Lester Fortnum and Madam Fortnum, and His Excellency the Governor of British Columbia Charles Boothby and Mrs. Boothby. The guests excitedly crowded around Jonathan and Anne. Jonathan repeated his promise to speak of it at the dinner table. Anne was animated as she recounted her happiness and relief that her husband was home.

The butler handed an envelope to Edward. Edward opened it, scanned the note, and whispered something to Hannah. Then, after a signal from Hannah, the butler announced that dinner was served. They all made their way to the dining room, in the proper order of precedence.

Jonathan's father sat at the head of the table, and his mother at the opposite end. Jonathan was seated to the right of his mother, as the male guest of honour. Anne was at Edward's right as the female guest of honour, and Sarah to his left. The chair to the left of his mother was empty.

Edward said: "One of our guests will be late. Let us begin, shall we?"

Before the first course was served, Jonathan found himself the centre of attention as all the guests eagerly implored him recount what had happened.

Jonathan gave a brief synopsis, and left out many details. He recounted how he'd been gravely ill, unable to leave, and in a delirium for most of the time. When he was strong enough, he found his way home. If any of his guests noticed gaps or inconsistencies in his account, they were too well-bred to mention it. They were effusive in their enthusiasm for Jonathan's return. Jonathan remembered how he'd dreamed of this scene during the dark days of his imprisonment, and now here he was. He took a drink of his wine, and savoured the attention and the joy he felt. His transition back into London society was going to be smooth. It would be as if he'd never left.

Halfway through the fifth course, the butler opened the dining room door and announced: "The Right Honourable Baron Zoltan Vladimir Georg Tovis von Klausenberg."

Edward said: "Very good. Our missing guest is here."

Jonathan sat in his chair, too stunned to move. Sarah, who sat on the opposite side of the table from her brother, was the only one who noticed the look of utter disbelief on Jonathan's face. The other guests were too distracted by the newcomer to notice.

Jonathan watched the baron stride into the room like an actor taking centre stage. He sauntered over to the place setting next to his mother, directly across from Jonathan. This could not be the same man he'd met in the Carpathian Mountains. That man had been a bloated, unkempt recluse who dressed in ghastly outfits. Jonathan vividly recalled the garish robe embroidered with dragons and swords, the knee-high socks and the slippers that came to a point. The man across from Jonathan was every inch a man of class and distinction. His aristocratic face was clean-shaven His shoulder-length grey hair was combed back and caught in a black velvet ribbon, giving him a charmingly eighteenth-century air that was also strangely modern and fitting. He had slimmed down and was impeccably dressed. Jonathan noticed that his eyes were the same mismatched blue-and-amber as he remembered.

Jonathan's parents greeted the baron effusively, as did the other guests. Anne caught the glance that the baron cast her way—full of an intimacy and recognition that nobody else noticed. She recalled the extraordinary evenings at his salon gatherings. Her attendance was a secret that was safe. She felt a sense of superiority toward everyone there. She was the one the baron had invited to his house, to mingle with fascinating, unconventional guests that these conventional people had no idea even existed. Anne's access to such a smart set allowed her to feel that, contrary to not being on their level, she was in fact more advanced, only they didn't realise it.

"I've just seen *Rienzi*," the baron said in a resonant voice as he took his seat. "That damned opera took longer than it should have."

The women tittered at his language, but not Sarah, nor Hannah. Sarah's face was grave. Hannah's face displayed the frozen smile that was her way of masking her true feelings of disapproval.

The baron continued: "My appetite is excellent, dear Lady Drake, so do not let your servants hesitate to bring me the earlier courses."

Finally, the baron's eyes rested on Jonathan. "Ah, Mr. Drake. Returned home safe and sound, I see. I was so relieved to hear that your journey back to London was … complete."

Jonathan was silent. He still could not believe the baron's transformation.

The baron turned his attention to the rest of the guests, and launched into a story with confidence that went beyond aristocratic arrogance.

"No doubt Mr. Drake told you that I could not linger on my estate any longer to enjoy his excellent company. You see, I'd had this strong premonition—a dream really, or a vision—that I should leave for Vienna right away."

"Why Vienna?" Governor Boothby asked.

The baron held up a gloved finger. "I am getting to that. So I was in Vienna, watching sessions of the Cisleithanian parliament in a fine building located on Ringstrasse. Have you ever been?"

"We have been to Vienna certainly, but not to the parliament," Lady Trask said.

"Our time in Vienna also excluded the parliament," Bishop Fortnum added.

Sarah knew that her mother had spent time in Vienna, but Hannah remained silent.

The baron resumed his narrative. "Then I should mention that it's the largest legislature in Europe, the western entity, if you will, of the Habsburg dual monarchy. Now, a noteworthy feature about the Cisleithanian parliament is that there is no official language by which business is conducted. Delegates may address the gathering in any language they choose, including German, Russian, Czech, Croat, Polish, Italian, Serbian ..." the baron counted off the languages on his fingers. "Naturally, this makes for quite a circus, especially when a representative from an insignificant faction decides to derail the proceedings by making a long speech in his native language. He may be insulting the other delegates, or even slandering the emperor, and nobody but his fellow countrymen would be the wiser. It is quite a show!"

"It *does* sound like quite the show," Lady Trask commented.

The baron chuckled. "Oh, it was, my dear lady. You see, while I was there, I met a most fascinating young man, a spectator like me, who watched the proceedings with as keen an interest as anybody I've ever met. He was a pale, skinny youth, with dark hair. But he had the most fascinating blue eyes. There were entire universes in the depths of his gaze, and yet to the casual observer, he was a nobody, an artist who spoke low-class German. But he did have a deep appreciation for music. In fact, he confided in me that, once, after seeing Wagner's *Rienzi*, he had a vision that he would one day be entrusted with a special mission to lead his people to freedom." The baron paused. "I myself had been wishing for the same vision this evening, when I was watching *Rienzi*, but the gods of inspiration were not paying attention to me, alas. Anyway, I believe this young man *will* rule. The future lies with commoners like him."

"Commoners like him?" Bishop Fortnum echoed. "Does your lordship really believe that?"

The baron nodded. "Oh, yes. That is the future. My Austrian friend and I spent many happy hours watching that chaotic parliament, and then afterward talking at a café. We both agree that the parliamentary system is a fraud. The future lies with the masses."

"That really is a revolutionary thing to say," Lord Borthwick interjected.

"It truly is," Bishop Fortnum agreed.

"Our dear baron is full of such insights," Edward said, steering the conversation away from the dangerous reef of socialist advocacy. These guests, after all, were loyal to the crown and parliament and would never advocate a worker's revolution.

"Yes, and our dear Mr. Jonathan Drake knows my viewpoints well," the baron said, gesturing to Jonathan. "Tell me, how was your journey back home here to London? I can see why you had been eager to return. It is indeed a wonderful city. I've enjoyed living here."

Jonathan stared at him, but said nothing. He was simultaneously trying to keep his composure while recalling his first meetings with the baron, and the nightmare months in the baron's dungeon. The images flowing in his mind's eye were overwhelming—he saw Mora and Iosip and remembered the pain and paralyzing fear. He brought himself back to the present moment and struggled to stay focused and composed.

Anne, embarrassed by her husband's silence, began talking. "Naturally, we were all surprised when he showed up on our doorstep. Of course, I had received word that he was in Budapest, but I didn't know exactly when he'd be home. You were traveling from Budapest, am I right Jonathan? Or was it Prague?"

The baron's eyes flickered, then he smiled. "Budapest! And Prague! Two of my favourite cities! Do tell us about your journey, Mr. Drake."

"He had told us some of the details," Anne added, "but not all. We'd love to hear more, Jonathan," she prompted him.

Jonathan's face was stony. Anne was baffled by his silence, especially after the dashing impression he'd made on the guests at the start of dinner.

Hannah glanced at her son, and then covered the uncomfortable silence. "Well, I'm sure Jonathan will be more than willing to tell us all about it later. Jonathan was instrumental in helping the baron find his new house in Belgravia," Hannah announced to the rest of the guests. "His firm sent him to the baron's estate in Klausenberg."

"Yes, he speaks fluent German, that is why he was able to go ..."

Anne began, and then let her sentence trail off when she noticed Jonathan staring at her.

The baron said: "German is a useful language, is it not, Mr. Drake? Especially when trying to communicate with difficult servants. Especially the female ones."

Jonathan could hear the taunt in his tone.

Anne was now flustered at her own clumsiness over an exchange she didn't understand, and that had taken a bad turn. She began: "Oh, naturally, your lordship should know that I didn't mean to imply anything other than—"

"Please, madam," the baron said, holding up his gloved hands, "no need to apologize. I have a rather odd sense of humour, as Jonathan well knows."

Jonathan clenched his fists under the table. How much time would he serve in gaol if he were to attack the baron in that moment? Would his parents disown him? He looked down at his plate and deliberated. A fruit knife was just within reach.

One of the guests asked the baron about politics in the Austro-Hungarian Empire, and the baron launched into a long monologue in his resonant voice and alluring accent. Edward and Hannah smiled brightly at the baron's exuberance, while the other guests listened, enthralled. Even Anne was taken with him, although she frequently stole nervous glances at her husband to see how he was reacting. Sarah listened politely, but to those who knew her, it was obvious she would rather be somewhere else. She had always hated these dinner gatherings.

Lord Borthwick piped up. "The baron is as articulate as Mr. Churchill. The two men should meet. I can arrange it."

At the mention of Churchill's name, the baron's face darkened. "One of these days, each of you here will realise just what a danger to world peace Mr. Churchill is," the baron said in a portentous tone.

"Has your lordship met him?" Edward asked.

"There is no need for that," the baron said. "His record speaks for itself. One day, England will regret his having been born to that American tart. When the blood of millions is spilled because of his warmongering, then perhaps each of you will see the truth of what I'm telling you. If he is stopped before it gets to that point, consider yourselves lucky."

Jonathan was again nagged by an urgency to speak with Churchill. He watched the baron closely to see if the last comment contained a more sinister message. He couldn't detect one, but then again, the baron was too clever to make an outright threat.

"We all have our disagreements with him, naturally," Edward said mildly. "I don't think Churchill is as bad as all that. He is certainly a bombastic arriviste, but that hardly amounts to the gravity you imply."

The baron stared at Edward with a stern gaze. "With respect, your lordship is naïve—like most English who do not understand the future. There are unseen forces, changes that will transform this world …" He smiled. "Ah, but let's not quibble over mere politics. The ladies are already bored."

Jonathan tensed. How dare the baron insult his father by calling him naïve. He said acidly: "Does the Baron von Klausenberg imply that Churchill deserves to die at the hands of people now in London who want to kill him?" Jonathan did not know where that idea came from, but it seemed the truthful thing to say.

The guests around the table gasped in amazement at Jonathan's bold comment.

The baron stared at him coldly. "What an extraordinary claim, Mr. Drake. Are you connecting me to something nefarious?"

"Would the accusation be beyond the pale?" Jonathan snapped. "After all, I've not just heard rumours, I've witnessed it. The coachman who brought me to your estate was whipped because he and I had helped a peasant with an overturned cart. I myself was not treated well by your servants. The cruelty of the Klausenberg dynasty is legendary in that region."

The baron laughed as if Jonathan had told a great joke. "Really. This is extraordinary. Mr. Drake visits my country, and comes away with such false impressions, as if we're all barbarians." He sighed. "But his comments are understandable for a man who suffers as he does. He *had* been gravely ill, and I *had* received word that he had died. But here is Mr. Drake now, as sound in *body* as can be." He smiled brightly. "Still, such prolonged illness can have an effect on one's *mental* capacity."

Jonathan said in a dead-calm voice: "Your servants poisoned me and tortured me. They planned to kill me."

The baron was unruffled. "My female servant was found dead, in a pool of her own blood, at the time you left my estate. What a coincidence."

Edward said: "What are you accusing my son of, exactly?"

"Nothing, my dear Lord Drake. I am simply noting facts." The baron turned to Jonathan, and his expression was one of pity. "I am so sorry for you. People with your condition are not without hope. In England, there must be some excellent institutions ..."

He let his sentence trail off, and took a sip of wine, as if he were the master of the house ending a trivial discussion with an inferior. He ignored the gasps of shock at the table as his words sunk in.

Edward stood up. "This is outrageous. You are accusing my son of—"

"I am accusing him of nothing," the baron interrupted calmly, without deigning to look at Edward. "Please accept my apologies if I have overstepped some unwritten boundary."

Edward deliberated for a few seconds, then sat down again and took a gulp of wine, greatly upset but trying to control himself. "Apology accepted. I hope that your lordship will understand that the previous news of my son's death has been a great strain on us all."

"Naturally," the baron replied.

Anne's face was pale with horror, Hannah's smile was frozen into a half-grimace, and Sarah watched in amazement as if she were at a stage play. The rest of the guests looked on—some upset, some amused, others offended that the baron had just insulted the son of the host and hostess by accusing him of insanity and murder.

Jonathan threw his napkin on his plate and stood up. "Mother, Father, I am sorry but I cannot be in the presence of this ... this ... blackguard."

Murmurs went around the table, but the baron was composed. He raised his glass. "Have a good evening, Mr. Drake," he said. "I'll drink to your convalescence." He took a healthy quaff. "Marvellous wine, as usual. You have excellent taste, Lady Drake."

CHAPTER TWENTY

When Jonathan arrived at his own house on Cadogan Square, an intuition stopped him from going through the front door. He went around to the back, and quietly slipped into the servants' entrance near the kitchen.

Joe was sitting at the table where the servants took their meals. Chompsworth was curled up at his feet. She wagged her tail at Jonathan.

"Are the babies upstairs with Minerva?" Jonathan asked.

Joe nodded.

"Have you even seen her?"

Joe shook his head no. He pointed to the table to indicate he'd stayed there the whole time.

Well, that was a relief. At least Joe had obeyed Jonathan's orders to stay away from Minerva. Perhaps they could both come to an understanding and keep their positions at the house. He and Anne wouldn't have to argue about it anymore.

He left his overcoat on a chair, and headed upstairs. He climbed the stairs stealthily to the top floor, where the nursery was located. The door to the nursery was shut tight, but he could hear a baby crying just beyond the door, and Minerva's voice. He couldn't make out what she was saying, but the tone of her voice was spiteful.

He went to an adjacent room—the room where Minerva slept—which connected through to the nursery. The room was surprisingly bare considering that the nanny lived there. The bed looked as if it hadn't been slept in. There were no personal items on the night side tables nor on the dresser. The air smelled sickly sweet.

The door to the nursery was ajar. Jonathan watched her. Minerva's back was turned to him, and she was struggling with a wiggling baby on the changing table.

"If you don't move, it won't hurt as much," she cooed maliciously.

The baby's cries intensified, and soon the other baby, hearing the distress, also began to cry. Jonathan could see the little legs flailing.

"Almost done," she said. "There. You've made your donation for the day. The master will be so pleased. Now it's your sister's turn." She held up a vial of blood, took a sip, capped it with a cork, and deposited it into her handbag.

It took Jonathan a few seconds to process what he was seeing. He flung the door open and strode into the room. She turned, surprised to see him. He grabbed her by the neck and shoved her against the wall. The babies were crying hysterically.

"Tell me what you were doing," he said in a voice that was deadly calm.

Her eyes were defiant and her reply was ready. "The doctor ordered it. He said it would help them. They've been very colicky."

"What is the doctor's name?"

"I don't remember. But I was under orders. Ask the mistress. She'll tell you."

"You're lying. You drank the blood of my baby," Jonathan said. "Why?"

She would not answer. Jonathan tightened his grip. "Why?" he repeated.

She choked for breath and scratched his hands with her long nails.

The memories of the tortures at the hands of Mora came flooding back to him, and his rage overwhelmed him. Jonathan intended to squeeze the life out of her so that she was no longer a threat. The cries of his children rang in his ears, and he didn't realise Joe was next to him.

The golem's powerful hands broke Jonathan's grip, and restrained him. Minerva doubled over, and her breath came in short, choking gasps. Then she straightened up, rubbed her neck, and glared at Joe and at Jonathan.

Jonathan said: "Get out of my house. If I ever see you again, I will kill you."

She gathered her belongings, casting insolent glances at Jonathan and Joe.

"See her to the front door," Jonathan ordered the golem.

As Minerva crossed the threshold, she turned and said with a sneer: "There are plenty of rumours that you've gone insane. You murdered the baron's maid. Now they'll find out you've tried to kill me. And ravish me. I'll tell them that."

Jonathan moved to accost her again, but Joe blocked him.

"Tell the authorities your lies," Jonathan said. "They'll find out what you did to my children. My father is a judge. You'll hang for your crimes."

Hatred flashed in her eyes. She quickly descended the stairs. Jonathan and Joe followed her, and watched her as she fled out of the front door into the dark, freezing night. The golem shut the door and locked it.

Jonathan said to him in a low voice: "I want you to follow her. Do not let her see you or hear you."

Joe didn't bother with an overcoat. He disappeared out the front door quickly and silently. Chompsworth stayed behind, barking in frustration at the front door that she couldn't go with Joe.

Jonathan returned to the nursery with the dog. Both babies were still crying hysterically. Jonathan picked them up, and tried to soothe them. He settled into the nearby rocking chair and began rocking them. He sang lullabies. After a long while, both babies fell asleep. He gently put them both in the cradle, and carried the cradle downstairs to the back parlour. The fire was embers, and the room was dark. He lit a lamp and rekindled the fire in the hearth. He poured himself a glass of brandy from a decanter in the cabinet, sat in his chair near his children, and tried to think about what to do next.

He wanted to talk to David and Sam, but he could do nothing until Joe returned. Besides, the hour was late. After a while, Joe slipped into the room and stood before him, the dog at his side.

"Did you follow her?"

Joe nodded.

"Did she go to a house?"

A nod.

"Do you know the address?"

Joe held up the correct number of fingers to indicate the digits of the house number.

Jonathan recognised it immediately as the baron's house in Belgravia. Jonathan described the house and the neighbourhood, and Joe nodded that Jonathan was correct. The golem mimed Minerva opening a door with a key and creeping into the house. From out of his pocket, Joe took out two letters. By dropping them on the ground, he communicated that Minerva had dropped them on her way to the baron's house. Both were addressed to Anne here at Cadogan Square—one from Anne's mother in Bristol, one from Jonathan's sister Sarah. Clearly, Minerva had been stealing the mail from Jonathan's house and bringing it to the baron's house.

Jonathan was too exhausted to decide on how to best proceed. But at that moment, he felt that he must do something to protect his household from the evil influences that had already infiltrated it. He ordered the golem to keep watch on the sleeping children. Then he went upstairs, took out of a drawer the mezuzah that the char-woman Ruth had given him. Downstairs, at the front door, he nailed the mezuzah to the doorpost. He returned to the back parlour, where the children were still asleep and Joe was keeping watch. He told Joe to get some sleep, then he settled into his chair, put his feet up, and closed his eyes, his hand on the cradle where his children slept.

When Anne came home an hour later, she was prepared to upbraid Jonathan for having left his own parents' dinner party so abruptly. She had been rehearsing what she would say to him on her way home. Chompsworth was there to greet her with a wagging tail. She expected to find Jonathan in his smoking jacket and slippers, reading by the hearth. Instead, he was asleep in his chair, still in evening dress. The two babies were nearby, sleeping in the cradle. She wondered where Minerva was. Out of the corner of her eye, she saw legs protruding from behind a side table, and realised that Joe was lying on the floor, eyes closed, hands folded across his chest.

Perhaps Minerva had negotiated another evening off, with no notice. She did that from time to time. Well, now that Jonathan was home, Anne would have to take a firmer hand and insist that the nanny abide by the rules. Anne went upstairs to her dressing room.

The next morning, Anne found Jonathan awake in the back parlour where she had found him the night before with the babies. He was still in his evening clothes. Joe and the dog were not there. Jonathan didn't notice that she was nearby. He wore a prayer shawl. Wrapped around his arm and head were leather straps with a tiny box affixed to each. Anne realised he was praying like a Jew. It shocked her. She did not know who Jonathan had become. She retreated from the doorway before he knew she was there. When she came back a little later, Jonathan was holding Lily, who was fussy. Jack was in his cradle, playing with a rattle and cooing.

"Good morning. Where is Minerva?" Anne asked.

"Dismissed."

Anger flashed in her eyes. "Dismissed? Why, Jonathan? And your hands are scratched. What happened?"

"Unwrap Jack and see for yourself."

Anne took the blankets and clothes off the baby until he was only wearing a cloth nappy. His arms and legs were bruised, and there seemed to be puncture marks everywhere, including two marks on the baby's neck. She was shaken, and she dressed him quickly.

"Lily has the same injuries," Jonathan said. "I came home to find Minerva extracting blood. Did you not know about any of this? Did you not suspect?"

Anne said defensively: "Dr. Chamberlain advised that they be bled every so often to cure the colic, and given laudanum when the episodes were especially bad, but I had no idea about this …"

"Who is Dr. Chamberlain?"

"Someone recommended by … Minerva." She was going to say "the baron" but she knew Jonathan would be furious.

"Didn't you ever bathe these children? Didn't you see any of this?" Jonathan demanded.

"Minerva took care of all that. That's what nannies do, Jonathan."

"I came home and found her up in the nursery. The babies were crying. She was extracting blood from them. She drank some of it. Did

227

you hire a vampire, Anne? What in hell is wrong with her? Or with you for that matter?"

Anne held up her hands. "I ... I didn't know. I truly didn't." She began to cry. Jonathan put Lily in the crib, and went over to his wife. He put his hand on her shoulder.

"Why didn't you ask my parents for help?" he asked, trying to soften his tone. "They would've done anything to help you."

"I had Minerva. I didn't think I needed their help." Anne wiped her eyes. "I'd never do anything to intentionally hurt these children. You know that, Jonathan."

His face was expressionless. "I know. Listen, I must get dressed and go to my office. Joe is in his room downstairs. Do not disturb him unless there is an emergency."

"Are you telling me I can't ask him to fetch things for me, or do chores around the house?"

"Exactly. He is not an ordinary servant. He is not to be treated as one."

"And yet we're spending for his upkeep? This is insane, Jonathan."

"I don't have time to discuss this now." He turned in the doorway. "One more thing, Anne. I do not want the baron, or any of his friends, or any of his servants in this house, ever." He left, closing the door behind him.

CHAPTER TWENTY-ONE

Anne's annoyance turned to dismay as she looked around the room. It was in complete disarray, with baby clothing, empty bottles, books, and dirty dishes strewn about. She was angry at Jonathan for more than his outrageous and embarrassing behaviour last night. He'd been away too long. Then he had appeared without warning, looking like a bearded stranger, thinking he could now rule the household with an iron fist, insisting that she not see her friends. He understood nothing about how hard it had been for her. Was she condemned to obey only his wishes, and not her own? Or could she reclaim her own independence and insist that the household be run her way, while she mingled in smart circles with a sophisticated set of friends?

She was seized with the sudden impulse to pack up her things and take the children to Bristol, where she could live with her mother, Mrs. Prudence Hastings, in the house where she had been born. But she realised that she would miss her friends here—friends whom she had cultivated at the baron's salons. Jonathan had told her that they were forbidden from entering the house, but he had said nothing about her seeing them outside the house. Of course, she would keep all that to herself. She remembered the good times at the baron's mansion, and she was determined to have more of those exciting evenings.

Her reverie was broken by Mrs. Rafferty shuffling into the room, and she was brought back to the dreary present.

The cook cleared her throat. "M'lady, I need to know what you'll be wantin' the rest of the week, because I'll be takin' some days to visit me grandchildren, like I told ye. Today's supper will be chops. And there's a beef stew and biscuits, which might even last clear though the week end. I made a barley stew and boiled eggs for the master, since he isn't havin' any meat these days."

"Of course," Anne said, still in the trance of her memories. She went over the menu and the shopping list with the old cook, her mind still distracted.

"Minerva has been dismissed," Anne announced in a piqued tone, "so you won't need to worry about her."

Mrs. Rafferty put her calloused hands on her hips. "Well, if ye don't mind me sayin', m'lady, it's about time that doxy was gone from here. Never liked her, never trusted her. The babies weren't natural under her care."

"What do you mean they weren't natural?" Anne asked sharply.

"Well, I had five of me own. One died as a child, another is off in New York, and three are up north. Anyways, 'tain't natural for babies to be always quiet and sleepin' as yours do. And when they cry, 'tain't a strong and lusty gale, like a healthy baby. It's quiet and weak, like a pitiful wheeze. Now, I know it's normal for babies to sleep a lot, but yours sleep too much, see what I mean? And they ought to be eatin' more, but I suppose with all that sleepin', they don't have much appetite. And they don't have much strength for cryin'."

"Maybe they're just sleepy babies," Anne said, trying to assuage an uneasy feeling.

"Well, that's just me penny's-worth, m'lady. At any rate, I'll have lunch ready for ye at noon sharp. And I'll be leavin' for home at one o'clock."

Anne fretted about Mrs. Rafferty's assessment of her children's disposition. Anne would devote herself entirely to them until a new nanny came, and everything would be all right.

The babies woke up, crying and hungry, and Anne spent the next several hours tending to them, with no time to do anything else. They seemed to be crying more than usual, Anne thought, but perhaps they only seemed more demanding than usual.

By four o'clock, Anne was exhausted and frustrated that they were so colicky.

While Anne was feeding Jack, the doorbell rang. She opened the door to find her sister-in-law Sarah standing there, wrapped in a dark green cloak with a hood drawn over her head. She wore riding boots that were splattered with mud. A light, misty rain had begun to fall.

"Is he home yet?" Sarah asked, referring to Jonathan. "I want to tell him how badly he upset Maman and Papa."

"I'm expecting him any moment," Anne said. Her eye caught the mezuzah on the door frame. She pointed to it. "I don't recall seeing that before."

"Perhaps my brother put it there."

"He has been rather contrary, has he not?" Anne said drily. Then she added: "Won't you have some tea?"

Once inside the foyer, Sarah removed her heavy wool cloak. Underneath she wore a dark-blue riding habit. She unfastened the ribbon that held her hair back, and her magnificent red hair cascaded down her back. She followed Anne into the back parlour. The children were each screaming in their cradles.

Sarah picked up Lily, murmuring words of comfort, and Anne held Jack.

"Poor thing!" Sarah exclaimed, putting the baby over her shoulder and patting her back. "She's out of sorts! You'd think she'd be cooing and smiling to see me!"

"They've been this way all day," Anne said peevishly. *Well, they certainly had the strength to cry today,* Anne thought. *If only Mrs. Rafferty were here to see it.* She rocked Jack back and forth to calm him.

"Where is Minerva?" Sarah asked.

"Jonathan dismissed her last night." Anne's mouth was drawn into a tight line.

"Oh, good," Sarah said. "I never liked her anyway."

"Why didn't you tell me before?" Anne snapped.

Sarah shrugged. "I didn't think you would have listened."

"Wouldn't I?"

"Who am I to tell you how to run your house?" Sarah said humbly. "I'll be asking you for advice once I'm married, whenever that will be," she added with a sigh.

Anne was disarmed by Sarah's unpretentious honesty. She knew Sarah wanted a husband and children. Yet Sarah wasn't competitive about it, and she didn't bear Anne any grudges for having that which she herself wanted. Anne suddenly found herself envying Sarah's freedom. Sarah didn't have to deal with crying babies, and a husband who had been absent for the better part of a year, and then had returned home a stranger.

After a while, the babies settled down, but they each wanted to be held. Sarah ate a scone while holding Lily in one arm, and let the baby chew on the edge of the scone, and eat spoonfuls of the clotted cream. Anne carefully poured tea with an outstretched arm while balancing Jack on her lap, and then fed him some of the clotted cream, along with peach jam. The two women were amused by the babies as they ate the delicious treats.

Anne glanced at the clock. "Jonathan said he'd be home by half-past three, and now it's half-past four already."

"He's usually punctual," Sarah observed.

"Yes." Anne hesitated, then said: "He's forgotten his keys almost every day since he's been home. I've had to be on hand to open the door for him, because we don't have a footman." She paused. "I don't understand who he's become."

"Neither do I," Sarah agreed.

The doorbell rang.

Sarah leaped to her feet. "It must be Jonathan. He's just in time to hear my diatribe. Lily and I will answer it. Right Lily?" Sarah headed for the foyer with the baby in her arms. "We're going to say hello to your papa—" she pronounced this last word with a French accent "—and we're going to tell him what's on my mind, and you're going to coo in agreement. Understood?" Sarah opened the front door and exclaimed: "Ozzie, you're just in time—"

She stopped mid-sentence. It wasn't Jonathan.

A smile lit up the man's face, showing white, straight teeth in a perfectly-trimmed auburn beard. "Oh, hello, Lily. Or is that Jack?"

"It's Lily," Sarah said. How did he know their names?

"Well, then, won't Lily introduce me to her charming companion?"

"Who are you?" Sarah demanded. The freezing wind stirred her long hair. Lily grabbed a tress of her hair and yanked it. Sarah freed it from the baby's grasp and tossed it over her shoulder impatiently. She could hear her mother's admonition that tying up one's hair was proper for an adult lady—especially when meeting strangers. Well, too late for that now.

He was still smiling. "My name is David Lowe. I am a friend of Jonathan's. And you are?"

"I am Sarah Drake. Jonathan's sister."

"A pleasure to meet you, Miss Drake. Is Jonathan here?"

"We're expecting him any minute."

"Along with Ozzie?" David quipped.

Sarah decided she liked his easy, confident manner. "Won't you come in, Mr. Lowe? Lily will catch cold if we stand here much longer."

David touched the mezuzah, then stepped into the vestibule. He removed his hat, and tapped the raindrops off it. "Are you disappointed that I'm not Ozzie?"

"Yes." On second thought, she added: "But maybe not. I was expecting Jonathan, you know. Ozzie is my nickname for him."

"I see. And does he have a nickname for you?"

Sarah hesitated, and colour came to her cheeks. "Yes, but it's not something I would disclose to someone whom I just met a minute ago."

David held up his hands. "I would never press you for a premature disclosure, Miss Drake. When will the esteemed Ozzie be home?"

"Any moment now." Sarah heard the faint accent in his speech that she could not place. She asked: "How many languages do you speak?"

"I've lost count. Yiddish, German, Italian, and English are primary, though."

"Yiddish? You are a Jew?" Sarah asked.

"I am."

They went into the sitting room. Anne was mending a bed sheet. Jack was playing with a rattle in his cradle. A fire blazed in the hearth.

Anne put down her needlework, and was embarrassed that David could see that she needed to mend a bed sheet, instead of having a servant do it, or buying a new one, as he probably did.

"Mr. Lowe. What a surprise," Anne said coolly.

"My dear Madam Drake," David said warmly, taking her hand as she offered it, "a pleasure to see you."

Anne murmured an appropriate reply.

Sarah wondered why Anne didn't look more pleased at this visit. Mr.

Lowe seemed to be a congenial man. Perhaps Anne was too vexed at Jonathan.

Anne said: "Please have a seat, Mr. Lowe. I'm sure my sister-in-law told you that Jonathan is not here yet. May I offer you some tea?"

"Yes, please. No cream or sugar, thank you." David had removed his overcoat, and Sarah couldn't help but notice his suit. The cut and fabric were elegant and modern, but different from the usual bespoke she saw in London.

"Scones?" Anne offered.

"No, thank you," David said. "Where is Joe? And the dog?"

Anne's mouth was drawn tight. "Downstairs."

David said: "Mrs. Drake, I need to have a word with you before Jonathan arrives, because I'm not sure how he's going to react."

Sarah rose to leave the room, still holding Lily. "I'll excuse myself."

David said: "Please stay, Miss Drake. It concerns your family. I've received word that Jonathan's reputation and career is … being threatened."

Anne gasped. "By whom?"

"It's not clear, exactly. A rumour is going around that Jonathan tried to defraud some aristocrat in a real-estate transaction, and that his—that is, Jonathan's— mental health is … unstable."

Anne put her hand to her forehead. So, the exchange between the baron and Jonathan at last night's gathering had now reached other ears, and rumours were gaining momentum. It was bad news, but perhaps still manageable.

Lily had fallen asleep in Sarah's arms, and Sarah gently put her in the cradle next to Jack. Then Sarah sat near Anne, and quickly pinned her hair up. She sensed that David was observing her without directly looking at her.

He stood up, put his teacup on the chimneypiece and lit a pipe. He was clearly deliberating how to proceed. The fire crackled in the silence.

"I normally don't put much stock in rumours," he said, blowing out the match and throwing it into the flames. "But in this case, you need to be aware of what's being said and protect yourself against any damage that may come out of such slanders."

Anne's eyes were downcast. "Is it truly slander, Mr. Lowe?"

"My dear Mrs. Drake, what do you mean?"

"What I mean," she said, her voice trembling with emotion, "is that I hardly know the man who is my husband." A tear rolled down her cheek. "And last night, his behaviour at his parents' house was … outrageous." This last word contained all the bitterness and fury she was feeling. "Ask Sarah. She was there. I hardly know what's truth and what's not. I'm afraid to tell my husband that Baron von Klausenberg has been a true friend to me during the long months Jonathan was gone. But my husband won't listen to me anyway. He is determined to insult the baron at every turn, and I am truly afraid of what he'll say to me when he finds out that I don't share his opinion of the baron."

Anne started sobbing, and Sarah put a hand on her shoulder.

David said in a gentle voice: "If you don't mind my asking, what do you mean when you say your husband behaved outrageously last night?"

Anne shook her head, refusing to answer.

Sarah's green eyes flashed with anger as she met his gaze. "What she means, Mr. Lowe, is that my brother made a total ass of himself last night. I was there to watch it unfold in all its dramatic glory." She described what had happened, and then added: "My mother is upset. Even my father is irritated, and he usually has great tolerance for these things."

David's face was grave. "Miss Drake, do you have any idea why your brother might be, how shall I put it, hostile toward the baron?"

Before Sarah could answer, Anne cut in: "No. I do not. Jonathan came back a stranger. He looks different. Too thin. A beard. He used to tell me everything, but now, he barely talks to me."

David asked: "Has he told you any of what his travels were like?"

Anne shook her head. "I've tried to ask him."

David deliberated with himself. He knew it wasn't his story to tell, and it was not his place to relate details that he didn't personally witness. He smoked his pipe, thinking about what to say next.

Sarah watched him carefully, her eyes narrowed. "What do you know that you're not telling us, Mr. Lowe?"

David's eyes met hers. "Discretion, my dear Miss Drake, is an important quality in a friend, don't you think?"

"Not if that friend's reputation is being compromised."

"I can tell you what I saw first-hand." David went on to recount how he had met Jonathan in Budapest, and how the masked intruders had broken into his aunt and uncle's house while he and Jonathan had been out to send a telegram to Anne. David recounted the episode watching his friend describe having visions in the spider's web.

"That must prove his mental stability is … not quite what it should be," Anne observed unhappily.

"It's not about his mental stability," David countered. "Jonathan knew things about my uncle, and my uncle's neighbour, that he could not possibly have known in the ordinary sense."

Anne's hands fluttered up from her lap, like two impatient birds. "All this proves nothing. Nothing at all. I want to know what we need to do now, to get my husband back to normal so that he doesn't keep making scenes when … when he's in the same room with … with someone he doesn't like."

"My dear lady, I am trying to explain."

"I don't see the relevance of it all," she sniffed. "And I don't understand why he didn't come home to London as soon as he reached Budapest."

"Because from there we went to Prague."

"Two men having a lark across the continent," she snapped. "While I was here struggling to care for our children. Disgraceful. Utterly disgraceful."

"Mrs. Drake," David asked gently, "are you religious?"

"We used to go to church. And anyway, I don't see the point of your question." Her resentment against him—and especially against Jonathan—was foremost in her heart and mind.

"Why did you ask Mrs. Drake whether she is religious?" Sarah asked.

"Because if she's not, then I don't know how to make her understand what I need to tell her."

"And what do you need me to understand?" Anne asked peevishly.

He quoted: "'There are more things in heaven and earth, Horatio, than are dreamt of in your philosophy.'"

Anne gave a bitter chuckle. "Sarah is the one to appreciate that answer, not me. I'm trying to find out why my husband delayed getting back to London, and you quote Shakespeare. Forgive me if I am less than convinced."

"Did Jonathan tell you that from Budapest, we went to Prague?" David asked. "We went there because we needed to find out what your husband was experiencing. Jonathan seemed to have a sudden, unusual ability for prophecy. If you think he's been a stranger since he returned last week, I daresay you'd have been far more upset had you seen him earlier."

David could see that his words frightened Anne. He pressed on. "Do you know what happened to him in Prague? Has he told you?"

"No."

"We went to a marionette museum in one of the oldest parts of the city. Your husband was almost killed in the cellar of that museum."

Sarah looked at him in fear, and Anne covered her mouth.

"Did you call the police? Did you find the attackers?" Anne rose from her chair and paced the room.

"That was the problem, madam. The attackers weren't ... human."

"They were wild animals, then?" Sarah said in a horrified voice. "In a city? That's preposterous."

"No, they weren't physical beings as we understand them," David said. "They were ... things of evil. Forces of another realm."

Sarah nodded. Anne went to the window to look out.

Without turning around, Anne asked: "How did he almost die?"

"We found him strangled by marionette strings in one of the cellar rooms. There was an unearthly wind blowing through the cellar, far colder than the worst winter wind. We all sensed a malevolent presence—even the curator felt it, and he is hardly a superstitious man. My uncle knew then that we were dealing with something beyond the ordinary. Jonathan knew it, too. He told us so when he regained consciousness."

Anne whirled around, and there were tears in her eyes. "How do you know it's not insanity? Just sheer insanity?"

"On my part or Jonathan's?" David challenged.

"Both," Anne retorted.

"Then you're accusing four men of being insane: Your husband, me, my uncle, and the museum curator."

"So be it," she said defiantly. "Jonathan wandered into a room and got himself tangled in some strings because he was having an episode. Someone left a door open somewhere, and the cold air came in."

"I am an expert when it comes to wine and wine cellars," David countered. "Subterranean cellars do not get as cold as that cellar was. It was far colder than the night air—a physical impossibility."

"Do you really expect me to believe ghost stories?" Anne cried.

"Yes, Mrs. Drake, I do expect you to believe in ghost stories, when they're true."

"Ghosts can't hurt us," she shot back.

"Evil forces can, and that's what you need to realize."

Just then, the door to the room opened, and Jonathan strode in. "I hope I'm not interrupting anything important."

He threw his coat over the chair. He went to the cribs where his children were sleeping. He gazed lovingly on Lily and Jack, leaned over and kissed them tenderly, and straightened up. Then he went to the fire to warm his hands. He seemed to be unaware that everyone was staring at him.

"I can't decide between a glass of brandy or some hot tea," he said. "So how about both."

"I'll fetch more hot water," Sarah said, grateful for an excuse to leave Jonathan and Anne in confidence.

"I will help you," David said.

David followed Sarah to the kitchen downstairs. Joe and the dog were sitting at the table. Chompsworth wagged her tail when she saw David and Sarah, and she went up to both of them to sniff them and have a pat on the head. Joe nodded an acknowledgment to them both. Then the dog went to the door and scratched to be let out. The golem went outside with her.

David and Sarah stood side by side in the kitchen, leaning against the work table that stood between the stove and the sink. They each kept their gaze focused on the flames of the gas burner that cradled the kettle.

"So, Miss Drake, how has your opinion of me changed since I knocked on the front door a half-hour ago?"

Sarah spoke in a quiet voice. "Contrary to Anne's opinion, I don't think you're insane, Mr. Lowe, if that's what you mean."

"Thank you. But if I were insane, it would be so much better for everyone, wouldn't it? It would mean that your brother and sister-in-law have nothing to fear. My words would be the mere ravings of a madman, as inconsequential as dust."

"That is why Anne prefers to dismiss you and all you have to say."

He turned toward her, and studied her profile. "Why don't you dismiss me, Miss Drake? Is it because you agree with Hamlet that there are more things in heaven and earth?"

"Perhaps. Or perhaps I have a certain courage, like Eleanor Duchess of Gloucester in Shakespeare's *Henry the Sixth*, part two. She attended the conjurer's séance to discover what the spirit had to say about the king's fate. That took courage on her part."

"Courage aside, I do hope you will avoid such gatherings. They are not good for one's soul."

Sarah gave a short laugh. "You sound like a Christian minister warning his flock away from trafficking with the devil. Oh, but that's inaccurate. You are Jewish, after all."

"Those of us who worship God have certain enemies in common."

She tilted her head to one side, and studied him. "Yet, it is curious that you don't dismiss that such gatherings have power."

"They have power, indeed, Miss Drake. But it is the sort of power that should be avoided."

"Poetry has power as well," Sarah observed.

"It does. But one need not avoid it. Poetry, like prayer, is good for the soul."

"I believe that a person can't fully appreciate poetry without some spiritual depth." She laughed. "A strange insight, isn't it?"

David watched the flames under the kettle. "Not really. Some of the oldest, most beautiful poetry was penned by one of the wisest, most spiritual man who ever lived."

"Oh? And who might that be?"

"King Solomon, author of the Song of Songs."

"Hmm," Sarah said, tapping her fingers against her chin. "I don't recall his poetry, although we may have read it in church sometime."

"I doubt it," David said. "Most clergy find it too erotic."

"Erotic? Really? Quote a line or two."

David's voice was hypnotic:

How beautiful are your feet in sandals, O prince's daughter!
Your thighs are like jewels, the work of an artist's hands

Your navel is like a curved bowl that never lacks wine;

Your belly is like a mound of wheat, garlanded with lilies.

Your two breasts are like two harts, twins of a gazelle.

Your neck is like a tower of ivory, your eyes like the pools in Heshbon, by the gate of Bat-Rabbim;

Your nose is like the tower of Lebanon which looks toward Damascus.

Your head is like the crimson Carmel, and your hair like purple; a king is caught in its tresses.

How beautiful and how lovely are you, O love, for delights!

He paused. "Of course, the Hebrew is even more evocative."

Sarah's eyes were closed. She liked the way he pronounced the names Heshbon and Bat-Rabbim—exotic, far-away places that she knew without asking he had visited. She tried to recall a forgotten lesson. "I remember reading about the Song of Songs once. I was told that they are allegories for the relationship between Christ and the Church."

David laughed. "Why can't Christians admit that some things in the Bible are earthy and human and erotic? Not everything is a Platonic ideal."

"I suppose that would ruin things."

"Would it? I'd think it would make life more interesting."

"That's not how Christians see it," Sarah retorted.

"So I've observed. But what good does it do to deny the fact that we humans are both spiritual and animal? We can acknowledge our earthly desires while we pursue spiritual perfection." He paused. "I like the part about a king being caught in her tresses. Any man who is lucky enough to entangle his hands in the tresses of the woman he loves so deeply must feel like a king when he is with her." David kept his gaze straight ahead, but he could see in his peripheral vision that Sarah was tucking a few loose strands of her hair into her hairpin.

His intimate tone had made her heart skip, and she felt a little flustered. She tried to sound flippant so as to regain her composure. "And are you lucky enough to be such a king, Mr. Lowe?"

"I thought so, once or twice. But I am not yet married to the woman who is my bashert."

"What is bashert?"

"The beloved one for whom I am destined, God-willing."

"And why are you not married to her?"

He said slowly: "Because I don't think she quite realises that she and I are destined for each other."

"Have you told her?"

"No, I have not told her. Not yet."

Boiling water from the kettle sputtered into the flame. Sarah was both relieved and annoyed at the interruption. She grabbed a towel to lift the kettle, and poured the roiling water into the teapot. She set the pot on a tray with a teacup. Then she filled a bowl with hot barley stew from a pot on the back burner, and set it on the tray, too. She could feel David's eyes on her the whole time.

"Would you like some barley stew, Mr. Lowe? Mrs. Rafferty is an excellent cook. One would never know it contains no meat."

"No, thank you, Miss Drake. I had a very late meal this afternoon." He stood next to her. "Please let me carry that for you," he said in the same intimate tone that had made Sarah's heart skip moments before. His hand brushed hers as he took the tray. For a few seconds their gaze met, and again she was flustered. She moved toward the stairs to regain her composure.

He followed her upstairs and into the room where Jonathan and Anne were sitting. The silence between husband and wife was tense. Anne was working on her sewing, and she was obviously upset.

David set the tray down. Anne made no move to pour, so Jonathan helped himself to the tea and stew, eating silently. Sarah watched them both. Occasionally she glanced at David, and her worried green eyes darkened with questions. His gaze told her to be patient.

Finally, Anne spoke. "Jonathan, we're all concerned about your behaviour. Especially considering what happened last night." She put down her needlework and looked at him.

Sarah gushed: "Oh, Ozzie, it was a frightful scene. Why did you have to insult Father's dinner guest? Maman is all in a tizzy today, and even Papa is vexed. You know he never really gets ruffled by such things, but he did last night. Even today I had to hear them discussing it at breakfast, and it was not pleasant."

241

Jonathan concentrated on his food, scraping the bottom of his bowl with his spoon. "This is very good stew. I prefer the heartiness of barley and potatoes over that of meat."

"Jonathan," Anne said, "are you going to tell us why you insulted the baron last night?"

Jonathan put down his bowl, took a sip of tea, and said: "He deserves worse. Much worse. He got off lightly last night."

"He is a friend of our parents," Sarah said, as if that explained everything.

"He is also my friend," Anne said with a defiant note in her voice. "During the months you were gone, he helped me tremendously, including finding Minerva."

Jonathan looked at her. "And we know what kind of a woman Minerva turned out to be, don't we, Anne? Doesn't that tell you something about the baron? That he employs a woman who would do that to little babies?"

"The baron didn't know!" Anne exclaimed.

"What did Minerva do?" Sarah cried. "What happened? Oh, Ozzie, you must tell me!"

"No, Jonathan, don't tell," Anne said with a hard expression. "It should remain between us."

But Jonathan held up his hands. "My sister and my good friend David have a right to know, Anne." Jonathan turned to the others. "Minerva was extracting blood from the babies, and she drank some of it. She took vials of their blood to the baron's house."

Sarah gasped at this horrifying news, and her eyes went to the cradle where the babies slept. Anne buried her face in her hands.

David murmured: "Good God. This is even worse than I thought. We need to tell Berg."

"And tell the authorities," Jonathan added

"Tread carefully there, my friend," David said. "There is a rumour going around that you tried to defraud the Baron in a real-estate transaction, and that you attacked one of his servants. Undue attention from the authorities and newspapers is a complication you want to avoid."

Jonathan chuckled bitterly. "Defamation. That is his strategy. He thinks he is so clever. Here in London, he doesn't have the same tools he had back when I was his prisoner at his estate."

"Prisoner?" Sarah repeated.

Jonathan didn't answer.

David broke the silence. "Jonathan, you owe it to your wife, and to your sister, to tell them. If the baron is accusing you of being insane, they won't be able to counter his accusations unless they know exactly what happened to you."

Jonathan stared dully into the fire. Then he described his journey to the baron's estate, and his time there, including the horrors he had experienced.

Anne sat there silently, her lips drawn into a tight line as she nervously jabbed the needle into the fabric and pulled the thread through. She felt that if she didn't keep her hands occupied, she would bolt from the room, screaming.

When Jonathan finished, Anne stood up, and her needlework fell to the floor. "I'm sorry, but I just don't believe it. Jonathan, you must have had a fever. You must have been delirious and imagined all this."

Jonathan removed his jacket, and unbuttoned his shirt.

"What are you doing?" Anne demanded.

"Offering proof," Jonathan said. He took off his undershirt and stood before both women, naked from the waist up. The fire light flickered off his scarred torso.

Sarah put her hand to her mouth. There was a look of horror in her eyes. "Good God. What on earth happened to you, Ozzie?"

Anne looked at Sarah, and then at Jonathan. "I see nothing to be concerned about. Except those bandages around your neck. Which you had not told me about," she added pointedly.

"You can't see the scars on his chest and back?" Sarah asked in amazement.

Anne shook her head. "No, I do not see any scars."

"Just like Berg," David observed. "He can't see them, either."

Anne's eyes narrowed. She thought about how much more she liked Dr. Berg than she liked Mr. Lowe.

As Jonathan dressed, Sarah gathered her things. She was clearly upset, and hardly able to speak. With a shake of her head, she declined

David's offer to accompany her back home. She wanted to weep, and was barely able to contain herself as she made her way to the front door.

After Sarah left, Jonathan announced that he would walk David back to his lodgings, and take the dog with him. Joe would remain at the house. Anne's face was inscrutable. She attended to the babies and to the remaining household tasks.

As the two men walked through the streets of Knightsbridge, Jonathan was lost in thought. David smoked a cigarette.

Jonathan said: "I think Anne took things as well as one could expect."

"That is a relief," David agreed.

"My sister hasn't got Anne's constitution. Anne's father was a doctor in Bristol. Many of his customers were sailors and dock workers, rough fellows. My sister's upbringing has been more … sheltered."

"Oh, I think you sister is far stronger than you give her credit for," David said mildly.

"Perhaps," Jonathan said vaguely.

They walked in silence for a few minutes.

David deliberated silently, then said: "Jonathan, I should tell you something. I'm in love with Sarah, and I plan to marry her."

"My sister? The one you met for the first time today?"

"The very one."

Jonathan threw back his head and laughed. It was the first time David had heard his friend truly laugh with total joy and abandon. Chompsworth sensed the gaiety, and she jumped and put her paws on Jonathan's leg, her tail wagging. She licked his hand.

When Jonathan had caught his breath, he said: "So she's the one who has one hundred percent of what you're looking for, eh Lowe?"

"Yes, one hundred percent," David affirmed.

"Well, let's see. You've known her not more than two hours. Did you get around to proposing to her when the two of you went to fetch the tea?" Jonathan laughed again.

"We talked about poetry. I hope your sister is aware by now, on some level, that I am smitten by her. She's not exactly oblivious to the fact that she is extremely beautiful."

"Would you like her more if she were oblivious to her own beauty?"

David shook his head. "No. I do not find naïveté alluring. I prefer perceptive women—especially a woman who has an accurate sense of her own worth, and the confidence that goes with it. Your sister has that confidence, but not the contemptuous arrogance that too many beautiful women have."

Jonathan chuckled. "Yes, you are right. For years now, there have been dozens of suitors throwing themselves at her like moths to a flame. She has burned so many love letters, the ashes alone would make a small mountain."

David's face was suddenly grim. "Is she like Atalanta?"

"Atalanta?"

"She was the beautiful maiden from Greek mythology who refused to marry."

"Sarah wants to marry."

"Does she take pride in her rejection of suitors?"

"Oh, no," Jonathan said. "I've walked in sometimes when she was in the midst of destroying a love letter. Tears would run down Sarah's face as she consigned the letters to the flames. 'Consigning letters to the flames' is her phrase, not mine, by the way."

"Did she say why she was crying?"

"She said she felt bad for dashing the young man's hopes. She also mourned the future she could not have with him, the children that would not be born to the two of them. And she never treated any of her suitors cruelly. She never gloated over rejecting them, never gossiped about a single one. She refused to talk about them to anyone—much to the consternation of the gossipy sorts who pressed Sarah for details. But Sarah held her tongue and did not say a word."

"Your sister is truly extraordinary," David said.

"Listen, old chap. Don't get your hopes up about Sarah. I don't want to see your letters among the fireplace ashes."

"Oh, that won't happen," David said confidently.

"Why not?"

David took a drag on his cigarette and blew out the smoke. "Because I don't plan to woo her in writing."

CHAPTER TWENTY-TWO

Sam Berg gently examined baby Jack. Anne sat nearby, holding Lily and anxiously watching the doctor's face. She dreaded the reproach he'd heap upon her for having allowed Minerva near the babies.

Sam adjusted his spectacles, then felt the baby's head, torso, and limbs. He examined each mark on the baby's body, noting the colour and shape of every wound he found. He repeated the exam with Lily while Anne dressed Jack. Both babies were slightly fussy, but nothing like what they'd been the night before, crying for hours without consolation. Anne's eyes were ringed with dark circles because she hadn't slept much.

"Why don't you tell me about your children's medical history," Sam prompted gently, "and about their nanny."

Anne described how Minerva took care of them almost from the moment Anne's mother had left to go back to Bristol, and how easy both babies seemed to be, at least according to Minerva. She told Sam about Mrs. Rafferty's misgivings that the children slept too much and "didn't seem right."

"What do you suppose Mrs. Rafferty meant by that?" Sam asked.

Anne nervously fingered the lace on her sleeve. "She told me that the children were not energetic enough. But last night, they certainly had energy. They cried until dawn."

"Tell me about Minerva."

"Did Jonathan not tell you why he dismissed her?" Anne asked.

"I want to hear your version."

"She was a godsend. I never had to do a thing when she was around. She asked only for a few hours off here and there." Anne didn't mention that Minerva would demand time off without notice, whenever she felt like it, and Anne believed she had no choice but to agree. Anne continued: "While she was gone, the babies slept. It was as if she had given them a magic potion to make them easy on me." Anne laughed mirthlessly, as if to convince herself that she was talking rubbish. Sam's face was grave.

"And when you had to take care of them, during her time off, were they always easy?"

"Always. I hardly had to change a single nappy, or bathe them. Minerva did all that." She paused. "I realise now that was a mistake. She had told me, once, that she bled them regularly because Dr. Chamberlain had told her that if they were bled, their health would improve."

"Had you met Dr. Chamberlain?"

"No. But Minerva had him call here once or twice when I was out. She gave me a full account later, and she showed me his written instructions." Anne burst into tears. "I know my husband must think me an uncaring mother. And my in-laws must think it, too."

"Have they told you that?"

"No, but ..."

"Then don't fret, Mrs. Drake. I personally think you deserve tremendous credit for taking care of two babies while your husband was away."

She took a few moments to collect herself. The she asked: "What is your diagnosis?"

"The nanny was probably giving the babies heavy sedation. That would explain their weakness and need to sleep more than normal. Now that they're no longer receiving a sedative, they're going through a kind of withdrawal, crying a lot, probably eating more than normal—which is good—and generally not following a regular schedule."

Anne was stunned. "Why would she sedate them?"

"It made her job easier, especially because she was taking blood regularly. The babies are anaemic, and now they need extra nutrition to fortify their blood." He made notes on a sheet of paper. "Here are instructions about what to do, and what to feed them, so they regain their strength. Beef-liver purée, boiled and mixed with enough water or milk to make it the consistency of porridge, that should do the trick. I'll be back to see how they're doing."

Anne's voice was heavy with exhaustion. "I got one hour of sleep last night, and I don't know how long I can go on like this. I need a nanny to help me care for them. But she needs to be a good person."

Sam was reassuring. "Don't worry, Mrs. Drake. We will help you find someone."

Agatha MacLeod sat at the edge of her chair. Her posture was stiff.

"I had worked for Lord Burneville-West, madam, but since his youngest child is now at boarding school, I've been let go. Here is his letter of reference. It's very good, as you can see."

Anne took the letter and read it. Then she handed it to Jonathan, but he held up his hand to say that he didn't need to read it. Anne thought this was strange.

Jonathan studied Agatha. She looked to be in her early forties, with a long face, ruddy cheeks, and greying hair pinned neatly back in a bun. She wore a sober brown dress, clean and pressed. Her black shoes were sensible, and were polished. A gold cross hung around her neck. She was a sturdy, large-boned, respectable-looking woman.

Joe sat in the corner, eating cake and scones. Chompsworth sat at Joe's feet, attentively waiting for crumbs or a dollop of clotted cream to drop onto the floor. Joe gave the dog a piece of scone with cream, and let the dog lick his fingers, then he picked up a piece of cake, let the dog lick off the frosting, and he ate the remaining cake in two bites. He wiped his mouth with his sleeve.

Agatha's eyes kept straying to Joe. She wondered who he was. His manners were dreadful. No servant of any household she'd been a part of would've allowed a servant to behave like that, much less sit in on an interview while sharing cake with a dog. And the madam and sir ignored him as if he weren't there. She wondered if she should even take a position in a household such as this.

"Where are you from, Mrs. MacLeod?" Jonathan asked.

"Mingary, Scotland, sir. That would be in the district of Moidart in Lochaber."

"I see. And what brought you to London?"

"Oh, I came here as a young bride, sir. That would've been some twenty-odd years ago. My husband worked on the docks. But he's long since passed, and I've been on my own for a while now."

"Have you any children, Mrs. MacLeod?" Anne asked.

Agatha's face constricted with pain for a moment, then she regained her composure. "I had a daughter, madam, but she died of the scarlet fever when she was nine. The good Lord didn't see fit to send us any more bairns after her."

"I'm so sorry," Anne said.

"Thank you, m'lady," Agatha said quietly.

"What do we need to know about you that we haven't asked about yet?" Jonathan said.

Agatha stuck out her chin and a proud, faintly defiant light shown in her eyes. "Well, sir, every Sunday I go to church." She pronounced it "chutch." "And I also go on the Days of Obligation. I am a Catholic. I hope that doesn't count against me, sir, but if it does, well then, we'll just have to say good day right now and I'll look elsewhere."

Jonathan held up his hands. "It's not a problem for me, Mrs. MacLeod."

"Nor for me," Anne agreed.

Relief swept over Agatha's face. "Thank you, sir. It's just that some people are peculiar about Catholics, and they don't always approve of going to mass …"

"No need to explain, Mrs. MacLeod," Jonathan said.

Anne excused herself to attend to the babies.

Agatha could not contain her curiosity. She nodded toward Joe. "If you don't mind me asking, sir, is he your man?"

"Yes, he is," Jonathan said.

"What is his name?"

"Joe."

"What is he?"

"Strictly speaking, he is a golem," Jonathan said recklessly, suppressing a chuckle. He felt he could trust this woman with his very life, if necessary.

"Golm?" Agatha repeated. "Is that Welsh?"

Jonathan though this marvellously witty. "Something like that," he agreed. "Joe Golm is a good Welsh name, is it not?"

Agatha gave a nod of satisfaction. "Welsh. That explains it, then. Does he always sit in when others are being interviewed for a position?"

"Well, this is actually the first time," Jonathan admitted. "You see, Joe is an excellent judge of character."

"But he doesn't say much, does he?" Agatha observed. "Not even a 'pleased to meet you, ma'am.' I know the Welsh are not always forthcoming, and their manners can be dreadful, but even this is beyond the pale, sir."

"That's because he is a mute."

Agatha looked chastened. "Oh, I see." She addressed Joe. "I hope you didn't take any offence at my questions, Mr. Golm. It's just that I've never—well, it doesn't matter anyhow."

Joe regarded her for a few seconds, then went back to his plate of cakes.

"Would you mind waiting, Mrs. MacLeod?" Jonathan said. "I want to consult with Joe for a few minutes."

"I can help your wife," Agatha said. "I wouldn't mind seeing the bairns."

"Yes, please find your way. The nursery is up two flights of stairs."

"Thank you, sir."

After Agatha left, Jonathan sat near Joe and said in a quiet voice: "Well, is she a good person?"

Joe nodded his head.

"Do you think she'd ever want to harm the babies? Or any of us?"

He shook his head no.

"Should we hire her?"

A nod.

"Thank you, Joe. I'll need to talk to Anne before we make a final decision."

CHAPTER TWENTY-THREE

Anne was grateful for Agatha's help, but also intimidated. The Scotswoman was dignified, stern, and frugal. She didn't tolerate indecision or what she perceived as feminine ambiguity. If Anne wanted help, or wanted more time to herself, she expected Anne to be forthcoming and give clear instructions, instead of relying on hints and allusions and expecting Agatha to guess her intentions.

Agatha took excellent care of the children. Jack and Lily grew stronger and plumper. Their colour improved, and they became livelier and more active, less colicky. Sam stopped by from time to time to examine them. He was pleased with their progress.

Agatha also got on well with the cook, Mrs. Rafferty. The two of them would sit in the kitchen together while Agatha fed the babies at the table, and Mrs. Rafferty peeled potatoes or rolled out a pie crust. Sometimes Joe sat with them, Chompsworth at his feet. Joe always drank plain water and ate bread and cake, while listening to everything they said.

Mrs. Rafferty nodded toward Joe. "He's a strange one, Mrs. MacLeod. I've never seen a man so attached to a dog like he is to that one. Why, he's like a dog himself. The two of them patrol around the house, guarding this door or that. I've even arrived in the morning just to find Mr. Golm asleep on the floor with the dog curled next to him, right near the kitchen door. Other times they're asleep near the front door, or at the foot of the stairs."

"That is strange," Agatha remarked.

"And here's another thing. Ye don't like beer or whiskey, do ye Mr. Golm?" Mrs. Rafferty said, half-teasing and half in amazement.

Joe shook his head no.

"That's a good sign in a man," Agatha said. "Drink has been the undoing of many otherwise decent men."

Mrs. Rafferty nodded her head. "Don't I know it, Mrs. MacLeod. Me husband, may he rest in peace, spent a small fortune at every pub in Dublin, and then in the East End when we came to London. But the strange thing is, Mr. Golm here doesn't go for tea, neither."

Agatha looked at him. "No tea, eh? Now then, that's not right. Not even for a Welshman."

Mrs. Rafferty had an idea. "Maybe if there were more sugar in it, he'd like it. He sure likes the cakes I make." She fixed a cup of tea, and put double the amount of sugar she thought was proper.

She slid it over to Joe. "There now, try it. It's not even hot anymore, so you don't have to worry about burnin' yer tongue."

Joe tasted it. Then drank the rest in one gulp. He slid it back to Mrs. Rafferty, clearly wanting more.

"Oh, now, would ye look at that, Mrs. MacLeod," the cook exclaimed. "He likes his tea with lots o' sugar. Just like a boy."

"No harm in that," Agatha said mildly. "Nobody ever got worse for drink on sugared tea."

Mrs. Rafferty fixed him another cup, and both women watched in amused satisfaction as Joe drank it right down.

"Joe, I know you can't talk, but can you at least read and write?" Agatha enquired.

Joe shook his head.

"Now that's not right, either," Agatha said. "Why don't we give you some lessons. Then you can improve your mind. And we can show you some table manners while we're at it."

"That's a capital idea, Mrs. MacLeod," Mrs. Rafferty said. "Everybody knows those in service are worth twice as much when they can read."

Agatha sat next to Joe with a blank piece of paper and a pencil. "Now this is the letter A. It makes the first sound you hear in the word 'at' or 'apple.' You try making the letter."

She gave Joe the pencil. He grabbed it in his fist.

"No, you have to hold it like this." She arranged his strong fingers around the pencil. He drew a shape on the paper.

"Good. Now this is the lower case 'a'." She guided his hand. "See? It's not so difficult."

"He learns fast, doesn't he," Mrs. Rafferty said while she peeled carrots.

The babies were sitting in the pram nearby, playing with rattles. Lily laughed, and Jack followed his sister's lead, and laughed, too.

Agatha looked over at them tenderly. "The little ones are happy that you're learning to read, Mr. Golm. When they're old enough, they'll learn to read, too."

Anne was upstairs in the living room, reading the latest letter from the baron.

> *My Dearest Anne,*
>
> *I heard you were at a dinner party Saturday last, hosted by of one of our mutual friends. I had another engagement, regrettably. How did you convince that difficult husband of yours to attend? But, I suppose he has to put up a good face in public, lest people suspect something unflattering. Have you received my last two letters? Or has your husband intercepted them? I miss your beautiful face, and your ethereal voice at my salons. Can you slip out one of these evenings and come visit us? Lucien has been asking after you. Karol's piano playing has never sounded better. Ursula invented a dance that is going to shock London, and you'll be one of the lucky few who can see it before everyone else claims to have seen it. I have heard that Minerva was replaced with a stern Scotswoman. Surely you could leave her in charge of the little piglets while you escape from the drudgery of soiled nappies and soured milk, and slip into the world of beauty, mystery, and art. I await your reply, my dear lovely nightingale.*
>
> *As always, I remain Your Ladyship's most obedient servant,*
> *ZTvK*

Anne carefully stashed the letter into the wicker box, as she had done with the other letters from him. She debated with herself about what she should do. She missed her friends at the salon. But in light of

Jonathan's revelations, she had become frightened. She had been careful to avoid any situation where she might run into the baron, both for Jonathan's sake and for her own.

She debated whether she should ignore this letter (as she had been doing). A terse reply was perhaps the best way to handle it. She grabbed a piece of paper and dashed off two lines. She explained that she was too caught up in her duties to spare any time away from the house, but she hoped his salon gatherings were just as lively as before. She signed the letter, "Sincerely, The Hon. Mrs. Jonathan Drake."

Anne re-read the part of the letter where Lucien had been asking after her. Anne's heart skipped a beat at the thought. She realised she rather fancied him. All the more reason she should stay away from the baron and from Lucien.

Three days later she received an invitation from Lucinda Fernleigh, Marchioness of Ullmeade, inviting her to a luncheon. Lady Fernleigh lived in Cheyne Walk—one of the most pedigreed streets in London, home to famous writers, painters, and composers. Anne knew her only slightly. She had met the marchioness during her engagement to Jonathan at a luncheon at her in-laws' house. Anne longed for a fuller social life, and here was an opportunity. She dashed off an acceptance.

Then she went downstairs to look for Agatha in the kitchen. She found the Scotswoman sitting next to Joe at the table, instructing him on how to write short words such as "cat" and "hat." Mrs. Rafferty sat nearby, slicing turnips.

"Mrs. MacLeod," Anne said, "I am going out to post a letter."

"Yes, ma'am." She gestured to the cradle near the fireside. "The babies ate like horses, m'lady, and now they're sleeping like angels."

"Wonderful." Anne said. She gestured to Joe. "How are lessons going?"

"Oh, very well, my lady. I think Mr. Golm will be reading and writing in no time a'tall."

CHAPTER TWENTY-FOUR

From the moment Anne stepped into Lady Fernleigh's house, she was astonished at Lady Fernleigh's daring taste. Unlike the dark interiors Anne was accustomed to, everything here was light and bright. The drapes were not the heavy, pelmeted creations of dark red or green velvet found in most London homes. They were gossamer clouds of white georgette that stirred with the slightest air current. How the staff managed to keep it all clean intrigued Anne. Lady Fernleigh must have an army of servants dedicated to capturing every speck of soot. There were at least two butlers, plus a distinguished-looking footman in smart green-and-pink livery. She wondered how many servants were downstairs.

Anne was the first to arrive, and the footman brought her to the dining room, at the far end of the ground floor. It was bigger than Anne's, with plenty of natural light. It overlooked a garden courtyard that contained a plain, wrought-iron bench under a tree. The courtyard was accessible through the double French doors beyond the dining table.

The walls of the dining room were pale green, almost white, with small framed sketches hung at regular intervals. The ebony dining table was polished to such a high sheen, it looked like a black mirror. The narrow black chairs looked like the thrones of fantastical creatures, with their exaggerated ladder-backs that were as tall as a woman standing. There was no crystal or brass chandelier over the dining table, but rather a collection of pink-and-green pendants decorated with stylized apples, hanging from the ceiling at various lengths. The electric bulbs glowed from inside each pendant, giving them a jewel-like quality. The effect was dazzling. Anne thought of her husband's offer to lay on electric throughout their own house, and she was determined to bring up the subject with him at the first opportunity.

On the ebony dining table was a bouquet of tropical flowers that looked as if they were made of red wax. The table was set with fine china and sterling on green place-mats. The sideboard was unlike anything Anne had seen before: a glossy black-and-white creation with simple, modern motifs of apples and leaves that fit perfectly with the rest of the dining-room.

Anne compared this house to that of her in-laws. The Drake mansion on Hyde Park was neoclassical, full of elaborate mouldings, trims, wainscoting, and carved ceiling medallions. Lady Fernleigh's house, by comparison, looked unadorned and sparse, yet very modern and chic.

Anne took a closer look at the pencil-and-charcoal sketches on the walls. They portrayed fantastical, repulsive subjects. A few were downright obscene, and Anne was shocked that they'd be displayed at all, much less in a dining room. The drawings reminded her of those that Lucien had shown her. Anne knew it was the mark of sophistication to appreciate such art, and she chastised her own old-fashioned mindset for finding them objectionable. But she didn't know how to free herself from that.

Her thoughts were interrupted by the arrival of Lucinda Fernleigh and two guests.

"Ah, Anne Drake," Lucinda said, sweeping into the room. She wore bottle-green harem trousers and a loose tunic blouse. The flowing silk trousers were caught up with a waist sash in saffron yellow. Anne had never seen such a daring outfit to receive guests. It was odd, but also dramatic, and Lucinda had the height and slim figure to carry it off.

"Good day Lady Fernleigh," Anne replied. "Thank you for your kind invitation."

"Let us dispense with titles," Lady Fernleigh announced. "It's all such a crashing bore. We can call each other by our surnames without titles, as the men do. Such stuffy formalities will not be tolerated in this house!" She gestured to the women next to her. "You remember Jane Carrington and Patricia Haig."

They exchanged greetings. Anne knew the latter two women by way of her in-laws. Jane Carrington was an heiress from a family of tea merchants, currently engaged to the owner of a Barbados sugar plantation. Patricia Haig was a full-figured woman from a wealthy family, married to an accomplished violinist who was also a music historian at King's College.

Four more women arrived, whom Anne was meeting for the first time. Every woman at the table was smartly dressed in a conventional style. Only Lady Fernleigh wore an outlandish outfit, and she wore it well. Anne was glad that she herself had worn her best day-dress, in a shade of robin's-egg blue that showed off her eyes.

The conversation started with guests complimenting the hostess on her superb taste in interior design. Lady Fernleigh chattered on and on about her adventures in choosing an interior decorator. She recounted everything in a bland, casual tone, but the undercurrent revealed a good deal of money and a pedigreed study of aesthetics. She explained why her interior designer's changes were a much-needed antidote to the heavy excesses of the Victorians. She talked about the Glasgow carpenter who had custom-built the sideboard in the dining room, and she promised to show her guests the new piano-forte in the music room that was in keeping with the newest aesthetic. The apple motifs were a play upon her title, the Marchioness of Ullmeade—"ull" being the Gaelic word for apple.

Anne was fascinated, but her heart sank. If the marchioness were ever to see Anne's house in Cadogan Square, she would think it provincial, out-of-date, and unimaginative.

The conversation moved to domestic concerns, such the best way to instruct the servants to clean silver, the merits of a hot-water apparatus for heating a room, and whether the latest hats from Paris were really worth the price.

"My husband and I are planning a trip to Paris for my new wardrobe," Anne said gaily, "so I will let you know if the hats on the continent are any better than the imports in our millinery shops."

Lady Fernleigh smiled benignly. "I am surprised that your husband is so eager to travel. Wasn't he on a long journey recently?"

"Yes," Anne said with faltering confidence. She hoped the rumours hadn't reached too far. "It was indeed a long journey, but he is back home now."

"Oh? Where was he?" asked Violette de Lyons, the striking daughter of a French comte and English baroness.

"He was on a business trip in the Carpathian Mountains, finalizing a real-estate transaction for a distinguished client."

"I understand his illness has been difficult for you and your family. I do hope he has a speedy recovery," Lady Fernleigh said with concern.

"Yes, we all offer our condolences," Jane Carrington said.

"But he was recovered before he got back to London," Anne corrected her, bewildered by their mistake.

A significant look passed between Lady Fernleigh and Jane Carrington, and Anne caught it.

"It is always difficult to balance the need for family privacy with modern forthrightness," Patricia Haig said in a matter-of-fact tone, as if she were describing settled science. "In my family, my grandmother had her own private apartments in the south wing. Back then nobody dared breathe the word 'insanity.' The euphemisms were 'eccentric' and 'ill.' Of course, among those of us who are modern and forward-looking, we don't view the problems of one family member as reflecting on anyone else but that individual. Certainly not on spouses, for example. Wouldn't you agree, Fernleigh?"

"Absolutely correct, Haig," Lady Fernleigh said.

So that was it, Anne realised. They all believed Jonathan was insane, just as David Lowe had tried to warn her. Anne could tell at a glance who at the table had heard the rumour. Those who had heard it looked at her with pity, the rest with astonishment and curiosity.

Lady Fernleigh said in a magnanimous tone: "I have never snubbed someone for the misfortune of events out of his or her control. My invitations are issued to individuals, not to family names and reputations."

"Which is why it is such a privilege to receive an invitation from you, Fernleigh," Violette de Lyons said. "That, and the fact that you have superb taste, and a marvellous cook."

"Why, thank you, de Lyons. It is indeed a privilege to be a hostess with such fine guests as those presently gathered at my table."

There were murmurs of assent from the others, and relieved comments about the food in order to change the subject. Anne was too mortified to look up. She pretended to study the meringue cake on the plate in front of her, and she could feel her face burning with shame. She wondered how she could find a graceful exit.

Her thoughts were interrupted by Lady Fernleigh's voice giving instructions to her butler. "Well, show him in, Bridges. I'm sure all of us would enjoy his company during dessert."

Moments later, the butler announced: "Baron Zoltan von Klausenberg."

The baron's charcoal-grey cape swirled behind him as he bowed low in the doorway.

"My dear ladies, I had no idea I was interrupting such a sumptuous ensemble," he said in his eastern European accent.

Anne looked around in a panic, wondering if she could make her escape now. The other women were riveted by him.

Lady Fernleigh chuckled and held out her hand. "Dear Zoltan, my friends would be most interested to meet you. They've only heard about you."

He took her hand into his black-gloved hands, and kissed her fingers. His gaze was as intense as ever, and as he was introduced to each woman in turn, Anne both dreaded and anticipated the moment when his gaze would be fixed on her. Would he add to the humiliation she'd just suffered? After all, he had accused Jonathan of insanity at her in-laws' dinner party, and his pointed remarks in his letter betrayed the intense dislike he had for Jonathan.

"And this is Anne Drake, wife of the solicitor, Jonathan Drake," Lady Fernleigh said.

The baron walked over to her, and without waiting for her to offer it, he took her hand in his gloved hand and kissed it, then held it longer than was necessary. Anne felt a curious tingling from his touch, and she was certain it was her own nerves. The exotic scent of his cologne added to her disorientation.

"We have been to more than a few gatherings together recently, have we not, madam?" he said, smiling.

Anne kept her inner turmoil in check. "Yes, a few."

Some of the other women looked at her with newfound admiration.

"In fact, it has been far too long since I have seen you ... and your esteemed husband, of course. We really must remedy that. I believe the

261

last time was at your in-laws' house."

He released her hand and went on to the next woman. When the introductions were finished the baron seated himself next to Lucinda and took a small box out of his pocket. He presented it to her with a flourish.

"The purpose of my visit is to give you this," he said, handing the box to her.

Lady Fernleigh opened the box and gasped with delight. "Oh, Zoltan! You had it repaired!"

She had again used the baron's first name. Anne wondered just how intimate their relationship was. She felt a small flicker of jealousy that he and the marchioness were on such excellent terms. She envied the fact that Lady Fernleigh had a large, well-staffed house, expertly decorated, all the while maintaining perfect composure as a poised, gracious hostess, who could wear outlandish outfits and look smashing in them. Anne wished she could be the centre of attention like that.

Lady Fernleigh held up a ruby pendant. "This has been in my family for generations. Legend has it that it was made in Venice in the seventeenth century."

"Oh, but it was," the baron interjected. "You can see how the design of the setting, and even the cut of the stone is unmistakably Venetian. It dates from, I would say, about sixteen-seventy-five, sixteen-eighty at the latest."

Some of the women murmured in admiration.

Lady Fernleigh continued. "This piece was badly damaged some years back. My mother told me the clasp had failed when she'd been wearing it. It fell to the ground, and a horse stepped on it."

"Infernal beasts," the baron muttered.

"I would like to know who restored it," Jane Carrington said. "I have some pieces of my own that need attention."

"Ah, now that is a challenge," the baron said. "The jeweller is a temperamental man who only takes a few private clients a year. Most of his time is spent working for noble families all over the continent, especially the Habsburgs and the Romanovs. But I will see what I can do."

Anne kept her eyes on the fruit ice that was set before her. She refused to meet the baron's gaze, and was relieved that his visit seemed to be coming to an end.

The baron announced: "I need to speak with Madam Drake. I know she is a woman of the highest propriety, so we will sit out in the garden." He gestured to the courtyard beyond the French doors. Then he signalled to the butler to bring Anne's overcoat. His blunt manner was shockingly un-English, but it also brought Anne a strange thrill that she was being singled out among all the women there. Murmurs went around the table.

From the dining table where the women sat, they all had a perfect view of the garden bench under the leafless linden tree.

Anne could think of no way out. She put on her coat as the butler held it for her. There was curiosity and envy on the faces of some of the other women. She wondered whether the marchioness and the baron had colluded on this ahead of time. It was bad enough that Jonathan's mental state had been the topic of conversation earlier. Now she was afraid of being made a further spectacle. She felt trapped, and also elated, and followed the baron outside.

The day was warmer than usual. Spring flowers were in bloom. The baron sat on the bench, removed his gloves, and let his hands rest on his elaborately-carved walking stick. Anne was again struck by his long, lacquered nails. She stood a little distance away and maintained a sullen silence.

"I see I will have to begin," the baron observed.

"I'm not the one who called this meeting," Anne retorted.

The baron laughed. "True. But it is in your self-interest to meet with me. You refuse my invitations to the salon, and I am not welcome at your house, thanks to your husband."

Anne said nothing.

"And what I have to tell you concerns your husband. There are rumours going around that his mental health is extremely unstable."

Anne glared at him. "You made that charge yourself at my in-laws' house, and now you pretend it comes from other quarters. I have nothing more to discuss."

Before she could take a step, the baron said: "Life will become a lot more difficult for you unless you hear what I have to say, Anne."

Anne remained standing, and kept her face blank. She could not see through the French doors into the dining room, but she knew all the women inside were watching them. She pretended to examine a bare rose bush in a stone planter. It had not yet begun to sprout leaves for spring, although the leaf buds were swollen.

"I regret my rash words toward your husband that evening at the Drake residence," the baron said. "Please accept my apologies. Your husband's enemies got word of what I said, and exaggerated that against him. His true enemies remain hidden, but I get the blame for it. I am not your enemy, Anne."

She met his gaze, and her eyes were full of anger. "Aren't you? My husband told me what happened at your estate."

The baron tilted his head thoughtfully. "Happened at my estate? I was gracious and kind toward him throughout his stay. With what has he charged me?"

"He said your servants held him hostage in a dungeon and tortured him."

"I knew nothing of this," the baron said sharply. "Did your husband accuse me of being there when this happened?"

"No," Anne admitted. "It was after you had left for London. He said you wouldn't let him go with you on the day you left. His food had been drugged. That's why he was too sick to travel."

The baron closed his eyes and nodded, as if a great mystery had been solved. "Drugged. And all this time I thought it had been mountain fever. When in fact it had been the handiwork of my own servants." He opened his eyes and his gaze seemed to burn through Anne to the garden wall behind her. "You have my word, madam, that I will avenge your husband's suffering. My servants will be held to account." The baron turned the conversation in another direction. "Surely Jonathan told you that I'd had one of the coachmen whipped for disobedience. And I'm sure he told you about the golden chalice in the town square, the one that no-one may touch unless he wants to lose a hand."

"Yes, he told me all this."

"I know it all sounds so disturbing to English ears. But that chalice is an effective reminder to all the townspeople that the authority of the law—my authority—reigns supreme. I am their king. You cannot know how primitive these people are, Anne. I know because they are my people. They are not like you English, who have an instinctive regard for order, for authority, for civilization. My people are like savage dogs who must be under the constant crack of a whip lest they go wild and tear each other apart. That is why I had the coachman whipped. It is a different world, and one that you cannot understand unless you have lived there. Even your husband, who is very intelligent and well-read, is not accustomed to our way of thinking. How can he understand it? It is an alien place."

"Then what about Minerva?" Anne said accusingly. Her heart broke when she thought of the harm inflicted upon her children.

"What about her?"

"She was … she was horrid."

"Ah, my dear Anne, no good deed goes unpunished, does it? I tried to help you by finding a nanny, and now you accuse me of some other crime that I do not know about. If there were not so many eyes fixed on us, I would wipe away that tear from your lovely face."

Anne wiped it away with the back of her hand. "I'm fine," she said.

"Then tell me about Minerva. Why did you dismiss her?"

"Jonathan saw her extracting blood from the babies."

"Was she under a doctor's orders to do this?"

"Well, she said she was," Anne admitted. "She put vials of blood into a basket. Jonathan said … he said …" Her voice trailed off. She didn't mention the part about actually drinking blood. It was too horrid to contemplate, and she was convinced that Jonathan had imagined that part.

"He said what?" the baron gently prompted.

"He said she went your house. She had a key and let herself in."

The baron's eyes blazed. "So that is where those damned vials of blood came from. I do not know who put her up to it, but you can see, Anne, that your husband is not the only one who has enemies in this city." The baron paused. "Did your husband follow Minerva to my house?"

"No," Anne said slowly.

"Then how did he know she came to my house?"

"Jonathan's man followed him."

"I see. And what is his man's name?"

"Joe."

"Just Joe? Has he no last name?"

"His last name is … Golm."

"Golm," the baron said slowly, rolling the name around in his mouth. "Golm. Fascinating name."

"It's Welsh," Anne explained.

"Is it?"

Anne felt as if she had already said more than was prudent, that she had given him some knowledge that might be used against her. She sensed that she had betrayed her husband in some way, without knowing how.

The baron lowered his voice. "Let us talk about our friendship, my nightingale. Won't you come to one of my soirées at least once in a while? Or, if they are not good enough for you, I will host a grand ball in your honour. I will invite the most distinguished guests in London. You can even bring Jonathan, if he would consent," he added dryly.

"I don't know if you got my letter—"

"Yes, yes," he interrupted, waving a hand. "You are busy with domestic duties. But not too busy to have lunch with a bunch of smart women." He smiled his most charming smile and nodded toward the French doors. "The fact is, they are boring and conventional, especially compared to the guests at my salon gatherings."

"Lady Fernleigh is not boring. Her costume is quite ... unconventional," Anne observed.

"She is not boring, but she is, at heart, conventional," the baron said. He looked down at the ground and said in a quiet voice, as if thinking out loud: "But the fact is, you could easily outshine her. You would make a better hostess than she is, because you are naturally smarter than she is. And prettier."

"Rubbish," Anne murmured, feeling her face flush, and wanting to believe that what he said was true. "I could never carry off the outfit she's wearing."

"True. That is not your style, and it would be foolish of you to try. At any rate, you outshine her in every way, except one," the baron went on. "You lack her financial resources. That is a pity, because you are more deserving of riches. You would use them more intelligently."

Anne felt anger at the baron's frankness, but also a strange pride.

The baron sighed. "But the other women in there, watching us now as if they are at a pantomime play ... do you think I would waste my time with any of them?"

Anne said nothing, but his words were the balm she was hoping for. She was eager to hear what else he had to say. He paused, as if deliberating what he should say next. A sparrow chirped from a branch high in the linden tree.

The baron said suddenly: "Do you know what I hate more than anything?" He waited only a moment, then continued. "I hate to see talent and beauty wasted. You spend an afternoon with women who could not care less about the deeper aspects of life."

"That's not true," Anne said, summoning a loyalty she didn't really feel. "Lucinda and Jane both play piano. Patricia's husband is a violinist. Violetta dances. One of the others—I forgot her name—paints watercolours."

"Ah, but I am not talking about prosaic culture. I'm talking about the deepest impulses of the human spirit. What would these women make of Lucien's portrait of you as Anat? How would they regard the brilliant Ursula? Our salon gatherings? Would they fit in?" The baron laughed. "They would be as lost as newly-hatched chickens among fine peacocks. They would be trampled. You think lunch with them is a worthwhile use of your time. What did you talk about this afternoon? Sherry stains on the upholstery? How to stitch needlepoints for bell pulls? That is how the typical Englishwoman wastes her time and convinces herself that she is so clever. Why not concern yourself with real art that touches the human soul? With visions of loyalty, undying love, of fealty to a cause higher than yourself? My dear Anne, you have so much more to offer. Even if we never see each other again, heed my advice. Do not let these people take away your spirit, your imagination. See them once in a while, that is fine. But do not trap yourself in their world. You are in the flower of your prime. Do not waste it. Please."

Anne said in a breathless voice: "Thank you for your concern."

The baron stood up. "I will not call on you at your house. I know I am not welcome there. But you are always welcome in my salon, and it would be a tragedy if I never saw you there again. Lucien and the rest of your friends would be heartbroken. And we are your true friends. Tonight, the salon gathering promises to be particularly brilliant. The invitation is open. Please don't worry about dress. Just arrive in all your splendid beauty, even if it is a simple muslin frock—the one you wore the day I met you."

Anne remembered back to that hot September afternoon, hours before her children were born.

The baron went inside. Anne followed him and took her seat at the table. He bade Lady Fernleigh and the rest of the women farewell, and added: "Madam Drake is an extraordinary person, as you all now have the pleasure of knowing first-hand. Thank you, dear ladies, for not minding that the two of us slipped out into the garden for a little tête-à-tête."

Anne kept her face blank, as if nothing important had happened, but she noticed that when the conversation continued after the baron's departure, the women who had treated her with distant, condescending formality earlier in the afternoon now eagerly sought her opinion on whatever topic they happened to be talking about. They wanted to know more about her, without directly asking her how she had come to be singled out by so eminent a person as Baron Zoltan von Klausenberg. His gilded touch clearly graced those whom he favoured.

The baron's words played in her mind. Anne couldn't help but compare this group to that of the baron's salons. Yes, it was nice to be in the company of women like Lady Fernleigh and the others, women who were rich and respectable. But she knew a part of her was bored and restless. She longed for the free, expressive atmosphere of the baron's salon, where she heard excellent music, saw talented artists and dancers perform unconventional works that nobody else in London had seen. Anne smiled to herself, wondering what these women would think if they knew she'd been a regular at the baron's salons, and if they knew what happened there. Would they be shocked? Envious?

As the marchioness said goodbye to her guests, she lingered with Anne, promising to invite her to dine, very soon. Anne left for home, and a feeling of triumph overtook her as she thought about her unexpected victory at Lady Fernleigh's luncheon.

CHAPTER TWENTY-FIVE

In the kitchen, Agatha and Joe sat at the table, a King James Bible open before them. The babies slept nearby in their pram. Mrs. Rafferty had gone home for the day.

With her finger moving across the page, Agatha slowly read the passage aloud.

"'… and there was no man to till the ground. But a mist went up from the earth and watered the whole face of the ground. Then the Lord God formed man of dust from the ground.'"

At these words, Joe suddenly started pointing at his own chest. His face was as animated as Agatha had ever seen it. She stopped reading and looked at him.

"You were formed from dust of the ground?" she asked.

Joe nodded his head vigorously.

"Well," Agatha explained, "we all come from Adam, and he was the first man to come from the dust. That's why we say at funerals, 'Ashes to ashes, dust to dust, from dust we came, from dust we shall return.'"

From the collar of his shirt, Joe pulled out a necklace of waxed twine and clay beads. Agatha adjusted her spectacles and examined the beads. Each bead had its own symbol. She didn't know that she was looking at Hebrew letters.

"What does it mean?" she asked.

Joe reached for the piece of paper and pencil. He wrote:

emet

Then under that he wrote:

truth

"The word is emet? It means truth?" Agatha asked.

Joe nodded. Then he crossed out the first e of emet and wrote next to it:

death

"The word 'met' means death?"

Joe nodded.

"That's something," Agatha said. "Add one letter to the word death, and you have truth. Maybe when we die, we learn the truths we can't understand in this life."

The clock chimed, and the babies, who were napping in a pram near the table, began to stir. Chompsworth was nearby. She pricked up her ears.

"The time got away from us, Joe. I have to take the babies for a stroll—I promised Mrs. Drake I'd have walked them by now. I won't be long."

Outside, the afternoon was grey, cold, and very windy. Agatha maneuvered the pram across the street to the park, taking care that the babies were not in direct wind. She walked along the black iron fence. The trees were still bare, but swollen leaf buds covered the branches, which were swaying in the strong wind.

"Spring is here, spring is here, the buds are all in bloom," she sang to the babies, who played with their rattles as she pushed them along in the pram.

They were well inside the park when Lily started to fuss. Agatha stopped to make sure both babies were properly bundled. Agatha straightened up. A man stood in front of them, on the garden path. His eyes were cold and intense. He wore no hat, and the wind blew his hair into a disordered mess. Agatha turned the pram around and walked quickly to the gate.

Once she reached the gate, she turned to look behind her, but saw no sign of him. She crossed the street and hurried toward the house. Once she was at the front steps, she turned to look across the street at the park. The man leaned against the fence inside the park, grinning at her.

Agatha was badly frightened and pushed the pram around to the servants' entrance as quickly as she could. She fumbled with her keys, glancing behind her to be sure he wasn't there. Once inside, she locked the door. She tried to catch her breath. Joe was at her side, looking at her with a puzzled expression. Chompsworth growled and jumped on the door. Agatha looked out the window, but saw nobody on the property.

In a shaking voice, she told Joe what had happened. As soon as she finished, Joe began checking that every door and window was locked. He drew the drapes and shades. The dog followed Joe as he did this.

Joe returned, wrote on paper and gave it to Agatha.

"'Did he hurt you,'" Agatha read aloud. "No, he didn't hurt me, thank the good Lord. But I was afraid even so."

Joe wrote again:

tell jonathan

Agatha read it and looked up at Joe. "Do you think I should bother the master about it? The man could've been drunk. Funny thing is, he didn't smell like it, or act like it."

Joe pointed insistently to what he'd written.

tell jonathan

"I'll tell him when he comes home. Has the madam come in yet?"
Joe shook his head.
"She's probably having a wonderful time at the luncheon."
Agatha turned her attention to the babies, and fed them porridge-and-cream while sipping a cup of strong tea. As the babies were finishing

their meal, Anne was making her way down to the kitchen, holding her umbrella, which looked mangled.

"Mrs. MacLeod, I'll need to go shopping for a new umbrella. Mine got shredded in the wind."

"Yes, m'lady." Agatha was wiping the faces and hands of the babies with a damp rag. "Did m'lady make sure that the front door is locked?"

"Yes, of course," Anne said. "I always lock up."

"Good. One can't be too careful these days." Agatha debated whether she should tell Mrs. Drake about the man in the park, or wait until Mr. Drake was home.

"And how are my little bunnies today?" Anne said. She sat at the table with them and playfully tapped each of them on the nose.

Agatha decided to tell her. "M'lady, I must tell you that there was a strange man in the park who looked menacing."

Anne didn't bother to look up. "Oh? Sometimes you see those types around, but not as often in this neighbourhood as in others."

"He gave me a fright. Do you think I should go to the coppers?"

"And tell them what? That a man in the park looks strange? Put it out of your mind, Mrs. MacLeod."

"Should I tell the master?"

"Absolutely not. He has enough to worry about. Can you fetch me a cup of tea?"

"Yes, m'lady." Agatha went to the stove to re-heat the water.

"I'll be in the back parlour. You may bring it up."

Anne went upstairs to the back parlour. She looked around and felt discontent. This morning, that room had been a perfectly respectable room, clean and well laid out, decorated in a way that her husband had complimented her for, and she herself had liked. Now, it was too small, too old-fashioned. The wallpaper and Axminster carpet struck her as outmoded. In fact, Anne thought her entire house lacked the modern style of Lady Fernleigh's house. And there weren't enough servants. As Anne tended the fire, she remembered the baron's words that if she had Lady Fernleigh's wealth, she could surpass that woman's achievements and reputation.

That was a pleasant fantasy, but she found it hard to imagine herself actually achieving it. But re-decorating her own house, now that was something to consider. How would she do it if money were no object? She realised she had never given it much thought before, besides deciding that she would like to grow orchids in one of the front windows overlooking Cadogan square. She could envision how nice it would be to have a full staff in smart livery, a carriage in full equipage—no, a motorcar would be better. With such a large staff, she wouldn't have to work so hard to keep things running smoothly. She wouldn't have to tend her own fires, or have the nanny bring tea—a proper maid would do all that. And she could receive visitors as graciously as Lady Fernleigh did, and have smartly dressed people come and go while she sat in a chair of cream-coloured shantung, her hair always perfect, and pass the hours in witty, cultured conversation. Her children would appear at a convenient time in to recite a poem or play a song on the violin for the guests.

Jonathan didn't seem to appreciate how hard Anne had worked in his absence, how she'd had to perform mundane tasks, such as lighting a fire or darning socks, that women of Anne's station should not have to bother with. The troubles with Minerva were excusable. She had needed a nanny, and Minerva had seemed to be the perfect choice. How could Anne have known otherwise? Jonathan needed to forgive her fully for that, put it behind them, and look toward the future to ensure that they had the standard of living they deserved.

She heard Jonathan come in the front door. She sat with her needlepoint while she waited for him. After a while, he opened the door, carrying her tea.

"Oh, hullo," he said, handing her the cup.

"The tea is cold," Anne said. "What took so long?"

"I was playing with Jack while Mrs. MacLeod was tending to Lily. She was in quite a fuss for some reason. Mrs. MacLeod told me there hasn't been a free moment to bring you this cup, so I said I'd deliver it."

"Oh." Anne couldn't help but think about how Lady Fernleigh would never be inconvenienced like that, and Lord Fernleigh certainly would never lower himself by playing servant. The marchioness had plenty of servants to ensure the tea was delivered steaming hot.

"Do you think we could give Joe more responsibilities around the house?" Anne said, trying to keep the resentment out of her voice. "After all, we're paying for his upkeep, but he doesn't contribute anything. And

I don't like the fact that he lurks about in various places, like a dog trying to find the best spot. It's terribly strange. He ought to sleep in his quarters, like a conventional servant. Instead, I find him sleeping on the floor in doorways, or loitering about in random locations. And the dog is always with him."

"I've noticed that as well. He stations himself where he can best protect us."

"From what?" Anne asked.

"Danger."

"What danger?"

"Strange things have happened, and I want to keep you and the children safe."

Anne thought about Mrs. MacLeod's hysterical tale of the man in the park. It was preposterous to think it was anything serious, and she had been right to instruct Mrs. MacLeod not to mention it to Jonathan.

"It's an unnecessary extravagance," Anne said. "Our house is perfectly secure. We live in a pleasant neighbourhood."

"Yes, but a threat can come out of nowhere. We have to be prepared for anything."

"I really think you're imagining things, Jonathan."

Agatha came rushing into the room, holding both babies. "He's out front, on the street! Come and look!"

"Who?" Jonathan demanded.

"That strange man who was in the park. He's out front, watching the house. Come look!"

Anne took one of the babies from Agatha and accompanied her to the front parlour.

"I know nothing about this," Jonathan muttered peevishly as he followed the two women.

Jonathan went to the window that overlooked Cadogan Square. The drapes were drawn over it. He peered through a small space in the drapes. Darkness had fallen. The man was standing in the pool of light cast by the street lamp nearest to their house. He wore no hat, and his hands were in his pockets. He grinned defiantly at the house. A steady rain was falling, but he seemed not to care.

Anne also peeked out, and the man's menacing look made her shiver. She withdrew quickly, and held her baby closer.

"That's the exact same one who was in the park today," Agatha said. "He doesn't look drunk, does he, m'lady?"

"No, he doesn't," Anne admitted.

"What happened in the park?" Jonathan enquired.

Agatha told him.

"And you didn't bother to mention it when I'd been downstairs fetching that cup of tea for my wife?"

Agatha bit her lip, clearly not wanting to mention that Anne had instructed her not to say anything to him about it.

Anne said calmly: "I told Mrs. MacLeod not to bother you with such a trivial detail. She had told me, but I hadn't thought it worth mentioning to you."

Jonathan turned to his wife, and gestured at the window. "You see for yourself how disreputable he looks, and how he taunts us by standing there so brazenly. And yet you have the temerity to question my judgement about retaining Joe? Really, Anne, where is your common sense?"

Anne said nothing. Her face was sullen.

The golem lurked in the doorway with Chompsworth.

"Joe, please come to the window here and get a good look at that man who is out there in the circle of light," Jonathan said.

Joe stood squarely in front of the window, swiped the drapery aside, and stood gazing at the man in full view. The others stood off to the side, out of view. Light from the street lamps came into the room, illuminating Joe's imposing stature. The dog put her front paws on the sill and peered out the window at the strange man. She let out a growl.

"Maybe you shouldn't let him see you so directly like that, Joe," Agatha whispered from off to the side.

"We can't undo it now. Let's see what happens," Jonathan said, staying hidden behind the drapes.

The strange man scowled when he saw Joe. He took his hands out of his pockets and walked away.

Jonathan turned to the nanny. "Mrs. MacLeod, when you take the children for a walk, please bring Joe and Chompsworth with you, always. The same for you on your outings, Anne."

"Are you saying I need to bring him whenever I visit with my friends?" Anne asked peevishly. "I thought he was not to be treated as an ordinary servant."

"He's not an ordinary servant," Jonathan countered. "He is here to protect us, and we should fully avail ourselves of that."

Anne slipped out of the room without saying a word to her husband. The doorbell rang. She didn't answer it, but continued up the stairs. On the landing, out of sight, she listened to determine who was there. It was David Lowe. She heard Jonathan suggest that the two of them retire to the back parlour. Anne proceeded to her dressing room to get ready. An evening out, among her friends, was just what she needed after everything that had happened that day. The invitation had arrived in the post just before tea, in flowery handwriting that was unfamiliar to Anne.

The baron's words (those that he had spoken to her at Lady Fernleigh's house) had impressed her more deeply than she had expected. If he really thought she could cut a smart figure in high society, then she owed it to herself and to her children to do exactly that. Yes, it was ambitious, but Lady Fernleigh was ambitious. So were the other women who'd been at the luncheon party that day. They all played their hands to the fullest advantage, they all fought for the best positions for their families. Why should Anne not do the same? Why should she not avail herself of the help that the baron could provide? He had full confidence in her, whereas her husband was unfailingly critical. Why should she not have confidence in herself, push ahead, and see how high it would take her?

As for Jonathan, well, in time he'd see the wisdom of her ambition. Surely he would eventually come to his senses and realise how unreasonable he was being with regard to Joe's place in the household, and his irrational hatred of the baron. If she could get the two of them to talk amicably, if Jonathan understood the baron's perspective, she was certain she could heal the rift between them.

All this went through her head as she arranged her hair and applied cosmetics. At last, she was dressed and ready. She descended the stairs.

David and Jonathan sat by the hearth in the back parlour, discussing in low voices the strange man who had accosted Agatha and the babies earlier that day. Anne breezed into the room, dressed for the evening.

David stood and remarked: "You are the picture of elegance, madam." Once again, he was struck by the perfume she wore. He knew it was ambergris, but he knew that enquiring about it would be a faux pas.

Anne smiled at him. "You are too kind, Mr. Lowe." Then she turned to her husband. "Goodbye, darling. I'll be out tonight. Violette de Lyons has invited me to a game of bridge."

Jonathan was taken aback with this sudden announcement. "I had no inkling. May we have a word, in my study?"

Their tête-à-tête in his study did not last long, and it ended with Anne leaving the house. David had taken the opportunity to go to the front parlour window to see whether the strange man was lurking out front, in the park. There was no strange man to be seen. He did hear the front door open then close, and he watched Anne walk resolutely in an easterly direction, her stylish umbrella tilted against the misty rain. He stayed at the window, waiting for Jonathan. A minute later, a cloaked-and-hooded figure on a fine-looking horse galloped to the front steps of Jonathan's house. The figure dismounted, and dashed up the steps. David was already opening the front door as the doorbell sounded.

Sarah swiped the hood off her head and pushed past David without so much as a greeting. She was wet and dishevelled, and her hair hung loose in damp auburn locks. Her forest-green cloak and dark blue dress were splattered with mud. She left footprints from her riding boots across the floor.

"Where is Jonathan?" she demanded, stopping in the front entrance hall and glancing up the staircase. "Ozzie!" she yelled. "Ozzie, come here quickly!"

The door of Jonathan's study opened. "Chippers! What's wrong?" he asked, hurrying to her side.

"I rode Tamburlaine bareback the whole way here, at a gallop. I had to get here as soon as I could. Oh, Ozzie, it's horrid. That odious baron has asked Papa for my hand. Maman and Papa had a terrible row about it, and Maman has threatened to leave Papa if he consents."

Jonathan's face went white.

"Refuse his offer, Miss Drake," David said. "You have that freedom."

Sarah shook her head in despair. "It's so complicated. Our family's reputation is at stake. I've never heard my parents so angry at each other. Papa wants to consider the offer, and Maman won't hear of it. Nobody had even bothered to tell me. I've had to eavesdrop on everything. I even read Papa's correspondence. I know that's wicked, but I'm so frightened. He's been negotiating with the baron. I can't believe he's treating my prospects like real-estate, to be traded away in a business deal." Her voice broke, and a tear rolled down her cheek.

David said: "Miss Drake, why don't you start from the beginning."

Sarah took a deep breath. She recounted how for months the baron had been insinuating himself into the family by sending tickets to the opera and theatre, even offering to take Hannah around town if Edward were unavailable. The baron had given up on trying to woo Sarah directly, because she refused all invitations from him. She didn't even reply to his letters. She admitted that she burned them as soon as she read them.

"I thought I was safe from him," Sarah added, "but I was wrong." She glanced at David. "I'm ashamed to talk about this next bit of news."

Jonathan said: "Mr. Lowe is our friend. If we can't trust him, we can't trust anybody."

Sarah continued. "As you know, our brother Michael is in Berlin, trying to make a name for himself as a composer. He racked up enormous debts before he left London. Our parents didn't discover the full extent of it all until weeks ago, just before Christmas, after he'd already been gone for over a year. They haven't had enough to pay it all off."

"Michael always was a spoiled, irresponsible little blighter," Jonathan muttered.

"It gets worse, Ozzie. The baron paid off every last creditor, without telling Father until now. So now we Drakes are in the baron's debt. He assured Father that the sum is trivial for him, but now he is presenting the bill, and I'm the payment. He hinted that if I don't marry him, he will find ways to make our secrets known."

"Father can go after him for defamation."

"The baron knows how to avoid those charges, the clever scoundrel.

He's counting on Papa to give in, because he knows that even a hint of scandal will destroy Papa's career. It will destroy our family. Oh, Ozzie, if it means saving our family's reputation, and keeping Maman and Papa together, maybe I should accept the offer, repugnant as it is." Her voice broke again, and she put a gloved hand to her mouth.

David said: "Miss Drake, you have my word that it will not get to that point. The baron will get his money back, and your parents won't have to worry about being beholden to him any longer."

Sarah said bitterly. "Ah, so then we'll just exchange one creditor for another. And what will be your price, Mr. Lowe?"

Jonathan found her sarcasm to be unwarranted, and he snapped: "Would you rather our parents keep owing the baron, of all people? And do you think David is such a blackguard to use you as a bargaining chip?"

Sarah was taken aback at his outburst, and she looked contrite. She turned to David. "You're not that kind of a man, Mr. Lowe. Please forgive me."

David said. "Forgiven, madam. You are under a great strain right now. But let me make myself clear. I'm trying to keep the baron from hurting more people. And, my dear Miss Drake, my proposal will not compromise your freedom to choose whom you marry, or even whether you marry. My aim is to remove any excuse the baron has to press his advantage with you. You will owe me nothing."

"When is the baron expecting a decision?" Jonathan asked.

Sarah's face was grave. "Maman is hosting a dinner tonight. He is one of the guests. She had wanted to strike him off the guest list, but Father won't hear of it. He assures her that the baron is an honourable man who will allow us time to come to a decision at least until next week. I think the truth is, Father is afraid of crossing the baron in any way."

"Who is going to be at this dinner party?" David asked.

"The usual dull gathering," Sarah replied. "Lord and Lady Edgerton, some editor from the New London Journal, Leonard and Rose Bixby, and others I don't remember." She added for David's benefit: "The Bixbys are old friends of my parents. He is currently an Ambassador to Malaysia. Of course, I am expected to be there. But I don't want to. Let me stay here and avoid it all. We can send a message with my regrets, on the pretext that I must help care for Jack and Lily."

"This is exactly the opportunity we need," David said. "Be strong, Miss Drake. You must attend, and you will not be alone. Jonathan, you must write to your father this moment and have your sister deliver the message that they need to set a place for an additional guest."

"I don't need to send a message," Jonathan said. "The hostess—who happens to be my mother—won't refuse to count me among her guests."

David shook his head. "You won't be going. I will."

Jonathan was silent a moment. Then he said: "I don't understand your method, Lowe, but I trust you."

Jonathan went into his study and sat at his desk. David stood next to him and dictated the message, with additional instructions that neither Sarah nor Jonathan could have invented on their own. Sarah stood there watching them both, her mouth agape.

"You can't just do that!" she said as Jonathan folded up the message and sealed it in an envelope. "Ozzie, you know how Papa hates snap decisions like that. He'll want time to deliberate, to map out his alternatives."

Jonathan stared at his sister. "And how much time do you think he really has, Chippers? The baron is not honourable. He'll force Father's hand and try to get his way using whatever methods available, legal or not."

David turned to Sarah. "How promptly is supper served at your house, Miss Drake?"

"Maman usually delays it by about fifteen minutes," Sarah replied. "There is always something she wants modified at the last minute."

"Good. Then I have just enough time to dress and catch a cab," David said, putting on his coat and hat. "You are welcome to share the cab, Miss Drake."

"I must ride Tamburlaine back home." Sarah hurried to the front door and let herself out into the misty darkness. She leaped onto her horse's back, and set off through the wet streets of London, her green cape and red hair unfurled behind her as the horse galloped away. David watched her until she was out of sight.

CHAPTER TWENTY-SIX

Sarah sat motionless at the dining room table, and twisted her napkin on her lap, out of sight. She kept her face neutral.

The table was elaborately set with china, sterling, white linen, and crystal vases of pink-and-yellow tulips and white narcissus. To her left sat Ambassador Bixby, a rather dull man with a leathery face from many years in the sun. Sarah pretended to be engrossed in his long-winded account of his consular service in Southeast Asia. His wife sat to his left. Mrs. Bixby was amiable and clever and had musical talent, but despite all that, she was even more boring than her husband. The Bixbys were slightly older than her parents, and had been good friends of the family for as long as Sarah could remember.

At the opposite end of the table from where she sat, Sarah glanced at Lord and Lady Edgerton, the Duke and Duchess of Rexford. The duchess was to her father's left, and the duke was next to his wife. Sarah had never liked either of them. The duchess's smile on her thin face could not sweeten a nature that Sarah perceived as essentially malicious. And, Sarah disliked the black-feather boa that she wore. It was hideous, with its long, pointed black feathers, like knife blades. It made her look like a sinister bird bringing an ill-omen. The duke was bald. He was just as slim and well-dressed as his wife, but whereas she was loquacious, the duke was reserved to the point of rudeness. Rather than converse, he preferred to concentrate on the food, and he ate everything put in front of him. Given his rank, he did not have to be a model of social grace. He and his wife were automatically included in the best social circles.

Next to the duke was Perkins, the editor of a London newspaper that had been making quite the splash for the past year or two. Perkins was a ruddy-faced man with thin lips and an aquiline nose. His wife was ill, and could not attend this gathering. He was a new guest, and Sarah had no opinion of him.

And then there was the baron, who sat to her father's right, and to the left of Mrs. Bixby. Sarah had purposely re-arranged the seating so that she was as far away from the baron as possible, and so that he was not in her line of sight. She had told the waitstaff not to tell her mother. She could tell that every guest had noticed the irregular seating arrangements, but nobody said a word.

Directly across the table from her, to her mother's right, was the place setting for David. Sarah tried not to glance at that empty seat, nor at the dining room entryway. Hannah had insisted on delaying the first course five minutes more to give David time to arrive. Servants in smart livery poured wine and champagne for each guest. When the five minutes had passed, she signalled the servants to bring in the hors d'oeuvre: quail eggs in aspic with caviar.

Sarah was disappointed that David had not yet arrived. She toyed with her food, wondering whether he was the kind of man to convince you that he'd do something, and then not follow through. If that were the case, she would hate him forever, and she would be sure to let him know what a vulgar cad he was, which would be sufficient reason for why she'd never speak to him again.

Sarah could tell that her mother was concealing an inner turmoil. Hannah usually wasn't quite that animated, even when hosting guests who were even more distinguished than this evening's gathering. Despite the lively chatter around the table, Sarah could feel that the air was heavy with tension. Hannah's sprightly conversation with those around her concealed her vexation at Sarah, both for rearranging the seating, and for Sarah's appearance.

Sarah had pinned her hair up satisfactorily, but not fashionably. She'd made the unexpected visit to Jonathan's house, and had had no time to have the lady's maid style it for her. Even if she'd had the time, she would've still done it herself. She had changed out of her muddied riding habit, and into a black dress that was more befitting a funeral than a dinner party. The neckline was high, the sleeves were long, and she'd wrapped a black lace shawl around her shoulders, and had fastened it at the neck with a cameo brooch. Her mother had frowned at the severe outfit, and had pulled her aside to ask why she chose to wear widows' frocks. Sarah made an excuse that she'd been feeling morose because she'd just read the poem "Isabella" by John Keats and she was in mourning for the tragic couple. She didn't admit that she knew about the baron's proposal, and had wanted to make herself look as unappealing a bride as possible.

The baron stood, holding his wine glass in his gloved hand.

"I propose a toast to our gracious hostess and host, Lord and Lady Drake," he said. "May our friendship always be strong, and may it grow stronger—and much closer, like a family, in the coming months."

"Brilliant!" Edward exclaimed, and quaffed his wine in two gulps.

"All of London awaits my announcement," the baron added significantly.

"What announcement?" the duchess asked eagerly. Her earrings and bracelets sparkled in the candlelight.

"What's that, Your Grace?" Edward said to her, pretending not to have heard.

"The baron said he has an announcement," she replied.

"It concerns your daughter, Lord Drake," the baron announced.

"Baron von Klausenberg might be referring to his newest protégé for piano," Sarah said. "The baron is a virtuoso, as everyone knows. He has graciously offered to teach me Chopin. But I am afraid I am just not good enough. There are more talented students than I."

"Yes, well, Chopin is not easy," Mrs. Bixby said mildly.

"Actually," the baron said, "there may be more talented students, but none as charming as Miss Drake. And, she is mistaken. It was not about learning Chopin."

"How forgetful of me," Sarah agreed. "Liszt, not Chopin."

"Actually," the baron began in his deep voice, "I plan to ask—"

"Mr. David Lowe of Venice, Italy," the butler announced.

Sarah breathed a sigh of relief. Everybody turned to see David in the entryway. He was dressed in evening clothes that had been custom-made in Milan. He looked elegant and aristocratic.

Edward immediately rose and strode over to David. They'd never met, but Edward was too distracted to introduce himself properly.

"The note was quite a surprise," Edward said in a confidential tone. They were far enough away that the guests could not make out the words.

"Does your lordship play chess?" David asked quietly.

"Yes."

"Then think of it as a prophylaxis that, with luck, will become a swindle."

"So let me see if I follow. You're here to frustrate some plan against me, and you hope to bring me to victory from a losing position."

"Exactly," David said.

Edward raised his eyebrows. "Surely it can't be as bad as all that. I'm not in a losing position."

"But you are, Lord Drake. And I'm here to reverse that."

David sauntered to the table with a regal confidence that made everyone fall silent.

David addressed Hannah. "Lady Drake, it is a pleasure to finally meet you. Please forgive me for being late." His momentary glance at Sarah gave her hope.

David took his seat across from Sarah. A servant poured wine. Conversation erupted around the table.

Hannah leaned toward David and said confidentially: "My son trusts you."

He matched her confidential tone. "I hope to always prove myself worthy of that trust." Then, more loudly: "This is an excellent wine, Lady Drake. A white burgundy from the Vosne-Romanée, premier cru, if I had to guess."

Hannah inclined her head. "Very perceptive. I take it you are an oenophile."

"One could say that."

Lady Edgerton said: "Mr. Lowe, if it's true you are from Venice, I was expecting a more continental accent. But you speak the King's English."

"Blame my years at Oxford, madam," David said.

"Oxford?" Mr. Bixby said. "I'm an Oxonian myself." He launched into a tale from his younger days. His storytelling was interrupted by the baron's resonant voice.

284

"The Duchess of Rexford has asked me to continue with what I was saying before our latest guest arrived," the baron announced, ostensibly to those at his end of the table, but in a manner that caught everyone's attention.

"It should wait," Edward interjected, cutting him short.

"I really think the baron ought to continue," the duchess said.

"That's right," said Perkins. "It's only courteous to let him continue."

Hideous old things, Sarah thought, frightened at the baron's persistence and their complicity. *The lot of them should just sink into the floor.*

"By all means, Baron von Klausenberg," Edward said in an obsequious tone, "please continue with what you have to say. You are quite determined, regardless of what I think."

Sarah clasped her hands in her lap and her knuckles were white.

"As you all know," the baron said, "I have become quite close with the Drake family. I first met Jonathan Drake when he came to my ancestral estate in the Carpathian Mountains last year. He helped me to complete the transaction that made my move to London possible. I count his lovely wife Anne among my dearest friends, along with the rest of the Drake family. We have enjoyed meals together, we share a passion for fine art and music, of course. Because of the high esteem in which I hold this family, I have asked Lord Drake to allow me to have his daughter Sarah's hand in marriage."

Gasps went around the table. Sarah was both horrified of the public spectacle, but also relieved now that it was all out in the open. She felt a strange calm, as if she were at a stage play, watching the drama unfold, despite the fact that she was the centre of attention. The guests glanced at her and then at the baron. David's eyes locked onto hers, and his gaze reassured her.

"Of course," Hannah cut in acidly, "the baron fails to mention that he gave us his word about keeping all this private until we've all had a chance to talk this over. Which we have not." Her smile was bright and bitter.

"And my consent has not been sought," Sarah added.

"Well, that's not cricket," Mr. Bixby said, frowning in disapproval.

"No, it's not cricket at all," Edward muttered, taking another gulp of wine.

"Even so," the duchess said with a giggle, "it is refreshing to have such an important matter out in the open, even if it is naughty of the baron to bring it up." She brushed a black feather away from her chin.

The duke was picking grapes off a silver epergne, eating them with relish while watching the scene unfold.

The baron continued. "Time is of the essence, my dear Hannah and Edward. You English like to drag negotiations on longer than necessary. I have made my proposal, and now it is up to the Drake family to accept it."

Edward rubbed his forehead. "Your lordship is perhaps unaware that in England, such decisions are not made in an instant, and certainly not at a gathering such as this."

The baron frowned. "You English have what you call freedom of the press, do you not? Then why do I not have freedom of the dining room? I am a man of great distinction, and I am saying the truth."

Mr. Bixby cut in. "My good baron, we English have rules of propriety, and rules of slander and defamation. Certain topics are just not discussed in front of guests, no matter how distinguished the speaker."

"Quite right," Mr. Perkins agreed. "As a newspaper editor, I do not have freedom to print whatever I want. Charges can be brought against me and my newspaper if my printed word defames someone."

"I hope you will keep that fixed firmly in your mind when you return to your office, Mr. Perkins," Hannah said pointedly.

Perkins grinned. "I am well aware, Lady Drake."

The baron waved his hand. "All this quibbling over details is exactly the waste of time you English excel at. And I have no time to waste. I need a decision now."

Hannah said: "I believe what you need is your hat and coat. My footman will show you to the door."

Before the footman could carry out the order, Sarah held up her hand.

"Wait, Maman. I want to put this all to rest before it goes any farther."

"Sensible young woman," the duchess said approvingly.

The baron smiled at her. "Yes, very sensible, my dear."

Sarah ignored him. She said in a clear, steady voice: "Mr. David Lowe of Venice, Italy, has proposed to me."

Hannah gasped, and so did most of the guests. David's momentary look of surprise transformed into an approving smile. The guests watched him raise his wineglass to Sarah in a silent toast. He kept his eyes on her the whole time.

The baron pointed to Edward accusingly with his gloved hand. "You did not tell me this!"

"I ... I did not know," Edward said in a bewildered tone.

"You have no control over your womenfolk," the baron said with contempt. He turned to Sarah. "Have you accepted?"

"I've accepted nothing," she said haughtily.

The baron said in a chiding tone: "I am disappointed that my supposed friends have put me in a position where I make myself look foolish, in public. Edward would not like me to make him look foolish in public."

"Too late," Hannah murmured.

The baron ignored her and continued: "We have a jury here." He opened his arms in a gesture to encompass all the guests at the table. "You English are so fond of juries. Sarah Drake has not given her answer to either suitor. Perhaps we can each present our case, and then she can choose the better man."

"This is outrageous," Hannah said.

The baron looked perplexed. "Outrageous, my dear lady? Surely, as the wife of a judge, you can appreciate how clever my suggestion is."

"We don't try our family matters in a public court, much less at a dinner party with our guests," Hannah said. "The matter is ours alone to decide. A fact which you seem determined to ignore."

The duchess put her hands together, as if in a prayer of gratitude. "This is just too delicious."

The baron continued. "I have announced my intentions, and yet this interloper—" he pointed at David "—insists that he is also a suitor. Since the conflict between two parties has already been made known to everyone here, why not decide it in front of everyone here?"

"Because it's nobody's affair but ours," Edward said.

"I've never seen anything quite like this," Mr. Bixby said in astonishment and disgust.

"Neither have I," the duke agreed, snatching an apple from the silver epergne and biting into it with a loud crunch. Nobody noticed his flouting of etiquette in refusing to use a fruit knife.

The butler quietly presented what looked like a telegram to Edward. Edward's face grew pale as he read it, and then he put the telegram into his pocket. "Very well, then. Let us proceed. Announce your decision, Sarah," he snapped. His face was distraught, and he took another quaff of wine, then signalled for a refill.

Sarah knew that something in the paper her father had slipped into his pocket was forcing him to carry on with the baron's charade.

Before she could speak, the baron announced in his resonant voice: "It is hardly fair for an intelligent woman such as Miss Drake to make a decision without comparing her suitors. I propose that we each present our case, and then hear the lady's decision on which of us is preferred."

"Is there really a choice?" Sarah asked sarcastically. "I feel like a brood mare on the auction block."

"Ah, but the brood mare doesn't get to choose her buyer," the duchess said in an amused tone. "But you do, my dear."

"Sarah is not a brood mare," Hannah pointed out, "and she doesn't have to choose either one."

"That's right, Sarah," Mrs. Bixby cut in. "You don't have to choose either one."

"Ah, the English talent for wasting time is on full display once again," the baron chided them. "Why don't we get on with this."

David sat back and rested his forearm on the edge of the table. He looked elegant and relaxed. "Yes, why don't we get on with it," he said. He glanced at Sarah, and his expression told her not to worry.

The baron fixed his gaze on David and pointed imperiously at him. "Why don't you tell us your name, where you come from, and what your ancestry is."

"I'm a wine merchant," David said. "I have lived in several places. My father is an ambassador to the Austro-Hungarian court. My mother is a physician."

Murmurs went around the table at this unconventional profession for a woman.

"And what is your race?" the baron enquired.

"My race?"

"Your religion, then," the baron said impatiently. "Catholic? Protestant?"

"I am a Jew."

"A Jew?" the baron repeated. "You say you are a Jew?"

"From the tribe of Levi," David said blandly. "I am a direct descendent of the Maharal of Prague, Rabbi Yehuda Loevy ben Bezalel."

"A despicable man," the baron muttered. "Guilty of unspeakable atrocities."

"Repeating the contemptible lies of gullible peasants is unbecoming in a man who claims to be worldly," David observed.

The baron's eyes narrowed.

"And what about you, Baron von Klausenberg," the duchess said. "Tell us about your background. I am sure it is quite distinguished."

The baron's eyes were hostile for a moment at her impudence in speaking to him that way, as if she were superior. Then his face softened, as if remembering that he'd have to humour these English if he were going to win.

"My racial ancestry is pure and distinguished," the baron said haughtily. "I come from a long line of nobility, stretching back to the Saxons and Magyars. My wealth is considerable. I own property throughout Europe. I am a man of highly cultivated tastes and refinements. And I am no Jew," he added. "Therefore, my offspring would not be tainted with the pollution of Hebraism."

Hannah sat up straighter in her chair and fixed her gaze on the baron. "If you marry Sarah, your offspring would be Jewish, because I am Jewish and therefore my children are Jewish."

"Hannah, I thought you had removed yourself from all that," Edward said.

Before she could answer, Mr. Bixby cut in: "In all the years we've been friends, I never suspected that about you, Hannah. Although it doesn't matter, of course," he added quickly.

"I had no idea, either," the duchess said in a tone that suggested it was somehow an indecent fact, and now she had had second thoughts about being there.

"Oh, but why deny it?" Hannah said brightly. "Baron von Klausenberg clearly thinks it is important, so we need to give him full disclosure, don't we?"

"Well, this certainly does change the equation, doesn't it?" the baron chuckled. "Or does it?" He let the question hang in the silence. "Every family has hidden secrets, does it not?"

"So you would marry a woman who has tainted blood?" David asked in a mocking tone.

The baron shrugged. "Did you think I didn't know about Lady Drake's background? Any nobleman, like myself, makes it his business to know these things before he makes a marriage proposal. Even so, I guessed it from the first moment I met Lady Drake, and yet I befriended her anyway. If Sarah marries me she could be a baroness—a rank clearly superior to being the wife of a Jew merchant."

"A rich Jew merchant," David added.

"Nouveau riche," the baron countered.

"Not so nouveau. The fortune has been in the family for over two centuries."

"My family fortune is over nine centuries old."

The duchess said: "It is so fascinating to hear two foreigners discuss the size of their treasuries with such pride. Pity that we English wrongly consider such talk vulgar—think of how much more interesting our conversations could be."

Mr. Perkins cut in. "At any rate, the baron has a point. One cannot hope to get ahead in society without the right connections, regardless of one's bank account. And let's be honest. Members of the Hebrew race are looked down upon in our society. Sarah would be better off marrying the baron."

The duke broke his customary silence: "One cannot find fault with this line of reasoning."

"Quite so," his wife agreed, her sparkling jewellery flashing as she spoke. "It really is in Sarah's best interest to marry the baron."

"It remains Sarah's decision," Hannah said.

"That's right," Mr. Bixby said. His wife nodded in agreement.

"But she still must take into account pedigree," Perkins interjected.

A butler appeared at Edward's side with another note. Edward scanned it, and stood abruptly. "I must take a telephone call," he announced, and left the room.

The baron rose and stood behind Edward's empty seat at the head of the table. "I will therefore lead us to the proper resolution." He ignored the murmurs that went around the table over his assertiveness in standing at the host's chair and commandeering the proceedings. The other guests glanced at Hannah to see how she took this brazen gesture. Her face was studiously blank.

The baron continued. "Now then, where were we? Ah, yes, the question of pedigree." He turned to Perkins. "You are absolutely correct, Mr.—"

"Perkins," the man said. "I am Henry Mortimer Perkins, editor of the New London Journal."

"Excellent, Mr. Perkins. I look forward to what you publish as a result of our little soirée here."

"Keeping in mind, of course, that defamation laws still hold sway," Hannah said. "And my husband knows the law."

Perkins smiled. "My dear lady, I am a man of perfect discretion. I would never wish to place myself in the cross hairs of the British justice system."

David cut in. "Tell me, Baron von Klausenberg, is it possible for a Jew to become a non-Jew?" he asked thoughtfully, as if contemplating a difficult equation.

"Why do you ask?" the duchess chuckled. "Are you thinking of converting to Church of England?"

David ignored her and waited for the baron's answer.

The baron grabbed Edward's glass and took a leisurely sip of wine. Then he sat down in Edward's chair. There were a few gasps at his boldness.

The baron answered blandly: "I already answered Mr. Lowe's question when I explained how beneficial it would be for Miss Drake to marry a man, such as me, who has a pure bloodline."

"You explained only how it would benefit her offspring," David corrected him. "You did not address whether, by marrying you and by formally adopting your religion, Miss Drake could become an authentic non-Jew."

"You are trying to trap me," the baron said in German.

David answered in the same language. "Not at all. I am trying to understand your theory."

"Theory? I have no theory, unlike the Jews who impose upon the world a vengeful god that forbids all manner of natural behaviour."

"Then answer my question," David said.

"Very well. The short answer is, no. She can never expunge her Jewish impurities."

"Why marry her, then?"

The baron smiled. Sarah sat motionless, wishing she could understand the conversation as her mother could. Hannah was gazing down at her plate, so as not to betray her comprehension.

The baron switched to Hungarian. "Look at her. She is a lovely thing, isn't she? Wouldn't you leap at the chance to conquer her?"

David responded in Hungarian. "You haven't answered my question."

"Which was?"

"Is there no way for a Jew to become a non-Jew?" David pressed.

"None at all. You Jews might speak every language, you might infest every country on Earth, but you will always have fixed Jewish characteristics. Nothing can change that."

"What are these characteristics?"

The baron let out an exasperated sigh. "A tiresome question. False ideas that you foist upon the world, traitors to your host country, wandering the earth with your stiff-necked resolve, undermining everything you come into contact with."

The baron's gestures were dramatic. The guests were transfixed by his oratory, and by the motions of his gloved hands, even though they could not understand the conversation.

"What, then, is to be done about us troublesome Jews?" David asked with a slight, mocking grin.

"Chmielnicki, but on a grander scale," the baron said coldly, tracing a large circle in the air with his gloved hands. "On a much, much grander scale."

"Ah, yes, pogroms. The tool of tyrants everywhere, throughout history. A favourite tool of your family," David said. "And yet the tyrants are always annihilated, and the Jews always survive. Curious, isn't it?"

"Not this time," the baron said calmly. "The flames of the next pogrom will engulf the world. The Jews will be destroyed in the dark fire—along with the others who resist us."

"That still doesn't explain why you would want to marry a Jew," David pressed.

The baron smirked. "Think of the abject submission, the numerous defilements. Marriage, for her, would be a perpetual punishment, until her very soul was destroyed and whatever remained would be totally subjugated to my will."

David's face turned as hard as stone. He said in a deadly voice: "I'd kill you now if I could get away with it."

The two men stared at each other in the tense silence. Then the baron said: "You fancy yourself like Moses, who beat the Egyptian slave master to death." His tone was mocking. "Jews always destroy the natural order of things."

"If by 'natural order' you mean tyranny," David retorted, "then you are correct. Cruelty is the tool of tyrants, and I intend to fight both."

"Cruelty is strength," the baron replied dismissively, flicking a gloved hand in the air as if to wave away a fly. "And of, course, there is science, which may solve the problem completely. I have seen experiments in which two people exchange blood. They are connected to tubes. As the blood of one goes into the other, the blood of the other comes in. I could entirely replace her Jewish blood with the pure blood of my race—even the blood of a common wench from my country would be adequate to use as a replacement. I could do the same to her children, too."

"Is there no limit to your depravity?"

Sarah saw the horror and disgust on David's face, and she felt terrified, even though she did not know what the two men had said.

Edward came back into the room. He stopped short when he saw the baron sitting in his place.

The baron rose, smiled, and said with a deferential bow: "I was keeping the throne warm for your grace." The baron remained standing to Edward's right.

"What did I miss?" Edward said ironically.

"A conversation I could not follow," Mrs. Bixby said. "The two gentlemen were carrying on in German."

"And Hungarian," the baron added. "Mr. Lowe and I should compare which of us knows more languages."

The duchess clapped her hands. "Oh, do that! It would be so amusing!"

The baron held up his hands. "Not now, my dear duchess. First, we must find out whether Miss Drake has any questions for her two competing suitors." His eyes rested on Sarah.

"I have no questions," she said calmly.

"Then tell us your decision, Miss Drake," the baron urged. "Whom do you choose for your husband?"

"She is under no obligation to answer," Hannah retorted sharply. Mrs. Bixby nodded in agreement.

Sarah looked at the people around her. The faces of her parents were creased with exhaustion and worry, as if their very lives were on trial. The faces of the duke and duchess were lively with interest in the difficulties of others that provided them with an evening of amusement. The eyes of the Bixbys were cast downward, as if they wished they weren't there. Perkins wore an expression of detached curiosity, as if he were gathering information.

The baron's gaze was cold and calculating, and a smile played on his lips. David's face betrayed no emotion, but Sarah saw a warm expression in his eyes that removed any lingering hesitation she may have had.

"I choose to marry Mr. David Lowe," Sarah said in a clear voice.

The table erupted into chatter. The baron narrowed his eyes. Then he clapped his gloved hands slowly, and everyone fell silent. "Brava, Miss Drake. Bravo, Mr. Lowe. Well played. Very well played indeed." With a flourish, he grabbed the nearest wineglass and took a sip, drawing out the moment as long as possible, like an actor who has full command of the audience. He put the glass down. "There is just one small detail that we have overlooked," he added.

"Is there?" Edward said listlessly. His face was chalky. Sarah was suddenly worried about her father. He looked exhausted and broken.

"Yes," the baron continued. "As you all know, Edward and Hannah have a son, Michael, who is now living in Berlin. I offered my assistance on some pressing financial matters."

"Is nothing about our family to remain private?" Hannah cried, glaring at the baron.

"It really is an outrageous public display," Mr. Bixby said.

The baron ignored them both. "Some people do not appreciate what I have done for them." The baron directed his gaze at Sarah.

"My daughter is not payment for a debt," Hannah said.

"You misunderstand me, my dear Hannah. Sarah fails to appreciate how I can save—no, how I *have* saved—your family. Pity, because now her life is going to be much harder. Each of your lives will be much harder And the debt needs to be paid. Otherwise, I will have to take legal action, I'm afraid. And that will be even more costly."

"You will be paid this evening," David said.

The baron's eyes narrowed. "I won't take money from a Jew."

"No need to do that, Herr von Klausenberg," David said amicably "Our distinguished host—" David gestured to Edward "—can write a cheque himself. His debt to you will be discharged."

"The cheque is here," Edward said, removing an envelope from his inside breast pocket. "You all are witness to it. Open it, Baron von Klausenberg, and let everyone see it is genuine, from my own account for the full amount, plus the interest that has accrued. You have my word of honour that the cheque will clear."

The baron took the envelope, and slipped it into the breast pocket of his jacket. His face was dark. "The Drake family will regret this evening," he said. The footman opened the door, and the baron marched out. Sarah breathed a sigh of relief.

CHAPTER TWENTY-SEVEN

Edward excused himself as soon as all the guests had departed, complaining of a headache and an upset stomach.

In the library, Hannah sank into a cushioned armchair. Her face was creased with exhaustion, and she had dark circles under her eyes.

David and Sarah sat nearby, at opposite ends of the leather sofa Hannah sensed the tension between them. Hannah thought Sarah looked triumphant and also awkward, like a young hound that had been successful in catching big game but wasn't sure what to do next. David was relaxed and dignified. Hannah was impressed with his manners. The man was regal, and utterly self-possessed. He had handled himself beyond all expectation that evening, and had possibly saved the Drake family from a treacherous fall. No matter what happened henceforth, Hannah would feel lifelong gratitude toward David Lowe.

"I should ring for Lawrence to build the fire," Hannah said wearily. "This room is cold."

"Let's not rouse poor Lawrence at this hour," David said, moving toward the fireplace. He revived the dying embers with more fuel. Soon the fireplace was blazing merrily.

"Thank you, Mr. Lowe," Hannah said. "It is much nicer not to have to wait for the warmth."

David resumed his seat. He glanced at Sarah, but she kept her eyes downcast. Hannah wondered whether her daughter would actually follow through on the path of marriage with this man. Hannah would not stop her either way, even though she herself had reservations.

Hannah broke the silence. "I hadn't planned for Sarah marry a Jew." She smiled to soften the impact of her words.

Sarah blurted: "Maman, Mr. Lowe hasn't actually asked me to marry him. I said that in order to defeat the baron, to get him to withdraw his proposal."

"I figured as much," Hannah said.

"It was a brilliant strategy, Miss Drake," David said approvingly. He turned to Hannah. "I would of course have sought permission from your lordship and your ladyship were I the one to have initiated the proposal."

"Naturally," Hannah said. She sat in silence, contemplating. Finally, she added: "You do realise that if anyone gets wind of this … charade … that the baron will be back with a vengeance. He will do everything to win. Of course, you both could announce the engagement in the papers, and then break it off when the baron has found someone else. That could take a while, and that means your prospects will be put on hold. Sarah, you probably did not think that far, did you?" Hannah was not angry at her daughter, she was angry at the baron for having forced them to such lengths, but her tone was sharp even so.

Sarah's eyes were downcast. She remained silent.

David said in a gentle voice: "Lady Drake, you daughter was put into a compromising position through no fault of her own. And she invented a brilliant evasion." He turned his gaze to Sarah. "Miss Drake, if you really do not want to marry me, you are under no obligation to do so. The immediate crisis has passed. I release you from your vow."

Sarah looked at him, and her face was grave. "But you never said whether you accept my proposal in the first place, Mr. Lowe, so how can you release me from my vow?"

In another woman, this would've come off as coquetry, but Sarah's face was open and earnest, as if she were trying to work out the logic of a puzzle that was of great importance to her.

Hannah raised an eyebrow. "Well, Mr. Lowe? Do you accept her proposal?"

David's smile was radiant. "Miss Drake, do you remember the day we met? You had answered the front door at your brother's house, and you were holding Lily."

Sarah nodded. "I remember every detail, including our discussion of the Song of Songs while we waited for the kettle to boil."

"After you left," David continued, "your brother and I took a walk. I told him that I was in love with you and that I planned to marry you."

"Ozzie never told me that!" Sarah exclaimed.

"That is because he is a man of discretion. When I told him that I planned to marry you, he laughed in a way I'd never heard him laugh before, as if the cares of the world had been lifted from his shoulders, and he could feel the mirth to the bottom of his very soul."

David's words touched a raw nerve within Hannah—it was a glimmer of hope that all would be well, that her son would be whole again, and her daughter would not live the life of a spinster—or worse, trapped in a marriage with the baron. Even so, she had to make sure it was a sound proposal.

Her retort was in the sharp tone of a mother protecting her daughter: "You have not actually accepted the proposal, Mr. Lowe."

David rose from where he sat, and kneeled in front of Sarah, like a knight at the feet of his queen. "I accept the proposal that we should be married, my dear Miss Drake. And I am formally requesting your hand in marriage."

Hannah said to her daughter: "Sarah, do you stand by your decision and accept this proposal?"

"Yes, I do," the young woman said quietly.

David took her hand, and kissed it. Then he arose and stood near the fireplace. He was overcome with emotion.

"I must admit I am somewhat disconcerted by all this," Hannah said. "After all, you two hardly know each other. There has been no courtship."

"There is no time, Maman," Sarah reminded her.

David was vaguely alarmed at this statement. Sarah's words were not spoken as a declaration of love, but as a fulfilment of duty, a tactical counter-measure. But when she raised her eyes to his, David saw something more—a spark of love that was kindling into passion. He realised then that she was carrying herself with the customary restraint and understatement that was proper for a young woman of her standing, especially in the presence of her mother.

In the silence of the night, the clock struck half-past one.

Hannah said: "It won't be an easy road, my dear Sarah, but you both have my blessings."

"Thank you, Maman."

"Thank you, Lady Drake. What about Lord Drake's permission?" David asked.

"I am speaking for Edward now," Hannah said resolutely. "Consider his permission granted. He won't stand in the way."

The hardness of her mother's tone frightened Sarah. She'd never seen this side of her mother before. Hannah continued. "I might as well tell you both this. Edward's absences from dinner this evening happened because the president of the Ravensbourne Bank is putting great pressure on him to decide in the bank's favour in the Desmond-Philips case. They are asking him to violate his conscience and integrity. He has been under such pressure before, but his enemies had no weapons against him. Now they do—or they think they do. I don't know how he is going to withstand the hideous pressure. I fear he won't."

"Has the baron anything to do with it?" David asked.

Hannah was silent a moment. "I have no evidence, but my intuition tells me that he, at the very least, knows what is happening and will use it against us if he thinks it expedient." She forced herself to smile. "The marriage of you two will be a bright spot in this dismal landscape. May your marriage be blessed."

"I will cherish her and keep her safe," David assured Hannah. "She is my bashert and my eishet chayil."

"I never thought I would hear my daughter's husband use those words," Hannah said, her tone suddenly becoming softer as she allowed herself to feel hope for the first time in a long time. "I am happy, despite the difficulties she now takes upon her shoulders as the wife of a Jew."

"What is eishet chayil?" Sarah asked.

"It means 'a woman of valour,'" David explained. "There is a proverb that says a woman of valour is more precious than rubies."

"I like that." Sarah's face suddenly darkened as she remembered something. "When you and the baron were talking in Hungarian, he said something that made you very angry. What was it?"

"I asked him what is to be done about us Jews, and he replied 'Chmielnicki, but on a much grander scale.'"

Hannah gasped. "I thought I'd heard him say that horrid name, but I couldn't be sure."

Sarah glanced from her mother to her fiancé. "I don't understand."

"Tell her," Hannah commanded.

David explained: "Chmielnicki was the name of a Cossack leader. In 1648, he led the Cossack armies and the peasants of the Ukraine in a revolt against the nobility. The Jews were caught in the middle. One of Chmielnicki's goals was to completely eradicate the Jews in that region. And he made a good start of it, too. Entire Jewish communities disappeared, untold numbers were tortured and enslaved. No Jew, no matter how helpless—or how young—was spared. There are stories—" David stopped talking.

"What stories?" Sarah urged. "Tell me."

"They're too unpleasant," David said.

Hannah said: "Sarah, you're a betrothed woman now, and you deserve to know." Hannah picked up the account where David left off. Her voice was toneless as she recited the atrocities. Sarah could not believe that her own mother—a woman of great breeding and discretion—could describe such dreadful things. Sarah had never imagined that one human being could do to another such wickedness—regardless of whether the victims were women, children, or babies.

Sarah's face was drained of colour, and she trembled in shock. David did not like to see her in such agonies. He put his hand on her shoulder.

"But Chmielnicki was not the only one," Hannah said. "There were other massacres, more recently, in which Jews suffered terribly. Some of my distant relatives were attacked in the Kishinev pogrom in 1903."

David added: "These past six years alone there have been massacres in Odessa, Kiev, and Bialystok."

Sarah asked: "Maman, is that why you left your heritage behind and stopped being a Jew?"

"Yes. I wanted to spare my children that same fate."

Sarah went to her mother and put her arm around her. "But, Maman, there are no real enemies to kill the Jews now. Not here in London."

Hannah retorted: "Did you hear how readily some of our guests agreed with the baron that Jews are a problem?"

"That's just a charade from guests who want to flatter the baron. Who is rising against the Jews now?" Sarah cried. "Nobody. We have nothing to worry about."

"Don't we?" Hannah said. "Few non-Jews know about the Chmielnicki massacres. And many either didn't care or they secretly approved of the Kishinev pogrom. The baron not only knows about them, he wants to see them carried out on a grand scale."

"So then why did you reveal that you're Jewish?" Sarah asked her mother.

"Because I'd been hoping that his Jew-hatred would cause him to spurn you. But I was wrong."

"Then he can't really hate the Jews that much," Sarah said, "and the danger is not as grave as you believe it to be. He still wanted to marry me, even after you told him I'm half Jewish. That means he loves at least one Jew."

"Sarah, he didn't want to marry you out of love," David said gently. "He had other motives."

"You mean, getting the debt paid back?"

"Among other things."

"What other things?"

David hesitated, weighing whether he should reveal the depths of the baron's depravity.

"Tell her," Hannah said. "She needs to know what he is."

David spoke reluctantly. "When I asked the baron why he wanted to marry you, knowing that your mother is Jewish, he told me he wanted to treat you as a slave, to degrade you and break your spirit. He also said he'd want to replace all your blood—and the blood of your children—with the blood of someone else, in order to purify you."

"How would he do that?" Sarah asked in disbelief.

"A complete blood transfusion. You'll have to ask Sam Berg for details, although it may be too depraved even for his vast medical knowledge."

Hannah closed her eyes and rubbed her forehead. "His evil and depravity is worse than I had suspected."

Sarah lifted her chin. Her eyes were defiant. "He can say whatever he wants. I've always loathed him, from the moment I set eyes on him. I would never have married him, even if everyone had wanted me to." She paused, then added: "I'll write him a letter. I'll tell him exactly what I think of him."

Hannah's eyes flew open, and she sat up straight. "No, Sarah. You are never to communicate with him again. Ever."

"Oh, Maman, you are being so melodramatic. A man like that cannot be allowed to go on, as if nothing has happened. Not to mention that he needs to be called to account for the way he treated Jonathan. And Papa. He can't be allowed such impudence. And he sat in Papa's chair this evening. It was an outrage."

David cut in. "Sarah, you must understand that the baron is a dangerous man. Your mother is right. You must stay away from him. Completely."

She was indignant. "Then who will fight for my family?"

"I will," David said quietly. "Your family are my family now. I have an obligation to protect you all. And it's more than just an obligation. It is my deepest desire, besides marrying you."

Sarah raised her chin. "We'll fight him together, then."

There was admiration in David's smile. "Yes. That's right, my love. We will fight him together."

Hannah stood up. "I must get some sleep. Mr. Lowe, I can see even now that I won't regret having you as a son-in-law. Goodnight. The footman will bring your hat and coat straight away."

"Goodnight, my lady."

Moments after Hannah left the room, the footman appeared at the doorway to show David out. David signalled, and servant withdrew, closing the door softly.

David turned to Sarah, who was standing near the fireplace. The flickering hearth made her hair glow like fiery copper.

She held out an envelope. "This is for you. It's an apology."

"Apology? Whatever for?"

"I accused you of using me as a bargaining chip when we were at Jonathan's house earlier today. I regret it."

He took the envelope, and opened the flap. He read the note and laughed.

"This note is too formal for a woman who will soon be my wife."

"Then let us consign it to the flames," she said with a wry smile.

He threw the note into the fire.

He took her into his arms, and whispered: "I hope your next letter to me is a love poem, penned by your own hand."

The clock chimed, but he didn't hear it, and neither did she.

CHAPTER TWENTY-EIGHT

Two days later, Jonathan came home from work to find a short, rotund man standing at his front door. Joe appeared with Chompsworth out of nowhere, and both warily eyed the stranger.

The man introduced himself as Inspector James Keane. Jonathan invited him in to the front parlour, and offered him a seat.

The inspector removed his hat and remained standing. He had a clean-shaven face, a double chin, and wisps of dull brown hair combed over his head.

He gestured at Joe. "You can dismiss your man, Mr. Drake, sir. This is going to be a confidential chat between the two of us. I won't take but a bit o' your time, sir."

Jonathan signalled to Joe that he should leave the room. The golem took Chompsworth with him, closing the door behind him.

Jonathan checked his watch. It was late afternoon, and Anne was not there. She'd left a note that she would be out, and would be home by tea-time.

"What was your name again?" Jonathan asked.

"Keane, sir. James Keane. I'm here to find out what you know about a woman named Minerva Vukovic. A foreigner. Seems she was your nanny for a time."

Jonathan assumed she had pressed charges. The best strategy would be to stay calm, answer all questions, and then hire legal counsel as soon as the inspector departed.

Jonathan said: "Vukovic? I didn't know that was her surname."

"She was in your employ, was she not, sir?"

"Yes, but my wife took care of all that."

"Is your wife here?"

"No."

"Then you'll have to answer the questions until such time as I can speak with the missus. And what time are you expecting her?"

"Soon."

"Well, then, let me proceed." The inspector asked question after question, jotting in his notebook. He kept repeating questions, such as how long Minerva had been employed, what her duties were, who her friends were, whether she was known by other names, and so forth. Jonathan found himself getting impatient and exhausted. He was relieved when the doorbell rang. He left to answer it, and came back with Sam Berg.

"Doctor Berg is my good friend, and I want him here," Jonathan said.

The inspector replied: "Whatever you wish, Mr. Drake. Tell me why your wife dismissed Minerva Vukovic."

That was a new question. Telling the truth would only strengthen Jonathan's case.

"My wife did not dismiss her. I dismissed her."

"Why did you dismiss her, sir? I thought your wife took care of those matters."

"Because Minerva extracted and drank the blood of my children," Jonathan said in a hard voice, "and I saw her do it."

"And why would that be, sir?" the inspector asked without surprise, as if this were a fact he'd heard regularly.

Sam spoke up. "Why are some people depraved, Inspector? You must ponder that question often."

The inspector said: "Please remind me who you are again, sir."

"I am Dr. Samuel Berg. I am a friend of Mr. and Mrs. Drake."

"Do you live here? In this house?"

"No, I do not, Inspector. I live just off of Sloane Square."

"And do you have medical knowledge about the children?"

Sam nodded. "Mr. and Mrs. Drake asked me to examine the children after Minerva was dismissed. I gave them my opinion, then prescribed a regimen to help the children recuperate."

"What was wrong with them?"

"Minerva had medicated them, probably with powerful sedatives, to keep them quiet. She also bled them excessively, claiming that she was following doctor's orders. There were puncture marks all over their bodies. The babies were weak and anaemic. Now they are thriving. Surely this is not your first case of abuse by a nanny without the parents' knowledge," Sam added.

Keane ignored the question and jotted notes in his notebook, and then addressed Jonathan. "And do you have a new nanny?"

Jonathan nodded. "Yes. Her name is Agatha MacLeod. Inspector, why this line of enquiry about Minerva? Is she in some kind of trouble?"

"Oh, yes," Keane said, chuckling morosely. "The worst sort. You see she's dead. Dead as a nit. Some bloke was crossing Albert Bridge yesterday, and he spotted the corpse bobbing in the water. Murdered."

"And have you narrowed down your list of suspects?" Sam asked.

Keane's eyes narrowed. "Well now. The list seems to be growing at the moment."

Jonathan waited. He wondered whether the rumours about his mental state had reached the inspector's ears, and he prepared himself for that line of enquiry.

"You see," the inspector continued, "she was impaled before she died. No major organs were ruptured. That prolongs the agony. It was done by someone who knows anatomy. That's why I'm especially glad you're here, Doctor. I want to ask you some questions."

Sam raised his eyebrow, and answered calmly: "Ask as many questions as you need to, Inspector Keane. I want to clear my name as quickly as possible so you can find the real murderer. In fact, I wouldn't mind seeing the body."

Keane rubbed his chin. "Right, then. Let's be on our way, doctor. We can chat as we go."

Jonathan was surprised that the inspector would allow a suspect to see the body. It suddenly occurred to Jonathan that Keane was far shrewder than he let on. Either he had decided that Sam Berg was not a suspect, or he still suspected him, and was going to use the next hour to observe Berg's reactions and enquire about his relationship to Minerva. It was a clever way to get Berg to trust him and give up whatever valuable information Keane was looking for.

Jonathan would not delay a moment longer in finding legal counsel, just in case Keane's sights settled on him. He would go straight away to see Geoffrey, his parents' solicitor. Time was of the essence, and the matter was too sensitive to contain in a letter. After the two men had left, Jonathan told Agatha he was going out to attend to some business, and then he donned his hat and overcoat and left the house.

Upstairs in the nursery, Agatha sat near the hearth, knitting. Jack and Lily were asleep in their crib next to her chair. Outside, a fierce storm raged, flinging rain against the windowpanes. Agatha looked up at the clock on the nursery chimneypiece. Joe had taken the dog outside to patrol the perimeter. She'd heard him go out just after Mr. Drake had left.

Agatha suddenly felt a chill rush over her, and an unaccountable sense of foreboding. She pulled her woollen shawl tighter, and hoisted herself to her feet. She picked out a log from the wood bin and carefully laid it on the embers.

She heard someone in the house. Joe must be back, making his rounds on the floor below. Any moment, she'd hear his familiar footsteps on the stairs, and Chompsworth would come bounding in the room, with Joe behind him, to check on her and the babies. She felt safe with Joe patrolling the house. He was a good man, and she often wondered why he had never married, and whether he'd even had a sweetheart. He seemed as innocent as a child, totally devoid of the sly lechery and importunity that plagued many men. She had watched Joe carefully since she first took the position here at the Drake house, and there was nothing about him that made her even slightly disconcerted. He was strong, but not threatening; obedient but not meek toward his superiors, deferential but not tyrannical toward those weaker than himself. His being a mute was something Agatha had become accustomed to, and it made him more agreeable because he didn't get on everyone's nerves with senseless chatter. Women had the unfair reputation of talking too much, but Agatha could wager year's salary on the number of men she'd met whose tongues ran twelve score to the dozen.

Agatha caught sight of a figure in the doorway as she straightened up from the hearth.

"Come sit, Joe," she began, and then realised the man wasn't Joe. It was the man she'd seen in the park.

He grinned, showing twisted, pointed teeth. He held a knife as he steadily advanced into the room. His eyes were dead flat, except for a spark of hatred.

Agatha positioned herself between the intruder and the sleeping babies.

"Get out!" she screamed. "Get out you damned devil!"

The babies awoke and began crying. The man slashed at Agatha's arm, knocking her off balance so that she fell to the floor. The man reached down into one of the cribs and grabbed one of the babies there.

Agatha screamed until she thought her throat would explode. The man backed out of the room with the wailing baby in his arm, keeping the knife pointed toward Agatha.

Agatha managed to get back on her feet. Joe suddenly appeared from behind and slipped a thick arm around the man's throat.

"Don't drop it!" Agatha screamed, running toward the intruder.

The man let go of the infant, and Agatha managed to catch the baby mid-air. She held the baby close, her heart pounding so hard she thought she was having a heart attack. The little screaming face was so contorted with terror that the colour changed from red to purple. That was Lily, she realised. The other baby, Jack, was screaming from the crib. Agatha went over and picked him up, holding both children close. She sat on the floor next to the crib, rocking back and forth, sobbing.

She looked up and saw that the man was on the ground, completely immobile. His head was at an odd angle. Joe's foot was on his neck, and he guarded him as jealously as a lion guards its fresh kill.

"Is he dead, Joe?" Agatha asked in a daze, above the wailing of the infants.

Joe nodded, and he would not take his foot off the man. Agatha concentrated on steadying her own nerves, and on soothing the babies.

She continued to rock back and forth, repeating gentle assurances in a trembling voice, but keeping her eyes on the body on the floor. It took a long time calm the babies. The whole while, Joe did not move from his spot. He was as focused as Agatha had ever seen him, ready to pounce on any threat that presented itself.

When the babies' crying subsided to whimpers and hiccups, Agatha relaxed a little. She gazed at the dead man's face.

"Joe, that's the man from the park. Remember? He stood outside the house that one night in the rain. The master and mistress both saw him."

Joe nodded.

"Where is the dog?" Agatha wondered aloud. "Why didn't she bark? Why isn't she here now?"

Joe looked around. Then he tilted his head and gazed at Agatha with a questioning expression on his face.

Agatha understood immediately. "No, you shouldn't go looking for the dog until the master gets home. Please don't leave. I don't want to be left alone. Especially not with that." She nodded toward the dead man. Then she started to weep quietly. Both children were calm in her arms.

"Joe," she said in a hoarse voice, "can ye put yer arm around me? Just for a moment? I'm so scared out of my wits I don't know what to do."

Joe moved to where she was, next to the crib. He sat next to her, on the floor, and put his arm around her shoulders. She leaned against him, still holding the babies in her arms.

Agatha didn't know how long they remained like that. They both heard activity downstairs. Joe knew it was Jonathan by the footstep, and he went to fetch him. Within seconds, Jonathan was at the door of the nursery, and his gaze was riveted on the dead man.

"What about the children?" Jonathan demanded.

Agatha said: "They're safe, sir, here in my arms."

"What the devil happened, Mrs. MacLeod?"

"It's the man from the park," Agatha explained. "He was comin' at me with a knife, and he tried to kidnap Lily, but Joe stopped him. Ye should've seen the evil in his eyes when he came at me and the bairns." Her voice shook and she fought the urge to cry.

"Why didn't the dog go after him?" Jonathan demanded. "That dog isn't afraid to chomp on an attacker." Jonathan had a sudden flash-back to the time in the ravine when the Chompsworth had fought off the beast at Jonathan's throat.

"We don't know, sir. She's gone missing."

Jonathan noticed that Agatha's sleeve was soaked with blood, and it had stained the swaddling that the children were wrapped in.

He pointed at her arms. "Whose blood?"

Agatha looked down. "It's mine. I guess his blade must've nicked me."

He took the children from her and placed them gently in the crib. Agatha pushed up her sleeve to expose gaping wound.

"Nicked you?" Jonathan said. "It's more than that. We must get this attended to. Wrap it tightly." He turned to Joe. "Stay with Mrs. MacLeod and the children. I'll call for a doctor." Jonathan muttered: "Damn Berg and his morbid curiosity. If he were here, he'd be more useful."

Jonathan saw the questioning look on Joe's face, and he knew the golem was wondering about searching for the dog.

"I don't know where Chompsie is at the moment," Jonathan said. "She's probably just on a short jaunt. Dogs sometimes want adventure. Speaking of adventure, why is my wife not home yet? And who removed the mezuzah from the front door?"

"She sent word she'll be traveling straight away to a dinner party," Agatha said. "She said she told you about it, but you didn't want to go."

"I don't remember any such thing," Jonathan muttered peevishly, "but then again, she probably didn't want me there anyway."

≺CHAPTER TWENTY-NINE≻

Inspector Keane waited until Sam Berg was finished tending to Agatha's arm.

Agatha kept her attention focused on the sleeping babies nearby. It kept her mind off the pain as Dr. Berg examined the wound, cleaned it, sutured it, and dressed it.

"It's not the worst cut I've seen, Mrs. MacLeod," he said cheerfully. "You must change the dressing twice a day. Don't get it wet. Try not to use that arm, otherwise the wound might pull open."

"Yes, sir," she murmured. The hand of her good arm rested on the blanket that covered Jack and Lily. They were sleeping like little angels.

Joe sat in a chair near the door, his face without expression, but his ears and eyes alert to everything. His posture was both relaxed and ready, and he looked as if he would spring to his feet at the slightest threat.

Jonathan paced nearby, lost in thought. The body had just been removed, and Jonathan could hear the men downstairs as they spoke to each other about carrying the body out of the servants' entrance so as not to attract more attention from neighbours than was necessary.

The inspector removed a pocket watch and glanced at it. "And where might be the lady of the house?" he added, as if it were an afterthought.

"Be damned if I know," Jonathan muttered.

Inspector Keane looked at him sharply. "What do you mean, sir?"

Jonathan gestured to Agatha. "Ask her. She knows more than I do."

"She's at a dinner party at the Wingate's," Agatha offered. "She told

313

me she'd be home quite late."

"Well, it's after midnight," Jonathan noted. "We'll see if she's as good as her word."

Inspector Keane caught the vexation in Jonathan's tone, and wanted to ask further questions on the relationship between Jonathan and his wife, but he sensed that now was not the time. Instead, he asked: "Is the good Mrs. MacLeod ready to tell me what happened?"

"It happened like this, Inspector," Agatha began. She recounted the events of that evening. She also told of having been accosted by the same man in the park, two days ago, when she had taken the babies out for a walk, and how they later saw him from the front parlour window, loitering in the glow of the streetlamp. Jonathan concurred with her account.

"Do you know who he is?" Keane asked.

"No clue," Jonathan said. "None of us had ever seen him before."

"And this is the same man who is now dead?"

"The very one," Agatha said. She sniffled into her clean white handkerchief and pulled herself together.

"And Mr. Golm," the inspector said, "I'll need to know your point of view."

"He's mute," Agatha said, "but he can write."

At the inspector's request, Jonathan furnished the golem with a large pad of paper and a pencil. Joe looked at the inspector quizzically, unsure about what he needed to write.

"Mr. Golm needs you to pose specific questions," Agatha prompted. She stationed herself next to Joe, and looked over his shoulder at the paper. She translated his notes as Keane asked questions.

After patient questioning, and Agatha's help, Joe's story was clear.

Joe had taken the dog out for a patrol of the outside perimeter shortly after Jonathan had left. On their patrol, there had been someone on the street, walking away in a hurry. It was a woman, and she looked unsteady on her feet, as if she were drunk or lame. Joe thought about following her with the dog to see what she was up to, but he got a sudden, strong feeling he should return to the house. The closer he got to the house, the stronger was the feeling that he needed to go upstairs to see Agatha and the babies. He was distracted, and he thought the dog was following at his heels, as she usually did. Joe ran upstairs, and that was when he found the strange man in the nursery, trying to take the baby. Joe wrapped his arm around the man's neck and strangled him. He didn't realise until later that the dog was not there with him.

Keane asked: "So you put your arm around his neck. Did you mean to kill him?"

Joe shook his head no. He wrote:

only stop him

Sam spoke up. "Well, it's clear Joe's aim was to neutralize the threat. I daresay that anyone bold enough to come into the house and try to steal a baby was deranged enough to not be stopped by an ordinary amount of pressure about the neck, hence the necessity of using force that proved lethal in the end."

Inspector Keane nodded. "I do agree with you there, doctor. It was a clear case of self-defence." He made notes and then looked at Joe and Agatha. "Has the dog returned home yet?"

"Not yet, sir," Agatha said, casting a glance at Joe. He met her gaze with a worried a look—a look that she had never seen on his face before.

The inspector said: "It is clear that the man had been watching the house, waiting to lure the dog away, so that he could slip in undetected and sneak up to the nursery."

Jonathan said: "Inspector, if you are finished, I'd like to go now and look for the dog myself."

"Be my guest, Mr. Drake."

Joe stood up, clearly eager to help Jonathan.

Jonathan said: "No, Joe, you need to stay here and protect the children and Mrs. MacLeod."

"No worries, Mr. Drake," the inspector said. "I'll be here awhile longer, looking around, and I'll keep an eye on your family. You bring your man with you if you want. All will be safe." He opened the inside of his jacket to reveal a revolver. He was hoping that Jonathan's wife would return home so he could ask her a few questions, but he kept this thought to himself.

"And I'll keep watch, too," Sam said.

Jonathan grabbed his hat and overcoat. "All right then, Joe, let's go find Chompsworth."

The two of them made their way to the servants' door that opened into the yard. They proceeded out into the dark yard. A chilly breeze blew through the moonless dark, rustling the trees. Jonathan had brought along an electric torch, and with a press of the button, he shined a narrow beam of light around the small, enclosed yard. It was empty. The two went through the gate and shut it behind them. Then they turned left and headed back toward the front of the house, along the pavement.

"Chompsie," Jonathan called, loud enough for the dog to hear but not loud enough to disturb the neighbours. "Come on, girl. Come back home."

Joe listened for any sound of the dog. He suddenly became alert, and put his nose up into the air, as if catching a scent. He took Jonathan's arm, guiding him across the street. They walked along the wrought-iron fence that enclosed the park.

Soon they came to the park gate. Joe went in first, pausing to sniff the air, with Jonathan close behind. Jonathan called the dog's name softly and swept the beam of light along the path and into the budding spring growth. Although the street lamps around the perimeter of the square were all lit, the trees and shrubs prevented most of the light from reaching the inner recesses of the park.

Joe suddenly stopped walking and raised his nose into the air, sniffing deeply. Then he veered sharply off to the left, stomping through flower beds and crushing with his heavy tread the spring flowers that were growing there. He dropped to his hands and knees, and crawled into the shrubbery, breaking off branches that were in his way with his strong hands. Jonathan crouched down and shined the electric torch toward the route that the golem was taking through the undergrowth. Joe stopped for a few seconds, re-adjusted his position, and began slowly backing out of the shrubbery. As he emerged, Jonathan could see that he had the dog in his arms.

"Oh, Chompsie, I'm so glad we found you," Jonathan exclaimed, putting a hand on her. Jonathan looked again at the dog, and saw that the fur was saturated with blood. Her throat had been so deeply cut that her head was nearly severed, but Joe was supporting her head so that it didn't fall off. In the glow of the torchlight, Jonathan saw a single tear glistening on Joe's cheek as he looked down at the animal in his arms, and then at Jonathan.

Jonathan was both enraged and terrified. He forced himself to say calmly: "Let's go back to the house and show the inspector. Then we'll bury her in the yard."

They went back out of the gate and walked along the fence. Just as they were getting ready to cross the street and arrive at the front door, Jonathan heard a motorcar on the square. He extinguished the electric torch, and turned to Joe. The golem was already retreating into the shadows, away from the glow of the streetlights, where they could conceal themselves.

From the shadows where they were hidden, they saw the motorcar stop in front of Jonathan's house. A man emerged, and circled around to open the passenger door. A woman emerged, taking the man's hand. He walked her to the bottom of the stairs that led to Jonathan's front door.

"Goodnight my dear Anat," said the baron in his resonant voice.

"Thank you, Zoltan."

To Jonathan's ears, his wife's voice sounded hollow and uncertain.

The baron added: "I hope our evening's amusement was not too … unconventional. But you are a woman of great strength, and your worldly experience continues to grow. Soon you shall have the enlightenment that will set you apart once and for all."

Anne murmured something that Jonathan could not catch.

The baron said. "Yes, but the more humanity sheds its inhibitions, the freer and more advanced it will be. Nothing can stop such freedom, or the possibilities that come with it. Be patient. Trust me. You'll see." Then he said: "I see that you removed that infernal Jew-amulet from your front door. That is progress, my dear Anat."

The baron kissed Anne's hand. Anne turned and ascended the steps without looking back. She unlocked the front door with her key, and went in.

The baron made his way back to the motorcar, but instead of getting in, he turned to face the direction where Jonathan and Joe were hiding. By this time, the golem was standing as straight and as still as an iron fence post, holding the dead dog as if it weighed nothing. The baron was also standing straight and still. Jonathan could not see the face of either because they were both in shadow (and he dared not move and call attention to himself). He sensed that there was some sort of connection between them, as if they were aware of each other's presence. After several moments, the baron got into the motorcar and drove away. Joe would not take his eyes off the motorcar until it had turned the corner and was out of sight.

They made their way to the back of Jonathan's house, to the yard. Joe gently laid Chompsworth on the lid of a coal bin against the wall of the house, and followed Jonathan inside through the door to the kitchen, to the stairs. Anne's voice could be heard even before they reached the back parlour where she sat.

"I was at a dinner party," Anne said in a loud, insistent voice. "I don't see how the location of it has any bearing on what happened here."

"Mrs. Drake," Inspector Keane said patiently, "I'm simply trying to find out all I can about the death of your former nanny, and about the person who tried to kidnap your daughter."

"How do you know it was a kidnapping?" Anne asked.

"Because he had the poor babe in his arms," Mrs. MacLeod interjected. "It wasn't as if he was just pinching the silver, like a common thief."

Jonathan motioned for the golem to wait and not go in the room just yet.

"Where is my husband?" Anne demanded.

Jonathan had the urge to go in the room and put his arm around his wife. But something made him hang back a few moments longer.

"Jonathan and Joe went to look for Chompsworth," Sam said.

"Then I'll tell you where I was," Anne replied with surrender in her voice. "The dinner party was in Belgravia, at—" and she gave the exact address of the baron's residence. She added: "It would be best if my husband did not know any of this. He thinks I was at the Wingates' dinner party. We had both been invited. But since he had no interest in going, I pretended to go but in fact I accepted another invitation."

"And why would your husband not want to go to either dinner party?" Inspector Keane asked.

"Because he regards the Wingates as crashing bores, and he despises the baron. So you see, my social life gets ruined because of my husband's strong opinions." She added: "It is rather too bad that he had not gone with me to the baron's dinner party. The police commissioner was there, Inspector. We had a delightful conversation."

The sense of betrayal Jonathan felt filled him with rage. He took a few moments to get a hold of himself before he went into the room. By this time, the inspector had moved on to other questions.

Anne turned toward Jonathan and Joe as they walked through the doorway. She looked alarmed.

"Good evening, Anne," Jonathan's expression was stone. "Or should I say, Anat. I trust you've had an unconventional evening."

She turned pale at his words, and she trembled.

"We've all had an unconventional evening," Sam said mildly, re-lighting a pipe. "Poor Mrs. MacLeod looks exhausted. And Mrs. Drake needs rest. In fact, we should all get some rest and resume this interrogation in the morning."

"Excellent advice, doctor," Anne said, heading for the door. She turned to Agatha. "Let me help you take those babies up to the nursery."

Each woman took a baby in her arms and left the room.

Jonathan said to Keane: "You'll want to have a look at the dog."

The men made their way to the yard. A cold drizzle fell from a black sky. Joe insisted on digging the grave himself. The dog was laid out nearby. Sam and Inspector Keane bent down to examine the wound on the dog's neck, by the light of an electric torch.

"Tell us again what happened," the inspector prompted Jonathan.

Jonathan recounted where they had found the dog, but he left off the part where he'd seen the baron drive his wife to the front door. He had a feeling he should withhold this information from Keane. If the police commissioner—who had more power than Keane—had been a guest at the baron's dinner party as Anne had noted, and was a friend of the baron, as Daisy had said, wouldn't the investigation be compromised? Such information could be used to damage not just Jonathan, but also Anne and other family members.

"It's a clean cut, so the blade must've been razor-sharp," Keane said.

"And the stroke was deft," Sam observed. "There was no hesitation."

"Was blood on the ground under the carcass when you found it?" Keane asked.

Jonathan looked to the golem for an answer. Joe shrugged. He obviously had not registered any such detail.

The inspector said: "Of course, that sort of thing is hard to see at night. In daylight, we can search the grounds thoroughly, if the rain hasn't washed it all away by then."

"If you don't mind, I'd rather not help you look for it," Jonathan said.

"Of course not," Keane agreed. "That's our job, Mr. Drake. One more thing." He scratched his ear, and hesitated. "I don't think there is a connection. But we've had two curious incidents. There was the body of a child found in that old synagogue off of Leadenhall Street three weeks ago, and another one found in a synagogue near the Marble Arch a week ago. We're worried that children are in especial danger right now."

"From Jews?" Sam asked with an incredulous note in his voice.

"No, that's not the conclusion," the inspector said slowly. "We think the bodies were put there to libel our Jewish residents. The rabbis at both synagogues have been extremely cooperative. They're convinced that what's at work here is something called a blood libel, because both children had been exsanguinated—that is, drained of blood. It is my theory, Mr. Drake, sir, that your baby could've been kidnapped for a similar crime."

"It wouldn't surprise me," Jonathan said in a hard voice.

Sam's voice was grave. "I'm sure the rabbis you spoke with explained that the blood libel is an old crime perpetrated against the Jews, in which they are accused of abducting and killing children and using their blood in religious rites. I'm sure they also explained that there has never been a shred of evidence for this heinous accusation."

"Yes, they did explain all that," Keane said. "And I must admit that in all the years I've been in this line of work, I've never seen this. We don't get much trouble from the Jewish quarter, so I don't have cause to concern myself with such matters."

"Of course," Sam said.

"But it is a frightful thing even so," the inspector said, rubbing his chin thoughtfully. "Maybe somebody is angry that more and more Jews are coming to London and buying up all the expensive properties. I don't know. Doesn't seem that this year is any different from last year on that account, so I don't understand why this is happening now, all of a sudden." He paused. "And another thing. We're getting reports of a curious kind of theft from the Jewish quarter. The holy goblets—"

"Those would be kiddush cups," Sam offered.

"That's right. Kiddush cups have gone missing from Jewish homes and synagogues. And the knives that the Jewish butchers use——"

"They're called shechting knives."

"Right. Those knives have gone missing, too. I'm told they can be very valuable, and those butchers are as upset as if they've lost their right hand."

"That's because the shochet—that is, the kosher butcher—regards the knife as an extension of his own hand," Sam explained. "He becomes so attached to his own knife that he won't borrow one from a colleague, nor will he ever let anyone else use his."

The inspector made a note in his notebook. "Yes, well, there you have it," he said, slipping his notebook into his coat pocket. "Now I'll be getting along."

Jonathan watched him let himself out through the gate. A damp breeze blew through the night. Jonathan shivered from the cold, and from the ominous information that Keane had shared with them. He suddenly thought of Mr. Miller, and wondered how these events were affecting him.

Jonathan gently lifted Chompsworth and handed her to Joe, who was standing in the grave. The golem wrapped the dog in his own jacket, and then laid the dog down onto the soft earth that he had just dug.

"She was a good dog. She saved my life," Jonathan said as he watched the golem backfill the grave with dirt.

Sam put his hand on Jonathan's shoulder. "She was a good dog indeed. We will all miss her."

CHAPTER THIRTY

Anne went to her dressing room, after having spent what felt like an eternity answering the inspector's questions. She sat at her vanity table, absently arranging her cosmetics and perfume bottles. The clock downstairs chimed three. There was the sharp smell of cleaning fluid that had been applied after the body had been removed. Even though it was the floor above, the smell had drifted throughout the house. She held a lavender sachet to her nose, but that did not help. She opened the bottle of ambergris perfume that the baron had given her, and dabbed a drop under her nose.

She was too upset to sleep. She had come home to find out there had been an intruder who had almost kidnapped her baby—that was more than she could bear at this late hour. Add that to the events that had unfolded earlier that evening, and before that, during the past two days and the shock was enough to overwhelm her.

What's done is done, she told herself, *and there was no way to un-ring the bell.* What she needed to do was to keep her wits about her. She was tempted to sleep upstairs in the nursery to keep watch over her babies. But she knew there was to be no sleeping, and she needed solitude to sort out her jumbled thoughts. Mrs. MacLeod was more than capable of keeping watch.

It had begun Friday at breakfast with the letter she had received in the morning post. She recognised the handwriting. Jonathan had already gone to his office, so she could read the letter at leisure at the table, while sipping a cup of tea.

My Dear Anne,

I want you to hear this news from me, not from some wagging tongue who cannot grasp the nuances. Last night, at the Drake's dinner party, I proposed that your sister-in-law Sarah become my wife. I know this is going to be a shock. Please hear me out.

Every great man, every great dynasty, must make decisions about marriage as an alliance, a strategy. A man of my wealth, nobility—and yes, my ambition—is no different. You British have a romantic streak, but some among you (even your occasional British sovereign) also recognise the need to cast aside romantic aspirations in favour of political strategy. My situation with regard to Sarah is just such a case. I have no love for her. I do not even like her. She is a spoiled, naïve waif. However, the alliance between the Drake bloodline and the Klausenberg bloodline would be a match of the ages for reasons that are too numerous to recount here. She has refused me this time, but I have other plans.

Suffice it to say, my dear Anne, that you are the one I love above all others. I have loved you, I think, from our first meeting, when you were heavy with child on that divan during that hot September afternoon, trying so desperately to hide your pregnant body under that shawl with the long fringes. Even if we do not formally marry, we are betrothed in our hearts, and our destinies are entwined. You still have the potential to become one of the most beautiful and sought-after women not just in England, but on the continent—even as far as St. Petersburg. I can help you attain that.

But I cannot help you unless you prove to me that I have your unreserved fealty. And, I must see you in person to explain exactly what that means.

Yours everlasting,

Zoltan

Anne's immediate reaction after receiving that letter was to burn it. Her next reaction was anger and incredulity that Jonathan had told her nothing of this latest development. Surely he knew. Surely his family had told him what had transpired. But nobody had bothered to inform Anne, and this was proof that they all were excluding her and did not really consider her a part of their family.

After an hour, the initial shock wasn't as great. She re-read the letter twice more, and slipped it back into a pocket of her dress. She would not burn it. She was, however, firmly resolved not to see the baron nor talk to him. The betrayal was too great.

She was not entirely surprised when another letter arrived in Friday's evening post, asking for a reply that she'd received that morning's letter. She slipped that letter into her pocket. And the next morning, Saturday, another letter came, asking the same question. Again, she refused to reply, and she resolved that she would go out that afternoon to distract herself from her inner turmoil. She did not let Jonathan know what was happening. She was testing him, to see whether he'd inform her of what had happened with his sister's spurning of the baron's proposal. He had still mentioned nothing to her. Nor had her in-laws bothered to inform her. She was angry at them all.

Anne knew that part of her anger stemmed from an intense jealousy of her friendship with the baron. She didn't want others to attain that intimacy. And, she had an intense envy that he was willing to elevate Sarah to a higher position in his life than the one that Anne enjoyed. Yes, the baron had tried to assuage Anne's fears about this, underscoring the fact that he loved her and did not love Sarah. He emphasized his willingness to give Anne a brilliant future. As a mother, Anne knew her children would benefit, reaching heights that they could not reach in their present situation. Yes, it was a cold calculation that excluded Jonathan. It was not without risk—especially the risk of scandal. But as the baron correctly noted, alliances were often strategic, and this alliance would be no less strategic and no less momentous for Anne and her children. But the baron had betrayed her, and she could not forgive him for that. Her own self-respect had to be more important than any advantage he could provide, if only Anne could swallow her own pride and let him help her. She would not swallow her pride. She would forsake the baron. And she would carry all the secrets with her, and not let her husband know what she knew, nor how much she resented him for his reticence.

Anne had not told Jonathan that recently she'd learnt from the baron that Jonathan had gone to some secluded convent, instead of coming home straight away. Were this fact to be known to the public, it would not reflect well on Jonathan's reputation, for various reasons which Anne could very well surmise herself: a man alone in a convent of women. Anne had waited to see how long it would take Jonathan to tell her about the convent, but he was not forthcoming.

The unforgivable part was his lack of trust in her, his unwillingness to reveal to his own wife what, exactly, he had endured. And it vexed her that he didn't reveal what was presently happening in his own family. The baron, by contrast, was forthcoming—almost to the point of rudeness. But Jonathan's reticence had put a chill on their marriage. It had pushed Anne away. The baron had warned her that Jonathan didn't really love her anymore. At first, she didn't believe that. But as Jonathan continually pretended as if his absence for most of the year hadn't happened, as he continued to exclude her, she realised that the baron was right.

And, she realised in that moment that her love for Jonathan had died.

It was a miserable position to be in. She was married to a man she no longer loved, and she could not marry the man she did love.

So when she'd left the house on Saturday afternoon to go on an outing to distract herself, she'd purposely worn a dress that could be worn to a dinner party. She had no intention of going back home to change. She'd go straight to the Wingate's that evening, and distract herself further. She remembered that she'd forgotten to tell Mrs. MacLeod of her evening plans, so she dashed off a note and had it sent.

When she arrived at the Wingate's house, the baron emerged from the shadows and intercepted her before she could ring the front doorbell.

"My dear Anne, you must let me at least have a word with you."

"You've treated me shabbily."

"But I can redeem myself," the baron countered. "Won't you at least hear me out? My motorcar awaits. We can travel the streets of London, and I'll tell you what is in my heart. If, after thirty minutes, you still loathe me, I will bring you back here and you can carry on with your evening."

With a face of stone, she followed him to his motorcar.

He started the engine. His gloved hand guided the steering wheel as he manoeuvred the car through the narrow streets.

"Your in-laws embarrassed me at their dinner party," he said. "Darling Sarah spurned me for the arrogant Jew named David Lowe, in front of everyone. She will lose whatever prestige she had, and nobody of standing or merit will want to associate with her. But, she deserves all that for her foolish choice. And David Lowe is the kind of man who ought to stay away from London."

"Did you actually propose to Sarah?" Anne asked in a choked voice.

"Yes." He glanced at Anne, and laughed at the pain on her face. He reached over and took her hand. "Now, my dear Anne, you must tell me what horrifies you. Is it the fact that I proposed to Sarah, or the fact that she and her parents treated me so outrageously?"

"All of it," Anne said hollowly. The truth was, she thought he deserved the outrageous treatment. But she didn't want to admit that the proposal is what rankled.

"Let's take the marriage proposal first, since that is probably what irritates female vanity the most. As you know, I have been friends with your in-laws since I came to London. I've felt sorry for Sarah from the first time I met her. She is pretty, but—"

"Most people describe her as quite beautiful," Anne said morosely.

"In my opinion, she is merely pretty. You are beautiful. But that is beside the point. Since the day I met her, I have always thought: What are her chances of marriage, really? It is almost too late for her. I thought my proposal would be a good match. I am rich, titled, cultivated—all the things that seem to matter most to your in-laws. They are rather climbers, aren't they?"

"Did you … do you … love her?" Anne asked.

"No, I do not. I told you all this in the letter, the very letter which you refused to acknowledge. The proposal was a matter of convenience. She needs a husband, I need someone who can provide me with heirs." He paused. "And there is something more," he murmured. "May I speak frankly to you?"

"Yes, of course," Anne said, breathlessly.

"I am only telling you this because I believe in complete honesty among friends. If I could choose a wife, I would choose someone like you, Anne, not someone like Sarah. She has too many flaws." He hesitated, as if unsure about whether he should go on.

Anne said: "We all have flaws."

"Yes, yes, but Sarah has an endless sense of self-entitlement. It pains me to say all this—she is your sister-in-law—but I feel I can confide in you. She has the snobbery of a rich girl who has had everything handed to her and has never had to work. Those flaws would never take hold in someone as intelligent and as sensible as you, Anne. You have been blessed with a more—how shall I put it?—a more realistic upbringing." He paused, and waved a gloved hand. "But, you are married, and therefore off limits. I always respect the propriety of those who take their vows seriously." He paused again. "I must admit, that the fact you are married has been a great source of personal tragedy for me these many months. Even now, it is difficult for me to talk about it." His voice broke a little.

Anne looked out at the buildings passing by as the motorcar threaded its way down Brompton Road. Her emotions were in turmoil.

"I don't know what to say," she murmured.

"No need to say anything. Your only flaw, my dear Anne, if I may be so bold, is that you do not understand your own greatness, so you do not insist on developing it. Nor do you insist that others recognise it and treat you accordingly. You also do not understand your effect on those of us who are artistic at heart. Lucien and I have spoken of it, as two men who know real feminine excellence when we see it."

Anne blurted: "You've spoken to him? About me?"

"Of course. We confide in each other. He finds you immensely lovely, you know. But like me, he would never press an advantage with a married woman."

Anne was silent for several moments. Then she said: "I must ask you something. Are you actually in love with me? You said so in your letter, but is it true?"

"My dear Anne, the answer is both yes and no. But this mixed answer is only because I am a man of great self-control, and you are a married woman of virtue and self-possession. Otherwise, the answer would be an unqualified, passionate yes. Could I lose my head over you? In a moment. You have already had that effect on Lucien, and I am no more immune than he is. I am simply not as susceptible—how do you English say it?—in having my head turned. He is much more susceptible, owing to his artistic temperament."

"Oh, but I didn't mean to turn his head!" Anne cried. "I don't trifle with men's emotions."

"My darling, I know that. He knows that. Sometimes people fall in love regardless of what the object of their love intends. Lucien is an experienced man, but he is still vulnerable to the arrows of Cupid. Faithfulness in body is not in his nature, as you may have guessed, although he is always faithful in spirit. Of that, you may be sure. It is an honour to be the object of his attentions, as many women have discovered."

The baron again reached for Anne's hand, and kissed it, while keeping his eyes on the road. Then released her hand. "Let us remain good friends, and not let it get more complicated than that."

Anne realised that all was not lost. She need not spurn this man and all he offered.

"You spoke of fealty," she ventured.

"Ah, so I did. Let us discuss it later. But first, you are to be my guest at my table."

At the baron's feast, Anne sat to the baron's right. The baron had placed a mantle of Siberian sable around her shoulders, murmuring how it is fitting for the goddess Anat to be robed in the finest pelts. Anne felt regal in it. Around her, on either side of the long banquet table, were fascinating people. She now knew it was only right and fitting that she should be there, and she basked in the attention. The baron had helped her to see her own greatness, and for that, she was eternally in his debt.

Servants brought in steaming platters of food and set them on the table. These servants were not dressed in the livery of typical London servants. They looked like flamboyant birds with their flowing turquoise trousers, tight scarlet vests, and emerald-green turbans affixed with a large sapphire and an ostrich feather. The dining room mimicked their theatrical garb, with gauzy hangings in bright yellow and pink, masses of perfumed flowers, coloured glass lamps, and overlapping Oriental carpets on the floor.

Anne was conscious of Lucien's frequent gaze. He was dressed in his usual powdered wig and lace-trimmed shirts. He looked like a dashing nobleman from a century ago.

"Enjoy, enjoy!" the baron cried from the head of the table. "Help yourself to the wine, which has been consecrated to the gods and goddesses of old. Ba'al, Molech, Ishtar … and of course, our darling Anat who is with us here tonight!" He raised his silver goblet to Anne.

There was applause around the table, and murmurs of "To Anat!" Anne inclined her head to acknowledge the homage.

The baron continued. "The assorted wine goblets on our table tonight are kiddush cups, from local synagogues and households. Some are glass, some are silver, some gold, others are pewter. All are now being used to hold the wine of pagan gods—an insolent violation of the commandments of the Hebrew Bible. Let us raise these goblets and drink deeply in honour of our idolatrous ancestors. Let us see ourselves as the enlightened who will topple the harsh deity of the Old Testament, and clear the path for the new deities of a new revolution. These new deities will be forged in the dark fire, and a new order will arise from the ashes!"

Lucien put his hand to his heart. "The baron's poetry fills me with passion! Let us drink!" He quaffed his goblet until it was drained.

Cries of approval erupted among the guests as they drank the wine.

The baron pointed to platters of meat. "What you see before you is roast swan, gathered in the dark of the night from the banks of the Thames by our obedient servant Vukovic."

Anne gasped. "But it is illegal to poach the swans! They belong to the Crown!"

The baron chuckled as he cut a piece of swan breast, and placed it on Anne's plate. "All the more delicious for the forbidden flesh that it is," he said.

"But what if someone should find out …" Anne let the sentence trail off.

"They won't, dear Anne, unless someone should happen to tell. And I do not think anyone here would do that."

"Certainly not I," one of the brooding Eastern European men said from halfway down the table. His accent was heavy. "The British monarchy is as corrupt as the Habsburg monarchy. Death to them all, I say."

"Dear Niko," the baron said indulgently, "your sentiments are in the right place, but you are sloppy about your anger. Do not let it spill out before the time has come. Stay focused."

"But the time *is* right," Niko countered. "In Serbia, we have been oppressed long enough and we——"

The baron raised his hand and the man fell silent. "The time has not come, and you have not mastered the rules. You think that only nationalism is the answer. But nationalism is only one possible weapon among many."

"I personally think Marxism holds promise," said a young actor whose name Anne did not remember.

The baron waved a hand dismissively, as if he were dealing with callow students. "You are all too short-sighted. Marxism, socialism, nationalism, communism," he said, ticking off the words on his red-nailed fingers. "The names are unimportant, so long as they are means to the same end: overturning the current order. The important thing is to support the most useful groups of a given time and place. It is of no importance what label they give themselves, even if they are but few in number. Words are tools. Commoners believe that words convey information and truth. But that is of secondary importance. Use words to get people to do what you desire, even if you are not telling the truth. That is the main usefulness of words, that is their true power, my dear friends."

"There is no denying that Gorky's novel, *Mother*, is a work of genius," Niko proclaimed.

"Perhaps," the baron conceded. "Speaking of Russians, where is the esteemed Vladimir Lenin? Rumour has it that he'd been here in London."

"He departed in June," someone shouted from the other end of the table.

"Pity," the baron said. "I so wanted to make his acquaintance. Such an intense man, with great promise. If he appears again in London, do notify me so he can join our feasts." He launched into a short monologue: "How does change come about? The answer is simple: Overturn all tradition, destroy all order, cast doubt on all certainty. Sow the seeds of discontent among the masses so that they revolt and destroy the existing order. They are like the peasants who clear your field of weeds and boulders.

Once they have done their job, you evict the peasants. Then you plant the field yourself, and allow the seeds of your vision to flourish. You make way for a true leader to deliver everyone from their suffering. Consider the roast swan here. Are we not waging war against the Crown this very evening by eating the King's birds? Yet if we don't rebel, the King wins and we lose. We must ourselves be the agents the change we are waiting for, otherwise, all is in vain."

He noted that Anne had not touched hers. "Eat the swan, darling Anat, and be the change that ushers in the revolution!"

That struck Anne as extremely profound, and she felt the thrill of rebellion rising in her gut. She cut into the swan breast, tasted it, and found that it was quite delicious. The illegal nature of it only added to her pleasure.

Just then, Anne noticed that the servant Vukovic was at the baron's side, whispering something. Vukovic was a tall, wiry man, with close-set eyes and a face that reminded her of a wolf. Anne had seen him once or twice before, and she thought he looked familiar, but she could not figure out why.

Vukovic left, and the baron turned his attention on Anne with a renewed intensity.

"So, where were we, darling Anat? Oh, yes. Overturning tradition. Let us take, for example, the suffragettes. They seek the vote, same as men. A noble cause, and one that is ripe for our revolutionary fervour."

"That's not where the true revolution for women lies," Ursula said. "Women will only have true freedom when they can live their lives, the same as men, in all respects." She emphasized these last three words with an obscene gesture of her heavily jewelled hands.

"I think the vote will accomplish that," Anne ventured.

Ursula laughed. "Do you? So when you are able to vote same as your husband, will you be his equal in other ways, too?"

"I, I suppose so," Anne said, uncertain about what Ursula was getting at.

Ursula continued. "We all know that Frenchmen have the reputation for having mistresses on the side. Is the same freedom accorded to their wives?" Ursula stared at Anne, waiting for an answer.

Anne felt uncomfortable. "I don't know. I never thought about it, really."

The baron cut in. "What Ursula is getting at, my dear Anat, is that men and women ought to have equal freedoms in all regards, including the romantic realm. It is hardly fair that women are expected to be virgins on their wedding night, but men are not. Why can't they both have the same pre-marital liberties?"

"Because of religion and tradition, which oppress us all," a playwright called from the other end of the table.

"Exactly!" the baron said. "Religion and tradition stifle the creative spirit, and kill pleasure." He pointed to Ursula and Lucien. "Those two there, however much they love each other, would never limit themselves with matrimony, or with monogamy, for that matter. Why should they? Would it not be better to give each person the freedom to leave when the arrangement was no longer suitable?"

"But if there are children . . ." Anne ventured.

"It makes no difference," the baron said. "We should not organise society for the benefit of the little parasites. They are dependent on adults and should do as adults wish. And it is far better to let the community raise them, rather than the parents, especially when one's youth and beauty are still in full bloom."

The baron leaned toward Anne and said in a low voice that only Anne could hear. "Tonight, there will be a special entertainment that only a select few will be allowed to see. The rest will go home. Please stay. What awaits you will be a revelation, a transformation into the fealty you asked me about."

What had followed had been too overwhelming for Anne to recollect fully as she sat at her dressing table later that night. Perhaps it had all been a dream. Ursula's performance, and later, Anne's own participation, must have all been hallucinations from too much absinthe. She'd been swept along. She hadn't been herself. They had taken her to some opulent room down the cellar stairs, and had dressed her in a long, plain muslin robe, and had put gold bracelets around her arms, and a tall conical headdress on her head. Then they'd called her Anat, the Goddess. They'd given her something to drink.

In a cellar room with a fire, they had chanted:

She plunges her knees in the blood of swift ones,
her thighs in the gore of fast ones

while daubing the blood of the dead one on the skirt of her robe. Then, after that, when they had sprinkled her with purifying water, they had chanted:

The Virgin Anat, the Mother of Nations,
She washes her hands.
Come together, O lads,
At Anat's feet bow down,
Prostrate yourselves, honour her.

And they had all prostrated themselves at her feet—all of them, including the baron. Later, when she was dressed in her own clothing, and seated in the baron's motorcar, Anne had said: "You promised to tell me about fealty." She was still in a daze.

The baron replied: "Do you know what happened to Minerva, the woman who used to care for your children?" the baron asked.

"She was found dead in the Thames," Anne said in a detached tone, looking out at buildings along the side of the road whose roofs were shrouded in fog. Her own detachment surprised her, but she embraced it. Detachment made it all so much easier to bear.

"Vukovic is her brother, you know."

Anne gave the baron a startled look. "I thought he looked familiar."

"He is proving himself to be a valuable servant," the baron remarked. Then he asked: "Do you know much about cultures where family honour is paramount?"

"I can't say I do."

"A brother will kill a sister who brings shame and dishonour to the family name. That is fealty. Not like you British who claim fealty, and then dare not make a decision unless every last insignificant family member has been consulted for her worthless opinion." He chuckled.

"No doubt the police could tell she had been impaled on a stake—unless, of course, they are as incompetent as they are stupid. They are probably thinking they need to find the doctor who managed to do it in such a way that no major organs were disrupted, so that death did not come too quickly. They forget that other professionals—artists such as Lucien, for example—have a vast knowledge of anatomy, too."

The baron glanced at Anne, and then went on. "Vukovic has become quite adept at procuring the Jew slaughtering knife. He has collected a number of them from shops and houses. Of course, the Jews believe they have a holy mandate from their vengeful god to slaughter animals quickly and painlessly. That is why they keep the blade sharp. But when a disloyal wench needs to learn a lesson, a dull, nicked blade is what's called for. Vukovic saw to that when Minerva's time came."

Anne was shocked out of her detachment by this information. "That is unspeakably cruel!" she blurted.

The baron chuckled. "My dear, as I have told you before, cruelty is another word for strength." He quoted: "'The goddess Anat gives battle. She cuts in pieces the sons of the two cities.'" He reached over and squeezed her hand. "You are becoming Anat. That is your fealty to me."

Now, as Anne sat in her dressing room and waited for the dawn to arrive, she thought about all that had happened, and she realised that she did not quite understand what the baron had meant by "becoming Anat." Yet, she could feel that a new strength was taking hold, a new resolve. She would not need to sleep, not now. She would stay awake until she heard Mrs. MacLeod getting ready for church, and then she would go and see to her children.

CHAPTER THIRTY-ONE

Jonathan was dressed in a morning coat and a top hat—the same top hat he'd lost in the ravine at the baron's estate. Strange that he'd be in day dress, when it was night time. He found himself alone on top of a hill, near a church. The heavy, arched double doors were open. He stepped across the threshold, into a dimly-lit interior, and walked toward the large rosette window at the other end. He was curious, and then suddenly afraid. There was something malevolent in the shadows. Suddenly, the altar erupted in flames. It was an alien fire, a dark fire, that rapidly progressed down the transept. Jonathan turned toward the doors, and ran outside, into the night. The path in front of him angled down steeply into the darkness. As he looked behind at the burning church, it had transformed itself into a burning synagogue. A demon emerged from the flames, and chased him. Jonathan ran down the path, stumbled, and then fell. His stomach dropped as he fell, and he realised he was falling down the ravine at the baron's estate.

He woke up, gasping for breath and sweating profusely. It took him a few moments to realise he was home, in his own bed. He made his way to the window and swiped the drapes aside. A grey dawn hung over Cadogan Square, and Jonathan peered down onto the empty street to be sure nobody was lurking there.

He washed and dressed for work. At breakfast, Anne was silent while Jonathan ate bread and jam. Jonathan was too distracted to attempt conversation, which was just as well. He had the feeling that she wasn't interested in his remarks, anyway.

At work that morning, Jonathan had trouble concentrating. He could not shake the feeling that the nightmare had left in his mind. His new clerk, a young man named Alfred with thinning blond hair, would occasionally glance at him with vague alarm. Jonathan plodded through his tasks, glancing out the window, and wished he could shake himself free of the nightmare that still hovered over him.

At noon, he decided to pen a note to David, to let him know he'd had another vision. It felt similar to the visions in the spider's web in Budapest. As soon as the letter was posted, he felt better.

When Jonathan arrived home late in the day, he expected the dog to greet him, wagging her tail, her brown eyes eager for attention. But then he remembered what had happened to her, and his heart ached.

He found David and Sam in the front parlour. Sam held Lily. David was talking with Agatha while she fed Jack from a bottle. Joe sat in the corner, watching everything with his calm, dark eyes.

"Oh, hullo there, Drake," Sam said. "I insisted that Mrs. MacLeod bring the children down from the nursery for a visit. I miss the days when my own children were babies."

Jonathan kissed each of his children on the top of their heads. "By the way, where is Mrs. Drake?" Jonathan asked.

"She went out, sir," Agatha said, her mouth drawn tight. "She didn't say where, sir. Now if you gentlemen will excuse me. I'll be gettin' these little angels ready for their bath." She gathered the children into her arms and left the room. David closed the door after her.

He turned to Jonathan. "I got your letter, and I hope you don't mind that I told Berg about it."

"Not at all," Jonathan said. "It's probably nothing."

"Tell us anyway," Sam urged him.

Jonathan recounted the dream of the burning church and the demon that pursued him.

David took a letter from his pocket. "My uncle Yehuda, the rabbi in Prague, wrote something in a letter that you may find interesting." He read aloud: "'I have dreamt a dream, three times, of a church burning and of a demon arising from those flames and pursuing a man down a hill. I believe the man is your friend Jonathan. Please tell him to pray and to study, and to be vigilant.'"

"So even Rabbi Loew shares my nightmares now," Jonathan said. "That's not much comfort."

Sam said: "Well, here's a bit of good news. Your father is doing much better, Jonathan."

"What do you mean, doing much better?"

"Nobody told you? Your father was bedridden. He had a fever and was delirious, but he's better now. I've been to your parents' house regularly to check on him."

"He probably told my mother to say nothing," Jonathan muttered in disapproval. Then he asked: "How is she holding up?"

"She's a strong woman. And your sister is remarkable, too."

"She is, isn't she?" David agreed.

There was a commotion coming from the entry hall. Joe got there first, and the other three men followed him. Joe grabbed a beggar-woman by the wrists. Anne was in her overcoat and hat, yelling at Joe: "Put her outside! She is an intruder!"

Joe did not obey her. Anne turned to her husband.

"Jonathan, tell him to put her outside! She doesn't belong here!"

"Release her, Joe," Jonathan said.

As soon as Joe let go of her wrists, the woman stopped struggling. She brushed her matted blond hair away from her face, and slowly turned around, studying the faces around her. Joe stood ready to restrain her in case she did anything dangerous.

"Who are you?" Jonathan demanded.

"I'm Daisy, sir. Madam Drake knows me, sir."

Anne was suddenly frightened as she recognised her former servant. She did not want to be blamed for this woman's current state. She said coldly: "I discharged you from your duties in the summer, Daisy, and I gave you excellent references at that time. I had received word that you had found a suitable position shortly after leaving my employ. I don't know why you've come back here. You must leave now."

"It's because I have something to say, m'lady. About the baron."

Anne felt a jab of dread in her stomach. She did not want to hear what Daisy had to say—and more to the point, she did not want Jonathan to hear what she had to say. The woman was clearly not right in the head.

"Then go to the authorities," Anne said. "None of us here can do anything about that. It's none of our business."

"I want to hear what she has to say," Jonathan said.

The dishevelled woman smiled slowly and turned to look at Jonathan. "Don't look much like me old self now do I, sir?" She pointed at his face, and her fingernails were broken and dirty. "I can see in your eyes you've been touched by the baron, same as me." She pointed to David. "And you're a handsome one." She pointed at Sam. "I like your face, kind and merciful, no danger there." She pointed at Joe. "Now you're a rum one, ain't ye?"

The clock chimed.

"You need to leave, Daisy," Anne said.

"She stays," Jonathan said.

"Beg pardon, sir, I could use a bite to eat," Daisy said. "It's been a while since I've had some hot porridge and cream. And some good meat."

"And you shall have it," David said. "Let us go downstairs and see what's in the kitchen, shall we?"

Sam followed the two of them downstairs.

"This is outrageous," Anne snapped at her husband. "And a waste of time. I don't need to hear what she has to say, anymore that I'd need to hear the ravings of a Hanwell resident. I'll be upstairs, taking care of my children with Mrs. MacLeod."

Jonathan said: "Anne, she may have valuable information."

"Then you deal with her," Anne retorted.

In the kitchen downstairs, Joe took a seat in the corner and watched Daisy eat while David and Sam sat near her at the table. A bottle of brandy sat in the middle of the table, along with bread and butter.

Jonathan arrived and pulled up a chair next to Joe. He gave the golem paper and a pen. On the paper, Jonathan had written: *Tell me what happened, Joe.*

Joe wrote:

she was outside front door
she say she want to see madam
anne yell at me and want her gone

Jonathan wrote: *Is she evil?*
Joe shook his head. He wrote:

soul not bad

His pen hovered over the paper as he thought about what word to use. Finally, he wrote:

tormented

Jonathan watched her. Daisy held herself upright, trying to maintain whatever dignity she possessed. She forced herself to eat slowly and politely, even though it was clear that she was half-starved. Jonathan remembered what kind of self-control that took—he'd felt it at the Abbey of Saint Hildegard, when he'd sat down to his first meal in months. He had great empathy and respect for Daisy, and as he sat across from her at the table, he said: "Please don't be shy about eating your fill, Daisy."

She nodded and said with food in her mouth: "I won't, sir, thank ye, sir."

The men chatted about inconsequential topics, smoked, and sipped some brandy. After the better part of an hour, Daisy sat back in her chair with a sigh, and put a hand on her stomach.

"Thank ye, m'lords. I haven't had such a meal in a long while."

"Now, Daisy, why don't you tell us why you're here," Jonathan prompted. "My man, Joe, says he found you lurking about the house."

"I'm here because I didn't know who else to tell, and I thought her ladyship could help because she knows the baron. I thought, she'll believe me. Nobody else will."

"Why wouldn't anyone believe you?" Sam asked gently.

"The baron told me nobody would believe me. So did Vukovic. So did Lucien and Ursula and all the rest of 'em. They're my betters, ye see, and I thought they're right. But then I heard some of 'em talkin', and I knew that even if they killed me for it, I had to tell someone."

"Start from the beginning, Daisy," Jonathan said. "Start from when you left this house."

"Well, sir, remember how the missus had to let me go. Right before the babes was born. I went to work for the baron. I thought it'd be a posh position. But it was hell. Not at first, mind you, but slowly-like. A rotten and stinkin' tide that creeps up and ye don't even realise it. I finally escaped, and I've been livin' under bridges and whatnot. The streets are cruel, but not compared to him and his friends. Swine and blackguards, they are. Depraved. The lot of them." Daisy hugged herself and began rocking back and forth. The men waited for her to continue. "At first, it was a good position. Decent pay, food, lodging, reasonable work. But then, I saw the horrors, the cruelties. You wouldn't believe me if I told ye. They said I'd get strong lookin' at things that frighten ordinary folks. They forced me to watch. Then they wanted me to hurt a ..." her voice trailed off. She was silent for a while, lost in her own thoughts. "And that's when I escaped." She shrugged. "I guess I did get strong. I ain't dead yet, am I?" She laughed hollowly.

Jonathan had his elbows on the table, and one of his hands covered his mouth. His face was pale. Sam kept an eye on him.

Jonathan blurted: "The baron told me he doesn't eat flesh. But someone was dropping off vials of blood to his house."

Her eyes focused on him, and she smiled a macabre smile. "Oh, that's right, sir. He don't eat flesh. But he never claimed he didn't drink blood, now did he? That's for his servants to gather and put it in a fine goblet for him. The old devil had us all fooled, splittin' hairs like that."

"Daisy," Sam said gently, "do you want me to come with you to the authorities so we can make formal charges against those who abused you?"

Daisy chuckled. "Oh, no, sir. I ain't tellin' the bobbies a thing. The commissioner himself is a close friend of the baron. That bloke is a copper-nose, always a drink in his hand. And he himself has participated in …" She stopped herself. "Vukovic'll find me, and they'll have to fish me out of the Thames like they did Minerva. After they let me die on a stake, that is. Like they did with her."

"Did Vukovic kill Minerva?" David asked.

She nodded. "And he being her own brother, too. The baron likes to say that cruelty is strength, and that's what Vukovic is. One look at his face, and even a daft blighter could see the wickedness there. And the bobbies won't even investigate what happened to Minerva. Case closed, they say, 'twas an accident."

Sam leaned forward a little. "So you came here to tell us what the baron and his friends did to you, is that it? You were hoping that Mrs. Drake would help you."

Daisy scratched her head, and wiped her nose on her napkin. "Yes, sir, that's it. It's been too much to keep to myself, and I had to tell someone. I knew Mrs. Drake has been friendly-like with the baron, and I come to warn her. She was good to me back when I worked here. There's another thing. There's been talk. The baron wants Winston Churchill killed—you know, the son of Lord Randolph Churchill."

Memories came flooding back to Jonathan. He suddenly recalled the cellar of the museum and the marionette that looked like the baron, how its red-stained mouth worked up and down, telling him that Churchill was a threat and needed to die. How could Jonathan have forgotten that?

Daisy was still talking. "I thought, Madam Drake was so nice to me, maybe she could help. She once told me her father is a judge, so he must know important people who could tell Mr. Churchill."

Jonathan was going to correct her mistake and point out that it was his own father who was the judge, but David turned to Jonathan and said: "That would explain the dreams, Drake. When you had that episode in Budapest, you dreamed of a burning chapel—a church—on a hill. Church-hill. Your most recent dream, the same. Uncle Yehuda's, too. It's no coincidence."

Jonathan stood and paced the room, agitated with what he'd learned. "But still I don't understand why Churchill," Jonathan said. "He's nothing but a spoiled, shameless self-promoter. He has no real power."

"I been thinkin' the same, sir," Daisy said, "and I been rackin' my brains, tryin' to remember everything the baron said about Churchill. Then it came to me. I don't exactly remember when, but he said Churchill will be the one obstacle—that was the word, obstacle—standing in the way when the master comes."

"Did he say who the master is?" David asked.

Daisy shook her head. "No, but he did talk about a foreigner, some artist bloke who'll one day rule the world. The baron said that even though he himself has wealth and a title, he is nothing more than a … the word was emis, emis … I can't remember."

"Emissary?"

"That's it!" Daisy said, slapping her hand on the table. "I don't know exactly what it means, though."

"It's an ambassador, someone who prepares for the arrival of a more important person."

Jonathan asked: "Daisy, did the baron mention when he was going to try to kill Churchill?"

"Didn't catch that part, sir. The baron ain't one to rush into things, that I do know, sir. He'll wait, and bide his time. I suppose it'd be at a time when the baron and Mr. Churchill are in the same place together, even if he has Vukovic do it. I do know the baron likes to be near the killings as they happen. He says it energizes him, even if he doesn't do it himself."

Jonathan remembered something she might know about. "I heard that there have been knives and goblets stolen from the Jewish quarter, and someone is blaming the Jews for abducting children and using their blood. Bodies have been found. Do you know anything about this?"

Daisy shrugged. "The baron hates the Jews somethin' terrible. Don't know why, since he's a foreigner, same as them."

"But what about knives and the dead children?" Jonathan pressed.

Daisy hugged herself and began humming, rocking back and forth. Her eyes got a faraway look. Jonathan repeated his question.

Sam caught Jonathan's eye and shook his head as if to say, "She won't talk anymore. Leave her be." Sam reached over and put his hand on her arm. She jumped and looked at him as if she'd never seen him before, then recognition flickered in her eyes and she smiled.

"Forgot where I was," she said.

Sam said: "Daisy, there was a strange man who came into this house and tried to kidnap Mr. Drake's children. Do you know who it could've been?"

She grinned. "Oh, the baron has lots of rough men to do his biddin'. Could've been any one of 'em. Probably Vukovic. Kidnapping's the least of what they do to the little ones." She folded her arms across her abdomen and started rocking again. "I need to go now."

"Can I help you find somewhere warm to stay?" Sam asked gently.

Daisy shook her head. "Oh, no, sir. The streets is the safest place for me. Vukovic can't find me there. I heard he prowls docks and gaols in search of men who'll do his bidding, but I know how to hide. My street friends look out for me."

"Can I hire a cab to take you to wherever you're going?" David offered.

"Thank ye, sir. But no. Better for me to get there myself, invisible-like."

"What if we need to find you?" Jonathan asked.

"The folks under Blackfriars bridge, they'll have an idea, sir. Ye might find me there some nights, warming my hands at their fire. Other times I'm in the labyrinths under the Adelphi Arches."

"Where is that?" Sam asked.

"Not far from the Strand. Next to the Thames."

David said: "Wine merchants I've dealt with have cellars in those labyrinths, and I've visited them in broad daylight. They unnerved me even then. They're damp and as dark as pitch. I'd be worried about getting hopelessly lost."

Daisy smiled. "And that's why they're the perfect hiding spot for the likes of me. A body could be there and no-one would ever find 'em."

Jonathan walked Daisy to the servant's entrance. As she stepped out into the night, she turned and said to Jonathan: "Take care, sir. There's danger everywhere. I can feel it. Can ye?"

Jonathan simply replied: "God speed to you, Daisy."

He watched her disappear into the shadows. Then he made plans to tell his father right away about what he had learned, so that his father could help him to warn Churchill as soon as possible.

CHAPTER THIRTY-TWO

Jonathan gazed down at his father's pale face, and waited for a sign that the old man was conscious again. He shook him gently. Edward's eyes fluttered open.

"Father, I need an introduction to Churchill."

"Why?" His father's voice was barely a whisper.

"Because his life may be in danger."

"Tell the authorities."

"I need to warn him personally."

Edward's eyes closed.

"Father, can you hear me?" He gently prodded his father's arm, but there was no reaction. Edward's cheeks and eyes were sunken, and his skin was dull and ashen. His breathing was so slight that Jonathan was terrified he may have slipped away.

Jonathan put his ear to his father's chest, and could hear his slow heartbeat and ragged breathing.

He had come to see his father as soon as Daisy had left. Now he was frustrated and frightened that he wouldn't be able to stop the threats. He paced the room, glancing at his father from time to time.

Sam arrived to take Edward's pulse, and make notes in a small book.

"You must let me know the moment he is conscious," Jonathan said.

"I will." Sam put the notebook on the side table. "Don't expect too much." He smiled kindly to soften the impact of his words.

"What do you mean?"

"Your father may regain consciousness, but he may not be coherent, even if he is able to speak."

"I have no other choice but to try to talk to him."

A nurse in a starched white uniform came into the room, but Sam motioned to her and she quickly left.

Jonathan followed her out. "Where is my mother?"

"In her sitting room, sir."

Jonathan made his way to his mother's sitting room, elegantly done up in mauve and cream. She was seated near the window, and in the brilliant sunlight, her handsome face looked lined and tired.

Jonathan put his hand on his mother's shoulder. She put her hand over his, and kept gazing out the window.

Jonathan said: "Mother, I need you to secure an introduction to Churchill for me."

"Whatever for?"

"I have received word that he may be in some kind of danger. Father is too ill to write on my behalf."

Hannah sighed. "You do realise that anyone with a modicum of fame always faces threats. Even someone like your father has had his share."

"Yes, I know. But can you do that for me?"

"Of course. I'll post it today."

The clock ticked on the chimneypiece in the silence. Finally, Hannah spoke. "Edward has been in decline since the evening the baron publicly embarrassed us in our own dining room. Edward retired early that night. The next morning, he would not get out of bed. I thought it would pass. You know how withdrawn your father can be when he's upset. After a day or two, he seemed to be back to his old self. He went out one evening, and when he came home, he went directly to bed and never recovered."

"Where did he go?"

"He never told me. My intuition is that he paid a call on the baron." She looked up at her son, and Jonathan saw fear in her eyes. "Something happened to completely break Edward's spirit. The baron is a very dangerous man."

"I know." Jonathan shared his mother's fear, which was compounded by the knowledge that his wife did not share it. He'd have to figure out how to convince Anne to see things his way.

As if reading his mind, Hannah went on. "The cleverness of the baron consists in knowing how to find the secret desire in your heart—the desire a woman nurtures about herself that she believes sets her above all others. In my case, it was being politically astute, and fancying that I would make a competent Member of Parliament. Of course, one small obstacle is that women are prohibited from serving in Parliament. But the law can be changed."

Jonathan's amazement prevented him from replying right away. Finally, he said: "I had no idea you had political ambitions, Mother."

"I've kept it well hidden. It's not exactly a conventional aspiration for a woman, is it? But I still harbour the ambition. Some of your father's greatest triumphs came as a result of following my advice. Do you remember the time he fell out of favour with the Earl of Westfield? Not only was Edward's career in danger, but so was our social standing. I engineered the strategy that not only revived his reputation, but that put him in an even more influential position than he had enjoyed before. On other occasions, he chose not to follow my advice, and it was clear he would have been much better off had he listened to me. That's when I began to think I could make a success of myself in politics."

"But why not content yourself with working behind the scenes, as the power behind the throne, as it were?" Jonathan asked.

Hannah shrugged. "I don't need more, but I desire more. It is human nature to want the dream or desire that has yet to be realised. Men fall prey to this all the time, and sometimes it ruins them. We women are not all that different in that regard."

Jonathan was thinking of his wife. He suddenly wanted to argue with his mother, as if winning the argument here would solve the tension between him and Anne. "But you are already so accomplished in other areas," Jonathan pointed out. "You have a beautiful house and a wardrobe that is the envy of London."

"Jonathan, you don't understand. If a woman is complimented on something she knows she is good at—such as dancing, music, her taste in clothing—she's accustomed to such praise, and those compliments are simply added to the collection. But if she is complimented on the thing she wants to conquer, the thing that she really pines for—that is the real treasure. She will think the giver of the compliment has some special insight into her heart and soul. And that is irresistible. I have noticed that men are susceptible to this same sort of flattery."

"Is this what happened with the baron?"

Hannah nodded. "Yes. And it was enthralling. He already had me in his snares, knowing I was eager for news about you. But on top of that, the baron knows how to convince a woman that she is already a master of whatever it is she seeks to master. He had me convinced that I could, with a little effort and with his support, change the laws, and I could win a seat and have a brilliant career as a politician. I almost fell for it. I realise now the time is not ripe for such a change. But it will be. Just not now."

Jonathan was too distracted with his own thoughts to pay close attention to what his mother had said. Jonathan wondered about the baron's hold over Anne. He wanted to know what it was that he had convinced her that she was master of.

Hannah said in a low voice: "There was a time I was angry at Sarah for not liking the baron. Now I realise she was a shrewder judge of character than I was. I'm ashamed of my own stupidity."

A knock at the door interrupted their conversation.

"Come in," Hannah said.

David and Sarah came into the room with an air of solemnity. The two of them stood in the middle of the Aubusson carpet.

Sarah ventured: "Maman, we've come to talk to you about something." Sarah glanced at David, and then continued. "We plan to get married as soon as possible."

"Why the rush?" Hannah asked.

David said: "Lady Drake, I've just been appointed to be His Majesty's Consul-General to Jerusalem—thanks to Lord Balfour. I may need to leave at a moment's notice. It would be easier for Sarah to travel with me as my wife, rather than as my fiancée."

"Congratulations, Consul-General Lowe," Jonathan said.

"That is a surprising position for a wine merchant," Hannah observed.

Sarah spoke with evident pride: "He's not just a wine merchant, Maman. He's involved with important world events."

Hannah looked sharply at David, and her eyes narrowed. "Then pray tell me who you are, exactly, Mr. Lowe." Her voice was dead-calm.

David drew himself up straighter. "As I mentioned before, my father is an ambassador. He lives in Venice, with my mother. For some years, I've been helping him under the aegis of my travels as a wine merchant. I have been able to see and hear things that no ordinary diplomat would have access to. The owners of public houses and inns sometimes overhear things their customers say after a bottle or two—things that would be of interest to those who can move world events. In vino veritas, as they say."

"So you're a spy?" Hannah said.

"I convey information to those who can put it to the best use. I've helped to broker negotiations. In two cases, I helped to prevent a war from breaking out. It's not a boring vocation."

Jonathan could see that his mother was intrigued. In light of what she had just revealed to him about her own political ambitions, he sensed that she would not disapprove of David's profession. She probably admired it more than she let on, but she was too self-possessed and shrewd to betray any of that.

Hannah said in a quiet voice: "If Edward dies, Sarah would have to observe a year of mourning and not marry until the year is passed. That would complicate things even more."

"Maman!" Sarah cried. "Don't talk like that! He's not going to die!"

"My darling, of course, you may very well be right. But in the meanwhile, I give you both my blessings." Hannah paused. "When all this is over, we'll plan an elaborate after-wedding celebration here at the house, and invite half of London. But now, there is no time to waste. Let us discuss what needs to be done in order that the marriage may take place as soon as possible."

The wedding was held the following afternoon at Hannah and Edward's house. Only immediate family were there, along with Sam Berg. Joe lurked in the background, watching everything. Agatha sat with him, keeping a hand on the pram where the babies slept.

The rabbi was a long-winded man from the synagogue in Aldgate. He took his time, pausing to expound on certain points. Hannah was impatient, but she restrained her impulse to hurry things along.

Anne sat next to Jonathan, wearing a stylish green dress, with matching shoes and hat. Jonathan noticed that she was even more withdrawn and cold toward him and his family. She had reacted to the news of Sarah's sudden wedding with what had seemed like contempt. Jonathan had been mystified by her reaction, but he didn't have the inclination to ask her about it. He knew they'd just end up arguing, and he had no fortitude for that.

There had been no time for Sarah to find a proper wedding dress. She wore a pale-yellow silk ball gown trimmed in lace, cinched at the waist with a lavender-and-turquoise sash. Her elegant bouquet of spring flowers had been sent from the local florist. Her veil was the one that Hannah had worn on her own wedding day. Hannah thought her daughter had never looked lovelier.

Edward sat in a wheelchair, dressed in a starched shirt and one of his best suits. Sam stood next to him. Edward still looked frail, but colour had returned to his cheeks somewhat, and Sarah was convinced that her wedding day was the start of his full recovery.

Edward said in a weak voice: "I give you both my blessings. David, I am proud to have you as my son-in-law. I know you will bring honour … and protection … to our family."

David caught the stress on the word "protection." He said: "Thank you, sir. The honour is all mine. I will always do my utmost. You have my word of honour."

"Good man." Edward smiled, but his haggard face made it look more like a grimace. "And my darling Sarah, you could not have chosen a better husband. Listen to each other. Always. Marriage is an equal partnership. I regret the times I did not follow your mother's advice. She is a wise woman, and a more skilled politician than I ever was. That is why it is important for you both to work together." Edward began coughing, and he held a starched handkerchief to his mouth. Sam gave him a glass of water. When Edward recovered, he continued. "Now, you all must celebrate. I will return to my room to sleep now."

"Oh, Papa, we can stay with you so you don't miss anything. The food can be brought up."

Edward shook his head. "No, my dear, I need rest, not food. I will be fine. I'm already feeling better, and by the weekend, I'm certain I'll be able to get out of bed and join you all for tea."

"And I'll be here to help him in his recovery," Sam assured her.

Sarah kissed her father on the forehead and pressed his hand. "That would make me so happy, Papa!"

"Now, go celebrate, my darling," Edward said in a hoarse voice. "Don't worry about me."

The wedding luncheon was held in the dining room, and the rabbi and David discussed theology and Jewish law. Clearly, the rabbi was enjoying himself. Hannah smiled and talked with great vivacity to Sam Berg, but Jonathan could see how watchful she was. There was a guarded shrewdness in her eyes that told Jonathan she was gathering information, and making calculations.

Anne looked subdued, and gave perfunctory answers when Sarah tried to draw her into conversation. As soon as she had finished, Anne announced that she had to excuse herself to check on the children, who were with Agatha downstairs.

After he had eaten, Jonathan went upstairs to check on his father. He waited by his bedside, listening to the clock ticking on the chimneypiece, and watching his father's face for any sign that the old man was regaining consciousness. He had questions he wanted answered. After a while, there was a knock on the bedroom door.

Anne came in and stood at the bedside, looking at Edward.

"How is he doing?" she asked in a subdued voice.

"He hasn't stirred."

"Agatha is downstairs, spoon feeding the children their dessert of biscuits-in-milk. They are gobbling it like little piglets."

"Where is Joe?" Jonathan asked.

"With Agatha and the babies, of course. Standing watch, as usual." Anne paused. "It would have been better if I could have had more time to prepare for this wedding. A new dress would've been nice."

Jonathan could hear the reproof in her tone. "I had no control over the timing, Anne. Nobody consulted me about anything."

"What was the rush?" Anne asked.

Jonathan gestured to his sleeping father.

"Anyway, I wasn't blaming you," she said, her tone softening. "I just like to feel as if I'm actually a part of the family sometimes."

"I've not been exactly forthcoming," Jonathan confessed. "I hope you can forgive me, and I hope we can find our way back to each other. I love you, Anne. I've never stopped loving you."

Anne bit her lip to keep herself from reacting emotionally to his appeal. Part of her—the old Anne—wanted reconciliation with her husband, wanted a new start. But there was the new Anne who had a brilliant future, but who first had to prove her complete fealty if that future were to open up to her in all its splendour.

To hid her emotions, she changed the subject. "Your sister does look lovely in that dress, even lovelier than I've ever seen her. I suppose part of her radiance comes from the fact that she seems so in smitten with Mr. Lowe."

"And he with her."

"He's so imperious. Do you really think he's capable?"

"Of loving her? Or of being a husband?"

"Both," Anne said.

"Yes." Jonathan paused. "Why do you doubt it?"

Anne shrugged. "A man that arrogant usually cannot love anyone but himself."

Her attitude irritated Jonathan. "Arrogant? He's not arrogant. I've no doubt of his love for my sister. He's positively dedicated to her. And, he's one of the finest men I know. And a great good friend to me."

"I didn't mean that the way it sounded," Anne said mildly. "He's just not my cup of tea, that's all." She gestured to Edward. "I'll sit with your father. You go down and celebrate."

"Let's call the nurse in to watch him and we can both celebrate. Lowe brought some especially rare champagne."

"The nurse is in the kitchen, eating her meal. Don't disturb her. I don't mind spending a little time here until she is finished. He was—I mean, he is—my father-in-law, after all. Go. Be with your family. I'll take some champagne in a little while."

Jonathan got to his feet. As he left the room, he glanced once more behind him. His wife was sitting stiffly next to his sleeping father, and the late afternoon light cascaded through the window behind her, shrouding her face in shadow, and illuminating his father's white face. The sleeping man looked as if he were already a cadaver.

✦ CHAPTER THIRTY-THREE ✦

By the time Jonathan arrived downstairs, the newlyweds had already departed.

"They are taking the train to Bath," Hannah explained. "They wanted me to tell you goodbye."

"Have you received a reply from Churchill?"

"Not yet," she answered.

"Please write to him again, Mother."

Hannah put her hand to her forehead. "I'll do that, Jonathan, but at the moment, I have other considerations. I am hardly eager to answer all the calls and letters I'm going to be receiving once the news gets out that your sister is married. I'm too exhausted receive anyone."

Jonathan did not like to hear his mother talk like this. She had never been one to yield to fatigue, nor to complain about her obligations.

"Then take a day or two of rest, Mother," Jonathan suggested. "In fact, you could forego the announcement altogether."

Hannah sighed. "That is another problem to solve. The rushed nature of the marriage ceremony is going to lead to all kinds of speculation, which is already bad enough after he—" Jonathan knew she was referring to the baron "—made a spectacle of himself at the dinner party. And if there is no wedding announcement, I fear it will make everything look even worse."

Hannah was lost in thought. Then she said: "The solution is one that David has already provided, and I was too exhausted to see it. The announcement of David's sudden consular appointment is the perfect justification. He and Sarah had to marry right away, given that he could be called up at any moment to leave for Jerusalem. Now she will be able to travel with him as his wife. I will ask Mr. Perkins whether he can run such an announcement in tomorrow's paper." She excused herself and left the room.

Jonathan helped himself to a dish of chocolates on the side-table, but he found that his appetite was not what it should be. He was too preoccupied with his father's condition. Sam came into the room, and took a seat nearby. They were the only two in the room. Joe had gone downstairs. Jonathan took advantage of the opportunity to ask Sam some painful questions.

"What are my father's chances?" Jonathan asked.

Sam removed his spectacles. "Hard to say. I've seen many people make a full recovery from conditions like your father's. And I've seen others who have remained invalids."

"What are his chances of … not surviving?"

"I don't know. I'm not God. Right now, the odds are not favourable."

"He said he'd be well enough by the weekend to have tea with us all. Do you think that is unrealistic?"

"Not at all," Sam said. "The human will can overcome anything."

"Are you telling me this to make me feel better, Berg?"

"I'm telling you the situation as I see it. Your father has an excellent chance of recovery, especially if his mind is set on it. Strong-willed people can force their body into strength. I've seen it many times."

Anne came into the room. Jonathan thought she looked pale and agitated.

"Don't get up on my account," she said, holding up her hands as the men prepared to stand. "I'm simply looking for something to drink."

"The champagne is excellent." Sam pointed to the bottle in the ice bucket.

"How is my father?" Jonathan enquired.

"The same as before," she said, pouring a glass of champagne. Her back was to him. She drained the glass quickly and refilled it.

"Are you not feeling well, Anne? You've quaffed your champagne rather quickly."

"I'm just a little overwrought from seeing your father like that."

"Champagne can be an excellent elixir for calming the nerves," Sam observed.

Jonathan stood. "I will go to my father now."

"The nurse is with him," Anne said quickly. "Why don't you stay here and chat with Dr. Berg and me. It would do you good not to dwell on your father too much." Her eyes darted to the door and back to Jonathan's face. She drank more champagne.

"I must speak to him," Jonathan said, leaving the room.

As soon as he stepped into his father's room, he noticed that the nurse was not there. At his father's bedside, he called "Father?" There was no response. He gently shook Edward awake. But Edward remained unconscious.

The nurse appeared in the doorway.

Jonathan snapped at her: "How long has he been alone?"

She was bewildered. "I thought Madam Drake was here with his lordship."

"How long has he been like this?" Jonathan demanded.

"I've just come up now and noticed it this moment, sir, same as you," the nurse said.

"But Anne said you were here. Oh, never mind! Get Dr. Berg up here right now, damn it."

The nurse rushed out. A minute later, Sam was at the bedside, feeling for a pulse and listening for his heartbeat. The nurse hovered nearby, while Jonathan, Anne, and Hannah waited a respectful distance away.

Sam broke the tense silence. "His heart is beating, but barely. There is nothing anyone can do except tend to him."

"I'll do that," Jonathan said.

"You need rest. I'm ordering you to go home with your wife and get some sleep. The nurse will be here to care for him."

Anne stared at Edward, and her face was ashen and expressionless.

When they arrived home, Anne disappeared to her dressing room. Jonathan made his way to his study, and sat at his desk with his head in his hands. The golem came into Jonathan's study, and handed Jonathan a slip of paper.

Jonathan closed the door of his study. Then he turned to the golem. "What the devil do you mean, Joe?"

Joe pointed at what he'd written. Then he wrote:

i see good and evil in hearts
her heart is gone dark

"I flat-out don't believe it. Anne loved Edward. She told me so herself. Please let's not speak of this anymore. You may retire for the night."

The golem left the room. Jonathan crumpled the paper, lit a match to it, and threw it into the fireplace.

Before breakfast the next morning, Jonathan received a note from his mother's servant. The news didn't surprise him. Anne watched his face as he read the note.

"My father is dead, and I am going to my mother's house straight away."

"Of course, I shall go with you," she said in a quavering voice. She wiped a tear from her eye. She wasn't prepared for the conflicted emotions that plagued her.

Jonathan said: "There won't be much for you to do."

"Oh, but I want to go," Anne said. "I loved him. He was like a father to me." She looked distraught, and her eyes filled with tears.

Jonathan was convinced that the golem was dead-wrong about Anne.

They travelled in silence to the Hyde Park house. The day was relatively warm, and the sun came out from time to time. The butler answered the door. Jonathan and Anne went upstairs to Edward's room. Hannah was already sitting at the bedside, dressed in black. Her face was pale and grim. A sheet was drawn over his father's face.

Jonathan embraced his mother. Anne stood nearby, and burst into tears. She buried her face in her hands.

Hannah went over and put her hand on Anne's shoulder, and murmured words of comfort.

Jonathan asked: "What time did he pass?"

"At about three twenty in the morning," Hannah said. "There was no sense in summoning you then. There was nothing to be done."

"Does Dr. Berg know?"

"Yes. I expect he'll be here shortly."

"What about writing to Sarah and David?"

"I did." Hannah shook her head sadly. "Her honeymoon will be cut short with the funeral of her father. I hope it is not an ill omen."

Jonathan was suddenly furious with her, and he knew his fury came from a place of fear. "You have never been superstitious, and now you talk rubbish. Really, Mother, I expected better from you."

Hannah was stung by this rebuke, but remained silent. Anne narrowed her eyes at Jonathan's outburst.

Finally, Hannah spoke. "My apologies for speaking foolishly, Jonathan. I'm just not my usual self, that's all."

The mourners stood by the graveside. It was not a large gathering. Hannah had informed only a few close friends, including the Bixbys. The funeral arrangements had been rushed to bury Edward as quickly as possible. Not only was this Jewish custom, which Hannah suddenly felt a pressing desire to observe, but she sensed another, more foreboding urgency that she could not define.

Rose Bixby had tried to persuade her to postpone the funeral for a few more days so that all the correct preparations could be made for a man of his standing. Hannah had refused. She wanted to have her husband buried in a simple coffin as quickly as possible.

"You can't settle for a pauper's funeral," Rose Bixby had argued.

"If you saw the bills I'll have to pay, Rose, you'll see it's not a pauper's funeral," Hannah retorted.

"But there are appearances. You have your social standing to consider."

"I have my own equanimity to consider," Hannah shot back. "I don't want an elaborate funeral, and Edward would not want it, either." She didn't add that she felt compelled to follow the Jewish tradition and bury the body as soon as possible. The tradition made sense to her not only given the demands of her current situation, but also on a deep spiritual level that she could not explain. She also didn't mention her sense of foreboding. Rose would not understand.

"Isn't that rather selfish?" Rose asked.

"Yes. Yes, I think it is, actually," Hannah said thoughtfully.

They left the cemetery and travelled to Hannah's house in Hyde Park. The rain started, and soon everything was wet and muddy—much to the consternation of Anne, who bitterly complained as she stepped out of the carriage. Jonathan tried to help her by taking her hand, but she broke away and made a dash for the front door, not even waiting for the footman and his umbrella. Once inside, she went to find Agatha and her children. Joe had stayed at Hannah's house with Agatha and the babies.

The funeral attendees helped themselves to a buffet in the dining room. Sarah and David had managed to catch a train back from Bath in time for the funeral.

"From a bridal dress to funeral dress," Jonathan murmured to David as they watched the black-clad figures of Sarah and Hannah from across the room.

"Sarah is a remarkable woman," David said. "And your mother is a tower of strength. I have not seen her weep once today."

"I've never once seen her cry," Jonathan said. "Not even when her own father died. I have often thought she is incapable of it."

They were silent a moment. Then David said: "By the way, Drake, I've been invited to a get-together this evening at somewhere called …" he tugged at his beard, trying to remember. "At the Proscenium. I have no idea where that is. A club, perhaps? It's strange that the invitation contained no address."

"Ah, the residence of the Viscount and Viscountess of Sudbury, right here in Mayfair. They don't bother with the street address because everyone knows where it is when you say 'Proscenium.' They're both theatre enthusiasts. They have a stage, as you'll see, hence the name of the house. My mother went to finishing school with the Viscountess."

"I have heard, but I've not been able to confirm, that Winston Churchill will be there to give a short talk about the book he recently published. I'd like to see about getting an invitation for you, but I've no idea how to contact the host or hostess."

Jonathan's reaction was immediate. "My mother can help with that. And if she cannot, I will just show up."

Hannah sat at her polished mahogany desk. The black silk of her dress made her hair look especially auburn, and the skirt of the dress pooled on the floor. She held the telephone receiver at her ear and waited for the connection to go through. Jonathan, David, and Sam stood behind her.

"Yes, I'd like to speak to the viscountess, please. Tell her it is Lady Hannah Drake calling."

Several minutes passed. A voice on the other end said: "Hannah, how strange to hear from you. Wasn't the funeral today?"

Hannah held the receiver away from her ear because the viscountess spoke loudly, enunciating every word. Everyone in the room with Hannah could hear her.

"Yes, the funeral was today," Hannah said in a subdued voice.

"Please accept my sincerest condolences."

"Thank you, Dora."

"Would you like me to call soon? Today is out of the question, but perhaps tomorrow or the day after."

"Yes, that would be fine. I have to tell you that I'm telephoning for a particular reason. Naturally, it is of great importance. I wouldn't dream of bothering you otherwise."

"Especially on a day like today."

"Especially. I heard you are having an event tonight. I'm wondering if I might be able to secure an invitation for my son. I realise this is forward of me, but he would appreciate meeting Mr. Churchill in person and getting him to sign a copy of the book."

The viscountess was silent. "Well, it is an unusual request, given your commitments ..."

Hannah knew she was referring to Edward's death and the customary mourning period for the widow and children.

"Yes, it is unconventional," Hannah said. "And I realise it is forward of me to request an invitation like this, and also somewhat rude. My apologies." Jonathan could tell she didn't really care whether she came off as rude. She was focused on accomplishing her mission, and she'd say whatever was necessary. Hannah added drily: "Edward had been making arrangements for my son to meet with Churchill, but obviously, that needs some...modification."

There was silence. Then the viscountess said: "If you don't mind my asking, how did you find out about our little get-together? I tried to keep it discreet."

Hannah let her pride become a boast. "My daughter is now married to David Lowe, who has been appointed as His Majesty's Consul-General to Jerusalem, thanks to Arthur." There was no need to say his last name. Both women travelled in the same circles as Arthur Balfour, and considered him a friend. Hannah added: "Consul-General Lowe is on your guest list for tonight."

"Is that so!" The viscountess's voice was now about twice as loud as it had been before. "I saw no wedding announcement in the papers."

"That's because the wedding was a small, private ceremony that took place yesterday. We wanted Edward to see his only daughter get married before . . . before it was too late." Hannah's voice broke, but she did not sob.

"Oh, Hannah, I am so terribly sorry. Please forgive me for being indelicate in your sorrow."

Hannah pulled herself together. "No, I beg your pardon, Dora. I'm just not in my usual self, that's all."

"Speaking of not being one's usual self," the viscountess said, "I have heard that your son has been . . . unwell. I'm concerned about his . . . ability to fully participate in our get-together tonight. Perhaps we should wait until another opportunity presents itself."

Hannah's eyes met Jonathan's. The poisonous rumours about Jonathan's instability had obviously reached many ears in London.

Hannah's voice became sweet with hidden deception. "Oh, but Dora, you are forgetting that I have two sons. My son Michael lives in Berlin, but he came back to London, fortuitously. Another opportunity may not present itself, given that he plans to return to the continent as soon as possible."

"Oh, I had no idea that we were talking about Michael!" the viscountess exclaimed, with obvious relief. "Of course, I will have him added to the guest list. And your daughter, too, since she is now married to Consul-General Lowe." The viscountess paused. "Do you think Sarah will come in her funeral weeds? Either way, please tell her I understand completely."

Behind her words, Hannah heard the unspoken question about propriety for those in mourning to attend social functions—especially so soon after a funeral.

"I will leave that up to her," Hannah said. "I realise this is all highly irregular, and again, my apologies."

"No need to apologize, dear Hannah," the viscountess replied. "I look forward to meeting your son-in-law, and seeing Michael, of course. It's been ages since I've seen him. And please know that I will call on you. Drop me a note and let me know when you're receiving."

Hannah hung up the telephone and turned to her son. "That settles it, then. Jonathan, you'll have to shave the beard but leave the moustache. You'll look more like your brother that way."

CHAPTER THIRTY-FOUR

Joe sat next to the cab coachman, and kept watch as they travelled from the Drake residence in Hyde Park to the Drake residence in Cadogan Square. The rain had stopped some time ago, but a thick fog had settled over the city. Neither the horses nor the coachman were daunted by the poor visibility. They knew the streets well, and could've found their way even in absolute darkness.

Inside the carriage, Jonathan sat next to Anne. Agatha was seated across from them, and she held both babies. Jonathan told Anne of his plans for the evening: Jonathan would go to the Sudbury's, and Joe would stay home with Anne, Mrs. MacLeod, and the children.

Anne sat in a resentful silence. Finally, she said to her husband: "I am deeply disappointed that I won't be able to accompany you, Jonathan. Your sister will be there with her husband, and they've been married mere hours." Jonathan could hear the anger and bitterness in her tone. "It's as if you'd rather not be seen with me."

"Anne, the viscountess thinks my brother Michael will be there, not me. It would be unseemly for you to be on the arm of Michael."

"Why don't you ask your mother again for help," Anne snapped. "She seems to work miracles on your behalf, and once in a while she could deign to work one on my behalf."

"If I couldn't get myself invited under my own identity, how on earth would I secure an invitation for my wife?"

"We could ask Mr. Lowe, who seems to know all the right people."

"He is newly-appointed."

"Even so, it rankles."

"I'll tell you what rankles," Jonathan snapped. "I'll be posing as my brother Michael, which tells you how much I'm welcome in that set. All because someone has been spreading lies about my mental state."

"You'll still get to attend, and so will your sister," she said bitterly. "I don't exist, do I?"

"Anne, it's not a social affair. Do you think I'm going there for amusement? It is a grim mission, and I don't even know whether my message will be received."

"Why the deception, Jonathan? Why?"

"It's complicated. And there are those who are out to harm us," Jonathan said.

"You mean, the baron," she said sarcastically.

"Yes, the baron."

"It's rubbish, you know."

He knew it was pointless to argue. He was already vexed that she'd forced him to reveal this much in front of Mrs. MacLeod. Fortunately, the good servant was wise enough to pretend that she was not listening.

As soon as the carriage stopped in front of his house, the horses nickered and stomped their feet. Jonathan leaped out ahead of the others to unlock the front door of the house. He didn't know why, but he felt a pressing need to be sure his house was safe before he let his family go in.

Joe stood at the bottom of the front steps and kept a watch up and down Cadogan Square, as if he expected trouble to appear out of nowhere. Anne and Agatha helped each other with the babies.

The rain had stopped. In the waning evening light that filtered through the fog, everything had a sickly yellow-green cast.

Jonathan turned the lock to his front door, but didn't hear the bolt retract because it was already retracted.

"Did I not secure the door when we left?" he muttered peevishly, hoping it was his own stupidity.

Jonathan pushed the door open, and the yellow-green fog made the vestibule and the front entrance hall glow with an eerie light. He crossed the vestibule to get a closer look at what was in the front entrance hall. It took him a moment to realise what he was looking at. He ran back outside, closing the front door behind him. He blocked Anne and Agatha, each of whom were holding a baby, from coming up the front stairs.

"Go back to my mother's house immediately," he ordered both women.

"Yes, sir," Agatha said, heading back to the cab.

The panic in Jonathan's voice scared Anne, and she stood her ground. "Jonathan, I don't understand. What's wrong?"

Jack started to cry in Anne's arms.

"Get back in the cab, Anne," Jonathan said.

Anne remained standing on the pavement. Agatha took Jack from Anne's arms and put him in the cab next to Lily.

Jonathan spoke to the coachman, who was keeping a tight hold on the reins because the horses were agitated. "Please take my wife and Mrs. MacLeod back to the house in Hyde Park from whence we just came, and have them stay there until I send for them. Dr. Berg is there. Drive him here right away. My parlour maid is very ill, and she looks contagious."

"Yes, sir," the coachman said.

"But Jonathan," Anne said, "we don't have a——" she was about to say "we don't have a parlour maid," but Jonathan had interrupted her.

"Anne, please. You need to go back to Hyde Park. Now." Jonathan's voice had a desperate, pleading note. He fought to keep his panic under control.

She reluctantly got into the carriage. He closed the door. Her face was at the window, hard as stone. "You never let me in to what you're thinking, you never tell me what you're doing. You treat me as if I'm an outsider."

Jonathan's face was anguished. "I'm the outsider. Can't you see that?"

"I'm still your wife. You could pretend that I matter to you."

"But you do matter, Anne. That's why I'm trying to keep you safe." He moved closer to her and said confidentially: "Tell my mother to arm herself with one of my father's pistols and tell her to give one to Thompson. He's a steady shot."

Anne glared down at him from the window. "Why the pistol? Of course, you won't tell me why. You're ordering me about like a common servant. I'm tired of being excluded from your plans."

"Right now, I need you to protect our children. Soon you'll understand, and then we can put all this behind us."

Her voice was suddenly calm. "Put it all behind us? But why wait? I'll put it all behind me now. I am finished with you, Jonathan. Finished."

"What do you mean?"

"Soon you'll understand." She drew the curtain across the window, and the cab pulled away. Jonathan did not wait to see it turn the corner. He ran back up the steps, with Joe behind him.

In the eerie light of the front entrance hall, Jonathan walked around the iron umbrella stand while Joe stood by, alert to any sound or movement. One of the umbrellas had been turned so that the crook handle was resting at the bottom of the stand, and the spiked ferrule was pointing up. Daisy's head was impaled on the ferrule. The rest of the umbrella protruded out of her neck, like some macabre black collar, dripping rivulets of blood that had congealed into a sticky mess. Her eyes were wide open, and her mouth was twisted into a blood-stained grimace.

Jonathan ordered the golem to search the rest of the house to see if anything else was amiss.

The doorbell rang, and then there was a knock. Jonathan ran to the front parlour, and moved the curtain just enough to see who was standing at the front door. It was Sam.

Jonathan opened the front door.

"How the devil did you know I wanted you here?" Jonathan demanded.

Sam handed him an envelope that had been opened. "Your mother received this just after you left, and I told her I'd deliver it, so I set off right away ..." his voice trailed off as his attention was caught by the macabre scene in the front entrance hall. He walked over and circled the gristly umbrella stand. He stooped to get a closer look at the head. "I've seen a lot, but never something like this. The tongue has been cut out. Poor girl. Have you notified the authorities?"

"No, and we won't do that. They'll detain me and interrogate me for hours. I've got to get to the Proscenium and warn Churchill. And, I've got to protect my reputation, which is already falling apart. Having the police here won't help matters."

"You ought to read what I gave you," Sam reminded him.

Jonathan pulled the note from the envelope.

My Dear Lady Drake,

Have your son introduce himself, and bring along this note. I'm always interested in new information.

Yours,

Winston S. Churchill

Jonathan said: "Well, that improves my chances of success this evening."

Sam was thinking out loud. "We'll burn the umbrella, and wash down everything with carbolic soap. And, we must find the rest of her. Let's search the house, starting from the bottom and working our way to the top."

Joe had returned, and he scribbled a note. He handed it to Jonathan, who read it aloud.

body at arches

Sam looked at him quizzically. "At the Adelphi Arches? Are you certain, Joe?"

The golem nodded.

"How do you know?" Jonathan asked.

He wrote:

strong feeling

"Did you find something else in another part of the house?"

The golem shook his head, and added:

rest of house not disturbed

Sam said: "It won't be difficult to transport the head in a hatbox, wrapped in oilcloth."

"I have no time for any of this," Jonathan said impatiently. "I need to get dressed and get to the Sudbury's."

"Joe and I will take care of it. Once we re-unite the head with the body at the Arches, we'll provide an anonymous tip to the authorities. And they can do a forensic examination on Daisy's remains, and give that poor girl a proper burial."

Jonathan said: "Sam, when you're finished with all this, I'd like you to go back to my mother's house and keep an eye on Anne and the children."

"Has she seen this?" Sam asked, gesturing at the bloody scene.

"No. I sent her back there with Agatha and the babies before they had a chance to come through the front door. I told her to make sure my mother arms herself with one of my father's pistols, and that Thompson is armed as well."

"If you're that worried, perhaps Joe should go to your mother's house now," Sam suggested.

Jonathan squinted his eyes and rubbed his forehead. "I have the feeling that Joe needs to come with me to the Proscenium. I don't know why. It just seems like that's what's needed."

Joe nodded in agreement.

Sam said: "Then while you dress, Joe and I will start getting things squared away here."

Jonathan went upstairs. He locked himself in the bathroom and shaved off his beard, leaving a moustache. Then he trimmed his hair with shears to the length he remembered his brother's hair, and he rubbed in some pomade and combed it in the direction he thought most resembled his brother's hair. He then changed into evening clothes. He went back downstairs. The hallway was now empty and smelled of carbolic soap Nobody would guess what it had contained just a short while before.

In the furnace room off the kitchen, a fire was consuming the bloodied umbrella, along with the blood-stained rags that had been used for cleaning. The umbrella stand was in a wash tub with carbolic soap.

"We burned whatever we could, and disinfected the rest," Sam explained. He pointed to a pink hatbox with a chartreuse lid. "I helped myself to that in your wife's wardrobe. I'll buy her a new one."

CHAPTER THIRTY-FIVE

Jonathan managed to slip into the crowded room without being seen by Lady Sudbury. It was a massive space, with arched ceilings that sloped down toward a stage. On the stage, an orchestra played, and some of the guests danced.

Jonathan scanned the room, and saw David and Sarah a distance away, holding glasses of champagne and talking to a half-dozen people who had gathered around the radiant couple.

As Jonathan approached, David caught sight of him and smiled broadly. He stepped toward Jonathan and guided him to a quiet corner.

"Is Churchill here?"

"Not yet," David replied. "But several other notables are, including the baron."

"Where is he?"

"I think he is near that large painting of the Persian harem, regaling guests with tales of the east," David said. "He was perfectly polite to me and Sarah, but the glint of malice in his eye was unmistakable. I can't let Sarah out of my sight, even to visit the powder room. I truly fear him."

"As do I," Jonathan said.

"He brought along his man, the one they call Vukovic," David added. "I happened to arrive when they did, and I heard him tell Vukovic to wait outside until the time was right. I'd never seen Vukovic before, but he's not hard to identify. He has the long face of a wolf—which is apt, because that's what his name means."

Jonathan's heart skipped a beat. "I should tell Joe all this."

"Where is he?"

"Among the coachmen outside."

"Who is watching your wife and children?"

"They're at my mother's house with Berg and Thompson. My father's pistols are at hand there." Jonathan paused, then said: "You remember that servant Daisy who came to see us. Her head was left in my house."

David's face was grim. "I wonder what our friend the baron knows of it. Did you alert the authorities?"

"Not yet. Joe believes Daisy's body is at the Adelphi Arches. Sam has agreed to bring the head there, and then provide an anonymous tip to the police."

Just then, applause erupted near the entrance. A light-haired, round-shouldered figure was making his way through the crowded room. Jonathan had only seen pictures of Churchill in the papers. In person, Churchill wasn't nearly as good-looking as his pictures portrayed him to be, but he was more impressive: larger with an exceptional presence that suggested a brilliant future. He had the charisma of a man who enjoys being the centre of attention, which was apparent from the confident way he interacted with those around him. Several people pressed him to say something, and he began to make an impromptu speech. Jonathan caught the slight stutter in Churchill's cultivated manner of speaking, but it seemed to only add to his authority and magnetism.

Jonathan joined the throng of admirers surrounding Churchill, and tried to get closer, but it was impossible to secure a word with the man After about fifteen minutes, Churchill made his way toward balcony doors nearby, and he slipped through with another man. Two muscular men in ordinary suits blocked the rest of the crowd from following. Jonathan waited off to the side until the crowd dispersed. Then he chose the more clever-looking of the two men, and showed him the note from Churchill.

"I must have a word with Mr. Churchill," Jonathan insisted. "I am Lady Drake's son."

"Apologies, sir, but Mr. Churchill has requested privacy for the moment. We're not to let anyone past these doors."

Just then, a woman's loud voice was at Jonathan's left ear. "Well, Mr.

Drake, you managed to join our little soiree, despite rather tragic events in your household."

Jonathan turned to see the Viscountess of Sudbury at his elbow. She was a tall woman with a long neck that was adorned with an elaborate diamond-and-ruby necklace.

"Good evening, my lady," Jonathan said.

She continued. "Please accept my deepest condolences. Your mother told me you'd timed your arrival from Berlin rather auspiciously, or inauspiciously, depending on how you view it."

"The condolences are much appreciated, my lady," Jonathan said.

Just then, Rose Bixby joined them. She greeted the viscountess, and then said to Jonathan: "How lovely to see you. My condolences on your father."

"Thank you, madam," Jonathan said. He needed to leave before Rose called him Jonathan rather than Michael. "Now I must excuse myself to have a word with my brother-in-law."

Jonathan made his way to the proximity of where David stood, but instead of approaching him, he found the nearest exit and went outside. He knew he could not keep pretending to be Michael Drake, and it was only a matter of time before he'd be discovered. He needed to talk to Churchill as soon as possible. The fog was thick, and Jonathan could only see a few feet ahead. He walked along the outer wall of the house until saw the outlines of a large balcony on the east side of the house where two men stood. It was at ground level, enclosed by a stone balustrade. He could hear men talking in low, earnest voices. In the fog, their voices sounded muffled and flat. He hoisted himself over the balustrade. The two men stopped talking and watched Jonathan's unconventional entrance.

"And who are you, emerging from the fog like that?" asked the man who was not Churchill. He was middle-aged, with a serious face and a large moustache.

"I am the Honourable Jonathan Drake, son of the late Lord Edward Drake, Lord of Appeal in Ordinary."

"Drake," the man repeated. He suddenly remembered. "That's right. I heard that he had died. My condolences."

"The funeral was today, actually," Jonathan said.

Churchill plucked the cigar from his lips and said: "The viscountess's parties are fascinating enough f-for you to interrupt your mourning?" He spoke with a stutter.

"I don't have much of a choice, sir," Jonathan said. "Mr. Churchill, I need to speak with you." He displayed the note that Churchill himself had written. "Your bodyguards wouldn't let me approach you."

Churchill waived his cigar. "Oh, I know, I know. It is sometimes n-necessary to be cautious. There have been stirrings of late."

"The threat isn't coming only from the ones you know," Jonathan said. "There is someone else who believes you will one day stop his faction from taking over the world."

Churchill laughed. "It must be someone in the opposition p-p-party, then. They let my father's political successes become personal affronts. Don't let them convince you of anything, my good man. It's all b-bluster. Stuff and nonsense from thin-skinned rogues. Right, Balfour?" He returned the cigar to his mouth and puffed a plume of smoke that instantly blended with the foggy air.

Jonathan realised that the man with the moustache standing next to Churchill was Lord Arthur Balfour, the former Prime Minister of England. He chastised himself for not having recognised him sooner, for not addressing him as he should have. But he had no time to dwell on any of this.

"Please, sir," Jonathan said, "it's more than that. There are those who believe that one day you will have tremendous influence on the world stage, that you will alter the course of events, and they want to stop you so that you don't thwart their plans."

Churchill's face suddenly became serious. He took the cigar out of his mouth and stared at Jonathan. "Just who are these people and what do they believe about me?" Churchill asked in a quiet, urgent voice.

"Really, Winston," Balfour interjected, "you're not going to simply accept all this at face value, are you?"

Jonathan turned to Balfour: "I am no crank. I am here in earnest with important information."

"That's what they all say," Balfour retorted with a smile.

Churchill waved his hand to silence him. He kept his eyes on Jonathan. "Tell m-me what you know, man."

"If you'll excuse me, gentlemen, I'll leave you to your conversation,"

Balfour said, and disappeared beyond the balcony doors.

"Well, sir," Jonathan began, "the man who wants to stop you says there is going to be a Great War. The Austro-Hungarian empire will fall. He says there is this chap, a common painter from Austria, who will one day rule all of Europe—"

Jonathan was interrupted. From out of the fog, a man with a knife leaped up onto the balcony, followed by another man, who jumped on the back of the knife-wielder and wrestled him to the ground. Jonathan grabbed Churchill's arm, and the two of them retreated just as bodyguards emerged from the balcony doors to subdue the two fighting men. One of the fighting men was Joe, the other was the same man that Jonathan had seen outside his house on the day when Agatha and the babies had been accosted in Cadogan Square.

The baron's resonant voice sounded from the lawn just beyond the balcony. "That man attacked me! Now he is trying to kill my valet! Arrest him!"

A crowd had gathered and was spilling out onto the balcony.

"It was the taller man who tried to kill Mr. Churchill with a knife," the baron said with absolute conviction. "I believe that man's name is Joe Golm."

"That is a lie!" Jonathan said. "The other man was wielding the knife!"

Joe was staring at Jonathan, vigorously shaking his head "no," to indicate that he did not want Jonathan to say anything more.

David whispered into Jonathan's ear: "Get a hold of yourself, Drake. Joe is my man. Not yours. You have nothing to do with him. Let me handle this."

David pushed his way to where Joe stood. The golem was still in the grip of one of the bodyguards.

The baron was making a speech, his gestures were dramatic: "... and he is clearly a danger to civilized men—"

"Who is Joe?" a man in interrupted. It was the Viscount of Sudbury, the host of the party. He was a tall man with an aristocratic face and rather unkempt hair. "All I see are a couple of servants who got into a squabble."

David spoke up. "That's right, your lordship. Joe Golm is my man. And he is mute. One cannot expect him to defend himself unless he is given a pen and paper to write down his version of what happened. The Baron von Klausenberg's scurrilous slander cannot continue without the man being able to answer for himself."

"And who are you?" the viscount demanded.

"I am David Lowe, His Majesty's Consul-General to Jerusalem."

"Ah, the Jew among us speaks up," the baron interjected. "I should have realised who was behind this nefarious plot." He stood at the balustrade, gesticulating with his gloved hands, like a foreign noble negotiating a treaty in a court not his own.

"What has a m-man's religion to do with his servant's actions?" Churchill asked, calmly re-lighting his cigar.

"Quite right," said the viscount. "Whom the servant belongs to has nothing whatever to do with the issues at hand, which need to be examined carefully."

"Ah, but that is where you are wrong," the baron countered. "I myself have information for a plot more sinister, something beneath the surface—"

Jonathan was about to tell Churchill who the baron was, but his attention was diverted by a tug at his sleeve. He glanced over and saw Agatha standing next to him. Her face had a look of fear. She said in a low voice: "Mr. Drake, your wife and children are in the baron's house."

From out on the balcony, Joe had heard what Agatha had said, and he began to struggle against the hands that held him. The questioning look in his eyes said to Jonathan: "Should I break away from here?"

Jonathan shook his head no, and the golem stopped struggling.

All attention was now on David, who was a commanding presence his evening dress, speaking calmly. That made it easier for Jonathan to slip away. He took Agatha's arm, and they escaped outside to the courtyard where the guests' private carriages awaited. Jonathan picked one at random.

"But this is Lord Featherston's carriage," the coachman protested.

Jonathan helped Agatha in. "He gave me permission to borrow it."

The coachman grumbled and climbed up to take his seat and the reigns. Jonathan told him the address. The carriage began to move.

"That's not the right address," Agatha said. "Your wife is at the baron's house."

"I know," Jonathan said. "We're going to get help from someone who knows the inside of that house better than the baron himself." Jonathan didn't know where his intuition came from, but he knew this decision was the right one. "Now, tell me what happened," he prompted.

Agatha took a deep breath. "She went to the baron's house straight away after the row with you, sir. As soon as the carriage pulled away from your house, she told the coachman to go there. I tried to argue with her, but she threatened to dismiss me on the spot if I made trouble. I couldn't leave those bairns, so I shut my mouth. We arrived at the baron's house. She would not let me talk to the coachman. The baron himself received her at the front door. He was dressed to go out. He told her he had some calls to make, and that he'd be going to the Sudbury house. She begged him to bring her along, but he was firm, and told her he could not do that. He reminded her: What would people say if he brings another man's wife to a social affair? Anne said she didn't care. She told him she'd just left you for good, and that if the baron wanted to marry her, she'd push for a divorce no matter the consequences. She told him you'd be at the Sudbury's, along with Mr. and Mrs. Lowe. She said it would serve you right to see that he, the baron, knew how to treat her better than you did by bringing her along. She was out of her mind, sir."

Anne's betrayal cut Jonathan to the core. He wondered if in fact Joe was right, that she had hastened Edward's death.

Agatha continued. "The baron persuaded her to stay at his house, to make herself comfortable. He promised to leave the Sudbury's at the soonest moment he could. Then the two of them would have a splendid feast afterwards, and celebrate her liberation. That's what he said. Liberation."

Agatha began to get teary-eyed, and she paused to blow her nose. Then she resumed. "So I stayed downstairs with the servants. I had the babies in my arms for a while, and I was pretendin' that I belonged there. They're an evil lot, those servants. I don't know where he found 'em, but they're wicked to the bone. Then someone sent for the babies, said Anne wanted them near her. I tried to go to her, too, but they wouldn't let me. I'm frightened, sir." Agatha began trembling uncontrollably. She struggled to keep her composure, but a sob escaped. "I haven't seen them since they took the bairns to Anne, somewhere in that house. I'd never have left them there if I could've helped it. But they took 'em away from me."

"Do you know where to?"

"I heard someone say something about a secret room."

"Was it the serail room?"

"That sounds like it," she said. "I couldn't go looking—someone would catch me. So I slipped out to find you and Joe." She started sobbing uncontrollably.

Jonathan put a hand on her shoulder. "Agatha, you are a woman of great courage. We are going to go find them."

The carriage stopped at the destination. Jonathan jumped out and ordered the coachman to wait. Agatha watched him bound up the steps of the brick building. The sign over the black door read: CHARLES CLAYTON COWLES, AGENT OF THE ESTATE. Jonathan tried the handle. It was unlocked. In the vestibule, he saw the same black iron umbrella stand that had been there all those months ago when he first had been there, and he had a sudden, horrifying vision of Daisy's impaled head. He opened the next set of doors. He ran down the black-and-white tiled corridor. His footsteps echoed. The door was unlocked. Cowles was sitting at his desk, smoking and reading a newspaper. The dim light from the lamp reflected in his wire spectacles. There was half a glass of beer next to him.

Cowles jumped to his feet. "I say, what is all this?" he demanded. Jonathan heard the fear and annoyance in his voice. "Who the devil are you, anyway?"

"I'm Jonathan Drake."

Cowles obviously did not recognise the name.

"I was the solicitor for the Belgravia house you sold to Baron von Klausenberg."

Cowles's tone changed and became much more friendly. "Ah, yes, now I remember. How are you Mr. Drake? It has been a while, hasn't it? Your journey was a success, I trust. Although it took longer than expected, as I recall."

Jonathan pointed to a wall that held the many sets of keys hanging on their pegs.

"Have you keys to that estate?"

"Of course."

"Give them to me."

"This is preposterous."

"It's a matter of life and death."

"Then the police should handle it."

Jonathan managed to locate the right set. He seized it and thrust it into his pocket. Then he took Cowled by the arm.

"What the devil are you doing?" Cowles squawked.

"You and I are going to the baron's house to rescue my wife and children."

"This is outrageous! Who do you think you are, breaking in like this and stealing keys?"

"My wife and children are being held prisoner, and you're going to help me find them. You know the layout of the house better than anyone." Jonathan gripped Cowles's collar and frog-marched him down the corridor.

"I object! I will not cooperate! We must call the police!"

"The police will blunder it," Jonathan said calmly. "Now if you don't cooperate, you will regret it."

Jonathan pushed him down the front steps into the waiting cab, and scrambled in after him, making sure that Cowles could not escape.

Agatha sat in the shadows on the opposite seat, her eyes wide with amazement. Cowles was just as amazed to see her there.

"I really must insist that you release me." Cowles twisted his hands together nervously. "My health is not good, and I cannot afford this kind of excitement right now—"

Jonathan gestured to Agatha. "This brave lady," Jonathan said in a low, growling voice, "managed to escape from the baron's house earlier this evening. She is going back there to help us rescue my wife and children. So I won't listen to a yellow dog like you tell me you don't have the guts to do what a woman like her is willing to do. Buck up, man, and stop being a bloody coward."

Cowles clamped his thin lips shut and slouched in the corner of the carriage. After a moment, he said: "I'll tell you the best way to get into the house if you let me get out at the next corner."

"You'll tell me the best way anyway, and I'll let you go when my wife and children are safe," Jonathan said menacingly.

Cowles folded his arms defiantly. Jonathan waited.

They sat in silence as the carriage made its way through the streets of London. Jonathan knocked impatiently on the roof of the carriage to implore the coachman to go faster, but the coachman ignored him and the horse plodded on at an agonizingly slow pace.

"I don't see why you don't let the police handle it," Cowles said, thrusting his lower lip forward.

"Because the police are slow and clumsy, and they'll get my family killed," Jonathan said through clenched teeth. Jonathan leaned toward Cowles and jabbed his finger into the frightened man's chest. "If you call them, I will personally hunt you down like the dog you are. You will regret it."

"What if I'm killed?" Cowles whined. "Doesn't that count for anything? I think I'm going to be sick!" He lurched for the door. Jonathan held him back, worried that it was a ruse to escape. At that moment, the carriage stopped.

The coachman said: "We're at the address you requested, sir."

Jonathan handed payment up to the man, and kept his eyes on Cowles, who emerged from the carriage and promptly vomited in the street.

"Thank ye very kindly, sir," the coachman said, ignoring Cowles's illness. The street was dark and the fog still swirled thickly. "If there's anything else you might need—"

"Be off," Jonathan said.

Without another word, the coachman flicked the reins and pulled away.

Cowles wiped his mouth with a handkerchief and gave Jonathan a baleful look. Agatha eyed Cowles with contempt.

A faint light came from the windows of a house across the street. The baron's house was dark and looming, like a great white mausoleum in the drifting fog.

"If you look at the keys," Cowles said hoarsely, "you'll notice one that is more square than the others. That's the one you want."

Jonathan found the key.

"Let's go around, past the service entrance," Cowles said. The three of them made their way down the side driveway, toward the mews. Cowles tried the door of one of the mews. It was locked.

"The smallest key will open this," he whispered.

"Sir, they're not in this building," Agatha said. "They're in the main house."

"There is a secret entrance from here into the main house," Cowles said nervously. "If you want to keep your arrival a secret, I recommend this route."

After a few attempts, Jonathan managed to open the door. The room was dark and musty smelling. Cowles groped his way along the wall. He yanked open a door, to an interior that was even darker than the room they were in.

"We have to go down this stairway," Cowles said. "It's a tunnel and the ceiling is low." As they descended the stairs, Cowles gave a running commentary to steady his nerves. "The theory is that the original owner built this tunnel so that he could escape unnoticed by servants, who would certainly have told his wife and gossiped unmercifully about his whereabouts. He was a rather randy chap, you see, and he liked a variety of amusements—"

"Ssh!" Jonathan said. They continued in silence.

Cowles whispered: "This tunnel leads to stairs, which go up to a landing. Beyond the landing are the doors to a pantry just off the kitchen."

They proceeded forward, and voices could be heard. They waited just on the other side of the pantry door. Through the lattice screen, they remained invisible, but they could see into the room beyond the pantry. Two women walked in and out of sight near the servant's dining table just off the kitchen. Each was carrying a baby in her arms.

Cowles stood behind them, panting with fear.

"And the baron, he don't like nobody to interfere with his plans," a woman's voice said. It was an older woman by the sound of her voice.

A younger woman's voice said: "But it ain't right, is it? I mean, they're just innocent babes and all."

"Then git out, girl. And remember, you'll end up like the other one—in the Thames!—if ye say a word. You know how the baron hates disloyalty. He'll find ye, no matter how clever you think ye are in hiding, and you'll regret it."

"My mouth is shut," the younger voice said with fear in her tone.

"Ye gotta do more than keep quiet. Whatever the baron commands ye to do, ye do. No questions. Even if ye feel sorry for the little 'uns, just like ye felt sorry for that little boy last week. That's how ye prove yer loyalty. That's how ye save yer own skin. Otherwise, he'll do things worse."

Jonathan could feel Agatha trembling violently next to him. She whispered: "I'm going to save Jack and Lily. Stay here and listen. I'll try to get them to tell me where Mrs. Drake is."

Before Jonathan could stop her, she quietly stepped out of the pantry and closed the door behind her.

She strode into the kitchen where the two women were. They had placed the babies in a basket on the countertop. Agatha had to restrain herself from taking both babies and bolting out of that infernal house. She forced herself not to look at Jack or Lily, who were both quiet for the moment. She could see that both babies knew she was there, and their bright little eyes followed her.

"The Baron wants me to get these babies ready," Agatha announced.

"Says who?" the older woman demanded.

"Says the baron himself," Agatha said aggressively, letting the woman know by her tone that she was astonished at her stupidity. "What is your name?"

The older woman said: "I was born Mary, but the baron calls me Medea." She pointed at the young woman. "She was born Kathleen, but the baron calls her Kali."

Agatha said in a commanding voice: "Mary, I just spoke to the baron at the Sudbury house. He told me to return here and personally supervise getting these children ready."

Mary's eyes narrowed: "I don't believe what yer tellin' me. You ain't one of us." She pointed to the gold cross that Agatha wore around her neck.

"Are ye daft, ye thick hussy?" Agatha shot back. "How do ye think I got my mistress here? By pretendin' to be a good Christian woman, of course. It's all a ruse. Has been for a while now."

Mary said: "Yeah, yer clever all right, but I still don't trust ye."

"Why not?" the younger woman asked. "Why dontcha trust her?"

Mary shrugged. "Just don't. And you can shut yer trap about it, girl."

Agatha rolled her eyes. "I don't give a damn what either of ye bloody wenches think. The baron'll be here soon, seein' all of us blethering on and on. And then we'll have hell to pay. He also said that the woman,

Anne, is to be given something to eat and drink. He doesn't want her to be weak. I'll bring it to her myself."

Mary grumbled. "He wants her drugged. He told me to give her some of this with drink, but no food." The woman held up a brown bottle with a stopper.

"Well, the plans have changed. I told him how she is, how she'll be pukin' her guts out if her stomach is empty. The baron wants her in good shape, not sick like a dog. No drugs until he gets back. Give her some food and water." Agatha added: "But if yer too lazy or too daft to do what I tell ye, I'll bring it to her."

"She's in that room, the sir-rail room below."

"The serail room," Agatha repeated loudly, as if correcting the woman. She hoped Jonathan and that nervous man Cowles had heard this crucial information.

"That's what I said, ain't it?" Mary sneered.

"How do I get there?" Agatha demanded

Just then, a man servant walked in. His eyes were flat. His face was covered with sores.

Mary exclaimed: "Oh, hullo Scab. You know when there will be carcasses soon, dontcha?" She laughed at her own joke.

"I heard there's a woman captive in the house," Scab announced. "I want to go see her."

"The baron said nobody is to see her," Agatha said.

"And just who the hell are you?" he demanded.

"The baron sent her with new orders," Kathleen said.

He walked over to the young woman and slapped her across the face. She lost her balance and fell to the floor.

Agatha wanted to help the young woman, but she didn't dare appear soft. Besides, her first priority was the babies and Mrs. Drake.

As if reading her mind, Scab made his way to Lily, who was chewing on her own fist. An evil grin spread across his face. He reached out to touch her.

"I wouldn't do that if I were you," Agatha said.

"Why not?"

"Because I'm in charge, and I said so."

He pinched Lily hard on the cheek, and she began crying.

"Now I'm going to have to tell the baron about yer impudence," Agatha said, restraining herself from picking up the baby. "He'll see the mark on her, and he'll wonder who did it. And I'll tell him."

"He lets me do what I want with all the captives," Scab said.

"Not these," Agatha snapped.

He made his way to Agatha and leaned into her face. "I don't like being told what to do." His breath was foul, and most of his teeth were missing. Probably from opium, Agatha guessed.

Agatha trembled inside, but she did not back down. "I don't care what ye like. I do the baron's bidding, not yers."

"Shut up." He ripped the gold cross off her neck and flung it across the room.

Agatha had to use all her strength not to go after the crucifix. It had belonged to her grandmother, and she derived great comfort and strength from wearing it. Well, God would just have to find another way to give her strength.

"Now ye've done it," Mary said. "She wears it as a disguise. That's how she tricked the woman into trusting her, by pretendin' she's a Christian."

Scab folded his arms. "I won't believe she's one of us until she proves it."

Mary chuckled. "Oh, she'll get to prove it all right. Just wait."

A slow smile spread across his face. "What time do festivities start?"

"Well after midnight, you know that. Although I heard he might be later than usual. Some ruckus started at the fancy house he's at."

"Well, it'll be midnight soon enough," he said. "And not all the guests are here. I guess I should go see if everything's ready."

He left abruptly, and Agatha breathed a sigh of relief. Without looking obvious about it, she scanned the floor for the gold cross, but she could not see it. The babies cried harder.

"I swear I can't take them crying anymore," Mary said in a threatening voice.

"I'll calm them," Agatha said in a hard voice, as if it were the last thing she wanted to do. She picked up both babies and began whispering words of comfort. Relief flooded through her as she felt their warm little bodies in her arms. She was careful to conceal her tenderness.

As soon as Jonathan heard Agatha say the word "serail," he turned to Cowles.

"How do we get into the serail room?" he whispered.

Cowles clutched his chest, and his voice was hoarse. "It's one level below the cellar. I showed it to you, a low doorway under the stairs. You have to feel for the lock and latch with your fingers, on the left. You have the key. It's the iron one that looks like a prison lock."

Jonathan held up the ring of keys that he'd taken from Cowles's office, and Cowles picked out the correct key.

"You're coming with me," Jonathan said.

"I can't," Cowles said, breathing heavily. "Don't … feel … well."

"We'll get you some help as soon as we rescue my wife and children," Jonathan said. "Now let's go."

"Can't walk," Cowles said, slumping against the wall. His legs were splayed before him, and his breath came in short gasps.

"Then wait here until I get back." Jonathan let himself out of the pantry. He proceeded in the direction of the green baize door. Just as he was about to open it, the younger woman named Kathleen appeared.

"Are you lost, sir?" she asked. She eyed his evening dress. "Guests are gathering upstairs. Shall I show you the way?"

"No need," Jonathan said. "I have special instructions from the baron."

The young woman heard her name being called, and she left him. Jonathan looked around for Agatha, but he did not see her or the babies, and he didn't hear them crying. Should he find the babies, or should he make his way to the serail room to find Anne? His indecision wasted precious seconds as he weighed every course of action he should take.

His calculations were interrupted by a woman in a black robe standing before him. She wore a scarlet-red Venetian carnival mask of long, red feathers, and she held another mask in her hand. Her hair came almost to her knees. She wore dozens of gold and silver bangles on each arm.

"I don't believe I've seen you before," she said. Her accent was American.

"My name is Siegfried," he lied, pronouncing the name as a German would, and affecting a German accent. "The baron requested that I join the festivities this evening."

"Usually, one has to be … initiated … before one is invited to events such as this. And I've never seen you before. And you have no mask."

"Oh, but I was invited," Jonathan said. "Back when I'd been a guest at the baron's estate in Klausenberg." He added in German: "It was not for the faint-of-heart. I am sure that if you had been there, you would not forget it, as I have not."

She clearly did not understand German, and Jonathan could see that he'd convinced her, at least in part, that he was an old friend of the baron. He took the carnival mask out of her hand.

"Thank you for the mask. I thought you spoke German," Jonathan explained. "You look like you are a member of one of the distinguished families from the region of Klausenberg."

"Do I? I suppose that's a compliment," Ursula said warily. She hesitated, and then drifted away, glancing suspiciously at Jonathan as she left.

Jonathan made his way to the green baize door, and quietly opened it. He wished he had an electric torch as he made his way down the winding stairs. At the bottom, he heard voices and saw a dim light at the far end of the cellar. The place was even more enormous than he'd remembered, when he'd been given a tour of the place by Cowles. And it was filled with more chairs now, and dim outlines of objects that hadn't been there before, including grotesque statues of chimera creatures that were half-human-half-animal. The symbols painted on the walls were the same symbols that had been carved into his torso, the same symbols he had seen on the baron's front door when he'd travelled to the Carpathian Mountains.

He had been a different man then, so innocent, so eager to travel to a faraway place to meet the baron and get paid for his adventure. He turned his mind to the task at hand and quietly made his way to the bottom of the staircase. He crept around the corner and found the door to the serail room under the staircase.

Jonathan heard singing on the other side of the door. It was Anne's voice. He felt for the keyhole and latch, and fumbled with the keys that he had taken from Cowles's office. Finally, he managed to unlock it.

A figure sat on the divan, clad in a long white tunic with white sleeves and a high neck. Heavy gold jewellery hung from her neck and wrists. On her head was a conical headpiece, and over that, a white veil that shrouded her face and torso.

"Hello, Jonathan," Anne said calmly.

He ripped off his mask and threw it on the floor, and then grabbed her arm. "Let's go."

"Go? But I've only just arrived. I left you this afternoon. I told you I was finished with you."

"Don't be stupid, Anne. The baron has evil plans—"

She interrupted. "Has Agatha been acting hysterical again? I told her to go away and never come back. She hates the baron as much as you do."

"Listen, Anne, I heard the servants upstairs talking—"

"All is well," Anne explained patiently.

Jonathan gritted his teeth in frustration. "If the baron is being so kind, why are you imprisoned here?"

"Imprisoned?" Anne repeated, laughing. She gestured to the sumptuous furnishings. "Does this look like a prison?"

Jonathan looked around the room. He remembered when he'd last been here with Cowles. The cushions of the low divans had been in tatters, the gilt brazier dusty and tarnished. Now everything had been restored. The cushions had been returned to their former glory: red dragons embroidered on a black silk background. On the walls hung panels of silk that stirred gently with the slightest movement. Oriental carpets lined the floor, and the brazier had been polished to a high shine. Several coloured-glass lanterns glowed on ebony tables inlaid with ivory. Ornate lamps hung by brass chains from the coffered ceiling. A thread of incense smoke wended its way from a brass burner. Despite the incense and luxury, the room smelled damp and decayed, as a cellar would. Or a mausoleum.

Jonathan pressed. "It's a prison, Anne." He held up the ring of keys from Cowles's office. "I had to unlock the door. You can't get out from the inside."

"That's only to keep me safe. There are some around here who would take advantage of me. Once the baron returns, he'll come get me, and the festivities will begin. I'm going to sing for everyone tonight, and we're going to introduce Jack and Lily, and I'll be the guest of honour. It will be a marvellous start to a new life."

Jonathan could only stare at his wife. Was she completely insane, or simply delusional? Did it matter?

He grabbed her wrist. "Anne, let's go."

She wrested herself out of his grip, scratching his hand in the process. "I'm not going with you, Jonathan, and the children are staying here with me."

"Where are they? Do you even know?"

Anne shrugged. "I don't know. But they'll be here soon. The baron promised."

"Anne, the people in this house are going to hurt you and the babies. I heard them say so. This is an evil place. Can't you feel it?"

"Nobody is going to hurt me. They're my friends. The baron is the only man who has ever truly understood me."

"I am glad you think so," said a voice from the doorway. "Because you know I love you more than life itself, Anne." The baron stepped into the small room, but left the door ajar. He smiled at Jonathan. "Have a seat, Mr. Drake."

The baron was dressed in a black silk tunic. It was embroidered with the dragon-eagle creature of his insignia. He had a scimitar on his hip.

Jonathan remained standing. "I insist that you let us go immediately. You are keeping us here against our will."

The baron gestured to the open door. "You are free to leave anytime, Mr. Drake. And Anne may go, too, if she wishes."

"I don't wish to go," Anne said.

"Then you must leave alone," the baron said to Jonathan.

Jonathan clenched his fists. "I won't leave without my wife. She is in danger here."

The baron laughed and turned to Anne. "Are you in danger, my dear?"

"Not at all, Zoltan," she murmured.

"I heard your servants talking about killing my children," Jonathan said.

The baron was silent a moment. "Yes? And what of it?"

Jonathan was speechless. "What of it?" He turned to Anne, and said in an incredulous tone: "Listen to what he's saying, Anne."

"Actually, I don't plan to do it by my own hand," the baron corrected him. "I was thinking that Anne herself could offer up the sacrifice. It is the boy who will be sacrificed." His hand rested lightly on the hilt of his scimitar. "The girl will live. When she is old enough, she will be my consort. Your blood line will live on, Jonathan. Not through your sister, as I had originally planned, but through your daughter. Surely that is a comfort to you."

Anne's face was suddenly full of horror and confusion as she realised what he had just said. She turned to the baron. "You told me you'd take us all under your wing, that you'd raise Jack and Lily as your own."

"Ah, but sometimes the plans must change, my dear Anne. In war, the conquering emperor slays the men and boys, and takes the women and girls into his household, as his property. This is war. All mothers know they may be called upon by their sovereign to give up their children to the sacrifices of war. I am your sovereign. Your fealty is to me by giving up your son. And, eventually, your daughter in marriage."

"I don't want to do that," Anne said. "That wasn't our agreement. You said you'd marry me, and my children would become your children."

"And so it shall happen as you wish," the baron said in a soothing tone. "But the prerogative of a father is to decide which child lives and which child dies."

"I don't want that," Anne said. Her voice had an edge of hysteria. "I don't agree to this." She turned to her husband. "This wasn't my plan."

The baron chuckled. "Anne, you know that I demand total fealty from you. Total fealty means that you must do what I tell you to do. Your namesake is Anat. Anat is both a fertility goddess and a destroyer. She is the Great Mother, the goddess who brings forth life and extinguishes it at her will. She is the Mistress of the Blood. By her body life is brought forth, by her hand it is snuffed out." The baron began to chant:

She hangs heads on her back,

She fastens hands on her girdle.

She plunges her knees in the blood of swift ones,

Her thighs in the gore of fast ones

"I don't want to be Anat anymore," Anne said, her eyes wide with terror.

"But my dear, it is too late for all that now. At every test of your fealty, you have done so well. Our darling Anat does not flinch from her duty. No leader could demand a more loyal follower. Her allegiance to me will be consecrated soon."

"Anne is not like that," Jonathan insisted.

The baron raised an eyebrow. "Isn't she? I know her better than you do."

The special emphasis on "know" provoked Jonathan's rage. "You blackguard. You've seduced my wife."

The baron held up his hand, and Jonathan noticed that his long nails were lacquered black.

"Not in the way you imagine," the baron answered. "But I have cultivated something deeper in your wife, something more lasting than mere lust. Lust is a useful impulse, but on its own it is too ephemeral, too easily transferred to someone else. What I have cultivated in Anne is an unquenchable thirst for a better world, for the brightest future imaginable. I've promised her that she, and others like her, will be the emissaries of a utopia. That is why she is willing to make whatever sacrifice I ask of her to in order that the new world may be born." The baron unsheathed his scimitar and turned to Anne. "Tell me darling Anne, would you be willing to sacrifice your children, by your own hand, if it means that a better world can come into being?"

Her eyes searched his. She shook her head. "You're asking the impossible, Zoltan. I can't give up my own children." Her voice caught on this last word, and a tear trickled down her cheek.

The baron said in a soft voice: "You are forgetting your lessons. Remember what I taught you. What is every mother's duty?"

"To send her children to war."

"That is right. And you are a mother. Is that your duty?"

Something inside her snapped. A spell had been broken. She looked at the baron, and for the first time she saw him for what he was: a cruel aristocrat who had used her for his own purposes. She was not the woman he thought she was. She was not the woman he was trying to force her to be. She realized that she wanted to stay married to Jonathan, to raise their children together.

"I don't want to," Anne said.

"What you want is insignificant, my dear. Your fealty to me comes first."

"No. Not any longer," Anne said. She tore off her veil and headdress. Her hair hung loose about her shoulders. Then she stood and reached for her husband's hand. "Take me home now, Jonathan."

Before Jonathan could take his wife's hand, the baron pushed Jonathan so forcefully, that Jonathan's head struck the wall. The baron stood over Jonathan, and kicked him in the head.

Anne screamed "Stop that! Stop kicking him!"

"Quiet, Anne," the baron commanded.

Starbursts clouded Jonathan's vision. He covered his face with his hands, and he could feel his own blood running into his eyes, and down his white shirt and black jacket.

"Why do you hate me?" Jonathan asked. "I helped you get here."

"Because you are an obstacle," the baron said. "You protected Churchill. And, if I am to have total possession of your wife, you must be removed."

"I don't belong to you!" Anne cried.

"Oh, but I beg to differ," the baron taunted.

Jonathan watched to see whether the baron would lift the scimitar against him, but the baron remained immobile, lost in thought. Jonathan calculated this would be the moment to rush him and grab the scimitar, but the baron read his thoughts, and said: "Now is not the time, Jonathan. Since you will not live to see the sun rise, let me tell you the future. In less than a decade, the world as it exists now will be gone. Nation shall lift up sword against nation. The war will be so great, that all countries, even the United States, will be drawn in. That war will kill off the best and brightest of this generation. It will be a mass-immolation, a dark sacrifice made more potent by the churches and governments endorsing it. It will demolish and destroy, and enable a new order to arise."

"And you think this is a good thing?" Jonathan asked, amazed at the look of rapture on the baron's face.

"It is a marvellous thing. Out of the ashes comes a new order. This is why I am here. I am the emissary who will hasten the destruction and the rebirth. Everyone will say that this first war will end all wars, but it will be only the beginning. There will be another, more destructive than the first. This century will be one of the bloodiest in history. And the blood will wash away the sins of the past. Each must give himself over to the collective, to the idea, just as our dear Anne will do. Or, as she is now named, Anat." The baron reached over and stroked her hair.

"I'm not Anat anymore," Anne said in a trembling voice. "I want my children to live. I want my husband to live. Please let us go."

"And yet you already have become Anat," the baron said in a voice that was almost a purr. "Shall we tell your husband of Anat's deeds? Or to be more precise, of your deeds as Anat?" The baron chuckled. "You hastened your father-in-law's death, at my behest. We had been aiming for you to smother him until dead, but you didn't quite succeed. Still, it was a valiant effort for a beginner."

Anne was quietly weeping. "I'm sorry I did that. I wish I could take it all back." She gazed at her husband, who was still lying on the floor, bleeding. "I'm sorry, Jonathan. I am so sorry!"

The baron's lips curled into a smile. "How very repentant of you, Anne." Then he swung the scimitar at her neck. Anne collapsed to the floor, and her white dress bloomed red.

Jonathan crawled over to his wife and took her his arms. He wept bitterly.

"Have you no ounce of humanity?" Jonathan cried in a hoarse voice. "You claimed to love her, and yet you cut her down like a sheaf of wheat."

The baron said: "Oh, but I do love Anne. True loyalty and true love mean that you will sacrifice anyone or anything to the ideal of the future." A thought struck him, and he ran his finger through the blood on the blade of his scimitar. "I do believe that makes six thousand, six hundred and sixty-six lives that this scimitar has taken. It is fitting that our darling Anne should be the one to bring about that glorious number of four sixes."

The baron reached over and ripped a panel of silk from the wall, exposing the stone. He then walked over to Jonathan who was still holding Anne. He dipped his fingers into her blood. On the stone wall where the silk panel had hung, he drew the top half of a circle, and a dot below it.

"I don't expect you to recognise this symbol," the baron said. "It is the ancient symbol of Ba'al, the god of the Canaanites, who demanded child

392

sacrifice. Anat was Ba'al's sister. You Jews conquered the Canaanites and ended the practice in that land, which is a pity, because it was a wonderful tool of control, and it was spiritually powerful. It was also a way for subjects to demonstrate their fealty to their sovereign." He traced over the half-circle with the point of the scimitar. "Ba'al's crescent is the curve of the blade that will behead the lion."

"Which lion?" Jonathan asked. He was dazed, and his throat was so dry that his voice was barely a whisper.

"The lion in Churchill's coat of arms, that holds Saint George's cross. The lion of Judah on the emblem of Jerusalem. In the end, the Canaanites will reign."

The baron wiped the blade of the scimitar with a corner of the silk panel that he had ripped from the wall. He held the gleaming, curved blade up and admired it. "The scimitar is curved like the glorious crescent of Ba'al. It cuts down obstacles in its path."

He set the scimitar next to Anne's body.

"Now, my dear Jonathan, it is time for the festivities. You shall wait here until I call for you."

The baron disappeared through the doorway. The door closed and the lock clicked into place.

CHAPTER THIRTY-SIX

Agatha waited off to the side, out of sight, watching the servants who came in and out of the kitchen. She wondered how she could take the babies out of the house without being seen. The rough bloke named Scab who had ripped the crucifix off her neck was keeping watch on all the entrances and exits nearby. Did he know about the secret passage that Agatha had taken to get here? She didn't know, but if he happened to follow her down that dark passage, he'd surely kill her and the babies. The very thought of being in that tunnel with him made her tremble with fright.

Agatha pulled herself together to think about what she could do. Jonathan had gone to look for Anne, and Agatha didn't dare try to find them both. She had to focus on getting Jack and Lily to safety. Nobody could help her. She had to do it alone.

Agatha's mind raced ahead. The basket was heavy and unwieldy. Holding it, or holding both babies in her arms without the basket, would mean her hands and arms would be free for nothing else. That meant she wouldn't be able to defend herself.

A sling. She could tie the babies against her torso with a sling, which is exactly what her mother had done when raising nine children. She looked around to be sure no-one was watching, then she picked up the basket with both babies, and slipped into a larder. That small room was a chaotic mess. Empty bottles and tins and papers were strewn everywhere. It smelled of food gone bad, spilled beer and garbage,

And it was obvious that vermin were taking advantage of the disorder. Agatha wondered how the baron could allow his servants to be so slovenly. She glanced around, not seeing what she needed.

She set the basket down, and hastily hiked up her skirt and ripped apart her chemise. She tied it into a sling around her neck and chest. Jack began to get fussy.

"Don't get upset, wee Jack," she said, trying to keep her voice steady. "We're going to be out of here soon. I need you both to be as quiet as church mice for a little longer."

She heard a noise outside the door.

"Whatcha doin'?" said a voice from the doorway. It was the young woman named Kathleen.

Agatha whirled around. "I've my orders to be here, girl," she replied in a severe tone, hoping the girl would be too intimidated to guess what she was up to.

"Well, I heard the baron is almost ready for them babies to be brought down to the celebration."

Agatha's heart raced in fright, but she maintained her self-control. She drew herself up to her full height and her eyes were blazing with anger. "You go tell them that we are almost ready. Dirty babies will only ruin the celebration, won't they? So I am cleaning them and giving them new nappies."

The girl laughed at the scatological reference. "Oh, he don't mind that. He says it pleases the Lord of the Flies. Funny name that, ain't it?"

The girl obviously didn't know the Bible. She didn't know that Beelzebub, the Lord of the Flies, was the devil himself. Or maybe she did, and that was worse. Agatha took no comfort in the fact that she herself had been right all along about the diabolical nature of everything connected with the baron and his infernal house. The air crackled with evil, dark shadows closed in, and she desperately wished her grandmother's gold cross were around her neck. It would give her strength. Well, she would have to push on no matter what.

"Well, be quick about it," Kathleen said, "or the baron will punish you."

As soon as the girl was gone, Agatha carefully placed each baby in the sling on her chest, praying as she did so that the Lord would protect them and get them all to safety. The sling weighed heavily on her shoulders, but she could manage. She smelled that her prediction about one of the babies having a dirty nappy had come true, but she had no time to change nappies. She just hoped whichever baby it was would not become too fussy.

Agatha began whispering to them. "We're going to be out of here soon. But we must be quiet."

As if on cue, Jack began fussing again, and Lily let out a whimper.

"Ssh," Agatha said desperately. "Please hush, my sweet darlings."

As soon as Agatha emerged back into the kitchen area, she knew the atmosphere was more frenetic, charged with the electricity of an evil storm that was about to break. The babies squirmed in the sling, and Agatha knew from the sounds of distress they were making that a crying jag was not far off.

Some of the guests were coming through the passageway, near where Agatha waited. They used the green baize door to descend into the cellar below. They all wore Venetian masks. Agatha was trembling so badly, she thought her knees would give way. She kept her face blank as she made her way to the pantry door where the dark passage back to the mews began.

"There you are," said Kathleen. "Let's go to the celebration. Everyone says baron is waiting."

"Just one moment," Agatha said imperiously. "I almost forgot. I have to fetch something that the baron told me to bring for tonight's festivities. I won't be half-a-minute."

Without waiting for the girl's answer, Agatha slipped around the corner, yanked open the door of the pantry, stepped into the darkness, and quietly closed the pantry door behind her.

CHAPTER THIRTY-SEVEN

David paced the floor of the library at the Drake house in Hyde Park. He had a pistol tucked into his waistband. The hour was late, and all the servants except Thompson had retired for the night. Thompson was methodically walking each floor, armed with a pistol and on alert to any intruders. Sarah sat next to her mother, and Sam hovered nearby, keeping an eye on Hannah. Sam was tempted to share the grisly news of Daisy, but he knew that he needed to keep that confidence for a while longer. The time was not right to disclose that horrible event.

"They refused to let Joe go free," David said in an irritated tone, "even though I gave them my word that I would guard him to be sure nothing happened."

"Did the baron's man also get taken into custody?" Hannah asked.

"Vukovic? Yes, they took him as well. The baron managed to slip away. I don't know where he went."

"Probably back to his house," Sarah said.

Sam shook his head. "That's would be a foolish move. He's undoubtedly guilty, and the authorities will easily find him there."

"But they don't think he's guilty," David corrected him. "As far as they're concerned, only Vukovic and Joe are persons of interest. Listening to the baron's little speech tonight, when this all erupted, even I believed him for a moment. He is a convincing liar."

"And what about Jonathan? Where is he?" Hannah cried, with panic beginning to rise in her voice.

"I'm sure he is fine," Sam said. "He was getting dressed when I dropped off that letter to him, and looking quite distinguished, I might add." Sam's conscience nagged him for misleading Hannah so completely, but he knew discretion was the better part of valour. "You must not strain your nerves, Lady Drake."

Sarah cut in: "If either of them has any sense, they ought to have left the Sudbury house as soon as possible. Jonathan is probably with Mr. Churchill this very minute, having a drink back at a private club."

Hannah sighed. "I wish you were right, my dear, but your poet's imagination gets the better of you."

Thompson opened the door to the drawing room. "Inspector Keane is asking to be shown in, my lady."

"Show him in, then," Hannah said.

A moment later, the inspector stepped into the room, his hat in his hands. "You butler didn't wait for me to ring before answering the door, m'lady. Very efficient, he is."

Hannah said nothing.

The inspector continued: "Begging your pardon, m'lady, but there is an important matter I must ask you about." He nodded soberly to the others in the room. Then he continued. "As I am sure you are aware, there was an altercation at the Sudbury house this evening. Your son was there. His man, Joe Golm, was taken into custody. He is a person of interest in an attempted attack on Sir Winston Churchill."

"Yes, go on," Hannah said.

"Well, my lady, Joe Golm has somehow escaped custody."

Sarah exclaimed "Oh!" and clapped her hand to her mouth. Keane looked at her.

"Do you have information that could help us, Miss, erm, Miss . . .?"

"Mrs. Lowe," she said. "No, no I don't have any information," she said, drawing herself up straighter. "It's just that I'm surprised anyone would escape custody like that."

David spoke up. "I'm sure I'm not the only one in this room wondering why you've come here. This is not Joe's residence."

"Has Joe Golm come here seeking refuge?" the inspector enquired.

"Why in the world would he do that?" Sam exclaimed. "He's Jonathan's man."

Inspector Keane turned to David. "Your name, sir?"

"David Lowe."

"Aren't you the man who stated at the Sudbury residence that Joe Golm was your man?"

David was unruffled. "Yes, and that was for the sake of expedience. I was trying to save Jonathan the trouble of becoming entangled with the whole mess."

As the inspector jotted down a note, he remarked: "Lying to the authorities is not the way to avoid becoming entangled, sir. It only makes matter worse."

"So I see," David said grimly.

"Jonathan Drake is already entangled," Inspector Keane said. "My men are on their way to Cadogan Square now. There have been reports of his mental instability."

Hannah rose to her feet. "All lies!" she cried.

The inspector gave her a sympathetic look. "That may be so, m'lady, but we must explore every angle."

Hannah lifted her chin defiantly. "Mrs. Anne Drake, my daughter-in-law who lives in Cadogan Square, will not appreciate being disturbed by your men at this hour," Hannah said in an angry tone.

Sam turned to the inspector. "Lady Drake's nerves are frayed, thanks to your indelicate manners, which is why she failed to mention that her daughter-in-law, Mrs. Anne Drake, is here, upstairs in the nursery, with the babies and the nanny."

Hannah glanced at Sam quizzically, but said nothing.

"Then let's have her down here so I can ask a few questions," Keane said.

"I am her doctor, and I forbid it at this hour. She is sleeping, and cannot be disturbed."

The inspector turned to Hannah. "Your son was accused of impersonating someone else in order to gain entry to the Sudbury house. He attended the party on false pretenses. Why did he do that?"

"It was a misunderstanding," Hannah said. "I have two sons. The hostess happens to be a long-time friend. She thought it was my son Michael who would be attending, rather than Jonathan." Hannah didn't care that she was lying. Too much was at stake.

"You realise that the attempted attack on Churchill is grave. Your son's deception does not help him. We will have to interview him. Where is he, by the way?"

"How am I supposed to know?" Hannah said coldly. "He doesn't live here."

"And yet his wife is here," the inspector observed.

David lit a pipe and threw the match into the fireplace. "Inspector, you already know that I was at the Sudbury house. So was my wife, Sarah. We saw what happened after accusations were thrown about as to who was guilty. I think you would do well to send your men to Baron von Klausenberg's house, and see whether his man Vukovic had any accomplices. I think you will find that place to be a rich vein of enquiry."

"We are pursuing our leads as we see fit," Inspector Keane said. "The baron will certainly come under our scrutiny when the time is right."

"That should be sooner rather than later," David said.

"Thank you for your advice," the inspector retorted, his mouth tightening "If Jonathan Drake should happen to show up, please ask him to contact me. And be on the lookout for the fugitive Joe Golm." He handed his card to Hannah.

After he left, Hannah turned to Sam. "Why did you tell me that Anne and the children are here?"

"Because Jonathan told me he sent them here," Sam replied.

"When did he tell you that?"

"Before he left for the dinner party at the Sudbury house."

Hannah rang for Thompson. When he appeared, she said: "Please see whether Anne is here with Jack and Lily."

He returned a few minutes later. "They are not here, m'lady."

Hannah put her hand on her heart, and her face was creased with worry. "They must be at Cadogan Square, then, soundly asleep, as we all should be."

CHAPTER THIRTY-EIGHT

In the absolute darkness of the tunnel, Agatha made her way forward. She tested each step along the uneven surface with her foot, being careful not to fall. Jack and Lily squirmed and whimpered in the sling. Agatha kept one hand on the stone wall, and the other out in front of her in case she tripped.

She realised, with grim satisfaction, that her theory about Cowles's disappearance had been right. The man was nowhere to be seen, and had undoubtedly fled at the first chance. He was a coward anyway, so it was no surprise he disappeared as soon as he could. How long it would take the police to get to the house, only God knew, but at least Jonathan and Anne would be safe soon enough.

The darkness unnerved her. She continued carefully along the tunnel, feeling her way with her hands and feet. She whispered comforting words to the babies to keep herself from panicking. Jack was now beginning to cry, and Lily made sucking sounds on her fist. Agatha's foot slammed into something covered with fabric, and she stepped back with a scream, almost falling. Both babies were startled by her scream and began crying. From somewhere in the darkness, above the din of the babies' cries, a low chuckle sounded, then an electric torch came on.

The man in the dim circle of light was the man named Scab who had ripped the gold cross off Agatha's neck.

"Escaping, are ye?" he said with an evil grin. He held up the electric torch with one hand, and then raised his other hand, which held a blood-stained knife.

Agatha backed away.

He gestured to the body at his feet. It was Cowles. "I caught 'em here, right where you see 'em. Now I'll do the same to you, and I'll return those little piglets to the baron."

"God damn you straight to hell," Agatha said.

From behind the man, Agatha saw a thick, muscular arm come out of the darkness and lock around Scab's neck. Over the wails of the babies, she heard the scuffle beyond the glow of the electric torch, which had fallen to the ground. Agatha was too frightened to move. The babies thrashed and screamed in the sling, their wails echoing through the tunnel. After what seemed a long time, a large, strong hand clamped over her wrist and pulled her along. It seemed to take hours to emerge from the darkness, but it was only minutes. Agatha could not stop shaking, even when there was enough light at the other end of the tunnel to confirm that Joe was guiding her. His head turned to the left and right as he scanned his surroundings, alert for the next threat. He led her outside, and down the alley in the opposite direction of the way she had originally come. The babies' cries continued. Joe turned left and then right, still keeping a hold of Agatha's wrist. They were now on a main thoroughfare. By this time, the babies' cries had quieted to a whimper. Even though the hour was very late, and a light rain fell, Joe managed to stop a cab.

He held the door open for Agatha to get in. She clung to him.

"I'm afraid, Joe. I want you to come with us."

He looked down into her face, and shook his head no. She could tell from the expression in his eyes that he expected to be back soon, that she needed to be brave and carry on.

"I said where to!" the coachman shouted. His horse stamped its hooves impatiently. "Ye deef er what? If ye don't tell me where to, I ain't drivin' nowhere,'cept away from ye."

Agatha found her voice. She told him the address of the Drake house in Hyde Park.

The coachman snapped the reins. Agatha put her head out the window and said to Joe: "He is in the serail room with Anne! Below the cellar!" Joe held up his hand to indicate he understood, then he strode off, back to the baron's house.

Seated in the carriage, Agatha looked down at the babies. Jack's breathing seemed to be shallow, and his eyes looked glassy when the glow of the occasional gaslights shined through the cab window. Lily was sucking her fist again, and mucous was running out of her nose. They each looked filthy, like neglected street urchins, and the smell was even worse now.

"We'll be home soon, we will, we will." She rocked back and forth and murmured those words over and over again, as if they were an incantation that would make the horses sprout wings so that the cab could fly through the streets of London. She stroked their heads and let her tears fall on them.

The cab finally stopped in front of the Drake residence in Hyde Park Agatha carefully stepped out of the cab. The coachman yelled: "That'll be 'alf a crown! Pay up!"

"Thompson will pay you," Agatha said, making her way to the front door and ringing the doorbell.

Thompson opened the door. His face registered shock at the sight of a wet and dishevelled Agatha carrying the babies in a sling. Before he could say anything, Agatha pushed past him, saying: "Pay that coachman."

Hannah emerged from the library, along with Sarah, David, and Sam. They helped her lift the babies out of the sling. Lily started crying first, and then Jack.

"They're hungry and thirsty and need to be cleaned," Agatha said, her breath coming in gasps.

She realised she was no longer able to stand. Sam saw that she was about to collapse, and he grabbed her arm. He and David helped her to a chair, she dimly heard Hannah ordering Thompson to wake two of the maids to draw a bath and help tend to the babies. Sarah and Hannah took them up to the nursery right away.

Sam put a glass in her hand.

"Please drink, Mrs. MacLeod."

Agatha took a sip, and then said in a choked voice: "You must send the police to the baron's house. Mr. Drake is there, with Mrs. Drake. Joe is there, too." She drank more.

David glanced at Sam. "If we send the police, and if they find Joe, they'll arrest him. We've got to get him out of the country as soon as possible. Sarah and I can take him back to Prague."

"Why does he have to leave? What did he do?" Agatha cried.

"He escaped police custody," David said. "He can't be put through the machinations of the legal system. He's, he's not—" David's voice trailed off.

"He couldn't stand trial," Sam cut in. "He's not really fit for it."

"Why not?" Agatha demanded. "He's mute, but his mind is sharp. And he's innocent. They'll let him off. The facts are in his favour. I'll testify."

"That's not it," David said.

"Is he insane, then?" Agatha asked.

"No, he's not insane. He's just not … normal."

Agatha snickered. "Well, sir, everyone knows that. They'll figure it out, and all will be straightened out sure as daylight." Her face suddenly became quite grave. "He saved my life. He saved the bairns' lives. He's a good man. For that, he deserves mercy. In fact, he deserves to be knighted."

"The authorities might not see it that way," David explained. "We can't have him incarcerated, not even for a day. He's not built for that."

Agatha was frantic. "If we don't alert the police, how will Mr. and Mrs. Drake get away from the baron?"

David's face was grave. "We have to pray that Joe can rescue them."

Sam spoke up. "I don't like this. We're pitting Joe's future against the lives of Jonathan and Anne. Suppose it's too much for Joe? We have a moral duty to inform the police and send as much help as we can. We must not gamble with innocent lives."

David considered this. "Perhaps you are right, Berg. Perhaps it is too much of a gamble to depend solely on Joe."

David walked across the room to the telephone, and placed the call.

CHAPTER THIRTY-NINE

The golem went back through the pitch-dark tunnel toward the baron's house. He didn't need a light. His eyesight in the dark was excellent. He stepped over the bodies of Cowles and the man named Scab as if they were just more obstacles to navigate. When he reached the pantry doors that opened into the house, he paused only for a moment to look through the lattice and see who was nearby, and to listen for voices. There was nobody. He quietly slipped through, and closed the doors behind him.

He could hear sound coming from ... that way. He turned his head to get a better fix on the location, until he perceived the sound was louder. Then he followed the sound through the corridor.

A single electric bulb cast a dim circle of light. He made his way to the green baize door and listened. The sounds were closer. With absolute stealth, he opened the door. He made his way down the stairs. At the bottom, he could see the flickering shadows on the wall. He moved closer to the fire, and saw a body lying on a low platform next to it, covered in a panel of crimson silk. Off to the side, Jonathan was tied to a metal frame in the shape of an X. His evening clothes were torn and bloodied. Iron spears were stuck into the ground, arranged around him like a circular palisade. On the walls, a few sconces held flaming torches.

The baron stood with his hands upraised, like a conductor directing a chorus. From around the pit, people in masks talked excitedly.

"Silence!" the baron commanded. He wore no mask. "We don't have much time. I sense someone here among us who does not belong ..."

407

The baron scanned the faces around him, and Joe knew that the baron could sense his presence, even though he was crouched in the shadows, behind the onlookers.

"But it does not matter," the baron added. "Nobody can stop the inevitable—not even enemies among us."

Some of the onlookers began chanting.

The baron nodded to the rhythm, and then spoke above the din. "Time grows short. Let us gather our strength. This man is our enemy." He pointed at Jonathan. Then he pointed at the covered body on the low platform. "Anat's body will be cremated in our purifying fire. Let us remember her as the faithful servant she was. Hallowed be her name."

The crowd murmured approval, and resumed chanting. Joe made his way along the wall, closer to Jonathan, but stayed in the shadows.

"Where is Lucien?" one of the onlookers asked. "He knows the art of pain."

"Lucien is not here," the baron said. "We must do this ourselves. I shall go first." The scimitar gleamed in the baron's hand. He positioned himself near the spears that encircled Jonathan.

Joe sprang forward from the shadows. The baron turned, and raised his scimitar to strike Joe, but the golem maneuvered out of the way. The baron swung it again. It glanced off an iron spear and pierced Jonathan's torso. Jonathan groaned. Many of the onlookers panicked, and ran for the stairs.

Joe pulled up an iron spear, and moved to stab the baron with it, but Ursula shoved Joe, causing him to momentarily lose his balance and his aim. Joe threw another spear at the fleeing baron, and missed again.

Joe made his way over to Jonathan. He reached up and ripped the restraints from Jonathan's wrists, and unfastened his ankles. He held Jonathan tightly, carrying him into the shadows, away from the fire pit.

Joe backed against the stone wall, still holding Jonathan in one arm and a spear in the other, and facing outward so he could watch for anyone who was not retreating. Jonathan's blood flowed freely, soaking Joe's clothes.

The chamber was now empty. The only sound was the fire, crackling and burning furiously.

"Let me sit on the floor," Jonathan said to the golem. Joe lowered him gently.

Jonathan slumped against the wall stared at the fire pit. His breathing was laboured. From out of the flames, Jonathan saw his father and Chompsworth walking toward him. Both figures glowed with an ethereal light. He reached his hand out to touch them.

"Jonathan, my dear son, you're going to come with us," Edward said, taking his son's hand. Chompsworth wagged her tail, and licked Jonathan's other hand. It felt more real than the pain that wracked his body.

"But, Father, I have to protect my children."

"Others will protect them. Joe must go upstairs and set fire to this house. He must carry out the bodies of you and Anne, and make sure you both have a proper burial. Then he must go to my house, gather everyone who is there, and flee to Prague. Once in Prague, Joe will go back to sleep in the synagogue from whence he was awakened." He addressed Joe. "Do you understand what I am telling you?"

The golem nodded.

Edward continued. "And after the golem is safely interred back in Prague, Hannah must go with the children and Sarah and David to Jerusalem. Sarah and David are to be the new parents of Jack and Lily. You must tell them all this, Joe."

Jonathan said: "Father, I know you are dead. But what about Anne?" He pointed to where her body was laid out, near the fire, covered in a panel of silk.

Edward said: "Do not worry. You will see her soon enough. Take care, my dear son. We will meet again." Edward vanished with the dog.

The golem sensed something, and he scanned the darkness to see who else was there, but he saw nobody.

Jonathan could feel himself becoming untethered to his body, and he wanted that release. The agony and pain he was suffering was beginning to decrease as he felt his soul begin its separation. He turned his face to Joe.

"Did you hear my father's words?" Jonathan said, his breath coming in gasps. "You must carry out the commands my father told you."

The golem nodded.

"The baron murdered Anne," Jonathan said. "He murdered her with his sword. Tell everyone that."

Then Jonathan saw the spider's web in front of him. The images there were of the night he had helped to awaken the golem. He recalled how, as he had circled the genizah with the candle, a feeling of profound peace and security had descended upon him. That same peace and awareness now descended upon him again. He let his breath go out one last time.

Joe grasped Jonathan's hand and pressed it to the necklace that he wore around his neck. Then he gently laid Jonathan on the ground. He carried the platform that held Anne's body, and laid it next to Jonathan.

He grabbed a torch from a wall sconce and made his way quickly to the stairs. Before he ascended, he paused. He tried to peer into the darkness behind the stairway, into the passage that led to the serail room. Joe could sense an evil presence there, and he wanted to pursue it, like a terrier stalking prey down a rathole, but the commands from Edward and Jonathan overrode this instinct. He had to do what they had told him to do. He sprinted up the stairs, holding the torch high.

He started on the top floor, going from room to room, and letting the flames of the torch lick draperies and tapestries. When he got to the bottom floor, where the kitchen was, some irresistible force drew him there. An object near the stove caught his eye. It was a necklace lying on the floor. A gold cross. He picked it up and slipped it into his pocket. Then went he back down into the cellar to retrieve the bodies of Jonathan and Anne.

The bodies were not where he had left them. They were now in the fire pit, being consumed by the flames. It was a dark fire, a sinister fire. The smoke ascended and disappeared into the black shadows of the ceiling.

At the edge of the fire pit, the crescent blade of the scimitar glimmered. Across the curve of the blade, the baron's black gloves were neatly laid out.

CHAPTER FORTY

Joe moved quickly through the dark, rainy streets. He could hear a clock tower chiming the late hour. At the Hyde Park house, Joe didn't bother to go to the servants' entrance. He went to the front door and tried the knob. Locked. Then he rang the bell. A pale-faced, exhausted-looking footman opened the door. Joe pushed past the servant and headed to the library.

Joe was wet from the rain, and his shoes squeaked and left muddy tracks as he walked across the marble floor. He flung open the door the door to the library. Sam stopped talking mid-sentence.

"Well, I'm dumbfounded," Sam exclaimed. "What on earth happened to you, Joe?"

David and Sarah immediately got to their feet and led the golem to the fireplace.

"Good heavens, Joe, we thought we'd never see you again," David exclaimed. "You must dry off. Let us ring for some hot tea."

"Maman sent the servants to bed," Sarah reminded him. "I'll fetch the tea."

There was another man there whom the golem did not recognise. Joe eyed the new man warily. The man was short and fastidiously dressed in a grey suit of expensive wool, with a neatly trimmed blond beard and red, plump cheeks.

David asked in a low voice: "Where is Jonathan? And Anne?"

The golem gazed at him dolefully, then glanced suspiciously at the stranger.

411

"This is Geoffrey Marsh," David said, reading the golem's expression. "He is the Drake family solicitor, and as trustworthy as I am. You can tell us anything."

David found a pad of paper and a pencil on the writing desk. He handed them to the golem.

Joe scribbled out the following and ripped the paper from the pad, and handed it to David.

jonathan and anne dead
edward said burn baron's house and return to synagogue in prague
and you and sarah and hannah and babies go to jerusalem
immediately

David dropped the paper onto the floor and walked over to the hearth. He held onto the chimneypiece for support, and stared into the fire without speaking.

Sam picked up the paper, read it silently, and handed it to Geoffrey, who swore under his breath.

Geoffrey turned to Joe and asked:

"Did the baron kill them both?"

Joe nodded.

"How did he kill them?"

The golem wrote:

sword
then baron put bodies in the fire

"Did you witness it?" Geoffrey asked.

no i did not see him do it
i found the bodies in the flames
and baron's sword and gloves near the fire
he wanted me to know he did it

"And Edward appeared?" David asked.

Joe nodded again.

412

"Edward? Edward Drake?" Geoffrey repeated. "You mean, his ghost? You can see the departed?"

Joe nodded.

"Oh, good heavens." Geoffrey rolled his eyes and pointed at the golem. "If they don't send him to prison, they're going to send him to an asylum. Of course, we could simply claim that he shares Hamlet's ability to talk to ghosts." He laughed hollowly at his own joke. Joe looked at him quizzically.

David said to Geoffrey: "You're going to help get him out of the country, Mr. Marsh. The authorities are looking for him. They're already furious that he escaped from custody earlier this evening."

Joe picked up his paper from the floor and pointed to the words that urged them to go to Jerusalem.

"Is that what Edward said?" David asked. "Are you certain?"

Joe nodded. He wrote:

danger is here i can feel it

"Here in the house?" Geoffrey asked.

not just house
all around

"Is the baron dead?" David asked.

i do not know

The front doorbell rang.

"I'll answer it," Geoffrey said. "Get Joe out of here. Hide him in that place we had discussed before."

He threw the golem's scribblings into the fire. David escorted Joe out.

Geoffrey took his time answering the door. A short while later, David strode back into the library with an imperious stride, as if he owned it. Inspector Keane was there, and he watched David with a hostile, suspicious gaze. Two policemen stood off to the side, observing everything. Sam sat in a nearby chair, doing a good job of looking relaxed and nonchalant.

"Your man absconded from custody," Keane said to David. "Tell us where he is."

David said: "I cannot tell you his whereabouts."

"Because you don't want to or because you don't know?"

"Are you accusing me of refusing to cooperate?" David demanded.

Keane backed down. "No, of course not, sir, it's just that he injured one of my men when he escaped earlier. We consider him a dangerous man. And so, I need to find out from you anything about him that will tell us where he could be."

Sarah appeared, carrying a tray of tea. "Oh, where is—"

David immediately interrupted her. "Your mother is in her room." David gave the inspector a hard look. "You are not helping her nerves." He went over to his wife and said gently: "Go upstairs and give your mother her tea. I have to talk to these gentlemen, and then I'll join you later."

After Sarah left the room, Keane said: "We received an anonymous tip that a servant named Daisy had worked for Lady Drake's son, Jonathan. She has been found at Adelphi Arches."

Sam said blandly: "Then perhaps you can ask Daisy for information that we cannot possibly supply."

"She'd dead, sir. Beheaded."

"That's dreadful!" Sam exclaimed. "Have you got leads?"

The inspector's eyes narrowed. "Not yet, sir, which is why we'll have to search this house."

"But Daisy was never employed here," David observed.

The inspector said: "I'm referring to your man, who escaped custody. Now, if you don't mind, my men will begin the search on the ground floor—"

"Oh, for shame!" Geoffrey interjected. "Two women are mourning the death of Edward Drake, and at this ungodly hour, you want to turn their house upside down looking for a common servant who strong-armed one of your men. Perhaps you need to find more manly men."

Keane glowered. "He's a suspect in an attempted attack on Mr. Churchill and Mr. Balfour."

"You ought to be looking for the Vukovic character," David said.

"We are, sir, but we need to also interrogate your man."

"Why don't you search the local pubs, then?" Geoffrey said. "These menservants can't stay away from their beloved whiskey for too long. And then if you don't find him there, search the gutters and brothel-houses. I'm sure you can find a few of your men who are altruistic enough to investigate that last venue."

"Don't tell me how to do my job, sir," Keane snapped. "If you don't permit me to search the house, I'll have to apply unpleasant pressure."

Geoffrey stood before Keane, nose-to-nose. In a low voice that was almost a growl, he said: "It's not up to me to let you search the house, Inspector, it is up to Lady Drake. And she must not have her house disturbed right now. It is disrespectful and unnatural so soon after her husband's death. And if you so much as insinuate that she is not cooperating with your investigation, I will bring you before a judge for impugning her good character."

"You have no grounds for accusing me of any such thing," Keane said with a scowl. There was a note of uncertainty in his voice.

"Don't I? I've been the family's solicitor for over two decades. If you think I don't know how to defend against slander and character smears, go ahead and test me."

The two men stared at each other. Keane said: "Well, it has been a long night. No reason not to pick it up in the morning. But if you should happen to see Joe Golm, notify us immediately. You do have a telephone, here, don't you?"

"Of course," David said.

"I'll be back here after sunrise, then," Keane said. He motioned for the two officers to follow him out.

After the inspector left, Geoffrey said: "Let's keep Joe hidden awhile longer. It would not surprise me if Keane or his men are lurking about, waiting to catch sight of him."

Sam asked in a worried tone: "Which one of us should tell Lady Drake and Mrs. Lowe about Jonathan and Anne? Bothe women are sleeping now, but when they wake up ..."

"Who is sleeping?" Hannah Drake asked, gliding into the room. She stopped and stood, looking from one face to the next. Her black dress made her face look as pale as alabaster, and there were dark circles under her eyes. Her auburn hair had been pinned up hastily, and strands of it escaped. She said in a tired voice: "Are Jonathan and Anne sleeping now? I'm so relieved that they're safe."

David walked over to his mother-in-law and took her arm. He led her to a sofa, and she sat. He sat next to her.

"Jonathan and Anne did not make it out of the baron's house. There was a fire—"

Hannah pulled her hand away. "No. Do not tell me this, David. Do not tell me that the monster took them from me. Tell me he didn't take them!" she cried. "Tell me that!"

Sam sat next to her and put his hand on her shoulder. She sobbed into her hands, rocking back and forth. Geoffrey poured a glass of whiskey from a decanter and handed it to Sam.

"Take a sip," Sam said gently, giving her the whiskey.

She looked up, staring vacantly. Then she took a sip.

David said quietly: "Joe says he saw Edward."

Hannah turned to him and studied his face, as if he were telling some macabre joke. "What do you mean, he saw Edward?"

"He saw ... an apparition of Edward. And he saw Jonathan's dog. Edward told him that we all must leave London and go east. Joe is to return to Prague, and the rest of us are to continue on to Jerusalem."

Hannah was silent as she contemplated this news. "How do you know Joe didn't imagine all this?"

David said: "That's not something Joe is capable of. His is a literal sort of mind. If he perceived it, it means it happened."

Hannah looked around the room in despair. "I suppose there is nothing to hold me here right now, anyway. A few of the servants can look after this place until I decide what to do. I'll need about two weeks to get it all sorted out."

"We don't have two weeks," David said. "We must leave immediately."

"That's not possible. How can I decide whom to retain and whom to give notice? And then there is the sorting and packing."

Geoffrey said: "I'll manage the house while you're away, Hannah."

"How will I know what to bring?" she asked in a plaintive voice.

"Things can be sent later," Geoffrey said. "Please don't talk to any of the household staff until after the inspector is gone. If Keane gets any inkling of these plans, that will make everything worse."

There was a knock at the library door. Agatha MacLeod stepped into the room. She clutched her rosary beads in her hands, twisting the strands nervously. She stood straight before Hannah, a grave expression on her face.

"Is it the children?" Hannah asked in a panicked voice.

"My lady, they are as safe as can be, and sleeping like angels right next to Mrs. Lowe."

Hannah sighed with relief.

Agatha said: "I came here to tell your ladyship that I want go with you and the bairns. On the journey east."

"How in the world do you know our plans?" Hannah exclaimed.

"I listened at the door, m'lady. I know it's wrong to eavesdrop, but what's done is done, and I can't stay behind here."

"I'm afraid that won't be possible," David said. "We are already seven of us as it is, counting Jack and Lily."

"And that also counts Mr. Golm, am I right, sir?" Agatha asked.

"Yes, Mr. Golm as well," Sam affirmed.

"And who will care for those wee bairns during the long journey?"

"We all can," Sam said.

"And when you get to your destination?"

"Then we hire a nurse there," David said. "There are nurses abroad, you know."

Agatha took a deep breath and closed her eyes. "It's like this. I can't bear to be apart from Jack and Lily. Or from Joe."

"Well, other arrangements are already being made ..." Hannah began, but Sam raised his hand to quiet her.

Sam said in a gentle voice: "Tell us what you mean, Mrs. MacLeod."

She opened her eyes, clutched her rosary beads tighter, and focused her gaze past those around her to the far wall opposite. "I love Joe Golm. And I love the bairns like my own, and I want to be their nanny in the new place."

There was silence except for the clock ticking on the chimneypiece.

"I see," Hannah said. "Well, it is all quite impossible, you know. I am sorry about that, Mrs. MacLeod. I thank you for your faithful service."

Mrs. MacLeod would not be dismissed. She looked at Hannah with a dignified face. "I wish your ladyship would give me and Joe your blessing, ma'am. I know most mistresses don't like their servants to marry, because they think it creates more trouble than it's worth, but I can promise that Joe and I would not be like that. We would be just as faithful and hard-working as ever. Even more so."

"It's not what you think, Mrs. MacLeod," David said. "The problem is, Joe is not the marrying kind. He's … different."

Agatha tried to smile through her pain. "Oh, I know he's different, sir. He doesn't drink, for one. And he's mute, for another. That right there would make most women want him for a husband. He saved my life twice. And it's not just that. I taught him to read. And to write. We've become close. I want us to be united, in the eyes of God."

"Please sit down, Mrs. MacLeod," Sam said gently.

She did as she was told. Sam continued in a gentle tone. "What Mr. Lowe is trying to say is that Joe is not a normal man. In fact, he's not a man as you and I understand the term."

"Well, I'm not one of those women who cares about *that* so much, sir. I'm not a young lass anymore. We can make allowances for any… shortcomings."

"That's not what I mean, Mrs. MacLeod. Joe is a … creation. He was created by another man."

"So were we all, sir. By our fathers."

David chuckled appreciatively at the good woman's logic. She looked up at him sharply, a frown on her honest features. "You mock me, sir," she said.

David defended himself. "I do not mean to mock you, Mrs. MacLeod. Please forgive me." He continued: "I am laughing in appreciation of the fact that you are a quick-witted woman, Mrs. MacLeod. What Dr. Berg is trying to say is that Joe is what is known as a golem. He is a creature who was fashioned out of mud, from the banks of a river in Prague, by a rabbi, about three hundred years ago. He was never born of a woman. He was brought into being to protect the Jews of Prague in the sixteenth century, when they were under attack from dark forces that would annihilate them. Then, he went to sleep in the garret of a synagogue there until we awakened him again. We did this some months ago, and brought him here to London. We are going to have to bring him back to Prague and return him to sleep in the garret, until such time as we need him again."

Agatha struggled to understand what he was saying. She bowed her head under the weight of this new information. She looked up again, and she briefly met the eyes of each of the three people who were looking at her. She said in a quiet voice: "If you tell me that the man I love is going away, lost to me forever, and if you tell me that Lily and Jack—the two children I love like my own—are to be taken to another country, without me, then I really will have nothing to live for."

Hannah was shocked. "But, my dear Mrs. MacLeod, you are a Catholic. Surely you don't mean—"

"No, m'lady," Agatha interrupted. "I would never take my own life by my own hand. It is a mortal sin. But I am not afraid to die. I would welcome the Angel of Death when he next hovers near, instead of fighting him like I have each time I've seen his black shadow. The same week Queen Victoria died, I was struck down with pneumonia. Almost met my Maker then, almost was re-united with my dead daughter. But I fought hard to stay on this earth. Next time, I won't fight. My heart has been broken, and it will not heal. The sooner God takes me to the next world, the better. That is all I have to say, m'lady."

As she rose to leave, Hannah said: "Mrs. MacLeod, this will not be an easy journey for any of us. We're going to places where the languages, the food, the customs, the weather are all so different from what we're used to. How would you even manage?"

Agatha took a deep breath. "Forgive me for my boldness, m'lady. But I must tell you this. I faced down the devil himself to save those two babies. The baron and his demon servants were going to hurt Jack and Lily. Not just to hurt, but to murder." Her voice trembled. "By God's grace, I carried Jack and Lily through that dark tunnel. We almost got murdered in that tunnel by one of the baron's servants, but Joe saved us. So, you see, my life is entwined with Joe's life. And my life is entwined with the lives of the bairns. Nothing can unravel that. No strange foods, no strange languages are going to ruffle me. That's because I've been to hell and back."

There was silence. After some moments, David clapped his hands in appreciation. "Brava, Mrs. MacLeod. You're going to be a fine travelling companion."

Sunlight streamed through the windows of the train compartment as the eastern European countryside passed by. David gazed out of the window, and wondered what the future had in store for those fields, for the working-men's houses that now sat solidly among the spring-green fields. For a fleeting moment, he saw the houses burned to ruins, and the ugly trenches of war dug there, like hideous scars on the land. The vision disconcerted him. Would Jonathan's visions of war and destruction—the ones in the spider's web—come true?

Sam sat across from him, reading a newspaper, and momentarily glanced out of the window, then returned to his newspaper.

Sarah was asleep, and her head rested on David's shoulder. Hannah dozed with a book open on her lap.

Agatha sat next to the babies, both of whom were asleep in their pram. She reached over to be sure the blanket was properly tucked around them. Then she sat back and put her arm through Joe's. The golem glanced at her with something like affection in his inscrutable mud-brown eyes.

Agatha knew that each mile that fell behind the train meant one mile closer to his resting place. Agatha would face that tragedy when it came. In the meanwhile, she was would live each moment with him now. She touched the gold cross necklace that was now safely clasped back around her neck, and she knew that it was the only jewellery that Joe would ever give her.

David glanced at Agatha, and admired the courage that he saw on her face. Then he looked at the golem, the creature he'd helped to bring back to consciousness in the garret of the Altneushul just a few months before. Psalm 139 came to David's mind, and he recited it silently:

I will give thanks to You
for I am awesomely and wondrously made
And my soul knows it well.
My essence was not hidden from You
when I was made in secret

I was knit together in the depths of the earth.
Your eyes saw my golam (unshaped limbs),
and in Your book they were all recorded;
In due time they were formed, to the very last one.

David looked over at the two sleeping babies, who were now his and Sarah's children. He silently recited two more lines of the psalm:

To me—how precious
are Your dear ones, O God!

Then he asked one more thing of the Creator: "Lead me in Your ways of righteousness and strength."

THE END

To see more of Christine Silk's work, visit christinesilk.com

Substack: https://christinesilk.substack.com

LinkedIn: www.linkedin.com/in/christine-silk-ph-d-0657201b

If you'd like to receive the latest news about *The Dark Fire*, and other books, email Publisher@ChartwellPress.com

X: @chartwell_press

⁓◠ GLOSSARY ◠⁓

Anaglypta. A brand of wall-covering going back to 1887 that is textured or embossed, and can be painted.

Anat. Also spelled Anath. Ancient Canaanite fertility goddess who, during the Hellenistic period, was identified with the warrior/fertility goddess Athena. Anat was the sister of the Canaanite god Ba'al. The Canaanite peoples practiced child sacrifice to Ba'al.

Antimacassar. A decorative piece of cloth or lace draped over the headrest of a chair to prevent the upholstery from getting dirty especially from the Macassar oil that was used on mens' hair during the Victorian era.

Arcade. A covered walkway with columns and arches running down one or both sides of a walkway.

Armoire. A large, free-standing cabinet for storing clothing.

Aubusson carpet. A French-style of carpet dating back to the 15th century that features intricate details such as flowers and scrolls.

Axminster carpet. A popular brand of carpet during the Victorian and Edwardian eras. It was woven in England starting in the mid-18th century.

Bairns. Scottish word for babies or children.

Balaam and his donkey. From Exodus 22-24. Balaam was sent by the king of Moab to curse the Jews, but instead Balaam ended up blessing the Jews because of God's will that he do so.

Bar mitzvah. Hebrew for "son of commandment." Age 13 is a milestone at which Jewish boys become bar mitzvah and take on the moral and religious responsibilities of an adult.

Bell pulls. Lengths of rope or embroidered fabric attached to a bell system in a house. When the bell pull was pulled, a bell would ring in the servants' quarters, alerting them that they were summoned.

Bashert. A soulmate; one's destined spouse.

Birkat hamazon. The blessings that are recited after a meal.

Blackguard. A contemptible or dishonourable person.

Black sun. A symbol that is a substitute swastika, regarded as a mystical source of energy capable of regenerating the Aryan race. Revived by former SS man Wilhelm Landig in the first half of the 20th century. See Goodrick-Clarke, pp. 3-4.

Bobby, bobbies. British slang for policeman, policemen.

Bounder. A well-dressed man who is vulgar. An unwelcome pretender.

Braces. Suspenders that hold up trousers.

Candelabrum. A candleholder with two or more branches.

Casement window. A window that swings out on hinges, like a door.

Challah. Bread that is shaped as a braided loaf, and typically served on Friday nights in homes that observe Shabbat.

Chimera. A hybrid creature from Greek mythology that is composed of different animals.

Cloister, cloister garth. A cloister is a covered walkway (such as an arcade) that links the buildings of an abbey or monastery. The cloister garth is the courtyard within a cloister.

Comte. French nobility. The English equivalent is count.

Copper. British slang for policeman.

Copper-nose. A drunkard.

Crowley, Aleister. Occult figure and magick practitioner who had a following in the UK and the US. See Symonds, *The Great Beast*.

Cybele. A Greek goddess dating back to the 7th century BCE. Also known by the name of Rhea. Priests in the Cybele cult (called galli) would mutilate and castrate themselves as a form of worship. See Davies, p. 157.

Davened shacharit, minchah, maariv. To daven means to pray. Shacharit is morning prayer, minchah is afternoon prayer, maariv is evening prayer.

Debrett's. A reference book on the peerage system in the UK that has been published continually since 1769. It is a who's who of nobility and titled families (see bibliography).

Doxy. A woman of loose morals.

Eishet chayil. Hebrew for "a woman of valour," from Proverbs 31:10.

Epergne. An elaborate table centerpiece (dating back to the 18th century) that holds fruit, nuts, or flowers.

Entablature. In architecture, a horizontal feature supported by columns.

Flyleaf. A page of heavy paper at the beginning of a hard-cover book.

Frock. An outer garment.

Funeral weeds. Sombre clothing worn by mourners at a funeral, and during the period of mourning afterwards.

Galon. Trim or braid with silk stripes that cover the side seam of dress trousers.

Gaol. British spelling of "jail."

Garret. British word for attic.

Genizah. A depository for storing holy manuscripts that are no longer used, such as worn-out prayer-books and scrolls.

Gilded rococo looking glass. An ornate mirror with a gold-like finish on the frame.

Gilt brazier with ball-and-claw feet. A brazier is a large metal pan that holds burning coals. "Gilt" is a gold finish. Ball-and-claw feet resemble a bird's talon gripping a ball.

Gimcrack. A showy, cheap object.

Gin pahit. A type of cocktail from the Raffles Hotel in Singapore, composed of soda water, gin and angostura bitters.

Gladstone bag. A type of luggage, named after William Gladstone, a 19th-century prime minister of the United Kingdom.

Golem. A supernatural creature made from mud, whose purpose was to protect the citizens of Prague in the 16th century. See Winkler, *The Golem of Prague.*

Gorky's novel *Mother*. Published in 1907, it tells the story of a working-class woman in Russia who helps her son to become a revolutionary.

Grand Tour. A months-long, educational trip that well-to-do citizens of the UK and Europe would embark upon to see Europe and Asia. The tour would include museums, cathedrals, and other architectural points-of-interest, including ruins and archaeology sites.

Great Mother. The archetype of the mother as both the creator and destroyer. A variation on this is the archetype of the Devouring Mother, or death goddess, as seen in various mythologies including Canaanite, Greek, Roman, and Hindu. See Neumann, *The Origins and History of Consciousness*, chapter 11.

Greek Revival. A style of architecture based on Roman and Greek features, popular in the England and the United States in the early 19th century.

Hanwell resident. An inmate of the Hanwell Insane Asylum in London.

Hashem. Hebrew for "The Name." It is used by observant Jews to refer to God.

Heraldic insignia. Graphic symbols that are displayed on coats-of-arms, flags, and stationery to identify a family, royal rank, military branch, and other social units.

Hussar. Light cavalry units.

In vino veritas. "In wine, truth."

Isabella. A poem by John Keats. Isabella refused an arranged marriage to a nobleman. She was in love with Lorenzo, a commoner. Her brothers murdered Lorenzo. Isabella exhumed his body and buried his head in a pot of basil.

Kippah. A head-covering worn by observant Jewish males.

Kochleffel. Yiddish for "pot-stirrer," meaning someone who stirs up trouble.

Lancet windows. A type of Gothic window that is narrow, with a pointed arch at the top.

Larder. A cool, ventilated room or cupboard used for storing perishable foods such as meat and dairy products.

Lavabo. A stone basin into which water flows, common in monasteries.

Layette. A collection of clothing for a new-born baby.

Livery. The uniform worn by servants.

Maimonides. Also known as Moses ben Maimon (1135-1204), and by the name the Rambam. Philosopher, jurist, physician. One of the most important intellectuals in Jewish history.

Mazel tov. Hebrew for "congratulations" or "best of luck."

Métier. An area in which a person excels, or has special talent or aptitude.

Mews. A place in cities where carriage horses are kept.

Mezuzah. A scroll (klaf) is inscribed with a special prayer, and then rolled up and placed into a case that can be made of wood, metal or glass. The scroll and the case together are referred to as a mezuzah. It is affixed to a doorpost in accordance with the commandment in Deuteronomy 11:20-21.

Mikveh. A ritual bath for purifying oneself.

Morning coat. A men's knee-length tailcoat. It is formal day-dress that one would wear to weddings, official functions, etc.

Nappy. The British word for diaper.

Netziv of Volozhin. Rabbi Naftali Tzvi Yehuda Berlin was the leader of the yeshiva in Volozhin, Belarus. He was the author of numerous works.

Novitiate. A novice in a religious order who has not yet taken vows.

Oenophile. A wine aficionado or connoisseur.

Oliver Haddo. A fictional character from William Somerset Maugham's novel, *The Magician*. In his introduction to the volume listed in the bibliography below, Maugham said that Aleister Crowley was the model for Haddo.

Outré. Beyond the bounds of what is considered proper and appropriate. Unusual, unconventional, shocking.

Pediment. A triangular piece above an entryway, sometimes supported by columns.

Pediment statues. In classical Greek and Roman architecture, pediment statues would depict animals such as horses and lions, and humans who represent ideal beauty.

Pelmeted creations. A pelmet is a framework above a window that conceals curtain fixtures and adds decorative interest.

Pogrom. An organised massacre of Jews.

Portmanteau. A large piece of luggage that opens by hinges into two compartments.

Pram. A baby stroller.

Prophylaxis/swindle. In chess, a preemptive strategy to anticipate and neutralize a threat from an opponent.

Psalter. A Book of Psalms. See Tehillim below for more detail.

Refectory. A large room in a monastery or convent where meals are taken

Regency demi-lune. A table that is a half-circle, in the style of the Regency period, which spanned from about 1811-1820.

Rum one. A strange, eccentric fellow.

Runner. A long, narrow carpet for spaces such as hallways.

Salver. A small tray for serving drinks, or holding mail and calling-cards.

Schubert's lieder. German poems set to music by Franz Schubert "Gretchen am Spinnrade" is a poem written by Goethe about a young woman at a spinning wheel who broods about her love for Faust.

Scimitar. A type of sword with a curved blade.

Sconce. A wall bracket used to hold candles, torches, and (after the invention of electricity) a wall-mounted light fixture that holds light bulbs.

Serail, seraglio. French and Italian words for the quarters in a palace that the women of the harem inhabited.

Shabbos. Also spelled Shabbat. The sabbath or "day of rest" as commanded in the Torah (Exodus 20:10) that begins for Jews on Friday at sundown and ends on Saturday at sundown.

Shammash. An employee in a synagogue, whose duties include secretarial work and assisting the rabbi.

Shiva. The week-long period of mourning after a family member has died.

Sideboard. A piece of furniture in the dining room with drawers and cupboards that hold the items needed to set the dining table.

Sir Francis Drake. (1540-1596) English explorer who circumnavigated the globe, and who also fought successfully against the Spanish Armada in 1588 as a commander.

St. Hildegard von Bingen. (1098-1179). German abbess, mystic prophetess, and composer.

Tallit. Also spelled tallis. A Jewish prayer shawl that has fringes at the corners.

Tanakh. Also spelled Tanach. An acronym that refers to the foundational texts of Judaism: Torah (the Hebrew Bible), Nevi'im (the Prophets), and Ketuvim (writings which include Proverbs and Psalms).

Tefillin. Small black leather boxes that are affixed by leather straps to a man's arm and forehead during prayer at certain times of the weekday, as commanded by God in Deuteronomy 6:8.

Tehillim. Called "psalms" in English. The Psalms are liturgical compositions for recitation or singing, of which there are 150. King David (who lived around 1000 B.C.E.) is usually credited with the composition of the psalms. "Tehillim" comes from a Hebrew root word for "praises." "Psalms" comes from a Greek word that means "a song sung to a stringed instrument." See Sarna, pp. 3-23.

Tokaji. A sweet wine, named after the region in which it is grown in Hungary.

Torah. Also called the *Five Books of Moses*, the Torah is the Hebrew Bible which comprises Genesis, Exodus, Numbers, Leviticus, and Deuteronomy.

Tromp l'oeil. French for "deceive the eye." In the decorative arts, it is a painting technique in which a 2-dimensional depiction looks as if it is 3-dimensional.

Tzedakah. Charitable donations in the form of money, food, clothing, etc.

Vestibule. An entryway or transitional space leading into a larger space.

Vow of the Nazarite. A vow taken in Biblical times in which a person would live a strict and holy life, including abstinence from any grape products such as wine and raisins. For more information, see this link: https://www.chabad.org/library/article_cdo/ aid/287358/jewish/ The-Nazir-and-the-Nazirite-Vow.htm#How

Welsh dresser. A large piece of furniture with drawers and cupboards below for storage, and shelves above for displaying objects or books.

Window tax. First imposed in England in 1696, and repealed in 1851, the window tax levied a fee based on the number of windows a dwelling had. See Oates and Schwab for a history and explanation of how the tax led to excess burdens on citizens, including negative health consequences.

ᴮIBLIOGRAPHY

Cassuto, Umberto. *The Goddess Anat.* Translated by Israel Abrahams. Skokie: Varda Books, 2005.

Chabad.org

The Chicago Manual of Style, Seventeenth Edition. Chicago: University of Chicago Press, 2017.

Davies, Nigel. *The Rampant Gods.* New York: Wm. Morrow & Co., 1984.

Debrett's Peerage and Titles of Courtesy. Hesilrige, Arthur G. M., editor. London: Dean & Son, Ltd., 1921.

Dundas, Alan, editor. *The Vampire: A Casebook.* Wisconsin: The University of Wisconsin Press, 1998.

Goodrick-Clarke, Nicholas. *Black Sun: Aryan Cults, Esoteric Nazism, and the Politics of Identity.* New York: New York University Press, 2002.

Harris, Cyril M., editor. *Illustrated Dictionary of Historic Architecture.* New York: Dover Publications, Inc., 1977.

Hinchman, Mark. *The Dictionary of Interior Design,* 3rd edition. New York and London: Fairchild Books, 2014.

Keats, John. "Isabella, or, The Pot of Basil." Online access: https://en.wikisource.org/wiki/The_Poetical_Works_of_John_Keats/Isabella

Kogos, Fred. *A Dictionary of Yiddish Slang and Idioms.* New York: Citadel Press, 1992.

Maugham, W.S. *The Magician.* New York: Penguin. 1967.

Manchester, William. *The Last Lion: Visions of Glory* 1874-1932. Boston: Little, Brown & Co., 1983.

Manchester, William. *The Last Lion: Alone 1930-1940.* Boston: Little, Brown & Co., 1988.

Oates, Wallace E., and Robert M. Schwab. 2015. "The Window Tax: A Case Study in Excess Burden." *Journal of Economic Perspectives,* 29 (1): 163-80. Online access: https://www.aeaweb.org/articles id=10.1257/jep.29.1.163

Paglia, Camille. *Sexual Personae: Art and Decadence from Nefertiti to Emily Dickinson.* New York: Vintage Books, 1991.

Pawel, Ernest. *The Nightmare of Reason: A Life of Franz Kafka.* New York: Quality Paperback Book Club, 1984.

Sarna, Nahum M. *On the Book of Psalms: Exploring the Prayers of Ancient Israel.* New York: Schocken Books. 1993.

Sefaria.org

Segal, Benjamin J. (translation and commentary). *The Song of Songs: A Woman in Love.* Jerusalem: Gefen Publishing House, Ltd. 2009.

Symonds, John. *The Great Beast: The Life and Magick of Aleister Crowley* Frogmore, St. Albans: Mayflower Books, LTD, Granada Publishing,1973.

Tehillim: A New Translation with a Commentary Anthologized from Talmudic, Midrashic, and Rabbinic Sources. Vols. 1 & 2. N. Scherman and M. Zlotowitz, general editors. Brooklyn: Artscroll Tanach Series Mensorah Publications, Ltd., 2013.

Trachtenberg, Joshua. *Jewish Magic and Superstition: A Study in Folk Religion.* New York: Behrman's Jewish Book Home, 1939. Re-print edition Mansfield Centre, CT: Martino Publishing, 2013.

Weingrad, Michael. "Brave New Golems." *The Jewish Review of Books,* Winter 2017. https://jewishreviewofbooks.com/articles/2390/ brave-new-golems/

Winkler, Gershon. *The Golem of Prague.* New York: Judaica Press, 1980.

Yorke, Trevor. *The Victorian House Explained.* Newbury, Berkshire: Countryside Books, 2021.